UNKNOWN
HORIZONS

UNKNOWN HORIZONS

The Lewis and Clark Expedition A Novel

TED BRUSAW
AND
RUTH KIBLER PECK

Cover Art by
JIM CARSON
jimcarsonstudio.com

Library of Congress Control Number:		2017914500
ISBN:	Hardcover	978-1-5434-5244-0
	Softcover	978-1-5434-5243-3
	eBook	978-1-5434-5242-6

Print information available on the last page.

Rev. date: 09/27/2017

To order additional copies of this book, contact:
Xlibris
1-888-795-4274
www.Xlibris.com
Orders@Xlibris.com
768004

CONTENTS

DEDICATION

My husband of 60 years, Ted Brusaw, passed away on August 7, 2015, and didn't get to see his last two historical novels in print. Ted's other published novels continue to attract readers. As I greet his last work with a smile, I know that somewhere, Ted is smiling, too.

Barbara Brusaw

It was challenging and fun to work with Ted Brusaw writing this historical novel that celebrates the momentous trip of discovery by Lewis and Clark. Ted was a master of research and expression--a successful writer with many admirable qualities. This book is dedicated to his memory and to the talented members of Wright Writers of Dayton who gave us months of critique, encouragement, and enthusiasm.

Ruth Kibler Peck

"We were now about to penetrate a country at least two thousand miles in width, on which the foot of civilized man had never trod. The good or evil it had in store for us was for experiment yet to determine, and these little vessels contained every article by which we were to subsist and defend ourselves."

Meriwether
Lewis

"The first white men of your people who came to our country were named Lewis and Clark. They brought many things that our people had never seen. They talked straight. These men were very kind."

Chief Joseph
The Nez Perce Nation

CHAPTER 1

Pittsburgh, Pennsylvania

August 1803

Tall, lean, twenty-eight-year old U.S. Army Captain Meriwether Lewis stood at a landing on the bank of the Ohio River in Pittsburgh, Pennsylvania. He peered into the thinning fog that hovered over the river, warehouses, and boat-building docks behind him, squinting to take in the entire scene. Shouts and laughter from dock workers as they went about their business filled the air that was already warm and steamy on this early August morning. Lewis inhaled deeply, relishing the distinctive aroma of morning dew and fog. He felt alive and honored as he imagined the trip ahead.

At last, it's time to begin this epic journey after all these months of preparation, he thought. He was eager to launch tons of supplies down the Ohio River on a keelboat and a pirogue to Saint Louis, the jumping-off point for exploring the Louisiana Territory. It was 1803, the year President Jefferson purchased the vast, unknown Louisiana Territory from France, adding an area three times the size of the present United States to the fledgling country. Lewis was thrilled that President Jefferson had commissioned him, his private secretary, to lead the team that would explore and chart this great area to the Pacific Ocean. The exciting but tedious preparation for the journey had occupied Lewis's every waking hour for many months.

"Okay, men!" he called to the group of eleven soldiers and three civilian workers who awaited his orders. "The locals say the river is too low for a keelboat to navigate. Let's show them what the army can do!"

The men cheered lustily, looking forward to the journey. Lewis's huge black Newfoundland dog, Seaman, cavorted with the men at the river's edge. Private Eric Bastone, a lively teenager, called Seaman into the fifty-five-foot keelboat as the others pushed it away from the dock and climbed aboard. This wasn't the ordinary keelboat that plied the rivers west of the Appalachian Mountains. It was fifty-five feet long and eight feet wide, with a thirty-foot mast that was hinged at the base so it could be lowered when necessary. A ten-foot deck at the bow provided a forecastle, and an elevated deck at the stern sported a cabin. On each side of the mid-ship deck were benches that could accommodate twenty-two oarsmen—nearly twice the number of men Captain Lewis had at present. The keelboat could be propelled by sailing, rowing, poling, or towing, and the thirty-one-foot hold could carry a cargo of twelve tons.

The group also had a white pirogue, a thirty-five-foot flat-bottom boat manned by six oarsmen and fitted with a mast. It now pulled in behind the keelboat as both boats moved slowly into the sluggish current of the river. The thinning early morning fog, common on the Ohio at this time of year, blanketed the river and the area surrounding it. To enable the keelboat to ride higher in the shallow water, Lewis had sent additional supplies ahead to villages and towns to be picked up as they moved down the Ohio River toward Saint Louis.

"The captain's going to be making history when he gets to the Louisiana Territory," Private Henry Cooper, a tow-headed young man, exclaimed to Private James Wharton. "I wish I could go all the way with him instead of just to Saint Louis."

"I don't know," Wharton said with misgivings. "This expedition will be small, and they could easily be killed by savage Indian tribes. Nobody knows anything about the unknown tribes in that unexplored territory."

"Yeah, but to go down in history like that, I'd take my chances. All these men will be famous."

"Maybe so," Wharton sighed, "but I think I'd rather keep my scalp than be famous."

Three miles into their journey, people who had gathered at the riverbank to watch them pass called to the keelboat to put in and demonstrate the air gun they had heard so much about. Lewis smiled. Looking toward the helm, Captain Lewis called, "Put in, pilot. Let's give them a demonstration."

"Aye, Captain." The old civilian river salt steered the craft toward shore.

The air gun was a pneumatic rifle that could be pumped up to six-hundred pounds of pressure per square inch, making it equivalent in power to the famous Kentucky long-rifle—but without as much noise or smoke.

"Set up a target anywhere you like," Lewis called out to the crowd after going ashore with one of the soldiers.

Two boys rushed to set up the target a challenging distance away.

"All right! Let's show them what it can do," Lewis ordered the soldier, who pumped up the air gun. He took careful aim, fired, and hit the target fifty-five yards away. A cheer went up from the crowd. Lewis said, "There you are, folks, a demonstration of the latest scientific invention!"

"Tell us about your mission, Captain," someone called out. They had all heard about a mysterious expedition into the wilds of the far western territory.

"As you probably know, the Louisiana Territory now belongs to the United States, and President Jefferson has sent us to explore it," Lewis responded. He didn't mention that they were going well beyond the Louisiana Territory, all the way to the Pacific Ocean because the area beyond the Continental Divide did not belong to the United States. In fact, an unmentioned part of the mission was to stake a tenuous claim to that extended area under the unwritten international rule of the right of discovery and exploration.

As they pushed off from shore, waving goodbye to the crowd on shore and continuing down the Ohio River, the crews scanned the shallow river for submerged sandbars, which the local people called *riffles*. Dense forest and thick undergrowth covered the land on each side of the river. Greenery was beginning to show patches of autumn brown in some places. Buzzards and hawks circled overhead, and crows cawed noisily to one another from nearby trees. Songbirds were mostly silent at this time of year, with the mating season over.

The first obstacle, Captain Lewis knew, would be Little Horsetail Riffle, a submerged sandbar, and they soon ran aground on it. In a scene to be repeated dozens of times in the next two weeks, Lewis stepped out of the keelboat and stood knee-deep in the river to assess the situation. He removed his hat, exposing sweat-drenched brown hair as the shallow water seemed to emphasize his bowed legs.

"Well, lads, here's the first sandbar of many we'll encounter. Let's dig a channel through it to free our boats and hope we can maneuver around the next one."

The young crew splashed into the knee-high water and went to work. They dug a channel ahead of the keelboat and then, using ropes, pulled and pushed it with all the muscle and stamina they could muster. After two hours of digging and straining, the crew finally broke the keelboat free.

"Well done, men!" Lewis praised them.

But barely two miles further down the river, the boats foundered on Big Horsetail Riffle. The men groaned, but Lewis prodded them with encouragement as well as challenge. "Come on men, you have the stuff for this trip! This is probably just a taste of what's ahead of us."

This time the work involved unloading the keelboat and stacking all the goods on the riverbank; however, Horsetail Riffle was such a problem that even after hours of digging and pulling, the boats were still mired in the river bottom. Local farmers wandered down to the river to watch, and finally Lewis turned to them.

"Can I hire a team of horses from one of you to help us over this thing?"

"I have a team of oxen that will do the job, with the help of your men," one farmer offered. "Oxen are steadier because they aren't skittish like horses."

"Good! Go get them. I'll pay you well."

The expedition continued down the river, battling the shallows all the way. When Captain Lewis finally called a halt for the night, they had gone only ten miles that day. He brought out a jug of whiskey to brighten spirits, and each man took a swig before Lewis took his turn. As evening darkened and stars dotted the sky, Lewis found himself daydreaming of the coming journey into the unknown. For fifty years, trappers and hunters had gone into the area between Saint Louis and the Mandan Indian villages on the upper Missouri River, but no known white man had ever ventured beyond the Mandan villages.

A noted cartographer had made a special map for Lewis, showing what was known of the Missouri River up to the Mandan villages. There were but three certain points on the map: the longitude and latitude of St. Louis, the Mandan Indian villages, and the mouth of the Columbia River on the Pacific Coast. The journey would be fraught with danger, but the rewards for the new United States of America could be enormous. And if he was able to complete the journey successfully, Lewis was confident the rewards for his military career would also be significant.

President Jefferson had charged him with keeping a daily journal with careful details of the terrain, the animals, the flora, and the unknown Indian tribes he would meet. Lewis lost himself in dreaming of the possibilities. He had spent months carefully planning this journey, even going to the arsenal at Harper's Ferry to supervise the building of an iron-frame collapsible boat that he and President Jefferson had designed for this mission, a boat that would be much lighter than dugout canoes. He'd had customized Kentucky rifles and pipe-tomahawks made at Harper's Ferry for the journey. He had also spent much time in Philadelphia buying supplies, including a dried soup that could be used when fish and game became scarce. Last year, President Jefferson had also arranged private tutoring for him in botany, astronomy, navigation, medicine, and other specialized fields at the University of Pennsylvania. In fact, Lewis had been studying these subjects in the President's library since becoming President Jefferson's secretary, a post he had held for the past two years. For some time, he and the President had talked about the expedition to explore the Louisiana Territory, and for the past months they had been actively planning it.

For Lewis, leading such a historic exploration was the dream of a lifetime. On the other hand, if he failed—and the odds against a small group of men being able to successfully cross almost three thousand miles of unexplored, trackless wilderness filled with unknown numbers of tribes of savages were great—he knew that history would judge him harshly. Although Lewis was confident he could rise to the task, a faint shiver of fear of the unknown enveloped him in the chill of the night on the dark riverbank. Around him, the comforting and familiar croaks of frogs and chirps of crickets soothed his fears.

The keelboat and pirogue crews awoke at daybreak with humidity so heavy that dewdrops falling from the trees seemed like gently falling rain. Soon the sun would appear, adding late summer heat to the humidity. They put out into the Ohio River again, moving slowly in the sluggish current. Before they had gone three miles, they hit the first sandbar of the new day. The men knew what to do and set to work.

"This is the lowest this stretch of the Ohio River has ever been in memory, Captain Lewis," a civilian crewmember whose father's farm was thirty miles north told him. "My pappy warned me about it before I left home to join you."

"Yes, I wanted to leave earlier, but it just wasn't possible," he told the man. Silently, he cursed the drunken boat builder in Pittsburgh whom he had hired to build the keelboat. The man had delayed their departure by staying drunk much of the time, while Lewis helplessly watched the river drop day by day. But the man was the only builder in Pittsburgh who had the skills to build the special boat, so Lewis could only grit his teeth and endure the delay.

CHAPTER 2

On to Clarksville

September 1803

The warm days and still air of September brought the usual dense morning fog all along the river, fog so thick that the men joked that they needed a paddle to get through it. As they progressed, fog obscured the sandbars in the shallow water and the boats went aground easily. Time after time, even after the fog faded into the sunlight of late morning, the men worked to free the boats from sandbars and debris. By evening the crews were exhausted and had traveled only six miles.

"Maybe I don't really want to go all the way after all," Private Bastone groaned as the men made camp. "Not if this is a sample of what it will be like all the way." He was grateful to stretch out on the ground for a few minutes rest.

"Maybe that's why Captain Lewis has replacements for us in St. Louis," Wharton suggested as he, too, slumped to the ground. "He knows we'll be so worn out, we'll be useless to go any farther."

The following morning, the fog held them up again. About an hour after they finally got underway, the pirogue following them sounded a distress signal with a trumpet Captain Lewis had provided for that purpose, and the keelboat halted to wait for it. When the pirogue finally pulled up, Corporal Warfington, the tall, friendly man in charge of the pirogue, explained the reason for the delay.

"We sprang a leak and came near to filling up with water. We had to empty the pirogue and repair it."

Captain Lewis, alarmed, said, "You're carrying our gifts for the Indians. I hope the water hasn't damaged them." He strode to the pirogue and lifted the oilcloth covering bags and boxes of beads, scarves, knives, and kettles, anxiously peering into the precious cargo. He referred to the items as gifts, but actually he planned to use them as currency to bargain for food and horses in and west of the Louisiana Territory. He poked and prodded, his expression becoming one of satisfaction.

"It looks all right. Let's spread it out to dry, just to be safe. Cover it with the oil cloth at dusk, men. We can reload it in the morning."

When they arrived at Georgetown, the keelboat and pirogue nosed in at a wharf. "Keep the men aboard the boats," Lewis said quietly to Warfington. "If they go ashore, they'll find whiskey and be useless the rest of the day."

As expected, the general store was the center of activity in the hamlet. Lewis found the proprietor, a thickset man with merry blue eyes.

"I'm Captain Lewis, leading a detachment of soldiers down the Ohio River to St. Louis, and I'm in need of another vessel to carry supplies. Do you know where I can buy one?" he said to the proprietor.

"I have a large canoe that might meet your needs, Captain. You can have it for eleven dollars. Come down to my dock and I'll show it to you."

Lewis bought the canoe and had the men transfer a portion of the supplies to it from the pirogue, but after a few miles on the river, the canoe began to leak so badly that they had to put in to repair it. Again, goods were unloaded and placed on the ground in the open air to dry out while all three boats were checked for leaks and repaired. The next day, with loads lightened by the redistribution of goods, sandbars did not offer such a hazard and the expedition passed Charlestown, a settlement of about forty houses in the Virginia Territory along the Ohio. By dusk a hard rain was falling, and the men scrambled to set up camp for the night.

The densely wooded terrain, the fall weather, and the difficulty of river travel were already known to Meriwether Lewis. As an army paymaster assigned in his early career to this area, it was all familiar. During those earlier days, he had learned the skills of a waterman by traveling the Ohio River in a twenty-one-foot bateau. The difficulties encountered on this first leg of his journey neither discouraged nor frustrated him.

Before turning in, Lewis sat by candlelight composing a letter to his mother and listening to the rain striking the canvas of his tent. In his absence, his mother was overseeing the Lewis family's two-thousand acre plantation back in Virginia. Although a frail woman, she had the will of a commanding general. She was respected far and wide for her knowledge of herbal remedies, and she grew a special crop of herbs that she dispensed with excellent effect to her children, slaves, and neighbors. She had taught Meriwether all about her remedies, a knowledge that would soon prove valuable in strange places under strange circumstances.

Dear Mother,

We have begun our journey to deliver our supplies to St. Louis, the jumping-off place for our journey of exploration. Tonight we are camped on the banks of the Ohio River. The river is so low that getting the boats over frequent sandbars has worn the men to a frazzle. But they are of good cheer and have learned to work well together. I trust Reuben, John, and Mary are doing well with their studies. When Reuben has progressed sufficiently, enroll him with Doctor Jarvis to begin his formal education. I know of nothing more important for a young man of his age than education. The same will be true for John when he reaches that age. Please greet my sister Jane and her husband on my behalf and tell them I wish them well.

Your loving son,
Meriwether

felt a twinge of guilt for abandoning his responsibilities as of his family, leaving his widowed mother in charge of not only two brothers and one sister at home, but also of managing the large plantation. But he knew she was capable and would be successful. Also, he felt strongly that the journey of discovery to the vast territory recently purchased by President Jefferson was too important to the future of his country to deny the call to participate.

The next morning Lewis and his team struggled through continued problems with sandbars until they reached Steubenville, on the Ohio shore. There, the Ohio River became deeper, and they were able to hoist their sails and cover several miles quickly with a favorable wind. However, the wind eventually became so strong that they had to haul in the sails lest the wind destroy them. The next day they arrived at Wheeling, a picturesque village of about fifty buildings on the Virginia side of the Ohio River. Here, Lewis checked on supplies that he had previously ordered sent here while he was still at Pittsburgh. He introduced himself to the proprietor of the general store.

"Oh, yes, sir. I've been expecting you. Your order is in the shed out back."

"I'll get my men to load them, but first I need to buy another pirogue to transport them. Can you help me?"

"We have a boat-builder who might be able to help you."

When they went in search him, Lewis talked with the craftsman and bought one of his pirogues, painted red, which was slightly larger than the white pirogue the team already had. The men filled the new pirogue with the new supplies, and Lewis—amid shouts of joy from the men—gave them freedom for the rest of the day. Lewis used his free time to write a report to President Jefferson.

Dear Mr. President,

Delays have plagued our journey down the Ohio enroute to St. Louis. A drunken boat-builder in Pittsburgh delayed us so long in departing that late summer has reduced the Ohio River to a record low, causing us many problems. Many times we have had to empty our boats to pass sandbars, and any number of times we have had to hire horses or oxen to pull our boats free of obstacles. The work has been strenuous for the men, but they are hale and hearty, and remain enthusiastic. I will continue to report to you as we progress.

Your Obedient Servant,
Captain Meriwether Lewis, U.S. Army

When the flotilla put out into the river the next day, it was hampered almost immediately by several difficult sandbars. The crew, now used to drudgery with keelboat, pirogue, and canoe travel in shallow water, went to work. At day's end they had traveled twenty-four difficult miles.

Next day, the men were surprised and amused by endless crowds of gray squirrels crossing the Ohio River, swimming to the Kentucky side.

"What do you suppose caused them to do that?" Lewis mused to a cluster of puzzled men. "Walnuts and hickory nuts are plentiful on both sides. How odd!"

Seaman, Lewis's huge black Newfoundland dog, had no questions or complaints about the unusual antics of the squirrels. He saw a chance for sport and took it. Plunging into the river, he overtook a squirrel, caught it in his jaws, took it back to the men on the keelboat, and then went back for another and another. He continued his sport until he was too tired to continue, as the men cheered him on. They were only too happy to clean and cook the squirrel meat for supper that night, appropriately sharing the feast with Seaman, the hero of the day.

As the flotilla continued, the river broadened and deepened, its banks now lined with stately hardwood trees showing the colors of autumn. Clearings became rare and villages even rarer, although this was not unmapped territory. Nevertheless, it was wilderness, and when the expedition camped at night, surrounded by thousands of chirping crickets and the deep chorus of frogs, Lewis heard again the comforting symphony of the wind whistling through trees, the familiar music he had come to love. Skies for the next two days were covered with low, gray clouds, and the air was stagnant with humidity. Now everything seemed damp, and the odor of mildew was evident in the supplies. Captain Lewis was alarmed when Corporal Warfington reported that rifles packed with the supplies showed signs of rust.

"We can't let this happen, men," Lewis said. "We have to keep the guns in good working order for hunting and protection when we reach the Louisiana Territory. From now on, each man will keep a gun with him to oil and clean daily. The same goes for the knives. A rusty knife won't do anyone any good."

That day they passed Letart's Falls, where the river fell four feet over a two-hundred-and-fifty yard stretch. The Ohio River deepened below the falls, so the crews ran up their sails and covered the remaining two hundred miles to Cincinnati in short order.

Cincinnati was a bustling river town, and Lewis was eager to pick up another shipment of supplies that he had ordered before leaving Pittsburgh. He also planned to go to the post office to see if any mail had arrived for him or his men.

"Warfington, have the men place our new supplies in the boats, then give them three hours to see the city and enjoy themselves. But advise the men to stay out of trouble. Whiskey is readily available here, and whiskey and soldiers don't mix well." Warfington smiled and saluted as Lewis walked away.

A packet of letters waited for Lewis at the post office. He was especially interested to see the return address of a letter addressed to him. It was from his old friend, William Clark, who had once commanded a rifle company in which Lewis had served. The two men had admired each other and become good friends. Lewis had recently written to Clark asking him to co-command the expedition to explore the Louisiana Territory.

The Clarks lived across the Ohio River from Louisville in a village known as Clarksville. Lewis knew that the personable, red-haired Clark was talented as a commander of men and respected by all. Lewis wanted Clark to share the duties of commanding the Corps of Discovery so

Lewis could concentrate on scientific studies of flora and fauna as well as relations with Indian tribes. With all his heart, he hoped Clark's answer would be "Yes," and he was eager to read his letter.

As soon as the opportunity presented itself, Lewis tore into Clark's envelope, hoping to see the answer he so wanted.

My friend, I join you with hand & heart and anticipate advantages which will certainly derive from the accomplishment of so vast, hazardous and fatiguing enterprise… William Clark

The sudden shout of jubilation from Meriwether Lewis may have startled those nearby on the streets of Cincinnati that day as the tall, dark-haired stranger read the letter, but Lewis didn't care—William Clark had agreed to accompany him on the adventure of a lifetime!

CHAPTER 3

Clarksville

October, 1803

Captain Lewis and his flotilla left Cincinnati for Clarksville, situated two hours farther down river, on its north bank. When Clarksville came into view, it was little more than a few log cabins on a wooded hill—but across the river, Louisville appeared to be a sizable town, spread out over many acres with a busy riverside landing where more than a dozen flatboats were unloading goods. As his flotilla tied up below Clarksville, Lewis directed Corporal Warfington to set up camp. Then he took off, climbing the steep path to the cluster of log cabins atop a high bluff.

The cool October air was bracing. Leaves were already beginning to cover the ground and a musty scent brought back memories of his Virginia home. In his mind's eye he saw the autumn beauty of familiar scenes of home and the fall activity of his family – the customary giant black kettle of apples cooking over a fire in the yard behind the summer kitchen, the sweet aroma of apple butter enveloping the house and grounds. He shook off the fleeting wave of nostalgia as he completed the climb. Two smiling men emerged from the largest cabin shouting their welcome.

"Meriwether! Welcome to Clarksville, my friend!"

"Hello, Clark!" Lewis yelled back at them. "I'm so glad to see you again," he said as the red-haired William Clark enthusiastically wrapped Lewis in a bear hug. "I can't tell you how happy I am that you are joining me for this expedition."

"Nothing could keep me from this mission except your refusal to take me." Clark stepped back, motioning to the older man. "Meet my brother, General George Rogers Clark. George, this is my old friend, Meriwether Lewis."

"I've heard and read much about you, General Clark," Lewis smiled, extending his hand. The famous general, who had led the Kentucky militia in securing the northwest wilderness during the Revolutionary War, shook hands heartily with Lewis.

"I'm pleased to meet you," the elder Clark said. "Come inside where we can talk."

Lewis noted that the famous man, deeply tanned and weathered, was showing a good amount of gray. William and George Rogers Clark had been born in Virginia to a family of the lesser gentry who had migrated to Kentucky when William was a teenager. George was the eldest and William was the ninth of ten children in the respected family. William had grown to adulthood across the river near Louisville.

As a fire danced and crackled in the huge fireplace, the three men— one a proven hero and the other two potential heroes—dined and drank together amiably through the afternoon and evening. Excitement and joy at the prospect of the adventure before the two younger men ran through the questions and answers they had for each other. They also discussed the old days when the two younger men had served together under General "Mad" Anthony Wayne.

"There is something I've been wondering about, Meriwether," William Clark said. "How did you become President Jefferson's secretary? An army officer seems a curious choice for such a position."

"Our families were neighbors in Virginia most of my life and we knew each other well. The President knew I had traveled extensively as an army paymaster as far as St. Louis, making me familiar with the organization and operation of the army. He needed a man with a good knowledge of the army because Congress was considering reducing its size, and my insights might prove valuable in deciding whom he should retain. There's also no doubt that I was in the right place at the right time."

"Did you live at the President's House in Washington or at Monticello?"

"During the past two years I have been living in the President's House—and I can't tell you how much I enjoyed meeting all the famous men who gathered around our dinner table. In such respected company I became quite the polished gentleman, believe it or not." Lewis smiled broadly and chuckled.

The two brothers were fascinated. "What kinds of things did they talk about?"

"Being such intelligent men with such varied experiences, they discussed natural science, geography, philosophy, Indian affairs, literature, history, music—all of this besides politics. It was quite an education for me! During those two years I was also able to read much of President Jefferson's personal library, from which I learned much about botany, geography, mineralogy, and ethnology. On top of that, he arranged for me to study things like medicine, navigation, and engineering under the tutelage of professors at the University of Pennsylvania—all excellent preparation for our exploration of the West."

"Tell me how you envision our expedition, Meriwether." William said.

"We'll be crossing territory belonging to the United States until we reach the Continental Divide in the Rocky Mountains, but we'll be outside of the United States from there to the Pacific Ocean. The President envisions our country eventually stretching from the Atlantic Ocean to the Pacific Ocean."

"Really!" General Clark said, surprised. "That's a very ambitious goal! Spain might have something to say about that. Maybe the Indian nations, too. Of course, the unwritten code—the Right of Discovery—might give us claim to the Northwest if you make it all the way to the Pacific Ocean and back."

"Is that the real purpose of the journey?" William asked.

"The primary purpose is to follow the Missouri River west until, hopefully, it reaches the Columbia River. The President wants to know whether there is a water route that can accommodate commerce stretching from the Mississippi River to the Pacific Ocean. He wants an accurate map, which I know is a particular talent of my red-haired friend here," Lewis said, slapping William's knee. "President Jefferson has many purposes. He wants to combine scientific, agricultural, and commercial information with the geographical data we gather. He's interested in mineral deposits, soil conditions, climate, and trade possibilities with the Indians. He wants us to record the names of the tribes as well as their languages, traditions, living conditions, laws, medicines, and customs."

"You have a great challenge before you," the old general said. "A truly enormous responsibility has fallen on your shoulders. But I know of no better men to handle that responsibility than the two of you." The two younger men smiled their appreciation.

Lewis leaned toward Clark and remarked, "We'll need cheerful, stout-hearted, physically fit men—men who get along well with each other and can withstand the extreme rigors of living outdoors in the natural elements for as long as two years."

"I think I have found some good men," Clark said. "Charles Floyd and Nathaniel Pryor are cousins, and both are men of character and ability who will make good sergeants, at least in my opinion. William Bratton is a blacksmith and gunsmith, which will be handy skills to have along. George Gibson is a fine hunter and also plays the violin, a good diversion to have along during the journey. George Shannon is only eighteen years old, but he is a very good hunter and they tell me he is also a good singer, which should go well with the violin, and the men will need entertainment. John Shields, at thirty-five, is considerably older than the rest, but he is also a blacksmith, a gunsmith, a boat builder, and an excellent repairman—overall, a nearly indispensable man to have along on such a journey as we are undertaking. Joseph Whitehouse is a hide curer and a tailor, which I suspect will be very handy skills on a long wilderness journey. Alexander Willard is another blacksmith and gunsmith, as well as a good hunter. They are all woodsmen, easy to get along with, and hale, hearty, healthy men.

"The word is out along the river," Clark continued. "I've been deluged with other men wanting to go along. I'm sure there will be no shortage of candidates to choose from. They feel that this will be the ultimate adventure for our country, and they are also hoping that Congress will give land grants to the men who complete the journey—just as the Revolutionary War veterans received. And, of course, I'll be taking my slave, York."

George Rogers Clark put another log on the fire as the two younger men continued planning and sharing goals for their expedition. Giant red sparks flew up the chimney and into the blackness outside. The general served bowls of venison stew which had been simmering in an iron kettle over the fireplace, piquing their appetites for hours with its aroma. Lewis thought of his men bedding down near the river and knew he was fortunate to be dry and warm in the Clark home. The cabin was sparsely furnished but adequate, with its table and chairs, shelves holding necessities, and cots with woolen blankets.

Lewis and Clark spent the next ten days in the area assembling their team and tons of equipment for the western expedition. They would leave as soon as possible.

CHAPTER 4

On to St. Louis

November, 1803

As the Lewis and Clark flotilla approached Fort Massac, a U.S. Army base on the Illinois bank of the Ohio River, Lewis signaled all the boats to pull in to shore. The November weather was nippy as the men jumped into the cold water to tie up the boats and Seaman raced ashore, sniffing at and inspecting everything. Lewis introduced himself to the fort commander, showing him the orders from President Jefferson to recruit volunteers from soldiers.

"Let's see if anyone is in the mood to volunteer for such an important journey," the commander said. "I suspect there'll be no shortage. You know how soldiers tire of garrison duty." He called the men to assemble, and Lewis addressed them.

"We are embarking on an expedition to explore the Louisiana Territory. We need hardy volunteers who can withstand the extreme rigors of life in the wild. The journey will probably take two years. It will be adventurous, but it will also be hard work and will no doubt include peril. If you are interested, we will consider you."

Many in the garrison volunteered, but only one man, a civilian, had the recommendation of the commanding officer. George Drouillard was an expert hunter, scout, and Indian translator, the son of a

French-Canadian father and a Shawnee mother. He was an expert in Indian culture and languages, as well as being fluent in French and English. Most importantly, he was a master of the sign language used by Indian tribes to communicate with each other—a critical skill for this journey. In his late twenties, with dark hair and complexion, Drouillard was intelligent, skilled in all he did, physically fit, slightly over six feet tall, and ramrod straight—a fine specimen of a man.

"We're delighted to have you join our party," Captain Lewis told Drouillard. "I look forward to making this journey with you," he replied, gripping Lewis's hand.

The party stayed at Fort Massaic only long enough for Lewis to take the latitude and longitude of the site as practice of the skill he had been taught at the University of Pennsylvania, a skill he would constantly use in the unmapped wilderness ahead. He then compared his numbers with the known figures for the area. They were correct, and Lewis felt like a student who had just passed a test.

The following day, the party reached the juncture of the Ohio and Mississippi Rivers, both swirling with mud from recent fall rains. Despite the muddy waters, Corporal Warfington brought cheers from the men when his fishing line landed the biggest fish any of them had ever seen: a catfish four feet long, ten inches wide, and weighing one hundred and twenty pounds. That fish fed all the men that evening.

Now that Captain Clark had joined the party as co-commander, Lewis often walked on shore as they continued toward St. Louis, Seaman always bounding at his side, a welcome companion. Lewis took every opportunity to practice his knowledge of botany.

As the expedition steered into the Mississippi River, the captains were shocked at the force of the moving water. The current was far greater that they had ever experienced. Rushing water, eddies, swirls, floating logs and other debris presented new challenges.

"We're going to have to have more men to deal with this current, Meriwether," Clark said.

"Yes, maybe twice as many as we have now. We can get them at Fort Kaskaskia, but that's another fifty miles. Meanwhile, we must keep all the men alert so we don't lose any of our supplies to this dangerous current."

"Yes, and more men means more supplies. We can get them in St. Louis."

Both men kept a watchful eye on their boats and floating obstacles as they progressed. Finally, after several treacherous days on the roiling river, they reached Kaskaskia, sixty miles south of St. Louis. The fort commander, a grizzled career officer with a short graying beard, introduced himself.

"Captain Leonard Dawson at your service," he said, raising a tanned, calloused hand in salute.

"Captains Meriwether Lewis and William Clark. Maybe you have already heard of our mission to explore the Louisiana Territory. We need more men to help us with our boats against the current of the Mississippi River." Lewis showed him the presidential order for recruitment.

A sizeable group of volunteers stepped forward when the request for volunteers was made, and the two commanders selected many men. Most would return to the fort with the keelboat after wintering next year with the expedition near the Mandan Indian villages on the Missouri River. The best of these men, however, would go all the way to the Pacific Ocean as key members of the expedition. Private Patrick Gass, a Pennsylvanian of Irish descent with the valuable skills of a carpenter, boatbuilder, and woodsman, was one. Sergeant John Ordway, an educated man who kept the fort's official records and performed other important bookkeeping duties, would prove his value to the expedition. Private Silas Goodrich was an expert fisherman, and Francois Labiche, half French and half Omaha Indian, was an experienced tracker, hunter, and boatman. Captains Lewis and Clark were pleased with these men and all the others added to their crew.

The flotilla set out at sunrise on December 1 with a frigid wind blowing up-river. Their first stop would be at the village of Bellefontaine in the Illinois Territory. As the boats pulled near the small dock, curious villagers came to the riverbank.

"Is there a Mr. Walden here?" Lewis called.

"I am Jesse Walden," a small, middle-aged man said, stepping forward. "But your provisions haven't yet arrived. They were due here yesterday. I'm sorry!"

Lewis grimaced with disappointment and addressed his crew. "We have to wait for them. We can't go on without them. Let's set up camp, men." It proved to be only a one-day delay, but the men were glad for even a brief rest from the oars and the dangers of the river. As the flotilla set out again, a hard, cold wind blew against them until mid-morning, when it suddenly reversed and enabled them to sail.

Finally, on a blustery and snowy day, they arrived at St. Louis, the westernmost major settlement in the United States. Built on a bluff above a flood plain, St. Louis had been settled forty years before and now had a population of about one thousand people.

"Clark, I'm going to stay here to order the extra supplies we need and find out what I can about the Missouri River and what's ahead for us with the Indians. Maybe I can find a local trapper or trader who is familiar with the area and the Indians. You take the men and boats on ahead and start building a fort where we can spend the winter."

The men were disappointed to miss St. Louis with its bawdy ladies and whiskey mills they had heard so much about, but they grumbled only among themselves.

After Clark and the expedition left, Captain Lewis looked up the town mayor, whose office was in an unpainted clapboard house on the main street. The mayor was working at his desk.

"I'm Captain Meriwether Lewis," he said. "I'm co-commander of a U.S. Army expedition sent to explore the Louisiana Territory. I wonder if you know of any trappers or traders who have been up the Missouri River and can advise me."

The mayor, a rotund, friendly man in his early forties named Rupert Gillette, beamed as he shook Lewis's hand. "I'm happy to make your acquaintance, Captain. I heard you were coming. Sit down and let's drink a toast to your mission." He took out a bottle and two glasses from a drawer of his desk and poured them a drink. "I'll be able to tell my grandchildren that I shook the hand of the man who explored the Louisiana Territory."

Lewis smiled and said, "As of right now, we have explored only the Ohio River, which didn't need exploring. But once we turn up the Missouri, we will be in new territory and need all the help we can get from people who have been up that way."

They touched glasses in salute and sipped the contents.

"You might look up Blaize Gaston," the mayor suggested. "He's a French trapper who has spent some time in that area. He lived with the Indians a couple of years and has an Indian squaw. You'll most likely find him at Twilliger's Tavern at this time of day."

Lewis located Twilliger's Tavern and Blaize Gaston, a seasoned, serious frontiersman in his thirties. The tavern was a log shack with two rooms, one for customers in the front and one for supplies in the back. Lewis introduced himself and his mission.

"Can you tell me about conditions up the Missouri and about the disposition of the Indians?" Lewis asked.

Gaston paused, the flames in the big fireplace nearby reflecting in his dark eyes. "The Indians are all right except for the Sioux farther on up the river. They are as mean as rattlesnakes, and they'll take half of what you got just to let you pass through their part of the river." He was clearly a straightforward, no-nonsense individual, which made him an ideal source for the kind of information Lewis needed.

"How many Sioux are there?"

"Hundreds," came the prompt reply.

"What about the other tribes?"

"All friendly except the Sioux."

"Thank you for the information, Gaston," Lewis said at the end of their conversation, rising from his chair. "I appreciate your candor." The men shook hands and Lewis left the tavern.

Large snowflakes were falling as Lewis walked toward the general store on the opposite side of the street. It was late afternoon and darkness would be coming on soon. He ordered the additional supplies needed for the thirty more men they had acquired for the expedition. Lewis also decided to buy four blunderbusses and a one-pounder cannon that could be mounted on a swivel in the keelboat, just in case they had to fight their way through the Sioux territory. The shopkeeper needed a few hours to gather his order, so Lewis rented a bed in the back room of the store for the night. Before he slept, he wrote a report to President Jefferson about the progress of the expedition to this point.

Dear Mr. President,

We have arrived in St. Louis, and Captain Clark and the expedition have gone on up the Mississippi River a ways to start building a fort where we will spend the winter. I have stayed behind in St. Louis to talk with as many people as possible who have knowledge of the Missouri River area. Because of the tremendous current of the Mississippi, we have had to double the size of the expedition until we reach the Mandan Indian villages. I have learned that we are very likely to have trouble with the Sioux Indians on the Upper Missouri River; therefore, I have purchased a one-pounder cannon and a swivel base to mount it on just in case, but I hope we do not have to use it. In order to be as prepared as possible, I have also purchased four blunderbusses should we be forced to fight. I have learned that the other Indian tribes are friendly. You will hear from me again when we reach the Mandan villages next fall.

Your Obedient Servant,

Meriwether Lewis,
Captain, U.S. Army

CHAPTER 5

Fort DuBois

Winter, 1804

Clark had come prepared with his design for the fort, which he named Fort Dubois, and he immediately set the men to felling trees for the needed logs. He charged Private Gass, chosen because he was an expert carpenter, with supervising construction of the fort. For weeks, through snow, sleet, and howling wind, the woods around the camp rang with the sounds of axes, crosscut saws, awls, hammers, and the loud profanity of Private Gass as the fort took shape. Clark also made design improvements to the keelboat, including the addition of lockers along its sides with lids that could be raised to form rifle supports. With the lids down, the lockers formed a catwalk where crew members could walk while pushing the boat forward with iron-tipped poles.

The countryside around the mouth of the Missouri River was pleasant land that had been largely settled by French immigrants. The soil along both the Missouri and the Mississippi was exceedingly rich for twenty miles or more up each river, providing excellent land for farming.

For twelve days, Captain Lewis remained in St. Louis buying supplies and continuing to talk with trappers and traders who had traveled up the Missouri. He also conferred with town leaders, forming friendships as he told about the coming exploration of the unknown western territory. Even in this outpost town, everyone was aware of President Jefferson's purchase of the Louisiana Territory. As the chosen leader of the exploration, Lewis was already a famous man to them.

Among Lewis's new acquaintances was a man who had traveled to the Mandan villages. He confirmed what others had said: the Sioux Indians were hostile, numerous, well-armed, and certain to demand a tribute for passing through their stretch of the Missouri River. Lewis decided to send the cannon to Fort Dubois immediately for installation on the keelboat. It could fire a solid lead ball weighing a pound, or it could fire sixteen musket balls at once. At close range, it would be a highly lethal weapon. He enclosed a note of explanation.

> *I have been warned by everyone who has been up the Missouri that the Sioux will demand a tribute to allow us to pass their area. The last thing we want is a fight with Indians, but if the Sioux become hostile, they must be made to understand that they are now under jurisdiction of the United State government and must submit to that authority.*

Lewis also sent along the four blunderbusses, which were extra-heavy shotgun-type weapons that could be loaded with musket balls, scrap iron, or buckshot. He recommended that two of them be mounted on swivels in the stern of the keelboat and one in each pirogue.

At Fort Dubois, the enlisted men began to hear tales about powerful warring nations of savages along the upper Missouri who were larger-than-life, fierce, and particularly cruel to white men.

"Sounds like these Indians are real ferocious," Private John Colter laughed. "I can't wait to meet up with them." These soldiers and frontiersmen were not men to be intimidated, and the stories merely whetted their appetite for adventure.

"Clark, I think you should go to St. Louis with me and talk with some of these trappers who have been up the Missouri," Lewis said as the two men sat in Clark's office at camp. "It will be good for you to hear their first-hand accounts, and you might think of questions that I haven't."

"Good idea," Clark agreed. "We can leave Sergeant Ordway in command of the fort while we're gone." They called all the men together.

"Captain Clark and I are both going into St. Louis," Lewis announced. "Sergeant Ordway will be in charge while we're gone, and no one will leave the fort without his knowledge and permission."

Ordway was an impressive man—tall, muscular, and personable. However, when the captains departed, trouble raised its ugly head within an hour. These were young and robust men, many of them fresh from the wilds of Kentucky and unaccustomed to military discipline. During the first evening, John Colter, Hugh McNeal, Moses Reed, Alexander Willard, and Peter Weiser were playing poker in the snug warmth of their quarters. Colter was due to go on guard duty, but he was enjoying himself as his winnings piled up on the table before him.

"Aren't you supposed to be on duty?" one of the players asked him.

Colter grunted as he studied his cards.

Five minutes later Sergeant Ordway came through the door. "Colter, you're late relieving Warner at guard," he said.

Colter looked up from the game. "I don't take orders from enlisted men."

"The captains put me in charge in their absence, and you are to take orders from me as you would an officer."

"I'm winning now. I'll go on duty when I start losing."

"Very well. I'll write you up and you can tell the captains about it."

The next day, this same group of men requested Ordway's permission to visit a nearby whiskey vendor. Knowing they would most likely become drunk and rowdy, Ordway refused. The men left without permission and, as predicted, returned to the fort drunk and useless. Ordway wrote another report for the captains. Other men went out on the pretext of hunting and instead found a whiskey vendor and got drunk.

When Captain Clark returned from St. Louis and read Ordway's reports, he severely reproached the miscreants who stood at attention before him. "Disobeying a direct order from a military superior is a very serious offense," he announced sternly. "In wartime, it is punishable by death, and any time we are in Indian territory, we are in a potential war zone." He paused to emphasize the importance of his words. "I know you are all good men. That's why we selected you. But it is imperative that you obey orders. Since this is your first offense, you are restricted to camp for ten days. But if another such offense occurs, you will be dismissed from the expedition and sent back to your former duty stations."

The episode had a sobering effect on the men. However, the expedition was at Fort Dubois almost four months and there was little for them to do. These were healthy young men, full of energy and a desire for fun. When they felt bored with the day-to-day routine of the camp, they drank and fought among themselves.

The situation got out of hand when John Colter loaded his gun and threatened Sergeant Ordway when Ordway gave him an order. Fighting was one thing, but threatening to kill Sergeant Ordway, the ranking sergeant and a key man in the expedition, was too much. Military discipline had to be enforced, and the captains ordered Colter court-martialed for mutiny.

"How do you plead: Guilty or not guilty?" Captain Clark demanded.

"I'm guilty as hell, Captain," Colter admitted. At 5'7" Colter looked small, but he was broad-shouldered and powerfully built. He had been a ranger with Simon Kenton in the wilds of Ohio, and Clark knew he was as tough as they came. "I did it, but I want to go on this expedition more than I ever wanted anything. I'll be a model soldier from now on if I can stay with the expedition."

Clark scowled at the contrite soldier before him. "This is your second offense and the second time you have defied Sergeant Ordway. I shouldn't give you another chance, but we need capable men. This is your final warning. If anything like either of these offenses occurs again, you will be dismissed not only from this mission but also from the army. There will not be a third chance, and I mean for the entire duration of our expedition. We will abandon you in the wilderness if you are found guilty of another offense. Understand that very clearly."

"Yes sir, Captain. I understand."

Captain Clark dismissed him with a wave of his hand.

Preparations for the expedition intensified as the additional supplies Captain Lewis had ordered began to arrive in the middle of March. Ice on the Missouri River was breaking up, the days were getting longer, the first show of buds appeared on bushes and trees, and the great geese and duck migrations were beginning. Spring was arriving at last. The entire company showed renewed spirit and enthusiasm. The captains called an assembly to announce the names of those who would continue the westward journey after the Mandan villages. The two captains stood together, but Captain Lewis did the talking.

"Twenty-seven men will go with our expedition to the Pacific Ocean. This group will be known as the Corps of Discovery, since exploration is the main purpose of our journey. Those who are not chosen for the Corps of Discovery will accompany us as far as the Mandan Indian villages, where we will all spend the next winter. Then those men will return to St. Louis in the spring with the keelboat, under the command of Corporal Warfington."

The men were eager to learn who had been chosen. In addition to the two captains, the Corps of Discovery would include three sergeants and twenty-two privates. The Corps would be divided into three squads that would be led by Sergeants Ordway, Floyd, and Pryor. The last two men were cousins, and among the names of the privates called were two brothers, Joseph and Reuben Fields. Some of the other men were old friends from home. Although not announced, everyone understood that Captain Clark's slave, York, would go along, as well as Captain Lewis' beloved dog, Seaman.

Some of the men selected had an acquaintance with Indians and had gained a familiarity with the sign language that different tribes along the Missouri River used to communicate with each other. Among the men in the Corps of Discovery, all but two were in their twenties and unmarried.

Undoubtedly, among the men not chosen there was disappointment, but all realized the importance of the mission thus far, including the months to come with the Mandans.

"That went well," Clark commented to Lewis as the men dispersed.

"We have an excellent group of men for the work ahead of us. I'm eager to get started!"

CHAPTER 6

Springtime on the Missouri River

May, 1804

When George Drouillard arrived at Fort Dubois from St. Louis with seven additional French oarsmen, Captain Clark saw the opportunity for a trial run to St. Charles, twenty-one miles above the junction of the two mighty rivers. He directed a full loading of the keelboat and manned it with twenty oarsmen, strengthened now by the addition of the seven French *engages*.

Spring rains were tapering off as a small group of settlers gathered at river's edge to watch the expedition leave Fort Dubois. They cheered, and the men responded with exuberant waves, excited to be leaving Fort Duboise at last. From here on, except for stopping at St. Charles to pick up Captain Lewis, the only people the expedition expected to see as they traveled up the Missouri River were Indians and occasional trappers.

"We're a company of goldarned Daniel Boones!" shouted George Shannon exuberantly as they pushed off.

"J-J-Just like C-Christopher C-Columbus!" stuttered Reuben Fields.

St. Charles, a village of more than 400 people, stretched for a mile along the riverbank. As the Corps of Discovery approached, curious French and Indian residents came to greet the expedition, a rare event for this community. That evening, after a dinner of roast venison and fried fish, there was fiddle-playing and dancing as the locals honored the Corps. The men spent a very agreeable evening dancing with the local ladies. William Bratton and Silas Goodrich were accomplished dancers who were in great demand as dancing partners.

The next day, Captain Lewis arrived from St. Louis, gleefully greeting all the men, who gathered around him. Smiling broadly, Clark clapped him on the back, "Well, Meriwether, I think we are at last ready to embark on our historic journey! Everything is in order. We have made adjustments in loading the boats, and I can think of nothing else we need to do."

"Excellent, excellent!" Captain Lewis smiled, his eyes alive with excitement.

"I'll send two men to fetch the four horses that I brought from St. Louis for the hunters."

"I've sent the Fields brothers to the Daniel Boone settlement upstream to buy corn and butter," Clark added.

Next morning, they pushed off aboard the keelboat and two pirogues. Excitement and confidence filled the men of the Corps of Discovery—a confidence that Lewis and Clark hoped would support them through the toils, dangers, and suffering ahead. The first five miles of the river ran alongside level and fertile prairie; then rugged woodland began. The pirogues, commanded by Corporal Warfington, were manned by the French *engages*, experts with the craft. The men of the Corps of Discovery made up the crew of the keelboat. They were supervised by three sergeants: one at the helm, another at mid-ship, and the final in the bow. The sergeant at the helm steered while tending the compass. The sergeant at mid-ship commanded the guard, managed the sails, supervised the men at oars, and served as sergeant of the guard at night. The sergeant in the bow was charged with keeping a lookout for other craft in the river as well as spotting Indian camps or parties on shore.

As they approached Boone's settlement, Clark called out, "Put into shore to pick up the Fields brothers!" It seemed that all the people at this small settlement were flocking to the riverbank, surrounding the blond-haired Fields brothers, and shouting greetings to the boats.

"G-Give us a hand, C-Captain Clark!" Reuben Fields called out. The foodstuffs the brothers had purchased were stacked on the wooden dock. Two men leaped from the keelboat and helped load the barrels aboard; then the boats were off again amid shouts from the onlookers.

Later that day, the expedition passed a large cave called "The Tavern," which the men had heard about at Fort Dubois. The mouth of the cave was one-hundred-twenty feet wide and twenty feet high. A huge rock nearby had been painted with unusual signs and images that both the Indians and the local French revered. A mile further, the group passed the mouth of the Little Osage River.

Camping that night, the captains inspected the men's weapons and ammunition and divided the Corps of Discovery into five messes. Every evening, upon making camp, Sergeant Ordway was to distribute the day's rations to each mess. The men in each mess were to cook it all and save a portion for the next day because no cooking would be permitted until camp the next night. Every day, Drouillard and his hunters would go out on horseback and return with their game. When they returned with bear or deer, Ordway would not issue lard or meat in order to conserve rations.

The captains established a daily routine. The expedition departed at first light each morning, weather permitting. When they camped at night, the Sergeant of the Guard would immediately post sentinels— one near the boats and the other a distance from the river. At each change of guard during the night, the two sentinels being relieved would reconnoiter the area around the camp at a distance of one-hundred-fifty paces and inspect the vessels to confirm security. Warfington and Drouillard were exempted from guard duty because Warfington had the responsibility of the pirogues and their lading, and Drouillard led the hunters and handled special duties ashore for the captains.

Captain Lewis had a close call as he walked alone along the shore. He had climbed a cliff, lost his footing, and slid three hundred feet down the face of the cliff before stopping his fall with his espontoon, a spear-like staff with a crosspiece that could be used as a rifle support. Twenty feet more and he would have been lost in the river.

"I always thought it was old fashioned of you to carry that espontoon," Clark remarked when he learned of the incident. "Now I'm wishing I'd brought one myself. "I'm sure glad I had it," Lewis responded with a smile.

That evening as the group set up camp, two Indians emerged from a stand of trees, one raising his hand in greeting. The second young brave carried a deer across his shoulders. "For you," he said laying the deer on the ground.

Captain Clark stepped forward, smiling and reached out to shake hands. "Thank you! Will you sit with us a while?" The cook fires had not yet been lighted, so the men sat in a companionable circle, passing a jug of whiskey, as was their custom. When the visitors rose to leave, Lewis presented them with a full jug, thanking them and wishing them well.

"That may be a good omen for us," John Shields remarked.

Because Privates Francoise Labiche and Pierre Cruzatte had been up the Missouri before and were also the best boatmen in the Corps of Discovery, Captain Clark ordered them to alternate manning the portside bow oar. The man not on portside bow duty would be the bowman, whose tasks included warding off floating debris with one of the iron-tipped pushing poles, calling out warnings about danger ahead, and watching for sandbars and whirlpools.

Cruzatte was half French and half Omaha Indian, a small, wiry man, blind in one eye, with eyebrows that grew together in one heavy line across his forehead. The men of the expedition had begun calling him "St. Peter" because his appearance gave the impression of impending doom. However, he was not a sad or negative person. He chewed tobacco and often challenged the other tobacco chewers to a distance-spitting contest—lively games that he usually won. When he became excited he spoke only in his native French, and his English was heavily accented. The same was true of Labiche, but his ability to speak several Indian languages brought valuable assets to the expedition.

Thunderstorms seemed to be daily occurrences during May. When a favorable wind was at their backs, the boat crews ran up their sails; otherwise, they had to row, pole the boats, or tow them from shore. The work of moving the huge keelboat upriver against the strong current of the Missouri was exhausting. The pirogues were a little easier because they rode higher in the water. The pirogues were also more maneuverable when turning away from floating obstacles in the river. To help dodge obstacles, the pirogue crews had only to lean to one side or the other, whereas the entire keelboat crew had to rush to one side or the other of their boat again and again. The young men of the crew turned it into a jolly sport.

"This is like riding a wild horse," Patrick Gass laughed.

"Yeah, mate. Only we can't get off this ornery horse," Hugh McNeal added, rubbing his nose—a habit of his.

The Missouri was at its springtime high—almost at flood stage—and the obstacles the boats encountered often included whole trees that had been uprooted when the riverbank caved in. Thousands of tree branches swirled in the muddy river and clumped together to form barriers that impeded the expedition. Men stood at the bows of the boats with their steel-tipped poles to fend off such dangers. Sandbars shifted in the river. Whirlpools and eddies were too numerous to count. Because the current was stronger in the middle of the river, the crews stayed closer to the shore, even though caving riverbanks presented danger. The expedition was finding that the Missouri River was more difficult to navigate than the Mississippi, but budding trees and springtime blossoms provided an air of freshness and rebirth to each day, spurring the men's enthusiasm.

Clark usually rode in the keelboat because he enjoyed being with the men. Lewis often preferred being alone, so he walked on shore to examine plants, soil conditions, animals, and minerals—some of the main objectives of the expedition. He might cover thirty miles on foot in a day, making his way back to the river to rejoin the evening encampment.

At a particularly treacherous stretch of the river, the crews encountered "The Devil's Race Ground," which Lewis had been warned about when he was in St. Louis. The shallow current here was very swift and changed directions constantly. The expedition entered it slowly, tentatively. Things went smoothly at first, but then the tricky current suddenly whipped the keelboat about, threatening to overturn the boat, men, and supplies.

"Quick, men!" Sergeant Floyd shouted, leaping over the side of the keelboat. All hands except the helmsman immediately followed him, attached a rope to the stern, and managed to straighten the heavy, awkward boat.

"That was almost a catastrophe!" Sergeant Floyd exclaimed with relief to Captain Clark.

"Probably the first of many," Clark said. "That was quick thinking, Sergeant. We need to all stay alert like that."

As the group sailed past La Charette, the last small settlement of white people on the Missouri, John Colter remarked, clearly relishing the challenge, "From here on, it is just us and the river."

Captain Lewis, standing beside him, agreed. "In the most literal sense, it is now 'All for one and one for all'. We have only each other from now on."

CHAPTER 7

Good times Through Beautiful Country

June, 1804

In a little more than a month, the expedition had traveled four hundred miles up the Missouri River. Lewis continued to record the latitude and longitude of key points each day, and Clark kept his evolving map up to date as the river snaked its way through pristine wilderness. The landscape was always changing, always breath-taking. The clear, cold water of abundant rivers and streams feeding into the Missouri, the massive trees in full leaf bordering the river, the beauty of bright green grasslands extending as far as the eye could see—each day the men were awed by the view before them. .

"This would make excellent farming country," Lewis observed. "I think the President made a very wise decision when France offered it for sale."

"If land like this continues across the entire Louisiana Territory, the United States will be a wealthy country," Clark agreed.

Late spring also had a disagreeable side. Clouds of gnats swarmed constantly around the men's heads in the daytime, and mosquitoes made them miserable both day and night. To ward off the irritating pests when they were in camp, the men stood in the smoke of their campfires as long as they could hold their breaths. They also smeared thick, smelly bear grease on their necks, faces, and hands to repel mosquitoes during the day. Ticks attached themselves to Seaman's skin, and when the men sat around the evening campfire, George Shannon began running his hand through Seaman's fur to search for and destroy the ugly pests. When he found one, he would pull it loose and toss it into the fire where it popped as flames consumed it. Seaman soon was searching out Shannon each time the fires were lighted.

The Corps of Discovery encountered two separate parties coming downriver. The first party had two canoes loaded with pelts and the second party had four rafts of pelts, probably both the bounty of winter trapping. Each time the Corps of Discovery passed trappers with their loads of skins, the men cheered and shouted in greeting as they passed.

Captain Lewis, continuing to roam on shore, found plants and shrubs that he had never seen before, including one he called Wood's Rose and another he called Gumweed. He recorded drawings and descriptions of these unknown specimens in daily notes. He included in his notes comments about this open and fertile countryside. As they approached the mouth of the greater Osage River, Captain Lewis called out for the keelboat to put into shore.

"We're going to stay here a couple of days to rest up, men, so let's make a good camp."

Many of the men cheered. When ashore, Captain Lewis decided to take the longitude and latitude of the spot where the Corps would camp, but he needed a clear view of the horizon to use his instruments. That meant that a stand of trees would have to be cut down, so some of the men got to work immediately with their axes while others set up camp.

At this point, the Missouri River was 875 yards wide, and the mouth of the Osage River was 397 yards wide. This rest break included writing in journals, dozing in the sun, and playing games. The hunters and fishermen, of course, were never entitled to an entire day off; whether working or playing, the expedition had to eat.

Captain Clark sought out Joseph Whitehouse, the former hide-curer and tailor. "Whitehouse, everyone has holes and tears in their clothes. Do you think you can make new clothes for us from our deer hides?"

"Well, I've never tried it with deerskin," he answered, stroking the stubble on his chin. "The hides will be a little tougher to push a needle through, but I'm willing to try."

Shortly after the Corps resumed its journey, the bowman called out, "Pirogue ahead!" All eyes turned up river. It was three trappers who had been hunting and trapping on the upper Missouri for an entire year.

"Looks like you had good luck," Warfington said, looking at stacks of pelts in their pirogue.

"Well, we have furs and skins, but we can't eat them," one of the trappers responded, looking through the many faces to identify a leader. "We are completely out of provisions, including gunpowder to kill game."

"Put in to shore, and we'll help you out," Captain Clark offered, motioning to his own men.

As all the boats pulled up to shore, Drouillard and his hunters arrived carrying five deer across shoulders and hanging from poles. Captain Clark gave the biggest deer to the trappers.

"We'll also give you enough gunpowder to get you to St. Louis," he told them. "That will at least enable you to feed yourselves."

"We are much obliged to you, Captain! We were in a bad way."

Lewis, watching with approval, was reminded of his boyhood days when his love of nature led him roaming across the Virginia countryside, sometimes ranging so far that only hunger would drive him home.

The spirit and camaraderie of the men of the Corps of Discovery were high. They were enjoying their adventure and each other's company. Every evening there was singing and dancing led by Cruzatte and Gibson, who both played the fiddle, and George Shannon's talented singing. The men loved to dance, and they didn't care that they weren't always graceful. Everyone enjoyed the entertainment, which allowed the men to poke fun at each other, have a good time, and forget about the tensions of the day that had just concluded. They vied with each other to invent new dance steps, laughing uproariously at some of the gyrations.

"As long as their spirits hold up like this, we'll have nothing to worry about," Lewis told Clark.

A short distance above the mouth of a creek that emptied into the Missouri, the expedition encountered a massive limestone overhang that projected out onto the river. Strangely, it was inlaid with red and blue flint, and it showed that great quantities had been gouged out of the rock.

"Flint makes good arrowheads," Drouillard said. "The Indians probably visit here often."

The boats stopped to investigate the site, but quickly decided to keep moving when they learned that the gouged-out areas in the rock housed dens of rattlesnakes.

For two weeks game had been plentiful, which was fortunate because during this time the men needed more food than usual to restore their energy. The reason was the absence of wind, when sails could not be used, requiring the men to expend their strength to row against the mighty current of the Missouri River. Often along these picturesque miles, their hunters brought in five deer by noon. All the venison that was not immediately consumed was cut into thin strips and dried in the sun or in the smoke of a fire. The prairie also abounded with hazel grapes and a very tasty wild plum that the men called Osage plums. The Corps of Discovery was eating well.

Once again, the bowman called out, "Rafts ahead!" Two rafts were approaching the expedition: one was loaded with pelts and the other with barrels—probably byproducts like bear grease or tallow. All three boats of the expedition put in to shore to talk with the trappers.

"I am Pierre Dorion," the leader of the party said. Then he introduced the rest of his party, who were all Indians. Dorion was a short, stocky, middle-aged Frenchman who had a jovial smile and weathered skin. "Where are you headed?" he asked.

"To the Mandan villages," Captain Clark responded. "If you have bear grease, we'll buy some." Then he added, "Where are you coming from?"

"From a Yankton Sioux village up above the Platte River," Dorion said.

"We have been told that the Sioux are very hostile," Clark said.

"There are two tribes of Sioux along the river—the Yankton Sioux and the Teton Sioux. The Yanktons are fine people, but the Tetons are the ones you speak of. I have lived with the Yanktons for nine years and have a Yankton wife."

"Do you speak the Sioux language?"

"Couldn't have lived with them nine years if I didn't."

"Do you speak any other languages?"

"Not Indian. Just French and English."

Clark gestured toward his men. "We have been sent by President Jefferson to represent the United States among the Indians. The United States has purchased the Louisiana Territory from France, and we are on a mission to explore it. Part of our mission is to send some Indian chiefs to Washington to meet President Jefferson. If we could persuade you to return to the Yankton Sioux with us and help us convince their chief to go on such an important journey, it would be a great help to us. We will pay you, of course, as an interpreter."

Dorion was silent as he considered Clark's request. "Well, I hadn't thought about anything like that," he said after a few moments.

"Spend the night with us and think it over," Clark urged. "You can give us your answer in the morning."

"Yes sir, I reckon I could do that."

After they had eaten that evening, all the men gathered around one of the campfires. Cruzatte played his fiddle, Shannon sang "Old Molly Hare" and "The White Cockade" in his rich baritone voice, and the men danced with abandon. Even two of Dorion's Indian party joined in the dancing.

"York, show these fellows some Nigra dancing," Clark called to his servant.

York was a big man, but he was agile and full of fun as he stepped, leaped, and swung with dances from his heritage. Dorion and the Indians clapped gleefully. By the time they turned in for the night, Dorion had been won over to the Corps of Discovery.

CHAPTER 8

Adventures and Problems

Midsummer 1804

Continuing up the wide Missouri, surrounded by lush countryside, the men noticed that the cliffs alongside the river were beginning to show wide strata of black. Out of curiosity they pulled over to investigate. Within minutes several men called out, "Coal!" to the rest of the expedition. Lewis, noting the discovery in his notebook, ordered the men to dig out a quantity to test in their campfires that evening. They found that the coal burned hot, but with considerably less flame and smoke than they needed to make venison jerky, so they bypassed the coal.

The area abounded with plums, raspberries, and several varieties of apples. As the Corps of Discovery continued, it passed prairie the men thought was the best land they had ever seen, which Lewis duly noted in his journal.

"I think I could make this my permanent home and settle down here," Hugh McNeal said, rubbing his nose.

"Yeah, but the only problem is there ain't no women," William Warner responded.

Each day, hunters in the expedition signaled the boats to come to shore and retrieve the game they had killed and the berries they had picked. At times, the expedition passed bad stretches of the river with shallow water, rocks, and swift current. At such times, the men walked on shore and pulled the keelboat and pirogues with tow ropes.

Problems appeared as some of the men began to be afflicted with boils and others came down with dysentery. Captain Lewis was glad for the basic medical skills he had been taught by his mother and the professors at the University of Pennsylvania. Captain Clark had seen other soldiers suffering from dysentery in the army, and he offered a suggestion to the men. "When you get a drink of water, dip your cup far below the surface of the river to avoid any scum." Even on the active Missouri, there were stretches where shallow, still water became contaminated during hot weather.

Arriving at the mouth of the Kansas River, the captains decided the expedition would camp several days to rest while Captain Lewis took celestial observations for their records. Private John Thompson, who had experience as a civilian surveyor, assisted the captains with both celestial observations and map making. Some of the men unloaded the white pirogue and turned it upside down for repairs while others put provisions out to air. Others found ash timber and made twenty oars. Drouillard and the hunters killed eight deer.

During the first night in this camp, there was a raid on the whiskey supply. Just after midnight, Private John Collins, on guard duty for the camp, decided to tap a barrel. Enjoying his secret drink in the dark, he tapped it again, and then again. Soon he was drunk. When his friend, Private Hugh Hall, discovered him, he decided to have a drink also. Soon, both men were drunk. At dawn, the sergeant of the guard discovered them and arrested both men.

The supply of whiskey was considered precious by all the men. Not only did each man look forward to his daily ration of one gill, but the captains had planned that part of the whiskey would be an attractive gift to Indian tribes along the journey. The expedition had brought along 120 gallons of whiskey, and when used as planned, it would last 104 days. Although it could be stretched by watering it down, it clearly would not be enough to last to the Pacific Ocean and back again.

Captain Clark immediately drew up court-martial papers, and the trial began just before noon. Sergeant Pryor presided, Private John Potts served as judge advocate, and four privates were members of the court.

"Private Collins, you are charged with the theft of whiskey that belongs to the Corps of Discovery. How do you plead to the charge?" Pryor asked.

"Not guilty." Collins fidgeted as he considered the significance of a court martial charge on his record.

The court speedily found him guilty.

Pryor intoned solemnly, "The court sentences you to a hundred lashes on your bare back with a rawhide whip." Collins swallowed hard and shuffled his feet.

Then it was Hall's turn.

"Guilty," he pleaded, deciding that pleading 'not guilty' was a losing proposition.

Pryor pronounced judgment again as Hall's eyes darted from man to man on the panel. "Because you were not on guard duty at the time of the offense, the court sentences you to fifty lashes. Court adjourned."

Captains Lewis and Clark approved the sentences, which were carried out that afternoon after the Corps of Discovery paraded for inspection. The other men had no sympathy for the culprits, and this punishment permitted them to unleash their anger in a controlled and satisfying way. Although the punishment gave the two men wounds that made sleeping uncomfortable for a night or two, the expedition didn't lose their services. Both were back at work a few hours after their lashing, quiet and contrite.

On the morning of July 4, the captains ordered the bow gun fired and distributed the daily gill of whiskey to each man early in the day as celebration of the twenty-eighth anniversary of the signing of the Declaration of Independence. The day was hot, sweat poured from the men's bodies, and Robert Frazier collapsed with sunstroke. Captain Lewis bled Frazier and gave him a dose of niter, which relieved his symptoms.

In the river near their camp was an enormous sandbar that was a half mile wide and completely covered with driftwood. The men discovered that the sandbars in this area of the Missouri were the habitat of a bird new to science, which Captain Lewis called the Interior Tern. They were fork-tailed birds that darted and swooped like swallows. The birds were noisy, squawking in a high pitch that in large numbers sounded like frightened pigs. They nested on the sandbars and lived on fish from the river. Their chicks were the same color as the sand, making them very difficult to see. Lewis was always excited when he recorded the description of an unknown species in his journal.

Hunters from the Corps came upon a herd of elk, which leaped into the river to escape them. Seaman, barking wildly, dove into the river in pursuit. He swam quickly to a young elk, broke its neck with one bite of his huge jaws, and returned it to shore. Meanwhile, the hunters shot two other elk in the river, and Seaman retrieved them also. The men laughed when the dog stood proudly on shore with the elk, shaking the water from his fur and wagging his tail as he waited for praise and pats.

"That dog earns his keep!" St. Peter said, flashing what passed as a smile on his sober visage. "Like having extra man in crew. Only he don't mind getting wet like men do,"

As usual, the boat crews blazed symbols on trees along the river so the hunters on land would know they had passed and could follow them. They also fired their cannon at times as a signal to those away from the main expedition.

The sergeant of the guard came upon Private Alexander Willard asleep on guard duty one night. This was a very serious offense that was punishable by death according to army regulations. The captains constituted the court this time because of the severity of the offense.

"How do you plead, guilty or not guilty?" Captain Clark demanded.

"Guilty of lying down; not guilty of going to sleep," was the response.

The captains found him guilty on both counts and sentenced him to one hundred lashes each day for four days, beginning that evening at sunset. This offense was among the most serious because it put the entire Corps in jeopardy.

"Them captains is acting awful high and mighty," Moses Reed groused to Newman. "What gives them the right to beat a man half to death because he can't stay awake all night?"

"Well, that was a rough sentence, sure enough," Newman agreed.

One afternoon, a violent thunderstorm struck with startling suddenness while the keelboat was near the upper point of a troublesome sandbar. As the storm increased in ferocity, the opposite shore caved into the river, tossing the keelboat violently in the roaring water, threatening its destruction. The men leaped from the boat into the water instantly, trying to brace the boat against the sandbar to prevent the loss of their largest boat and crucial supplies. It required all the men's strength and determination, but they saved the keelboat. In less than fifteen minutes, the storm suddenly subsided. Almost immediately the river again became calm and smooth. A gentle wind rose in their favor, and the crew ran up their sails, floating serenely up the river as if nothing had happened.

"We never had weather like this back home!" Private John Shields muttered as the men again stood on the deck, dripping wet, their faces filled with relief.

"I expect we're going to see a lot more things that are like nothing we ever saw back home," Captain Lewis agreed.

As July wore on, the Corps of Discovery came to higher plains and had to struggle to handle the boats in the heat, even sometimes stopping for three hours at midday to rest.

In the bottoms, grass often grew to a height of four feet. Lewis documented wild timothy, lambsquarter, cockleburs, grapes, plums, and gooseberries, their plants varying slightly from the familiar strains in the East. Something the Corps was seeing frequently were man-made mounds, which they assumed to be Indian burial grounds.

Finally, the expedition came to the mouth of the River Platte, where the captains chose a campsite they named Camp White Catfish because the ever-whistling Silas Goodrich had caught a large white catfish at that spot. The camp was on a wooded island about ten miles beyond the

Platte, at a point that would be convenient for making observations. The men pitched their tents and prepared to stay a few days. The wind blew hard here and raised so much dust that Captain Clark couldn't work on his map in the captains' tent. He tried the keelboat, but it rocked too much in the wind. He finally quit until the wind died. Mosquitoes were such a problem that sitting still for even a moment was extremely disagreeable. The men stayed in motion or tossed their mosquito netting over themselves for protection.

The Platte, which trappers in St. Louis had described to Lewis as a "mile wide and an inch deep," was bursting with animal and plant life. Lewis learned that the Platte was rarely more than four feet deep but was at times as much as three miles wide. At its mouth, it was only three-quarters of a mile wide.

"Drouillard, I was told that three nations of Indians live on the Platte River," Captain Lewis said. "Take St. Peter with you and see if you can find any of them. If you do, invite them to a council with us."

While the expedition waited for Drouillard and Cruzatte to return, the men made a flagstaff and raised the United States flag in anticipation of the council with the Indians. While they waited, they put the contents of the boats out to dry, and some of the men dressed skins or made new oars. But Drouillard and Cruzatte returned with disappointing news.

"The chiefs and young men are out on the prairie hunting buffalo," Drouillard said. "They won't return for days."

"We can't wait for them," Lewis said, obviously disappointed. "We have to keep moving." To Clark he muttered, "The first tribe we've encountered and we miss them. I hope this doesn't bode ill for us."

Drouillard, while out hunting a few days later, came upon three Oto Indians dressing an elk they had killed. Using sign language, he greeted them in a friendly manner. They made him a present of some of the elk meat, and he invited them to return with him to the keelboat. The captains greeted the Otos, gave them a gift of whiskey, and sent Private La Liberte with them to their village to invite their chiefs to the Corps of Discovery's camp for a council. The men made camp in an open place to wait for the Oto Indians, hoping for a council.

The prairie here was covered with grass a foot high and timber that included willow, cottonwood, elm, sycamore, hickory, walnut, oak, and mulberry. Goodrich whistled as he caught several catfish, and the hunters killed turkeys, geese, and ducks.

"Goodrich, you're the happiest person I ever met," John Colter told him.

"Why do you say that?"

"Because you whistle all the time,"

"I just like music!" Goodrich explained.

"Then why don't you sing with Shannon when Cruzatte plays in the evenings?"

"Because I can sing only a three-note range, but I can whistle anything," Goodrich grinned.

Lewis took latitude and longitude while Clark worked on his map as the expedition waited for the Otos to arrive. Joseph Fields trapped a badger, an animal totally new to the men of the Corps of Discovery, although Cruzatte and the other Frenchmen knew about it. One of the trappers caught a live beaver, which the men found surprisingly easy to tame. Catfish were plentiful, and John Potts caught three very large ones. The captains named the creek in which he caught them Potts Creek.

CHAPTER 9

Indian Country

August, 1804

The first day of August was Captain Clark's birthday and to celebrate the occasion, the cooks prepared a lavish meal of venison, elk, and beaver tail with dessert that included the abundant fruits in the area: cherries, plums, raspberries, currants, and grapes. The men enjoyed the special meal as much as Clark did. Afterward, Cruzatte brought out his fiddle, Shannon sang "College Hornpipe" and "Sir Roger de Coverly," and the men danced. The men toasted Captain Clark with their daily gill of whiskey.

Captain Lewis enjoyed the celebration, but he was becoming more and more anxious about their failure to meet groups of Indians in this country where he knew they lived.

"We must make contact with them," he reminded Clark in frustration. "An important part of our mission is to inform all the tribes that their new nation intends to embrace them if they will put down their weapons for a more peaceful way of life."

"Yes, but can we persuade them to give up their warrior way of life and become farmers? I don't know, but I do know we must be patient," Clark counseled. He paused before adding, "The tribes are out hunting buffalo now, but they'll show up soon, I feel certain."

The Missouri River snaked its way through a country of lush green vegetation that was beginning to show a blush of late summer brown. The surface of the river sparkled, almost blinding the men in the hot afternoon sun, and the prairie grass on both sides of the river had grown to heights of almost eight feet.

Early in August, to the relief of the captains, a delegation of six Oto Indian chiefs and seven warriors arrived at the Corps' campsite, accompanied by a French trader named Giroux to serve as translator. They came in boats made of animal skin—boats that would not turn over! The Otos were dressed in buckskin and moccasins, much like the men of the expedition, but the Indians were also adorned with feathers and porcupine quills and armed with bows and arrows. Every soldier in the Corps of Discovery was alert for any possible threat. La Liberte, the soldier sent to fetch the Otos, did not return with them, even though the Otos said he had left the day before. Lewis and Clark were surprised by his absence.

The soldiers raised the American flag and then drove poles into the ground on which they draped the keelboat sail to provide shade for the meeting. To reflect the importance of the council, Captains Lewis and Clark changed into their full-dress uniforms despite the sultry August heat.

"Ask how many are in their tribe," Lewis told Giroux when the formality of introductions was finished.

Giroux, a short, wiry man with a face weathered from years of out-of-doors life, answered the question himself. "There are about two-hundred-and-fifty of them. They are farming and hunting people who live in semi-permanent villages. Their big chief is out with their young men hunting buffalo, but a few of their lesser chiefs are here. They have brought gifts for you." At that, several of the younger Indians presented five watermelons as a happy murmur arose from the soldiers standing by.

"Ah! Watermelon," Lewis smiled, nodding to the presenters. "Thank you! In this stifling heat, we all will enjoy them!"

Lewis reciprocated with gifts of tobacco twisted together into what was called a "carrot," as well as a quantity of pork, flour, and cornmeal. After the presentation, Clark called the Corps of Discovery to attention and they performed some marching drills for the entertainment of their visitors. Captain Lewis addressed the Otos through Giroux.

"All the land west of the Mississippi River to the great mountains, where the river flows both east and west, is now part of the United States of America," he began with an authoritative but friendly tone of voice. "All of our brothers in this land now have a new father who has adopted them as sons." He explained that the United States would become the trading partner of all Indians, and that everyone would benefit. The six Oto chiefs delivered short speeches, acknowledging their new father and pledging cooperation.

"The chiefs also said they want gunpowder and whiskey," Giroux told Lewis.

Lewis presented a canister of gunpowder, fifty musket balls, and a bottle of whiskey. Then Clark gave them trinkets, which pleased the Otos greatly. They smiled and nodded to each other approvingly, and said something else to Giroux.

"They said the French had never given such fine presents," Giroux explained.

"Good!" Clark responded. "It's comforting to know that we have an advantage."

As the expedition traveled deeper and deeper into unknown territory, Private Moses Reed had become increasingly troubled. One evening he found the opportunity to talk with John Newman out of earshot of the other men.

"How can we survive hundreds and hundreds of miles of wilderness with only savages to turn to in time of trouble? I'm afraid we're all going to die out here—killed either by Indians, starvation, or accidents. We haven't seen the worst of it yet. It's more dangerous than I ever imagined!"

"Well, maybe you're right, but I think we'll make it," Newman replied, trying to keep his squeaky, high-pitched voice to a whisper. "The captains always seem to know what they're doing, and I trust them."

"Well, I don't because they don't know what's ahead. I think this trip is doomed." Reed's dark eyes were intense, filled with fear. At that moment, Reed decided to desert the expedition, and he knew he would have to do it alone because it would be too risky to try to recruit Newman, as he had planned. He decided he would return to the Oto village and make it from there back to civilization.

When the Corps pulled to shore to make camp the next evening, Reed approached Clark. "Captain, I left my tomahawk back at the council site. I'd like permission to go back and get it."

Clark considered the importance of the missing weapon and gave his permission. "Just be sure you're back in time to take your place at your oar in the morning."

Reed had stashed his clothes and extra ammunition outside the camp. Retrieving them, he took off into the wilderness to find his way to the Oto village. Rain fell all night and by morning, the rain and wind were so fierce that the expedition was delayed for two hours. Even so, Reed had not returned.

"Has anyone seen Reed?" Captain Lewis asked among the men as they busied themselves getting ready to shove off.

No one had, and Newman kept his suspicions to himself. Finally, the expedition departed without Reed, stopping at noon for Lewis to make and record observations. By the end of the day, Reed still had not returned.

"I'll check his personal belongings," Clark said to Lewis, and he soon discovered that Reed's belongings and ammunition were gone.

"Reed has deserted!" a surprised Clark told Lewis.

"It looks like it," Lewis agreed. "This is disappointing because the men all seem in such good spirits. Let's send a detail to find him and bring him back."

The captains selected a four-man detail, headed by George Drouillard and including Privates Reuben Fields, Bratton, and Labiche to find Reed and bring him back.

"If he won't surrender, kill him," Lewis instructed Drouillard coldly. "Army regulations demand death for desertions. If he won't surrender, let him pay the debt he owes."

Captain Clark added, "At the Oto village, if their big chief has returned from the buffalo hunt, bring him back with you if he is willing. Also, see what you can find out about La Liberte while you're there. We'll wait for you near the Omaha village."

Drouillard and the three men departed directly for the Oto village, the only logical place for Reed to go. They traveled all the following day, camped that night, and at midmorning of the second day approached the Oto village with care, looking for Reed.

"There he is," Field whispered, pointing.

"Men, prime your muskets. Be ready to shoot if Reed runs," Drouillard ordered.

With their guns loaded and ready, the men quietly entered the village and surrounded a visibly shocked Reed. He started to raise his musket, but quickly realized he would be killed before he could fire.

"Reed, you are under arrest for desertion," Drouillard said. "My orders are to bring you back or kill you. Which will it be?"

Reed was so frightened he could barely speak. "You men know this is an impossible expedition," he pleaded, searching their faces for agreement. "We will never make it through this wilderness with savages waiting to kill everyone." His musket fell from his shaking hands. "I want to live, not die," he pleaded.

"I'm not here to argue with you, Reed." Drouillard motioned to his companions. "Tie his hands behind his back while I look for the chief of the Otos."

Drouillard found the chief and invited him and others from his village to come to the Corps of Discovery camp for a council. Then he asked about La Liberte, and the chief summoned the French trapper. Private Fields stepped over to hear their conversation.

The two men spoke French, but Fields could tell that Drouillard asked him about being gone from the Corps of Discovery. La Liberte was surprised and taken aback, strongly denying a second question Drouillard asked him. Drouillard motioned back toward the way his group had come, and La Liberte seemed to agree, but he asked a question and hurried away.

"Did La Liberte desert, Drouillard?" Fields asked.

"No. He is going for his gun and clothes and is coming with us. " The Corps of Discovery never saw La Liberte again.

Meantime, the expedition had continued and come upon the gravesite of the famous Chief Blackbird, an Omaha chief whose memory was so revered by his people that they still brought food to his grave four years after his death. The grave, located atop a three-hundred-foot hill, was a mound of earth six feet high. To honor him and to please his people, the men placed a flagpole and flag on the mount.

"The Omahas say he is buried astride his horse," Clark said.

"I think very few leaders in history have been so loved," Captain Lewis added, in awe of the legends about the mighty chief.

They camped in a nearby cottonwood grove that night, and the next morning Lewis summoned Sergeant Floyd.

"Floyd, take Cruzatte, Shannon, Warner, and Cooper and see if you can find the local Omaha village. If you find them, invite them to a council with us."

Floyd took along a flag and some tobacco as presents. However, locating the Omaha village proved to be a challenge because the men had to struggle through dense thistles and huge sunflower plants that rose to a height of ten feet. They finally came upon an abandoned Indian village of three hundred dwellings that had been burned some time before. A few miles further, the group came upon the current Omaha village, where an old chief greeted them. Cruzatte spoke the Omaha language and communicated fluently with him.

"We have come from a faraway land to make friends with our brothers, the Omahas," he said. "We come to invite your chiefs to come and talk with our chiefs."

The old chief nodded. "Our chiefs and young men have gone to hunt buffalo. Only women, children, and old men are here now," he explained.

"Just our luck," Floyd said when Cruzatte translated for him. "Ask him about the burned village."

"We found a large village that had been burned. Why was it burned?"

"There was much sickness. Half of our people died. We burned the village to stop the bad sickness."

The men returned to the camp alone, and when Floyd reported on the trip, both Lewis and Clark were disappointed.

"Damn!" Lewis said. "Apparently all the Indian tribes are out hunting buffalo. The time of year is preventing us from counseling with these tribes. I had hoped we could meet with all the friendly Indians before meeting with any hostile ones."

"We'll keep trying," Clark said. "I'm sure they can't stay out more than a week at a time."

Game was scarce in these grasslands, so Captain Clark took a crew of ten men to make a brush drag and take it to Omaha Creek, where they caught 318 fish. Their success took them the next day to a nearby creek that had been dammed by beavers. This time, they caught more than 300 salmon, pike, bass, and perch. The men had a great fish fry that evening, along with much fiddling and dancing. During the festivities, Labiche arrived with the news that Drouillard's detachment was returning.

"Do they have Reed?" Lewis asked.

"Yes, and some Indians are with them."

Drouillard arrived with Reed, two Oto chiefs, seven Oto warriors, and the Oto's French interpreter, Giroux. Lewis and Clark greeted the party warmly, ignoring Reed to make him feel insignificant. The Otos were covered only with breech cloths, blankets, or brightly painted buffalo robes. After introductions and the usual exchange of presents, Lewis explained to their guests that the expedition was going to conduct a military trial for the man who had deserted. The captains created the court with Captain Lewis as the presiding judge. A nervous Reed was brought before it.

"Private Moses Reed, you are charged with the very serious crime of desertion in the face of potential danger," Lewis began. "How do you plead, guilty or not guilty?"

"Guilty," Reed responded, hanging his head.

"How do you plead to the charge of theft of a musket, a shot pouch, gunpowder, and musket balls?"

"Guilty."

"You deserted your post in potentially hostile territory at a time when every soldier is vitally needed at his post. Under the Articles of War of the United States Army, you could be executed for this offense. But since you surrendered and returned to face the consequences of your action, it is the sentence of this court that you run the gauntlet four times and then be discharged from the army. You will give up all soldierly duties as unfit to be a soldier and be assigned to hard labor as an oarsman with the French *engages* without pay until you can be returned to St. Louis."

The Oto chiefs pleaded with the captains on Reed's behalf when they learned what "running the gauntlet" meant.

"The Oto never strike anyone, not even children," Chief Little Thief explained to Captain Lewis.

"This man's absence from his duties could have endangered the lives of our entire party," Lewis explained. "We cannot let such disloyalty go unpunished. It is our law."

The two chiefs nodded to each other with understanding, and Chief Little Thief said, "We punish disloyalty with death." The Oto delegation witnessed the punishment without further comment.

Each soldier in the Corps of Discovery cut nine sturdy switches from trees and formed two lines with a four-foot path between them. At a given signal, Reed was forced to walk nude through the path as men mercilessly beat him with their switches. After four trips through the gauntlet, Reed's body was a bloody mess.

During the council that evening, the captains entertained the Otos by demonstrating a magnet and by firing the air gun with its powerful blast. The Otos were impressed, but they soon became troublesome by begging for whiskey and gifts, not satisfied with the presents already given to them.

"We have already given you all the presents we have," Captain Clark explained. "Let us be happy in the friendship between us." However, he had to give them a dram of whiskey before the Otos were willing to leave.

CHAPTER 10

The Yankton Sioux

August 1804

Sergeant Floyd became ill during breakfast, suddenly doubling over with excruciating pain in his stomach and crawling away from his mess group for a little privacy in his discomfort. The breakfast fare—hard biscuits, bear jerky, and tea—would not stay down. The men summoned Captain Lewis to see if his knowledge of medicine and herbs could help Floyd. Captain Lewis treated him, made him a bed in the keelboat cabin, and designated York to look after him. Sweat broke out on Floyd's forehead, and he clutched his stomach, groaning. He was gravely ill with an unknown ailment, and the entire expedition was concerned not only about his survival, but also fearful that the sickness might spread to the rest of them. Seaman stretched out on the floor beside Floyd's bed and remained there, compassionately sensing the seriousness of the situation and licking Floyd's hand now and then.

Floyd's cousin, Sergeant Pryor, also kept vigil at his bedside, trying to cheer him by recalling boyhood memories. Captain Clark took a turn as Floyd's caregiver when the others needed sleep. The next morning York and Pryor prepared a cool bath for Floyd in the hope that it would lower his fever, but before they could put him in the tub, Floyd grasped Captain Lewis' hand and said, "I am going away. I want you to write a letter for me." Suddenly, his eyes glazed over and he stared into the distant horizon and stopped breathing.

The men of the expedition were shocked and saddened at Floyd's sudden illness and death. He was only twenty-two years old when he died on August 20. The men carried his body to a hill overlooking the river, where they buried him with full military honors. Captain Lewis conducted the funeral service, and his comrades placed a large stone on his grave that bore his name, rank, and date of birth.

"I hope this will be our only death on this journey," Clark told Lewis when they were alone.

Lewis shook his head sadly. "So do I, but a journey into the unknown that will last at least two more years? It isn't likely." A constant weight on Lewis' mind was the responsibility for the well-being of all the men in the Corps of Discovery.

The next day, the captains held an election to replace Floyd as sergeant. The winner was Patrick Gass, a choice approved by the captains. The popular Gass, recruited back at Fort Kaskaskia, was a natural leader and a companionable wit who loved to tell jokes.

As the Corps of Discovery continued up the Missouri, the grasslands again became densely wooded, with stately oak trees on the bluffs and thick stands of cottonwood, elm, and maple along the river. Ashore, hunters found a new species of small red berry that the Indians called 'rabbit berries' growing on bushes that often reached a height of ten feet. The expedition passed cliffs of red rock, a substance the French trappers said the Indians fashioned into decorative smoking pipes and flutes. This area was known as neutral ground, where warring tribes could come and quarry the stone as they mingled in peace by mutual consent.

In the oppressive heat of late summer, the men of the expedition pressed onward, looking longingly at the cool shade on shore. Private Joseph Fields, one of hunters, excitedly hailed the boats from the riverbank.

"We killed a buffalo!" he shouted triumphantly.

None of the men had ever seen a buffalo up close, so twelve men volunteered to help butcher it and bring the meat to the campsite. That evening the men dined on buffalo hump, buffalo tongue, and buffalo steaks. The favorite meat of the Corps was the tail of the beaver, but buffalo hump and tongue ranked next as their meat of choice.

A gale-like wind blew the sands of the sandbars in the river in such thick clouds that the men could hardly see. The sand was so fine that it stuck to everything it touched, and the trees and grass for half a mile were covered with it. At a distance, the sand rose in the air like a column of smoke. The men, whose faces, hands, and clothing were now covered with sandy grit, groped their way slowly, almost blindly, on the river until finally deciding that safety required them to make camp.

That evening one of the horses got away, and Drouillard and Shannon left camp to find it. When Drouillard returned, he not only hadn't found the horse, but he had become separated from Shannon and lost him as well. Two other men were sent to search for Shannon and the lost horse as the expedition set off the next morning. The men found the horse and took it to the new camp that evening, but they said that Shannon had gone on ahead of the expedition.

"I suspect he thinks he's behind us, which is going to make him hard to catch up with," Captain Clark speculated.

As they continued up the river, a teenaged Sioux swam out to one of the pirogues and signaled that he wanted to talk. When the expedition put ashore, two more teenagers appeared. Through Dorion, the captains learned they were Yankton Sioux and that a large band of them was camped nearby. Their village was nine miles from the river. The captains arranged a council with their chiefs for the next day. During the evening, Lewis found tracks on the riverbank verifying that Shannon was ahead of them, not behind.

"Let's send a man ahead to catch up with him," Clark suggested.

The captains selected John Colter, who had served as a ranger with the famed Simon Kenton and was their most experienced woodsman. "Take several days' rations with you," Captain Clark instructed. "Travel as fast as you can because Shannon is probably in a bad way by now from lack of food."

By early the next morning a heavy fog had settled over the entire area, so heavy that the men couldn't see the seventy Yankton Sioux gathered on the opposite shore. When the fog began to clear at about eight o'clock, some of the Indians swam the river to have breakfast with the expedition. At nine o'clock, the captains sent the pirogues across the river to ferry the rest of the sixty or so Indians over. They were a strong, handsome race, and the chiefs looked regal in their buffalo robes painted in designs of bright colors.

"Welcome to our camp," Captain Lewis greeted the chiefs. "We are happy to see you."

The smiling chiefs nodded and spoke in their language, reciprocating their greeting through Dorion. Four of the Sioux chanted and played on a curious instrument made of buffalo hide that had a tuft of hair tied to it. The face and chest of the leader of the musicians was painted white, and the other three were painted in various colors. The squaws wore white buffalo robes, with their long, black hair combed back over their shoulders. Both men and women wore decorations made of porcupine quills and feathers.

"Sergeant Pryor," Lewis called, "run up the flag and fire the cannon as a salute." The Indians were duly impressed by the display and the roar of the cannon. Captain Clark gave each of the visiting musicians a carrot of tobacco, and the four Sioux musicians continued to chant and play their instruments while the soldiers prepared the camp for the council.

"We are happy to meet our brothers, the Sioux," Lewis began the council. "We have come a long way to meet you and welcome you into a new family. Our great chief, President Jefferson, has sent us to welcome you into that family and explain how our new relationship will benefit you."

He gave his standard speech about the goals of the Corps of Discovery, then he passed out medals and small gifts to the chiefs. To demonstrate their friendship, the Sioux staged mock war dances that began and ended with wild whoops while the musicians continued to play and chant. After the war dances, the Indians organized a competition to show off their boys' ability to shoot with bows and arrows, and the captains offered highly valued blue beads as a prize. One lad hit the mark every time he shot.

"That boy is uncanny!" Clark marveled to Ordway.

"Yeah, I wouldn't want to go against him in battle without a gun," Ordway agreed.

Captain Clark demonstrated the air gun for the Indians, who ran after each shot to see the new bullet hole in the tree. They chattered excitedly at this new marvel. At dusk, the soldiers built a huge bonfire in the middle of camp, and one at a time, the brightly painted Sioux warriors leaped into the firelight, each dancing and singing songs of his great feats in battle and the hunt and how many horses he had stolen. Some of the dancers wore necklaces of grizzly bear claws that were as long as three inches each.

"Throw gifts to them," Dorion counseled the soldiers.

The men threw knives and tobacco to the dancers, delighting their guests.

The Indians camped alongside the expedition that night. The next morning, another formal council was held with their new friends, the Yankton Sioux. The chiefs sat in a row and pointed finely carved and brightly colored peace pipes toward the captains who sat opposite them. This time, the chiefs were the ones who made speeches. They asked for whatever the white men could give them, but what they wanted was guns, powder, ammunition, and whiskey. They agreed to make peace with the Pawnees and Omahas and to go to Washington to meet President Jefferson. The captains were very pleased with their cooperation.

The soldiers ferried the Indians back across the river in the pirogues. At the Indian's request, the captains left Dorion with them for the winter to help arrange peace with the other tribes. Dorion would also organize an expedition of chiefs that he would lead to Washington in the spring.

CHAPTER 11

The Teton Sioux

September, 1804

Sailing with a cool and gentle breeze, the Corps of Discovery enjoyed the sweep of the open, timberless prairie, which was ablaze with miles of colorful wildflowers. As they set up camp on a large island, the hunters returned with news that excited Captain Lewis.

"We saw some kind of a strange goat, but we couldn't get close enough to shoot one," Drouillard said. "They can run like the wind!"

"Damn," Lewis muttered, but then brightened. "If there was one, there have to be more. Let's keep a sharp lookout tomorrow."

Colter returned from searching for Shannon with no news except that while searching for Shannon he had killed a buffalo, an elk, and three deer. Captain Clark sent men with sleds to retrieve Colter's bounty.

Captain Lewis, walking on shore, came upon a colony of small mammals that lived in tunnels in the ground. Lewis was amused by the animals, so he called the boats to shore so the men could see them. The little creatures popped up out of their tunnels, sat on their hind legs, and scolded the men, bringing laughter from everyone who saw them.

"Go back to the keelboat and get some shovels," Lewis ordered one of the men. "Let's dig one of them out of its tunnel."

He was intrigued by the strange, little, furry animals that hid in underground tunnels, but they escaped all attempts to dig one out. Lewis had another idea.

"Bring some barrels of water, and we'll flood one out."

Finally capturing one animal, the men built a cage for it, and Lewis decided to send it to St. Louis for safe-keeping when the keelboat returned in the spring.

Autumn was already touching the landscape, and the expedition passed groves of cottonwood trees with fading leaves and small plum trees loaded with ripe fruit. The hunters were excited to return with an antelope—the "goat" they had seen earlier—as well as a jackrabbit, both species new to science. Elated, Captain Lewis described and catalogued both species and stuffed them to be sent to St. Louis with other new finds.

A strong wind rose and the men hoisted sails, running comfortably and fast until the mast on the keelboat suddenly broke. Retrieving a cedar tree that was floating in the river, they stopped at an island to make and erect a new mast. On both sides of the river herds of buffalo, elk, deer, and antelope were grazing peacefully.

The next morning, as the keelboat rounded a bend in the river, the men spied George Shannon waving wildly to them from the riverbank. The men applauded and shouted to him. Seaman, who had formed an especially close bond with Shannon, went wild with excitement at the sight of him, jumping and barking frantically.

"Praise be!" Captain Clark called to him as the boat swung close to shore. "We had almost given up hope for you!"

"So had I!" the tow-headed Shannon exclaimed in a choking voice, his blue eyes brimming with tears he could not hold back. "I thought you were ahead of me, and I've been chasing you for sixteen goldarn days!"

Shannon was very weak and nearly starved. He told about running out of ammunition and shooting a rabbit with a stick instead of a musket ball. But for the last twelve days, he had been without meat, surviving on wild grapes, berries, and plums. Finally, knowing he was too weak to go any farther, he had decided to sit on the riverbank in hopes that a trapper or trader would come down the river and rescue him.

The men gathered around him, shaking his hand, expressing their joy, and congratulating him for surviving the ordeal.

"For want of ammunition, you nearly starved in a land of plenty," someone observed.

In his honor, the captains named a nearby creek Shannon Creek, and everyone cheered again.

The Corps of Discovery gradually entered high plains where buffalo, elk, and deer were plentiful. Unlike domesticated beef back home, wild game was lean, and the men, with all their strenuous activity, needed the energy provided by fat. One buffalo, four deer, or the equivalent, was required to feed the Corps each day. With the exhausting work of rowing, poling, and towing the boats against the powerful current of the Missouri River, each man consumed an average of nine pounds of meat daily. They ate their fill of the lean game the hunters killed and whatever wild fruit each area afforded, but the nourishing fat was nearly absent from their diet.

When Colter came in to report that he had killed a buffalo and needed help to bring the meat in, Gass took some men and returned to the location with him.

"I hope the wolves haven't gotten it," Gass said on their way to where Colter had left the buffalo.

"Nah, I left my hat on the carcass so my smell would scare them away."

But when they reached the location of the kill, the wolves had indeed devoured the buffalo—and destroyed Colter's hat as well! He took some kidding when the men learned about it.

"The Indians would call you 'Scares Wolves Away,'" Shannon teased him.

One day while Captain Lewis was walking on shore looking for new flora and fauna, he came upon the fossilized skeleton of a fish that was forty-five feet long. He drew a sketch of it and then hailed the keelboat to come to the riverbank to collect the bones to send back to Washington in the spring. The men were fascinated and talked about it for hours. No one could come up with a plausible explanation for a huge fish skeleton being on land.

The September air was getting chilly, despite bright sunshine that lit up orange and red leaves with golden light. The captains issued flannel shirts to the men to wear under their buckskin shirts, which eased the nip in the early morning chill when the breath from every man rose in the air like little white clouds. They were entering the territory of the Teton Sioux now, and the next day three Teton Sioux teenagers swam the river to meet the expedition. Drouillard spoke to them in sign language.

"They say there is a band of eighty lodges camped at the mouth of the next river and another band of sixty lodges a short distance above the first," he reported.

"Ask them to invite their chiefs to a council with us tomorrow," Lewis instructed.

Private John Colter, hunting on shore with the expedition's only remaining horse, shouted to one of the pirogues to come and get two elk and a deer he had killed. While Colter and the pirogue crew were getting the carcasses on board the pirogue, Colter's horse disappeared from the tree where he had tied it. Although Colter was short and quiet, he was a tough fighter who was not to be taken lightly. Seeing three young Sioux nearby, he started toward them to accuse them, but Captain Clark intervened, wanting to prevent a fight if possible. Instead, he challenged the Indians himself through Drouillard's sign language.

"You have stolen our horse and you must return it," he demanded. "We came here as friends, but we will fight if we have to."

The Indians looked at one another and then gestured their innocence. "We know nothing of your horse," one of them signed. "But if one of our people took it, we will get it back for you. We will talk to Black Buffalo, our chief."

Clark answered through Drouillard, "Invite Black Buffalo and your other chiefs to come to meet with us tomorrow."

So these were the dreaded Teton Sioux, the sign for whom was a finger drawn across the throat.

"I think we would be wise to anchor the keelboat a hundred yards out in the middle of the river and keep all hands on board except our sentries," Clark suggested. Lewis readily agreed.

The three Tetons stayed with the expedition's sentries all night, and things seemed pleasant and peaceful. Privates Richard Winser and Robert Frazier gave the Indians tobacco and smoked with them. The young braves signed that their village had eighty lodges that housed roughly ten persons each and that their village moved from one campsite to the next with dogs that pulled poles on which the Tetons loaded as much as eighty pounds of baggage.

The next morning Lewis and Clark received word from Black Buffalo that he and many of his tribe would come to council on the following day.

"Sergeant Gass, have the men raise the flag and put up the keelboat sail as a shelter for the council tomorrow," Lewis ordered.

The captains also decided to keep most of the men on board the boats again and keep the cannon ready to fire in case they had to fight the Tetons tomorrow. The next morning, every man in the Corps awaited the arrival of the Teton Sioux with foreboding. When they assembled at the river, Lewis greeted them with a handshake and gifts.

"We are happy to meet you," he told Black Buffalo and the lesser chiefs through Drouillard. Black Buffalo was an impressive, well-built man of about forty years of age wearing beads, feathers, and paint to indicate his importance in the tribe.

Lewis gave him a red coat and a cocked hat with a feather in the band. He gave the lesser chiefs some gifts as well. The Teton chiefs seemed to have difficulty understanding Drouillard's sign language, and the captains realized what an asset Dorion would be if he were still with them. The chiefs said little at first, but then they made it clear that they wanted more presents. Black Buffalo pointed to the red pirogue and then to himself.

"No," Captain Lewis said firmly, shaking his head. He turned to Private John Dame, "Demonstrate the air gun for these river bandits, Dame. Maybe that will impress them."

The chiefs were duly impressed, but they remained sullen. When Lewis began his speech about the Corps of Discovery, he quickly realized that the Teton Sioux chiefs understood nothing he said. He ended his speech and had the men perform military drills instead as entertainment. Then he handed out medals and other small gifts that did not satisfy the chiefs. They scowled and talked to one another in angry voices.

"Let's invite them aboard the keelboat," Clark suggested. "They might like that."

Lewis motioned for the chiefs to get into one of the pirogues, and its crew rowed them to the keelboat. Lewis ducked into the keelboat cabin and returned with a bottle of whiskey and some glasses. He filled each chief's glass half full. This finally pleased the chiefs, but they wanted more. Lewis, not wanting to get them liquored up, refused. One of the chiefs again scowled and raised his voice in anger. At that, Lewis showed them his astrological instruments and his spyglass, but nothing made them happy. Lewis demonstrated the keelboat cannon, but even the roar and power of the cannon failed to faze them.

Losing patience, Lewis snapped an order: "Sergeant Ordway, bring one of the pirogues and take them back to shore."

When the chiefs realized what was happening, they became even angrier, and when Clark and a detail of seven soldiers boarded the pirogue and motioned to the chiefs to follow them, they refused.

"All right, men, get back in the keelboat and force them into the pirogue!" Clark ordered.

The men returned to the keelboat and forcefully pushed the chiefs into the pirogue. As Clark took the chiefs to shore, Lewis stayed on the keelboat where he could command the cannon, blunderbusses, and riflemen. When the pirogue reached shore, the chiefs refused to get out, and some of the Teton warriors on shore surrounded it and grabbed the bowline.

"Let go of the line!" Clark shouted, gesturing.

The chiefs glared at him and spoke to each other in angry voices. They gestured fiercely at Drouillard, who interpreted to Captain Clark as best he could.

"We have more warriors on shore than you have on the boat," the Tetons signed. "You must give us one of your pirogues if we allow you to move up the river."

At this demand Clark drew his sword, and the warriors readied their bows and arrows, edging closer. The whole assemblage—the Corps and the Teton Sioux—were on edge, and ready for battle.

Clark still tried to reason with the Indians. "We have weapons and medicine on our boats that can kill twenty times the number of warriors you have on shore."

Aboard the keelboat, Captain Lewis ordered the men to prepare for action. They loaded the cannon with musket balls, and the riflemen knelt, resting their muskets on the raised locker lids to steady their aim—all in full view of the Indians.

Black Buffalo finally decided that the price of collecting additional tribute might be too high. He got out of the pirogue, followed by the other chiefs, and took the bowline from the warrior who held it. Clark approached the chiefs, smiling, and extended his hand.

"Let's forget about all of this and be friends," he said.

Black Buffalo turned his back to Clark.

"All right then, you bastards!" Clark said angrily, knowing they would understand only his tone of voice. "If you stupidly insist on fighting us, you will die."

Completely disgusted, Clark returned to the pirogue and the men cast off. Black Buffalo, apparently having second thoughts, splashed into the river, calling loudly to Clark. He wanted to return to the keelboat with Clark, so Clark allowed the chief and two warriors to climb into the pirogue. When they arrived at the keelboat, Black Buffalo indicated that he wanted to spend the night aboard.

"Why do you suppose he would want to do that?" Lewis asked.

"I don't know," Clark responded. "Maybe just for the novelty of it."

The captains agreed to allow Black Buffalo to spend the night aboard the keelboat, but they doubled the guard while he was there.

The next day, the captains were surprised when Black Buffalo invited them to visit his village. They agreed in hopes of lessening tensions. The Indians came to get Captain Clark with a buffalo robe, spreading it on the ground and motioning him to sit on it. Then six Indians hoisted him aloft and carried him to their council house on their shoulders. Then they returned and carried Captain Lewis to the lodge in the same manner.

The village consisted of about a hundred tepees made of buffalo hides. The warriors painted their faces and chests for the council and decorated their hair with hawk feathers. Their squaws were cheerful, fine-looking women, but it was clear that they were slaves to their men. Lewis noted many female captives in the village who proved to be from the Omaha tribe, and Cruzatte spoke their language fluently. They told him that in a recent battle between the Teton Sioux and the Omaha tribes, the Sioux had destroyed forty lodges, killed seventy-five Omaha men, and captured forty-eight women and children.

Hundreds of Teton Sioux now gathered to stare at the soldiers. One especially large tepee sat in the center of the village, and the chiefs led Lewis and Clark inside. Sitting in a circle were elders and painted warriors who were passing around a pipe, the smoke rising in fragrant tendrils. The women had prepared a feast of dog meat for the gathering. Then Black Buffalo made a speech with many gestures, trying to overcome the language barrier.

"We are poor," Drouillard translated. "The white men should give us something."

Lewis responded without sympathy, showing his displeasure at the demand. "We have given you all we can afford to give, and until you change your ways, you deserve nothing more. You must stop harassing travelers who pass by on the river." Black Buffalo and his elders understood Lewis's refusal and anger through his tone of voice.

The soldiers watched as the Indians performed a scalp dance around the campfire to celebrate their recent victory over the Omahas. They played tambourines made of stretched animal skin on hoops, and some of them beat sticks on drums made of dried and stretched hides. The women, highly decorated with feathers and colorful beads, leaped up and down, waving the scalps their mates had won in the recent battle. The men of the Corps had heard about the Indian practice of scalping their enemies, but few of them had ever seen a scalp, and they were repulsed by the savagery of the display. Every now and then one of the Indians advanced and recounted his own war exploits in a chant. This was then taken up by the other young men as the women danced. As the soldiers tossed beads and tobacco to the performers, they noted that the recently captured Omaha women sat downcast and sad-faced.

Suddenly, a young warrior broke out of the dance and gestured angrily at the soldiers, apparently because he had not received as many gifts as the dancing women. He grabbed a drum from one of the players and hurled it to the ground, breaking it. As he stalked off, he grabbed two other drums and flung them into the fire. Two squaws retrieved the drums, and the dancing continued until midnight. The solders were surprised that the Sioux chiefs tolerated such behavior from one of their young men.

Black Buffalo offered young women to Lewis and Clark for the night, but the captains refused, having pledged to set a perfect example for their men. Again that night, Black Buffalo asked to sleep aboard the keelboat. The captains agreed, but again doubled the guard. Cruzatte had learned from the Omaha prisoners that the Sioux planned to overpower and rob them during the night.

Clark whispered to Lewis, "As long as we have their big chief on board, they won't attack us."

"That's probably true. But let's be prepared for anything."

The tribe had special warriors who seemed to function as a police force. Whenever they approached, all the villagers scattered to avoid them. Lewis had seen one of them beat two squaws who were arguing. That night the Indian sentries along the perimeter of the village sang out the occurrences of the night at regular intervals.

Next morning, the Corps of Discovery was eager to be on its way, but Black Buffalo went ashore and returned to the river with his warriors.

"This looks threatening!" Lewis said quietly to Clark.

A warrior grasped the bowline of the pirogue and refused to let go. Black Buffalo indicated that he wanted more tobacco, apparently to save face. The captains controlled their anger, and Lewis tossed a carrot of tobacco onto the riverbank.

"Now show that you are chief by controlling your young men!" Lewis said, trying to sign his demand. He walked to the cannon to emphasize his determination, but Black Buffalo continued to ask for more tobacco.

The captains became angry, and the Indians were ready to fight.

In one last attempt to end the standoff peacefully, Lewis tossed another carrot of tobacco to the warrior holding the bowline, and he released the bowline.

"Cast off! Man your oars!" Clark called out then added, "Let's get out of here as fast as we can!"

In his haste, the pilot of the pirogue struck one of the keelboat's lines, and the pirogue swung around broadside, breaking the line and crashing into the keelboat. The Indians on the bank laughed, pointing and gesturing with great hilarity at the spectacle of men who couldn't handle their own craft. The pirogue was badly damaged and had to be repaired before departure, a job that lasted until nightfall. The men had every reason to believe the Teton Sioux would attack during the night, but they didn't, although the Corps spent a restless and sleepless night.

In the morning, the men were exasperated to see Black Buffalo and two hundred warriors on the riverbank, gesturing for them to stay.

"No, we must keep moving," Clark indicated by pointing upriver.

"We will not allow you to go on!" Black Buffalo made clear by pointing back downriver and making a chopping motion with his hand. A few of the warriors carried ancient British shotguns, a few brandished spears, and the rest were armed with bows and arrows as well as tomahawks.

Lewis conferred with Drouillard, who signaled Black Buffalo. "Come and talk with us in the keelboat cabin."

Three chiefs went with the captains into the cabin, but talking proved futile.

Black Buffalo crossed his arms over his chest, stared at them belligerently, and demanded, "You cannot pass unless you pay."

Lewis replied, "You now belong to the United States of America. We were sent here by the great chief of the United States to make friends with you, not to fight you or pay you to allow us to pass on the river. The river does not belong to you. It belongs to the United States of America. We have powerful medicine on our boat that can kill all of you and your entire village."

"You must pay," Black Buffalo insisted in sign language.

"We will not pay you, and if we fight, many of your young men will die. Our weapons have great power. You cannot fight our weapons. We are continuing up the river."

"No!"

"You are not going back to your village peacefully?" Lewis asked.

"No!"

Lewis stepped out of the keelboat cabin.

"Sergeant Pryor, call the men to their battle stations and raise the sail," Lewis ordered, then returned to the cabin.

"If you don't leave now, we will throw you into the river." Lewis told Black Buffalo.

"One more tobacco," the chief demanded, again trying to save face.

"I will not be trifled with!" Lewis said angrily, rising to his feet as did the chiefs. "Leave our boat!"

"One more tobacco."

Lewis threw a carrot of tobacco to the warriors holding the line. "Now show you are chief by controlling your warriors," he challenged the chief.

Black Buffalo, the other chiefs trailing, left the boat, took the line from the warrior who held it and released it.

The Corps of Discovery set out immediately with a favorable breeze. They would not camp on shore again until the Teton Sioux were far behind them. The Corps of Discovery knew now that the Teton Sioux were indeed the pirates of the Missouri River.

CHAPTER 12

Meeting Friendly Tribes

October, 1804

Days later, when the expedition camped on a large sandy beach, a man called to them in French from the opposite shore. One of the Frenchmen with the Corps answered him and discovered that some of the Frenchmen in the expedition actually knew him. He came across the river to visit.

"Do you speak English?" Captain Lewis asked.

"Certainly," the man answered.

"Are you going downriver?"

"Yes."

"We have just had a bad experience with the Teton Sioux. Are any more of them ahead of us up the river?"

"No more," the man said. "They are all behind you now."

"But they are in front of you. You still have to deal with them."

"That isn't a problem. I know I have to pay them for safe passage, and I am ready to do it. They let me go by as long as I pay them."

The French trapper remained and visited with his friends, talking until nearly midnight. The captains were relieved that they were finished with the Teton Sioux, but as a safety precaution they delayed sending out the hunters for another day.

Flocks of geese now winged their way south, honking loudly in their V-formations overhead. Large herds of elk and antelope crossed the river, migrating. A party of five Indians, one with a turkey slung over his shoulder, hailed them.

"Ignore them," Captain Clark ordered the men.

Days shortened and nights lengthened. The nights were very chilly and mercifully killed off the mosquitoes. The river sparkled in October's bright sunlight under brilliant blue skies, and the grassy prairie stretched as far as the eye could see. The Corps of Discovery found that autumn on the Missouri River was delightful. During October, the thick, wiry grass was golden brown, shimmering in the soft breeze while long shadows up and down the hills and valleys created a beautiful vista of light and shade. In the chilly fall air, the men built their fires a little larger as they gathered closer around them, discussing what they had done and seen that day and what they expected the next day.

The men awoke to frost. As they put out into the river, they encountered a herd of antelope swimming across the river. They killed four of them as well as one deer. Because their supply of meat had been depleted several days before, fresh game was most welcome, and they stopped to clean, cook, and eat their fill at a deserted Arikara Indian village.

Two passing Sioux Indians asked for food, which the captains gave them. They said they were going to visit the Arikaras. The Corps was now entering the territory of the Arikaras and soon came upon four Arikara villages. Captain Lewis took several men with him to one of the villages while Captain Clark formed a guard around the boats as a precaution.

"It's good to hear the English language again," a resident said as he approached Lewis and his party. The group was surprised to see someone who looked like an Indian but spoke English.

"You are an American!" Captain Lewis exclaimed.

"Yes, but I have lived with these good people for thirteen years and feel more like one of them now. My name is Joseph Gravelines."

"You must speak their language then," Lewis said.

"Yes, I speak Arikara, Sioux, French, and English."

Lewis's eyes widened in interest. "Are you familiar with the area upriver? The land and its people?"

"Of course."

"We have been sent by President Jefferson to make contact with as many Indian nations as possible and try to establish trade and commerce with them. Your language skills could be a great advantage to us. I would like to hire you to go with us as interpreter," Lewis offered.

After a bit of haggling about wages, Gravelines agreed.

Lewis extended his hand and asked, "Can you arrange to bring a delegation of Arikara chiefs to our camp tomorrow morning for a council?"

"I'm sure I can," Gravelines responded.

The Arikara Indians, about two-thousand strong, were farmers who raised beans, squash, and pumpkins. They proudly showed off their carefully tended vegetable gardens to the captains and offered them vegetables as a gift. The expedition rejoiced in the vegetables because they had eaten very few for months. The Arikaras, whose men decorated their hair and arms with feathers and quills, were friendly and industrious. The women wore moccasins, fringed leggings, and a long shirt of antelope skin, generally white and fringed, that was tied at the waist.

The men of the Corps of Discovery were astonished to see what the Arikaras called 'bull boats' arrive at the riverbank. The strange-looking boats were made of a single buffalo hide stretched over a bowl-shaped willow frame. Each boat could hold five or six braves, in addition to three squaws to paddle it. Soldiers gathered around one to inspect it.

"They must be hard to steer," Joseph Barter said.

"Yeah," William Warner agreed. "They must have one squaw on each side to row and one in the back to use an oar as a rudder."

"These boats look like they would be easy to make," Thomas Howard added.

After smoking with the Arikaras at the council next morning, Lewis gave his basic Indian speech, with Gravelines interpreting. Then the captains distributed gifts. The council ended with the chiefs promising to consult with their warriors and to respond to Lewis's speech the next morning.

York was a marvel to the Arikaras. They gathered around him with great curiosity, even touching his skin to see if the black would rub off. They had never seen a black man before, and they called him Big Medicine—a term they used for the magic of the Great Spirit to explain things they didn't understand. York was amused by their awe, and when a group of children approached him, he pretended not to see them until he wheeled and roared like a wild animal. The children screamed and ran in terror, and York laughed until tears rolled down his cheeks. He picked up a heavy log and lifted it above his head to show off his strength. He signed to the children that he had been a beast in the forest until Master Clark captured and tamed him. The soldiers laughed as they enjoyed York's antics, but Clark intervened, quieting York lest the Indians take him seriously.

The Arikara way of showing appreciation was to offer their guests their handsomest squaws, and if the guests declined, the chiefs were insulted. Therefore, to show their friendship, the men of the Corps, including York, enjoyed the favors of the Arikara women. Later, however, the soldiers realized with regret that these favors had infected them with venereal disease.

This Arikara village contained about sixty lodges, each made of a round frame covered with willow branches and grass and then a thick coat of earth. The Arikara traded their agricultural products with neighboring Indian tribes for other necessities. The captains gave them a mill to grind their corn and showed them how to use it. The Arikaras were astonished at how quickly the machine could grind the corn, a task that usually took them hours of labor at the grinding stone.

At the council next morning, the chiefs agreed to everything Lewis had said. They also asked the captains to make peace between their people and the Mandans, with whom they were at war. One of the Arikara chiefs asked to go with the expedition to the Mandans to talk council with them to help make peace.

When the Corps of Discovery continued its journey, the countryside featured more timber than previously. Twenty or so miles upriver from the Arikara villages, the expedition came upon large stones on the bank that resembled a man, a woman, and a dog. The chief told them a story of a young man and a young woman who were in love, but whose parents forbade them to marry. The couple, taking their dog, went off to mourn. Legend says that they lived on wild grapes until they finally turned to stone.

As the days and weeks passed, Moses Reed, the soldier who had tried to desert the Corps, remained an unhappy malcontent, continuing to poison the mind of his close companion, John Newman. For some time Reed had agitated Newman against the captains, saying how unfair and arbitrary they were. Finally, Newman grumbled against the captains to other men.

"All our lives are at stake on this dangerous and useless expedition," Newman harangued. "We should have more say in decisions that affect our lives, and we should be able to elect our own officers. This isn't an ordinary Army mission, and everybody, including the captains, should stand guard and do their fair share of the work."

When Lewis heard about Newman's complaints, he arrested Newman for mutiny. Reed, no longer a soldier, was beyond the captains' power to punish, but Private Newman was subject to the Articles of War. The captains convened a court-martial with Sergeant Ordway as head of the court. The jury of ten privates found him guilty of mutiny, sentenced him to seventy-five lashes and discharge from the army. Like Reed, he was also sentenced to join the French *engages* in the red pirogue as a civilian oarsman without pay.

"Captain Lewis, I throw myself on the mercy of the court," Newman pled in his squeaky, high-pitched voice. "I've been a good soldier, and I want to finish the expedition with everyone else. I promise I will never rebel again."

"Newman, you have been a problem ever since we arrived at Fort Dubois back in St. Louis," Captain Clark lectured him. "Your quick temper and bellicose ways have been a problem, and your attempt to lead an insurrection is beyond the pale."

"But when they make fun of my voice, Captain, I have to fight back." Newman responded meekly. "I didn't mean no harm by what I said about you and Captain Lewis."

"Whether you *meant* harm is beside the point. You could have *caused* harm. You went too far, Newman, and there is no turning back."

The men awoke to heavy frost the next morning. Walking on shore with Bratton and the Arikara chief, Lewis saw buffalo, elk, and great herds of antelope on the plains below. After two miles, they encountered a canoe with two French trappers coming downriver. "Ask them where they have been and where they are going," Lewis instructed Cruzatte.

"We have been upriver, trapping beaver, but we were robbed by a hunting party of Mandan Indians who took our guns, ammunition, axes, and thirty beaver skins. They left us with nothing."

Lewis replied, "We are on our way to visit the Mandan. In fact, we plan to winter with them."

The trappers perked up, and one of them said, "We'd like to join you. Maybe you can talk them into returning our possessions."

"That's between you and the Indians," Captain Clark answered. "If we are to winter with them, we have to get along with them. Your problems aren't our affair, but we will provide you with a gun and ammunition so you can hunt and feed yourselves."

The expedition was now entering the territory of the Mandan Indians, and the bowman spied a large group of Indians watching them from shore.

"Helmsman, put in," Lewis ordered.

Lewis called out to the Indians and waved to them to come and talk. More than twenty Indians arrived, some of them women. With Gravelines interpreting, Lewis spoke to them.

"I am Captain Lewis. My great chief sent me to greet all the Indians and to welcome them into a new family."

"I am Black Cat, a chief of the Mandans. Welcome to our country." Probably in his thirties, Black Cat looked lean and fit. The two men shook hands. The Indian hunting party and the Corps of Discovery all began to shake hands.

"Come, visit our village," Black Cat invited the white men.

At the village, Black Cat introduced them to a chief named Big White, who showed them around the village. The Mandans had a long history of trading with white men and had learned a few words of English and French from trappers and traders. Like the Arikaras, the Mandans were farming people, and Chief Black Cat pointed out fields where his people grew corn, beans, squash, and sunflowers. The village consisted of forty circular huts, similar to the Arikara lodges, that were built around a large clearing with a tall cedar post and a larger lodge at the center. The Mandan collection of villages served as the marketplace of the region. The Mandans and Hidatsas were allies and lived close to each other. There were five villages in the area—two Mandan and three Hidatsa. The Hidatsas were also known as the Minnitarees or the *Gross Ventres*, French for "Big Bellies."

"Other tribes come to trade," Chief Black Cat explained. "They bring horses, furs, buffalo hides, blankets, clothing, and guns. In summer, our villages fill with traders from the Crow, Cree, Kiowa, Cheyenne, Assiniboin, and Arapaho tribes. White men also come to trade."

The lower Mandan village was led by Black Cat and his second chief, Raven Man. Further upriver was another Mandan village led by Chief Big White, with Little Raven as his second chief. Their lodges were round and very large, each accommodating several families.

The Corps of Discovery sailed on to the next villages with a fine breeze behind them. They saw a number of Indians on horseback strung out along the south riverbank. When the Corps stopped to eat, the Arikara chief onboard with the Corps went to speak with them, and one of them returned with him and spent the night with the expedition. The next day, the Corps stopped at noon at a hunting camp of Mandans that included women and children. An Irishman was also with the Indians, trading with Mandans for the Northwest Company of Canada.

"The United States has purchased the Louisiana Territory," Lewis informed him. "You are now in America.'

"Yes, I know," the Irishman said.

"News travels surprisingly fast in the wilderness."

The expedition stayed two hours before proceeding upriver, where they encountered the second and third Mandan villages, one on each side of the river. They camped a little north of the Mandan villages at a convenient place to hold council with the whole Mandan nation. The captains found three Frenchmen living among the Mandans, including a man named Jessaume who had a squaw and a child.

"With your permission, we would like to spend the winter here," Captain Lewis told Chief Black Cat.

"Good," Black Cat responded, nodding his head.

"We will build a fort to live in," Lewis added. "We need to find a place with big trees for logs to build the fort as well as plenty of game and fresh water."

Black Cat said, "We will help you find such a place."

Chief Black Cat, Captain Lewis, Captain Clark, and the new interpreter Jessaume traveled up the river some distance, but they did not find a place to build a fort for the winter.

"There must be five thousand people in these villages," Clark marveled. "That's more people than live in St. Louis and Washington combined!"

"Yes, and about a thousand of them are warriors," Lewis added. "It's a good thing for us they are friendly."

The captains prepared for a council with the Mandans the next morning. Many Hidatsas from their villages farther up the river came for the council as well. They all met under an awning made with the sails from the boats, stretching around the meeting area to keep out the wind. Captain Lewis gave his speech through an interpreter and then distributed presents. The chiefs promised to make peace with other tribes and to go to Washington to meet President Jefferson in the spring. The council ended with a firing of the cannon, and the nations returned to their villages and hoisted the American flags Lewis had given them. The captains gave Black Cat a corn mill, which greatly pleased him and the people of his village.

Captain Clark took a detachment of eight men and two Mandan guides in a pirogue and embarked on a second unsuccessful search for a place to build a fort for winter quarters. The large trees required to build a lodge were scarce in this area. Mandans came to the Corps' camp that evening with a gift of cornbread made with ground corn mixed with fat, and the captains gave them presents in return.

Black Cat invited Captain Lewis to his lodge, and because the captains assumed that Black Cat was the big chief of all the Mandans, Lewis and an interpreter went eagerly. Black Cat was dressed in the red jacket and cocked hat that Lewis had given him.

"It would fill my heart with joy to have peace with the Arikaras," he said. Then his expression changed, and he added, "You were not kind to us when my people came for council and you gave us little presents. We expected great presents."

"I could give only what we could bring in our small boats. We have many, many miles ahead of us to travel to the great ocean, and we gave you all we could." Then he added, "Many white men will come after us who will bring you many great presents." Black Cat's dark eyes lit up at Lewis's vision of the future.

CHAPTER 13

Fort Mandan

November, 1804

The captains went again in search of a place for winter quarters, threading their way through dense brush for miles. As they hiked, Lewis discovered the Silver Leaf Breadroot plant, a new plant that he happily recorded in his log. They finally came upon a site they decided was suitable for their fort, near where the mouth of the Knife River emptied into the Missouri. The location offered plenty of fresh water, wood, and game—and it was across the river from one of the Mandan villages.

"This ought to be an excellent location," Clark said with satisfaction, "and being so close to one of the Mandan villages will be a real advantage for trading with them."

The captains began to design a fort that could withstand attack from less friendly tribes.

"The Sioux aren't so far away that they can't attack us, and we must be prepared,"

Lewis said, the dangerous days with the Teton Sioux still fresh in his mind.

They laid out the position of the huts in the fort with two rows joined at one end forming an angle. Each hut would contain four small rooms, with roofs covered with earth and sod for insulation. The roofs were to be made "shed fashion," sloping to expel rain or snow, and projecting a foot over the walls. The outer walls of the huts would also serve as part of an eighteen-foot palisade. There would be a sentry post with the swivel gun from the keelboat mounted like a cannon.

Sergeant Gass, the Corps of Discovery's best carpenter, was again given responsibility for supervising the construction of the fort. The men established a tent camp where they could live while building their new fort. Each night as the men lay in their tents, they heard the chirping of hundreds of crickets hiding in the coarse grass, the deep-throated frogs on the riverbanks, and the wind rushing through leafless trees. Some of the birds in the area were species that Lewis recorded in his log during the winter months.

Surveying the partially completed fort, Clark said with satisfaction, "This fort should keep us warm and secure for the winter."

"Once it's finished, all we'll have to worry about is providing ourselves with food," Lewis added, "but that isn't going to be easy."

"We'll probably have the nearby area hunted out in a month or so," Clark agreed. "Maybe we should set up a hunting camp twenty or so miles up the Knife River where a permanent detachment of hunters can stay to provide us with a continuous supply of game."

"Good idea. We can rotate the men for that duty, and that should help ensure us enough meat for the winter," Lewis added.

The next day, Captain Clark took six hunters and set out in one of the pirogues up the Knife River to establish a permanent hunting camp while the rest of the men continued to build the fort.

Lewis had hired the Frenchman Jessaume as an interpreter, and he now moved into the new camp with his squaw and child. Having a child in camp was a novelty to the men, and many of them enjoyed playing with him in their off hours. Jessaume's squaw even helped with cooking for the mess group to which they were assigned. Lewis also hired another Frenchman, Baptiste LePage, to replace John Newman, who had been relegated to unpaid status in a pirogue. LePage had trapped in the upper Missouri country, and both captains thought his experience would be useful.

Eventually, the men raised one line of huts and began filling the cracks in the construction with grass, pieces of old tarpaulin, and mortar, applying a thick coat of earth over it all to seal the huts and make them as warm as possible. Then all hands worked to raise the second line of huts. Finally they began building the chimneys, working as quickly as possible so they could all move into the shelter before the really bad weather arrived. Already, heavy frost and bone-chilling air greeted them each morning. The Hidatsa and Mandan Indians, curious about the white men's construction methods, visited them every day as the men completed the fort.

"We're running out of meat, Captain," Sergeant Ordway told Lewis one evening. "We'll be completely out in a couple of days."

"Surely, the hunters will return soon," Lewis said hopefully.

Water was freezing at night, prompting the men to hasten the pace of their construction work even more. The hunters had not returned, and just as the meat supply was running out, the chief of the lower Mandan village arrived with a gift—about a hundred pounds of buffalo meat strapped on his wife's back.

The Corps was delighted to receive the meat, but William Carson observed, "Damn! They don't treat their women very well."

"None of the Indians do," Joseph Whitehouse responded. "They treat their wives like pack animals. Look how she's struggling under the load. And I've never seen one complain. It's their way of life, but really I'm not sure we do a hell of a lot better."

Captain Lewis gave the chief's squaw some trinkets and a small axe for her labor.

Lewis sent a scout to search for the hunters and learn the cause of their delay. Two Frenchmen had gone out on a trapping expedition some days before, returning with twenty-two beavers, but they had not seen the hunting party from the Corps.

Each morning the trees were now covered with frost so thick that it fell off in chunks when the sun came up. The soldiers, who had never seen such a frost "back east," worked by firelight until one o'clock in the morning to complete the 24-by-14-foot smokehouse, and they raised the roof on it the next day in anticipation of the hunters' return.

Chief Black Cat visited the fort, with his squaw carrying a load of corn for the expedition. Black Cat was very interested in the customs of the white man and came to the camp often to study them. Captain Lewis was continually impressed with Black Cat's integrity and intelligence.

All hands were employed at different kinds of work now, some daubing the smokehouse, some cutting firewood, some hunting, and some doing other chores.

"Here come the hunters!" Joseph Barter shouted jubilantly on a cold afternoon, waving to attract attention.

The hunters tied up their heavily loaded pirogue at the riverbank, and men gathered to help unload the meat they had brought—five buffalo, eleven elk, thirty deer, and all sorts of small game. The eager men splashed into the shallow water at the riverbank, hoisted large pieces of meat onto their shoulders, and headed for the smokehouse where the meat would be smoked over fires kept burning twenty-four hours a day.

"You are a very welcome sight!" Lewis exclaimed to the returning Clark and his hunting crew. "We were completely out of meat except for part of a buffalo that the Indians gave us."

Clark smiled at the eager reception. "The hunting was so good that we kept at it until we had killed all the meat we could haul back. I thought it was important to bring back as much game as we could."

Toussaint Charbonneau was a forty-four year old French Canadian who lived with the Hidatsas and spoke Hidatsa and French, but not English. He was a trapper, laborer, and interpreter of the Hidatsa language. He had two teenaged Shoshone wives from a tribe that lived in the Bitterroot Mountain range on the eastern side of the Rocky Mountains, some six-hundred miles west of Fort Mandan. One of his two wives, Sacagawea, presented the captains with a gift of two buffalo robes. In return, Lewis gave her blue beads, highly praised by Indians. Sacagawea sewed the beads onto a belt around the waist of her deerskin dress. A slender young woman with braids down her back, Sacagawea was a cheerful, outgoing fifteen-year-old who was about six months pregnant.

The captains agreed to take Charbonneau and one of his wives with the expedition in the spring to interpret for them when they reached the Shoshone nation, and Charbonneau chose Sacagawea. She could talk to the Shoshones in their own language and to Charbonneau in Hidatsa. Charbonneau could then translate Hidatsa to French for Drouillard, who could pass the message to the captains in English. It was a convoluted method of communication, but Lewis was confident it would work.

"Having a squaw with us will also show any tribes we encounter that we are not a war party," Clark offered.

Charbonneau had won both Shoshone girls in a bet with the Hidatsa warrior who had captured them in a raid on the Shoshones six years before, when Sacagawea was only nine years old. His "wives" were actually his slaves, and he owned Sacagawea just as Clark owned his slave, York. The fact that she would be the only female on the expedition made her feel special, and knowing that she would be the interpreter with the Shoshones made her feel important and proud. She was excited to be going to the village of her birth, although she had been gone so long that she wondered if any of her own people would remember her.

Like all Mandan and Hidatsa squaws, Sacagawea wore a dress and leggings made of deerskin, topped by a knee-length robe made from buffalo hide that doubled as a blanket at night. Her clothes were decorated with beads and porcupine quills, and her moccasins were made of buffalo hide, with the furry side turned in.

A problem arose concerning one of the squaws staying in Fort Mandan with one of the interpreter's wives. Her husband beat her, stabbed her, and was ready to kill her when Colter and Shields intervened. The man was angry because he said his squaw had slept with Sergeant Ordway. Captain Clark ordered Ordway to give the man some presents to mollify him. Then the captains ordered that none of their men have sexual intercourse with this particular woman under penalty of severe punishment. That evening Black Cat arrived, learned of the situation, and lectured the husband as well. Both the man and his wife left, dissatisfied with the whole episode.

One village of Hidatsa Indians was told by traders from the Northwest Company that the Americans intended to join with the Sioux and attack their village from their newly built fort. Captain Lewis, with an interpreter and six men, set off upriver on a diplomatic mission to visit the Hidatsa village, twenty-four miles away. The Hidatsas had learned from the Mandans that the soldiers were peaceful, however, and there was no problem. After Lewis held council with the Hidatsas elders, three of their chiefs let him know that they wished to see the new fort. When they came to visit Fort Mandan, the soldiers, curious about the name "Big Bellies," shook hands with the chiefs and tried to converse with them.

"Why are you called Big Bellies?" Private Charles Chaugee asked through an interpreter.

The chief responded with a laugh, patting his stomach. "Because we always choose the warrior with the biggest belly as our big chief."

"Is that a joke?" Chaugee asked the man next to him.

"Of course it's a joke. Look at him grin," Jean LaJeunesse said. "Why would they really choose the warrior with the biggest belly as their chief?"

A Mandan visitor to the fort told the captains one late November day that a raiding party of Sioux had attacked five Mandan hunters, killing one, wounding two others, and stealing nine horses. The captains huddled to discuss the raid.

"I think we should offer them our help in fighting the Sioux," Clark said.

Lewis was thoughtful for a moment. "They have been very kind to us, and we damn sure have no love for the Sioux."

Clark gathered twenty-three volunteers and led them across the river to the Mandan village.

"We will help you fight the Sioux," Clark said to Chief Black Cat through interpreter Drouillard, expecting him to be pleased.

Black Cat was surprised and a little alarmed at the sight of such a formidable armed fighting force standing before him. He looked at Clark curiously for a moment and then slowly shook his head. "The snow is too deep, and the Sioux have too much headstart," he signaled. "If you will go with us in the spring, after the snow is gone, we will make war on the Sioux."

"But if they can travel in the snow, so can we," Clark had Drouillard respond.

"You don't know this country as we do," Black Cat communicated. "We cannot catch them now. We will even the score another time. You do not understand our ways. We thank you for your offer to help."

Clark and the soldiers returned across the river, and Clark reported the episode to Lewis, shrugging his shoulders in perplexity.

"That's surprising, to say the least," Lewis said. "All Indians love to fight."

"I guess they think we are meddling in their affairs, which they feel we don't understand," Clark said with resignation, "and of course, we are and we don't."

The members of the expedition needed an enormous amount of food every day, and even more as winter gripped the land. To get through the winter, the Corps would need large quantities of corn, beans, and squash from friendly tribes in addition to the game provided by their own hunters. This winter would be a challenge to the Corps of Discovery.

CHAPTER 14

Frigid Weather, Warm Friendships

December, 1804

English-speaking visitors were rare to the Corps of Discovery these days, so when a smiling Scotsman who had been trading with the Indians showed up at Fort Mandan, he was warmly greeted. He was a jolly person with red hair and fair skin, a bit short and stout, with a brogue and a hearty laugh.

"Where be ye lads goin'?" he asked Captain Clark as the two red-heads shook hands.

"We're exploring the Louisiana Territory—the area the United States just purchased from France," Clark responded as Lewis came to greet the visitor.

"Aha! And how far might that be?" he asked as he and Lewis's shook hands.

Clark deferred to Lewis, who answered, "As far as the dividing ridge, the western boundary of the Louisiana Territory." It was a cautious answer, and Lewis added, "Come inside and we'll talk a while."

The captains entertained the Scotsman for a couple of hours. When he rose to leave, he said, "Fare thee well on your journey. 'Tis mighty fine country you'll be seeing."

The captains watched him until he was out of sight.

"I suspect he was fishing for information to feed to his company and the British government," Lewis speculated.

"I'm sure he was," Clark agreed, "But he seemed a friendly fellow."

Both Great Britain and the United States had made tenuous claim to the area between the Louisiana Territory and the Pacific Ocean, but it was very much up for grabs as far as each nation was concerned. Clearly, however, whichever nation could first claim the right of exploration would gain an advantage. The unsuspecting Indians had no idea their homeland was in the covetous hearts of both nations.

The men of the Corps were now bringing in huge logs to build the stockade fence, or palisade. They also built a platform on top of the smokehouse where sentries could walk their assigned beats, surveying the countryside from a vantage point. The weather became so cold that the captains suspended all work except cutting firewood. When the snow and wind eased a little, Black Cat came to the fort to report that great herds of buffalo were only a few miles from the river.

"If you would like to hunt with us, we will lend you horses," Black Cat signaled through Drouillard.

Captain Lewis took fifteen men and killed ten buffalo, while the Mandan warriors killed fifty. For the next two weeks, the captains alternated leading large hunting parties before the buffalo migrated out of the area. The American soldiers quickly learned that the Indians were better riders than they were. Riding at break-neck speed, the Indians could guide their horses with their knees, and they shot their arrows with such force that an arrow sometimes went entirely through a buffalo. Colorfully dressed squaws followed the hunters to butcher the buffalo before wolves could get to the kill. The Indians had a custom that any buffalo that didn't have an arrow in it or other mark of ownership was fair game for anyone to take. It was also the custom of the Indians to share the buffalo meat with everyone in the tribe, both those who had hunted and those who had not.

One day, after killing eleven buffalo, the soldiers stayed out all night, sleeping in buffalo robes in sub-zero weather. They found a ravine that shielded them from the prairie's relentless winds, gathered wood, and built a fire that they kept going all night. They took turns as sentry during the night, as much to keep the fire going as to provide security. They slept in fetal positions, their feet toward the fire, trying to make their bodies as compact as possible to preserve their body heat within the cocoon of their buffalo robes. In the frozen emptiness of the night, under the icy points of millions of stars in the black sky, the lone sentries heard the mournful sounds of the wind as it moaned across the open prairie. They could also hear the eerie howls of a lone wolf in the frigid distance, expressing his hunger, calling for a mate, or simply announcing his presence to the wilderness. His howl rent the night, the very definition of loneliness on the vast prairie.

The next day, the hunters killed nine more buffalo while the temperature sank to forty-five degrees below zero. The Indians could stand the cold to a degree that amazed the soldiers, who sometimes heard about or met Indians who had actually spent a night out on the prairie without a fire and with only a buffalo robe, thin moccasins, and antelope-skin leggings.

Back at the fort, Lewis remarked, "For the safety of the men, I think we had better change the guard every hour because of the extreme cold."

"Good idea," Clark agreed. "We don't want to risk frozen fingers, toes, or noses."

Captain Clark lined his gloves with fur and had a cap made of the hide of a lynx that had fur nearly three inches long. The captains called in all the hunters to shelter. Frost even formed on the outside of the chimney where a fire was kept burning all night. The only work the men were assigned was cutting wood for fires, while the sentries were now changed every half hour. In the incredible cold, two members of Ordway's mess went to a Mandan village and traded trinkets for corn and beans. Soon, other soldiers were doing the same. Even on these bitterly frigid days, the men found Mandans playing games out of doors.

"They've got to be freezing their asses off," Colter laughed.

"Yeah, but they seem to be having fun," Shannon responded with wonder.

Four men from the British Northwest Company, including Laroque and Heney, visited the fort to trade robes and furs. Heney impressed the captains as a very intelligent man. He described the American fort in a report to his headquarters.

> *The fort is constructed in a triangular form, with houses on two sides and amazingly long stockade pickets in front. The whole is made so strong as to be almost cannonball-proof. The two ranges of houses do not join each other but are joined by a piece of fortification made in the form of a semi-circle that can defend two sides of the fort, on top of which they keep sentry all night. A sentinel is likewise kept all day, walking the fort.*

The weather moderated somewhat on December 19, and the men worked on the stockade fence in rotating shifts, with half the men out at a time, changing shifts every hour. Many Indians continued to visit the fort, bringing corn and beans to trade for mirrors, beads, and buttons. The palisade fence was finished on Christmas Eve, and the men immediately began building a blacksmith shop. To celebrate Christmas, the captains distributed flour, pepper, and dried apples to the four messes.

Christmas Day, 1804, was clear and cold. The captains told Sergeant Ordway and his crew to fire the cannon at daybreak, and the men were called into formation for a prayer of thanksgiving. Lewis led the men in prayer.

> *Heavenly Father, we offer thanks for seeing us safely through our journey thus far. We give thanks for the birth of our Savior on this day so long ago, that we might know salvation. We pray you will go with us to the successful conclusion of our journey and see us all safely home. We pray this in the name of Him whose birth we celebrate this day. Amen.*

The captains handed out a gill of whiskey to each man, and they feasted, danced, and relaxed the entire day. They had requested that the

Indians not come to the fort on this day so they could honor the day in privacy, which the Indians respected.

At first, the Mandans gave their corn freely or traded it for trinkets, but when they realized how much the soldiers needed it, they began to drive harder bargains. The captains could not part with any more of their trading goods because they still had a long way to go to the Pacific Ocean, so they had to find another way to buy corn, beans, and squash from the Mandans and Hidatsas. The problem was solved when the Indians discovered that John Shields had set up a blacksmith forge to repair tools. They were fascinated by the bellows and Shields' ability to make iron items. The Indians had accumulated many tools from white traders, and these old tools had been damaged with use. The Indians were very fond of metal arrowheads and metal implements they used to scrape buffalo hides.

Black Cat appeared one day with a broken axe. He handed it to Shields and pointed to the broken part questioningly. Shields took the axe and examined it. He nodded and said, "Sure, I can fix it."

Then all the Indians began bringing their broken tools to the fort to be repaired, and Shields charged for his work in corn, beans, squash, and roots. Soon he was operating a thriving business, with other soldiers stoking the fire and helping to operate the forge. When he had repaired all the Indians' broken tools, he began making new tools and weapons, such as battle axes and hide-scrapers, which he sold to the Indians for food. Five men were kept busy cutting timber to make charcoal for the forge, and two others made a charcoal pit as a kiln to heat the wood to turn it into charcoal. Other men gathered dead grass from the prairie to cover the charcoal pit. Two other soldiers made sleds for the Indians and received corn and beans in payment.

The captains provided medical services to their neighbors. The Indians had noticed that they were skilled at doctoring frostbite and other ailments. Mothers began bringing sick children to them, and they paid for the captains' services with food. It was Mandan and Hidatsa food as much as their own hunting prowess that enabled the Corps of Discovery to survive the winter.

The daily routine at Fort Mandan included hunting, trading, repairing equipment, coping with the weather, and conversation. Holidays and special occasions brought the Indians and the white men closer together. Many Indians, including women and children, visited the fort regularly, and many of them provided work for the blacksmith shop. They also brought corn, beans, squash, edible roots, and bread made of corn and beans mixed together. The close interaction of the Corps of Discovery with the Mandans and Hidatsas during the winter of 1804 established a true bond of friendship among these communities.

CHAPTER 15

Bitter Cold and Rattlesnake Potion

January-February, 1805

On New Year's Day, half of the men went to the lower Mandan village at the invitation of the village chief to dance to the music of an Indian tambourine and Cruzatte's fiddle. Clark called on York to dance, and the Indians were again astounded that a man so big could be so agile. One of the Frenchmen danced on his hands, delighting the Indians, and frivolities continued until late into the night.

A week or so later, the Indians held a buffalo dance and invited the soldiers to join them in their communal lodge for festivities, which began with the music of rattles and drums. The old men of the village, dressed in their finest, filed into the lodge where they sat down and waited. Soon the young men entered with their wives. Pipes and tobacco were prepared for the old men, and a smoking ceremony ensued. Then the drums began to play. As the drumbeat swelled in intensity, one of the young men stepped forward and offered his wife to one of the old men. She smiled coyly at the old man and reached out her hand in a gesture of acceptance.

"Take her and enjoy her, to lure the buffalo to us," her young husband implored the old man.

Coaxing the old brave to rise, the young squaw led him from the lodge, and the two returned some time later. This ritual was repeated by the other young couples, much to the surprise and interest of the men from the fort who learned that the primary purpose of the ceremony was to induce the buffalo herd to come near for killing, thus producing food and buffalo hides. The Mandans believed that the hunting skills of the old braves would be transferred to the young men through sexual relations with the young wife. If the selected old man was reluctant to accept the young wife, the husband usually threw a robe into the bargain. To the good fortune of the enlisted soldiers and York, the Mandans also attributed big medicine and great powers to the men of the Corps of Discovery—so throughout the three days of the Buffalo Dance, the men were quite happy to be there. Sure enough, there was a great buffalo hunt a few days later.

The men joked among themselves about the ritual. Shields exclaimed, "Hey! This is an Indian custom we should take back home with us!"

"Yeah," Shannon replied, laughing, "coon hunts would take on a whole new goldarn meaning."

As the weather continued blustery and cold, Captain Clark worked at drawing a map of this country, soliciting input from Indians, trappers, and traders. One day the Mandans came in from the prairie with a load of buffalo meat, but reported sadly that two of their young men had frozen to death during the night and others were missing. Privates John Thompson and Peter Weiser had also gone out hunting, become separated, and only Thompson returned in the evening. He had suffered severe frostbite, and the captains were afraid that Weiser may have frozen to death. Just as a search party was preparing to leave the fort, Weiser stumbled into the fort amid cheers from the men.

"I was able to get a fire going and keep it alive all night," he said. "I was never so cold before in my life, but I'm still alive due to the fire and my buffalo robe. I didn't sleep a wink, but I stayed alive."

One of the two Mandans who were thought to be frozen to death was carried to the fort the next day alive, but with badly frozen feet, and

Lewis kept him in the fort to treat him. He had been left for dead, but when his father and some friends went to retrieve his body, they found him alive. He had regained consciousness, made his way to some woods, and survived by making himself a bed of branches.

The weather continued brutally cold, sometimes so cold a man's penis would freeze if he wasn't quick about relieving himself. None of the men had ever experienced such cold, and the shifts of sentries were again shortened to thirty minutes. Hunters who returned to the fort with frostbitten toes and fingers learned from Lewis to soak them in cold water.

The captains kept the men busy, not only because there was much real work to be done, but also because they knew that idle soldiers soon stir up trouble. The men hunted, cured hides, made clothing and moccasins, collected wood to make charcoal for the blacksmiths, and built wooden sleds to haul game and supplies across the frozen ground. They also continued visiting the Mandan villages to trade, socialize, and learn Indian ways.

Many of the soldiers worked at chipping away the ice from the keelboat and pirogues, which had become cemented into the river with ice. They also hauled stones on sleds from a bluff below the fort. The idea was to heat the stones, put water into the pirogues, and place the hot stones in the water to heat it in hopes of coaxing the pirogues loose from the ice. But they found that when the stones got hot, they burst. Sergeant Gass went up the river to another bluff to look for a different type of stone that would not break up with the heat. When they also burst, the captains gave up on the plan.

Captain Lewis was usually friendly and welcoming to strangers, but when Francois Laroque, of the British Northwest Company, came to Fort Mandan, he spoke sternly to him: "You are giving British flags to the Indians and leading them to believe that England is the controlling power here. That is not true and you must stop."

"I am not guilty of that," Laroque replied.

"I have also been informed that you plan to appoint chiefs among them, and I forbid you to do so. The United States owns this territory, not Great Britain."

Laroque raised his hands in a gesture of innocence. "I assure you, Captain, I have no such intentions."

Lewis knew full well that Laroque was guilty as charged, but he was satisfied that he had made his point. He decided to drop the matter, but he remained alert for any proof of further such actions.

As February began, everyone at the fort was busy making ropes, canoes, charcoal, and battle axes to trade for corn. Game became so scarce that Captain Clark took sixteen men, two horses, and two sleds to go down the frozen land to hunt in a new area. They planned to stay until they had a full load of meat. Meanwhile, the Mandans continued to pay Shields for making battle axes and scrapers to dress their buffalo robes.

Charbonneau returned from Clark's hunting party in only a few days. "We killed thirteen elk, thirty-three deer, and three buffalo," he reported proudly. "Captain Clark sent me ahead with the horses loaded with meat, but I left them eight miles downriver because they couldn't cross the ice without horseshoes."

"Sergeant Pryor, take two men and two horses that have been shod to get the meat," Lewis ordered. "Bring back the unshod horses by land."

The horses had been borrowed from the Mandans. Lewis knew the Mandans didn't treat their horses very well, so when the horses first arrived at the fort the captains had ordered them to be fed corn moistened with water. The horses refused to eat it, preferring instead the bark of cottonwood trees—the diet the Mandans had given them. The Mandans were wild and severe riders, and during a buffalo hunt their horses often went without food for days. When they returned to their villages, the Indians took their horses into their lodges to protect them from the cold, but they gave them only cottonwood boughs and bark to eat.

"I can't believe their horses can survive this way, but honestly, they seem quite fit," Lewis, shaking his head, marveled to Clark.

"I guess it's just a matter of what they get used to," Clark responded.

Returning to the fort after dark one day, Private Thomas Howard scaled the wall of the fort rather than calling the guard to open the gate. A Mandan Indian saw him and scaled the wall as well. The guard reported this event to Captain Lewis, who was much alarmed because this demonstrated to the Indians how easily they could enter the fort. Lewis had the Indian brought to him.

"What you did was very dangerous," he said through Drouillard. "The guard could have shot you."

The Indian was frightened. "He thought it was good because the soldier did it," Drouillard translated.

"The soldier should not have done it, and he will be punished." Lewis had Drouillard assure him. "Explain to your village that they will likely be shot if they try to climb over the wall."

The Indian seemed greatly alarmed, so Lewis gave him some tobacco and sent him on his way. Howard was put under arrest and learned that he was facing court-martial. He had been a soldier for several years and should have known better, Lewis decided. Charged with setting a bad example for the Indians, Howard was found guilty and sentenced to fifteen lashes, but the court recommended leniency and Lewis forgave the lashing.

Meanwhile, Sacagawea, living with Charbonneau at the fort, was ready to give birth. Lewis was concerned about her ordeal because he knew the birth of a first child could be troublesome and could threaten the mother's life. He had no experience with childbirth, so he consulted Jessaume.

"Sacagawea has been in labor since yesterday," Lewis began. "I'm concerned about her and the child. Do you know of any roots or potions we can give her to ease her pain and bring about the birth?"

Jessaume scratched his bearded chin and thought for a moment. "She young, strong. She be all right," he said. "But sometimes small potion of ground-up rattle of rattlesnake move things to finish."

"Good! I have such a rattle among my medicines. Come with me, and we'll prepare it for her." The two men hurried off to Lewis's quarters, where Lewis ground the rattle into powder, then mixed it with water. The two men walked quickly to Charbonneau's lodge where Sacagawea lay in labor, and she eagerly drank the potion.

Within ten minutes, a baby boy was born! Whether the snake rattle contributed anything to the birth, no one would ever know. Charbonneau named the new arrival Jean-Baptiste after a friend, but Sacagawea called him "Pomp," the Shoshone word for "first born." All the men of the expedition had become fond of pleasant, gentle, intelligent Sacagawea, whom Captain Clark had taken to calling "Janie," and they were proud that her baby was born in their fort.

On a trip to one of the Mandan villages, Sergeant Ordway found himself fascinated by a flirtatious young Mandan female who seemed as fascinated with him. She had a smiling, roundish face and attractive figure clothed in a deerskin dress decorated with colorful red beads and porcupine quills.

"Ordway," he said, pointing to himself.

Then he pointed to her and raised his eyebrows in question.

"Malawi," she smiled.

Making a definite move, Ordway again pointed to himself and then to her, and then back and forth with a questioning expression.

Smiling again, she nodded. He took her hand, and they went for a walk. Deciding they had to learn how to communicate, he pointed to a tree and said "Tree." Then he pointed to her questioningly, and she told him the Mandan word for a tree. It quickly became a game, and they laughed as they learned new words from each other. Ordway began to visit her as often as possible, and suddenly winter didn't seem quite so long or boring to him.

Winter evenings inside the fort continued to be a time for relaxing in front of open fireplaces with music, dancing, and conversation. While leaping and spinning might not have looked like dancing to anyone else, the men of the Corps enjoyed such antics, which limbered muscles that usually were stiff from the day's outdoor work. On many evenings, friends from the Mandan villages joined them for the merriment. Everyone laughed when York "danced" with Seaman by getting him to rear up on his hind legs and put his forepaws on York's chest. York would put his hands on Seaman's sides and sway with the music for a minute or two. When the men grew tired of dancing, the story-telling would begin. They swapped hunting and fishing tales, and sometimes they wistfully told quieter stories of their lives back home. When things became too sentimental, Cruzatte would challenge the other tobacco chewers to a spitting contest, and the scene became raucous again.

Seaman padded contentedly from hut to hut, usually settling down in a doorway to watch people come and go, often getting a rewarding pat on the head from passersby. Lewis sat for hours hunched over his desk, describing the new plants and animals they had discovered. He wrote about the Indians, their customs, and his own ideas for trading with them, as well as the soil conditions and the minerals the expedition had encountered.

Near the end of February when winter paused for a sunny day, Chiefs Big White and Big Man visited the fort and told Captain Clark that several of their braves had gone to consult their Medicine Stone three miles away. The stone was about twenty paces wide and had a level surface. They believed it forecast the Mandan tribes' future in the coming year—war, peace, and other events. The Indians smoked at the stone and spent the night in nearby woods. The next morning they returned to find marks covering the stone, marks which predicted events of the coming year. The braves who 'read' the stone said that game would be scarce until spring and that wolves would compete with hunters for the meat—which, of course, was true every year.

When Drouillard, Frasier, Goodrich, and Newman left the fort with three horses and two sleds to bring back a load of meat from the hunting camp, they were suddenly surrounded by a large party of Sioux warriors who thundered down upon them, whooping and shouting gleefully. Some of the Sioux seized two of the white men's horses, cut off their collars, jumped on them, and took off at a furious gallop. The soldiers kept their grip stubbornly on the gray mare because she had a nursing foal at the fort.

"No! You damned thieving bastards! You can't take a mare from its foal!' shouted Frasier, pointing to the mare's udders and holding onto her for dear life.

One of the older Indians interceded and allowed Frasier to keep the mare. When the Indians had gone, the men, angry and disappointed in their loss, returned to the fort for more horses and sleds.

Lewis was angry and exclaimed to Clark, "We can't let this go unchallenged! You stay here to command the fort while I take a force of men to find and punish the Sioux."

He led a party of twenty men out to find the guilty Sioux. At the place where the Sioux had attacked, they found one of their sleds and followed the trail of the Sioux to two old Indian lodges, but they were empty. About six miles farther, they saw Indian lodges with smoke rising from them. Leaving their horses and sled with one man, they sneaked up to the dwellings, only to find them empty and on fire. They continued until they reached the expedition's old hunting camp, but they found that the Sioux had torn down Clark's meat pen and made off with all the meat it had held.

Finally despairing of ever catching the thieves, Lewis decided to give up the chase and turn to hunting. When the detachment finally departed to return to the fort, they took along two sleds, each loaded with approximately 2,400 pounds of meat. One was pulled over the river's ice by the gray mare, but the other had to be pulled by fifteen soldiers in harness. The men pulling the sled were utterly exhausted when they camped that night. The next day, the ice began to melt, which made the going wet and slippery for the men pulling the heavy sled. When they finally arrived at the fort, the men pulling the sled were so fatigued that they fell into their bedding and didn't stir for hours.

All winter long, the pirogues and keelboat had been encased in thick ice on the river, so when a late winter sun began to melt the ice, the men worked to free the boats and bring them ashore. They chipped the ice away from the first pirogue, then the second, struggling to pull them from the strong grasp of the frozen river to the safety of the riverbank.

To free the keelboat took many hours of chipping away, prying it loose, using poles as levers, and finally hitching the horses to pull it to land.

Two French trappers came from an Arikara village with some warriors who said they had met a large band of Sioux who bragged that they had stolen the white men's horses and meat. The Sioux told them that if they saw any man from the Corps of Discovery, they would kill them because they are "bad medicine." The Sioux said, "We will make war in the spring against the white men and the Mandans."

Captain Lewis felt content with the way the expedition had gone thus far, except for the fracas with the Sioux. Only one man of the Corps had died, and he to sickness rather than hostility. The men had successfully survived a winter of unimaginably brutal weather, working together and sharing fun as well as hardships. When he considered what lay ahead of them in the mountain range, however, anxiety descended on him like a blanket of fog. The future was unknown, sure to be challenging, and his and Clark's responsibility for thirty lives weighed on his mind.

CHAPTER 16

To the Yellowstone River

March-April, 1805

Ice on the Missouri River was beginning to break up, signaling the men of the Corps of Discovery that they would soon be able to resume its mission. Sergeant Gass gathered one group of men with tents and several days' rations and set out for a distant site to build dugout canoes. Others stayed at Fort Mandan making new tow lines for the pirogues. The local Indians continued visiting the fort to have their tools and weapons repaired at the blacksmith forge, paying for the services with corn, beans, and dried meat.

A Hidatsa Indian named One Eye came to the fort to see York for himself because he didn't believe the stories others had told him about meeting a black man. York, always good-natured, stood still while One Eye tried to rub the color off his skin, even spitting on his fingers and rubbing harder to find a white patch. Laughing at the Indian's obvious surprise, York removed his cap, bent his head toward One Eye, and invited him to feel his short, kinky, black hair. One Eye reached out tentatively and then broke into a wide smile when his fingers sank into York's wooly hair. Both men were laughing as they shook hands, and the Indian departed, convinced that York's color was no hoax.

Sacagawea and her baby were popular with the men and a real novelty for the expedition. But noting that her husband, Toussaint Charbonneau, had developed a haughty attitude, the captains held a meeting with him. Believing that Sacagawea, as interpreter with the Shoshone Indians, would be indispensable to the Corps of Discovery's mission, he became puffed up with self-importance.

"I do no labor, stand no guard," he informed the captains.

"Yes, you will," Lewis replied with the voice of authority. "You will do the same work the soldiers of the Corps of Discovery do."

Charbonneau scowled and shot back, "No!"

"In that case, you would just be a burden to us," Clark said brusquely. Lewis stood and looked into Charbonneau's eyes. "If that's your answer, take your squaw and leave our camp now." Then he turned away.

Shocked at the order, Charbonneau took Sacagawea and Pomp and moved back to his Hidatsa village. However, after four days he and his family returned.

"I go, do what you say," he promised.

The captains agreed, secretly relieved that they would have the Frenchman's strength and experience as well as his pleasant squaw and her tribal language skills.

Gass and his team had returned with four dugout canoes, and he and Shields were now making a new steering rudder for the keelboat in preparation for its return trip to St. Louis. However, the captains had begun to have second thoughts about resuming their journey with only four dugout canoes.

"I would rather have too many than too few," Clark admitted. "It won't cost anything to make one or two more."

"My conclusion also," Lewis agreed. "Let's have the men make two more."

Fort Mandan was a beehive of activity, with everyone making final preparations for the next leg of the expedition. Two men went to the Northwest Company's camp to trade wolf pelts for tobacco, while other men made oars and poles for propelling the canoes through treacherous waters, and others shelled corn. Tents and bedding were put out in the open, airing out under the warm spring sun. Ducks, geese, and swans were migrating north, and the Indians set fire to the dry grass to allow new grass to grow for their horses and to attract buffalo. On those days, the air was smoky, but the ever-constant brisk wind helped to sweep away the smoke. Excitement was in the air.

By the end of March, ice floes were coming down the river in great chunks, and dead buffalo began floating down the river as well, evidently drowned as they tried to cross the river on thinning ice. As the Mandan and Hidatsa Indians pulled the dead buffalo carcasses from the icy water, the men of the Corps paused in their own preparations to watch them.

"Look at them!" one man exclaimed.

"That's amazing!" joined another. "It's almost like dancing, the way they can jump from floe to floe!"

The Indians worked together to pull the dead buffalos to their side of the river.

"This must be something they do every spring. They are experts at it!" came another admiring comment.

Spring brought joy to the men of the Corps of Discovery, who had survived the most brutal winter any of them had ever experienced. They were healthy except for a few with venereal disease. They sang as they packed their goods, preparing to resume their journey into new territory, ready to conquer whatever lay before them in the West. Few nights passed without a dance.

The first day of April began with lightning, thunder, rain, and hail. After the storm, the men gave their careful attention to preparing the keelboat, pirogues, and dugout canoes for departure. Everything that was being returned to St. Louis—live animals in cages, stuffed animals, pressed plants—was loaded in the keelboat.

Captain Lewis's copious notes and drawings and Captain Clark's detailed map of the journey thus far were also packaged and stored aboard the keelboat.

"If we don't make it back," Lewis said quietly to Clark, "at least our country will know what we did up to this point."

Clark smiled with assurance. "We'll make it back, and we'll have much, much more to show our country than this load we're sending back to St. Louis now."

The captains inspected weapons, ammunition, food, medical supplies, trade goods for the Indians, and tools. Lewis gave last minute instructions to Corporal Warfington who was commanding the keelboat on its return to St. Louis.

"Be on full alert in Teton Sioux territory, and be ready to shoot your way through that stretch of river if you have to," he said.

"Yes sir, I understand, Captain," Warfington returned. "We'll be ready, and if necessary, show them they can't bully us."

The keelboat pulled away from Fort Mandan, piloted by Gravelines, who was taking two Indian chiefs to visit President Jefferson. The crew of six soldiers and two French *engages* waved until they were out of sight. Troublemakers Newman and Reed were aboard the keelboat, being returned to St. Louis. Corporal Warfington also took along several other Indians and trappers as passengers for some portion of the journey downriver.

Captain Clark, with the two heavily loaded pirogues and six dugout canoes, prepared to embark upriver as Captain Lewis made ready to walk the route ashore in search of new species. Clark had distributed goods and provisions in the eight vessels so that in the event of loss, the Corps would still have something of everything. The Corps of Discovery was now twenty-eight soldiers plus Drouillard, Charbonneau, Sacagawea, Pomp, York, and the dog Seaman. Just before pushing off, the Mandan girl, Malawi, appeared with a bundle strapped to her back.

"Ordway!" she called to Captain Lewis.

Lewis looked at her and then his eyes darted to the canoe Ordway commanded.

"Sergeant Ordway!" he called. "Someone is here to see you."

Ordway climbed out of his canoe and went to Malawi. Their communication consisted of few words and many gestures. Then Ordway turned to Captain Lewis.

"She wants to go with me like Sacagawea goes with Charbonneau," Ordway explained.

Surprised, Lewis again looked at her. Then he shook his head.

"We can't do that, Ordway. If we did, every man would soon have his own squaw—and we'll be lucky to feed ourselves through the mountains. Sacagawea is coming because we need her to translate for us when we reach the Shoshones."

Ordway looked at the ground, then to Malawi, whose eyes were brimming with tears, her face contorted with disappointment as she realized that it was a negative decision.

"I understand, Captain." He turned quickly to embrace the young woman, then returned to his canoe and jumped into position, ready to go.

Sacagawea and Pomp were popular among the men of the Corps. Traveling with a baby who gurgled and smiled despite hardships or the weather, provided tender amusement for the men. They enjoyed watching him and playing with him. Usually he was strapped into a wooden carrier on Sacagawea's back, a placid and sweet *papoose*.

It became obvious very quickly that Sacagawea would contribute more than simply translation services to the expedition. On the first day, when the party stopped to eat, she knew where to find wild artichokes that mice had collected and buried. She found a sharp stick and dug up a huge pile of the vegetables, showing the men how to cook and eat this welcome addition to their meal.

The two pirogues and six lighter, more maneuverable dugout canoes made their way easily up the Missouri River. The captains intended to leave the pirogues at the Falls of the Missouri River, where Lewis planned to assemble the iron-frame boat that he and President Jefferson had designed, covering it with elk skins. The white pirogue, slightly smaller and more stable than the red pirogue, was the "flagship" of the flotilla. Rowed by six oarsmen, it carried the Corps' astronomical instruments, medicine, trade goods, journals, notes, and casks of gunpowder. Sacagawea, Pomp, Charbonneau, Drouillard, and the two captains (when one of them wasn't walking on shore) all traveled in the white pirogue. The flat-bottomed pirogues were clumsy water craft, but experienced crews could easily handle them. The six canoes were round-bottom dugouts hewn from cottonwood trees, fitted with sails, with a crew of four oarsmen. The expedition often made twenty miles a day alongside level and fertile plains that had neither trees nor shrubs, although the bottoms along the shore were timbered. The men could plainly see coal strata in the bluffs along the riverbank. Lewis noted all these features in his journal. As the weather warmed at the end of April, mosquitoes once more became a pesky nuisance.

Each day the captains sent out up to ten hunters to bring in enough meat to feed more than thirty people. The countryside had turned green, and the hunters had found large patches of spring onions which added a pleasing flavor to meat stews. Sometimes strong spring headwinds prevented travel on the river, and so the men had a day now and then in camp, providing time to air out damp items, repair boats, make moccasins and clothing, and cure meat. The captains used that time to record astronomical data and to update maps of the area recently traveled. They also recorded careful notes on the geography, soil, minerals, climate, and native peoples of each region.

Whenever the expedition met a party of Indian hunters, the captains stopped to smoke and talk with them to establish friendly relations. Timber in this area was cottonwood, elm, ash, box alder, and dwarf juniper. Underbrush consisted of swamp willow, redberry, and chokeberry. Magpies, grouse, crows, hawks, and field larks abounded. Bluffs alongside the river still showed strong strata of coal.

Fighting the swift current of the river, the expedition passed high plains and bottoms alive with springtime growth. The men by now had cast off their warm clothing and worked in loincloths because much of their time was spent in the water, pulling the vessels and freeing debris from their path. One day at sunset they saw Indians on horseback who kept their distance from the expedition.

"L-Look at those g-g-guys" Reuben Fields said to his boat mates as he waved to the Indians, hoping for a response.

"They don't seem interested in talking to us," Colter commented. "We must look pretty fierce."

"Nah," Fields said laughing. "I-It's the s-s-sight of you in a loincloth that s-s-scares them." Everyone in the canoe laughed.

As the expedition struggled up the river, the spring grasslands nurtured vast herds of buffalo, elk, and antelope. The grasslands also indirectly supported the coyotes, foxes, wolves, and bears that lived off the hoofed animals. Large swarms of insects hovered above the animals, which brought immense groups of darting birds to feed on the insects. Antelope often crossed the river, and although they were fleet runners, they were weak swimmers and easy to kill in the water. Even Seaman could catch and kill an antelope that ventured into the river.

Keeping pace with the flotilla on shore, Lewis one morning came upon the remains of an Indian hunting camp. Nearby was a scaffold about seven feet high under which lay a body wrapped in a buffalo skin. Near the body was a leather bag containing moccasins, beaver tails, a buffalo-skin scraper, dry roots, and a small quantity of Mandan tobacco. Lewis was interested, but didn't want to linger in this place sacred to native peoples.

Because the wild animals of the northern plains had seen so few human beings, they were not afraid of the men of the expedition. They showed no alarm when the men approached to inspect them out of curiosity. Lewis came upon a buffalo calf that looked up at him but didn't run away. At that moment Seaman came bounding up to Lewis, and the calf snorted and darted behind Lewis for protection. The calf followed Lewis until he got back into the boat at the water's edge. The men discovered that buffalo cows defended their calves only as long as they kept up with the herd; if they fell behind, the cows seldom returned to find them.

While Charbonneau was steering the white pirogue one day, a sudden squall struck the boat, causing him to panic and turn the pirogue sideways to the wind, tilting the boat over so far that it threatened to capsize. Charbonneau, who couldn't swim, was frozen with fear and cried out to God for mercy. Cruzatte leaped up, shoved Charbonneau aside, turned the pirogue into the wind, and shouted for the crew to pull down the sail. It was a close call because the white pirogue carried all the captains' official papers and instruments, as well as all the medicine. Only goods and provisions were distributed among the canoes.

"We'd better keep an eye on Charbonneau," Lewis confided to Clark that evening. "He doesn't seem to know how to handle the pirogue in a crisis."

Clark added dryly, "Apparently he doesn't handle fear well either."

The Corps of Discovery's worst enemy was the wind, which was blustery most of the time, sweeping down the open spaces of land. Some days it was so strong that the men stayed in camp because they couldn't row upstream against it or tow the boats through high, wind-driven waves. Despite being the rainy season of the year, this country was dry, and the wind stirred up great clouds of dust and sand, blowing it into the men's faces and causing sore, irritated eyes. Sometimes, the only recourse was to pull into a sheltered inlet until the fury of the wind lessened.

One day in late April the expedition pulled into a cove until winds calmed, and Captain Lewis, Sergeant Ordway, and Private Fields crossed the Missouri to go up the Yellowstone River to take and record observations. They set up a camp on the bank of the Yellowstone, about two miles above its mouth.

"Fields, hike up the river for several miles and see what you can learn about it," Lewis said.

During Fields' absence, Lewis recorded three astronomical readings at three-hour intervals during the day, showing Ordway his method and purpose. When Fields returned, a buffalo calf had trailed him the last four miles,

"The only thing I found was this strange-looking horn," he reported, producing a large curving horn of what would prove to be that of a bighorn sheep.

"That's an ungodly looking thing!" Lewis said, taking the horn to inspect it. "Now all we have to do is find the animal that goes with it. When we do, science will probably name it after you." He smiled and added, "Maybe something like a *Josephus Fieldus* goat."

Fields grinned and self-consciously cracked his knuckles.

After leading the buffalo calf to an area spotted with buffalo dung, an area of possible rescue by a buffalo herd, the three men returned to camp with the horn. Captain Clark was busy with his maps, calculating distances.

"My figures show that the Yellowstone River is 1,888 miles from the mouth of the Missouri," he said, "and that we have traveled 279 miles since we left Fort Mandan." Both captains kept meticulous records of everything pertaining to the exploration of the wild and beautiful western lands.

The hunters were eager to test their skill and courage against the most feared animal of the region—the grizzly bear. They had first heard about them from the Indians at Fort Mandan, who said they were gigantic, ferocious, and fearless. They had told the soldiers hair-raising tales about their experiences. Captain Lewis and Drouillard didn't have long to wait for their first encounter. They were walking on shore when they were suddenly startled by thrashing sounds in the brush behind them. Wheeling around, they found themselves face-to-face with two massive grizzly bears ready to attack them. Reacting instinctively, both men fired quickly but only wounded the grizzlies, which reared up on their hind legs bellowing their rage. As the two men feverishly reloaded their rifles, one of the bears ran away but the other one charged at Lewis just as Drouillard fired again. This time his shot hit the grizzly in the head, and it slumped lifeless to the ground.

Lewis was shaken but safe, and he smiled as he said, "Well, we've fought the grizzly, but I can't say I'd care to repeat the experience. I see why the Indians fear them." Although Lewis had hunted black bears in the East, he had never seen such fearlessness in a bear. It took four men to haul the meat from the grizzly back to camp.

CHAPTER 17

Fighting Grizzlies and the Elements

May, 1805

"Captain Lewis!" Bratton called from outside the captains' tent at sunrise. "Joseph Fields is mighty sick."

"What's wrong with him?" Lewis asked, slipping his shirt on over his head as he fell in step behind Private Bratton.

"He's burning with fever and running at both ends."

"Sounds like dysentery. Let's have a look."

Huddled under his blanket, shivering and bleary-eyed, Fields lay silent as Lewis put his hand on the private's forehead and then checked his pulse.

"How do you feel, Fields?"

"Terrible, sir," he answered softly, his voice barely audible.

"I'll be right back with something to help you feel better," Lewis said. "You just rest."

In a few minutes Lewis returned with Glauber salts and laudanum, his standard treatment for dysentery and fever. He was glad Fields seemed to be an isolated case—he had seen an entire camp stricken before, even with fatalities. He was accustomed to treating common boils, abscesses, and sore eyes from the constantly blowing sand—all uncomfortable, but not a threat to life itself. For boils and abscesses he used poultices, and for sore eyes he used a wash of two parts white zinc sulphate and one part lead acetate.

Despite the sick man among them, the expedition pushed off as soon as possible. The country continued to be level and fertile, with well-timbered bottoms. Bald eagles were numerous in this wild area, nesting high in the trees. Elk and buffalo were also plentiful. The wind was blustery, as usual, and when the first strong gust hit the flotilla, Charbonneau, for the second time, mishandled the white pirogue. The captains, both on shore contrary to their own rules, watched helplessly as the pirogue tipped and water washed over its sides.

"Cut the halyards!" Lewis bellowed into the wind. "Haul in the sails!"

But those in the boat couldn't hear him. Cruzatte, the best river man in the Corps of Discovery, shouted at Charbonneau to turn the boat into the wind, but Charbonneau was again panic-stricken, fearing for his life in the rushing river. The pirogue filled with water to within inches of the gunnels, and articles from the boat began to float away. As the crew scrambled to regain control of the boat, Sacagawea reached over the side, retrieving most of the threatened articles from the river.

That evening, Clark told Lewis, "I don't want to trust Charbonneau to steer the white pirogue again. We can't afford to lose it."

"I agree," replied Lewis. "We can't risk losing our journals, maps, and instruments. Their loss would surely cripple our mission."

"Janey was the calmest one in the boat. There she was—little Pomp sleeping on her back—and she still was able to pull nearly every item back into the boat. She knew how important they were to us." Clark was smiling as he recalled the scene.

"Yes, in a *just* world, Charbonneau would be *her* property instead of the other way around."

Early May had turned cold, and one day brought several hours of snow. The canoes and pirogues were always in peril because the river was crooked, the current was strong, and the river banks collapsed into the water without warning. Now, for almost one hundred and sixty miles, the landscape was dominated by high, rugged bluffs. Lewis called this area the "Desert of America" because it was such high, dry country. Dwarf cedar grew among the pine trees on the hills. Beaver were plentiful along this part of the Missouri River, and their meat was a welcome change—especially the men's favorite, beaver tail.

From the boats, the hunters spied a grizzly bear lying in the open about three hundred yards from the river. Six men went after the grizzly, which seemed unaware of their presence until they got within forty yards. Four hunters fired while the other two held their guns at ready should more shots be needed. Even though all the first four shots struck the bear, it charged the men! The other two hunters fired, breaking the beast's shoulder—but it still charged! Unable to reload their guns quickly enough, the hunters fled toward the river, the bear gaining on their every stride. Two of the hunters leaped into the river and the others hid among the thick brush on shore, reloaded their guns, and fired again. Their shots went into body of the huge bear, but they also revealed the men's hiding place. The bear swung around and headed for their thicket. The men dropped their guns and leaped over a twenty-foot bank into the river. Enraged, the animal plunged into the water after them! Finally, a man on shore shot the monster in the head, and killed it. When they pulled the bear from the river and butchered it, they found that eight balls had penetrated its hulking body.

Not long after this episode, the rudder on the red pirogue broke and the expedition had to stop until Shields and Gass could repair it. Drouillard used the lull to shoot a beaver in the river. As usual, Seaman leaped in to retrieve it, but when he dove under the water the wounded beaver bit the dog's hind leg. Seaman surfaced with the beaver in his jaws and swam ashore, hobbling on three legs toward the hunters, while his fourth leg gushed blood. Lewis examined the leg, applying pressure to stop the bleeding, but the flow didn't stop because the beaver had bitten through an artery. Lewis tied a piece of buckskin around Seaman's leg just above the wound to lessen the bleeding, and the men lifted the badly wounded dog onto a blanket and carried him to camp.

It seemed to Lewis that Seaman's leg would never stop bleeding. While he cut away the fur from the area and stitched the ragged wound, York comforted the dog, crooning softly and petting his head. Lewis had never before treated a wound that bled so much, and he feared that Seaman would die from losing so much blood. Sacagawea made a bed for him in the white pirogue and draped a blanket over a stick frame to shield him from the sun. Lewis worried about infection, but by the next evening Seaman was able to eat a little broth with chopped meat, and on the following morning the dog was able to stand on his three good legs. Sacagawea and York faithfully tended the much-loved dog for days, and after a week Seaman was playful again—much to the delight and relief of everyone.

Late one afternoon, Bratton, who had been out hunting, ran to the river shouting, "Bring the pirogue to shore! Hurry!" Bratton was out of breath and very frightened of something.

Its crew swung the white pirogue to shore as Bratton dove from the bank, splashing feverishly to safety in the pirogue.

"What happened?" someone yelled.

Breathless and panting, Bratton shouted, "A grizzly!" He gasped for air and added, "I shot him and he came after me!"

The bear was not behind Bratton, so Lewis took seven men to find it, tracking him by a trail of blood. They found him concealed in very thick brush and shot him in the head. When they dressed the carcass, they found that Bratton had shot him through the lungs. Even such a severe wound did not prevent the bear from chasing Bratton a half-mile and then returning the same distance and digging himself a bed that was two feet deep and five feet long.

"It's hard to believe that the bear was still alive when we found it!" one man said.

"Such strength and ferocity must be necessary in country like this," Clark said. But he also knew that the necessity of facing grizzlies was beginning to unnerve the men.

On a sunny spring morning a few days later, Lewis climbed a bluff and beheld for the first time the snow-covered Rocky Mountains. His heart skipped a beat at the magnificence and the beauty, but he also viewed the Rockies with foreboding. He could only imagine the hardships and suffering the expedition would experience as they crossed them, for the size of these mountains was on a completely different level of magnitude than the familiar Appalachian Mountains back east.

Progress on the Missouri River was slower now because it was filled with seemingly endless bends. In addition, the high bluffs came down to the water's edge denying the men access to the shore. The shallow river was filled with huge boulders, and strong headwinds slowed travel. For the most part, the men towed the pirogues and canoes with elk-skin tow lines that became weaker because they were constantly wet. Often, the lines broke, usually when the men were guiding a craft around the rocks. These vessels were in great danger of turning broadside, being carried downstream out of control, and overturning. The men were working in the river, combating both slippery mud and sharp rocks that cut and bruised their feet. The captains' pride knew no bounds as they witnessed the men's discipline, abilities, and capacity for brutally hard work.

The country on both sides of the river continued level and fertile, and great quantities of buffalo and other wild life were plentiful. Clark and Drouillard killed the biggest grizzly to date. The hunters had learned a great deal of respect for the grizzly, which was more likely to attack than flee when they encountered men. Their formidable appearance and the stubbornness with which they died had weakened the resolve of many of the hunters to face down the grizzly.

The Corps of Discovery came to a stretch of river that again required them to tow the vessels much of the day. Fortunately, the banks were firm and devoid of vegetation, which favored the use of tow ropes. This was rugged country with high hills covered with pine and cedar trees. The expedition passed the base of a cliff where rotten, stinking corpses of buffalo, evidently driven off the cliff by Indians, were piled high. The Indians had taken only what they could carry and left the rest to decay. The men watched a pack of wolves gorging on the putrid meat. They were so stuffed and lethargic that Clark walked up to one and prodded it out of his way.

One night, when everyone was sleeping except the guards, a buffalo bull blundered into camp. The four fires burning in the camp confused the buffalo, and the terrified animal began to charge wildly about. Seaman chased it, barking and adding to its terror. Some of the men sat up, dulled by sleep, while others reached for their guns. The bull's panic increased as the men on the ground began to move, and its hooves came within inches of sleeping bodies. Then it charged the tepee where the captains, Charbonneau, Sacagawea, and Pomp were sleeping, apparently mistaking the tepee for a living, threatening enemy. Just in time, Seaman diverted it from the tepee and chased it out of camp.

"Damn! Don't these beasts sleep at night?" Hugh Hall asked. "What the hell was he doing wandering around in the middle of the night?"

"Probably looking for a heifer," John Boley said dryly.

As they traveled on, the river became more and more challenging, bringing a terrifying moment to Captain Lewis. The tow rope on the white pirogue broke at a particularly dangerous part of the river, causing the pirogue to swing around, strike a rock, and almost turn over before the quick-acting men were able to save it. When they were again in calm waters, Lewis was so relieved that the white pirogue—and thus the expedition, in his mind—had been saved from disaster that he decided to reward the men.

"Well done, men," he shouted! "All the work we have done is wrapped up in the contents of that pirogue. If we had lost it, we would have serious problems. Pull over to the shore and let's celebrate."

On shore, he raised a jug to salute his team, and then removed the cork and poured drinks for all. The men milled about with their drinks.

"I think Captain Lewis values the white pirogue as much as he values his own life," Drouillard commented to Ordway.

"Well, he's put his life and career into this expedition, and the record of it all is in the white pirogue," Ordway said compassionately.

The flotilla passed cliffs that were two- to three-hundred feet high, nearly perpendicular, and shining white in the sun. Falling water had carved fantastic lines in the sandstone that allowed the imagination to see endless images.

"There's the Virgin Mary," Labiche cried out reverently, crossing himself.

"Hey! I see George Washington!" Private Whitehouse said excitedly, pointing.

"You could probably see Mary's Little Lamb if you wanted to," Shields dryly observed, ending the game.

Lewis wrote in his journal that those cliffs were a remarkable sight where a thousand figures and even buildings could be imagined.

A strong wind seemed always to blow downriver, forcing the men to tow the boats, requiring exhausting effort from them. Their elk-skin ropes were worn and prone to break as the men struggled to pull the boats against the current, their bare feet slipping on the muddy riverbanks. Earth and stones falling from the bluffs above added danger to their work. Part of the time, the men waded in water up to their armpits while rocks on the riverbed bruised and cut their feet.

Land on both sides of the Missouri was rolling prairie, bare and desolate. One night they camped at the mouth of a stream they named "Blowing Fly Creek" because the air was filled with swarming flies. Flies infested everything, and members of the expedition had to constantly shoo them out of their food as they ate.

That night, the sentinels raised an alarm because a tree that leaned over the tepee where the captains and Drouillard's family slept somehow was in flames. Everyone sprang into action, quickly dismantling the tepee and moving it to a safer location. The moment the tepee was out of danger, the entire top of the burning tree crashed to the ground exactly where the tepee had stood. High winds had fanned the fire, blowing in every direction and spraying burning embers over the camp, even damaging the tepee in its new location.

"How do you suppose that happened?" someone wondered aloud.

"That damned wind must have picked up a spark from one of the campfires and blown it into the tree."

"Day or night, we can't escape the bloody wind!" was the disgruntled response.

As the team continued up the Missouri, they saw large areas of prickly pears as well as hundreds of stubby pines and dwarf cedars. Fierce wind continued to be an unyielding adversary, and the expedition found itself enveloped in a gigantic cloud of dust and sand that made it impossible to work, cook, eat, or sleep. When the wind finally calmed a little, the landscape as far as the men could see was caked with fine grains of sand. The men washed themselves in the river, where the cool water soothed their skin. Captain Lewis prepared his mixture for sore eyes, and the men were grateful for the medication.

Though it was late May, standing water was still freezing at night here in the high country, sometimes to a thickness of one-third of an inch. When the breeze was in their favor, they hoisted the sails and enjoyed Mother Nature's assistance on the river. Now they were surrounded by mountains that were very rocky and covered with scrub pine. They sensed foreboding because game had become scarce. There were few bottoms now, with hills coming close to the river on both sides. In this new terrain, the rapids in the river became more and more tempestuous. When they came upon the most violent rapids yet, they doubled their crews and used both tow lines and poles to control their boats.

The Missouri suddenly spread to three times its former width, and the expedition came upon islands covered with cottonwood trees. The land became less forbidding and more fertile, and the river bottoms again bore timber. The expedition encountered an Indian camp that had been abandoned about two weeks, and Lewis counted the remains of one hundred-twenty-six campfires. Sacagawea examined some abandoned moccasins and assured the captains that these had not been Shoshone Indians.

As the Corps of Discovery pressed onward, the current against them became too rapid for oars, and the river was too deep for poles. They had to use tow ropes. The rocky bluffs now rose to a height of two to three hundred feet, often forming grotesque shapes. Huge columns of stone rose from the ground as though the result of a master sculptor's labor.

The Corps of Discovery was witnessing a new part of America that was indeed wondrous to behold. The captains, despite being stunned by the natural beauty, knew they were entering the Rocky Mountains, with its monumental challenges still ahead of them.

Chapter 18

The Great Falls of the Missouri

June, 1805

The countryside along the banks of the Missouri River gradually became more level, making towing the boats easier, a blessing to the men whose feet were bruised and battered from rocks on the riverbed. According to what the Mandan Indians had told them, the Corps would soon arrive at the Great Falls of the Missouri, where they planned to assemble the iron-frame boat. With game abundant once more, Lewis began collecting elk hides to cover the iron-frame boat.

Grizzly bears were seen every day now. While hunting, Drouillard and Charbonneau were suddenly charged by a grizzly when they intruded into his territory. Shooting frantically, Charbonneau wounded it—then, his gun empty, the terrified Charbonneau froze as the bear rushed toward him! Drouillard took careful aim and shot the bear in the head just in the nick of time. The animal's furious charge ended with its lifeless carcass at Charbonneau's feet. Shaking uncontrollably, still immobilized with fear, Charbonneau stared dumbly at the carcass.

After a moment of silence, Drouillard said sarcastically, "You're welcome!"

Finally coming to his senses, Charbonneau mumbled, "That monster would have ripped me to shreds."

"Tell you what, the next time you make some of that buffalo sausage, you can give me an extra portion, and we'll call it even," Drouillard grinned.

"*Mais oui, boudin blanc.* My pleasure." Then he smiled and added, "But I think you sell my life pretty cheap."

The expedition arrived at a wide fork in the Missouri River. "Make camp here," Lewis instructed the men, and to Clark he said, "We have to decide which of these two forks is the Missouri. What do you think?"

"I'm surprised the Mandans didn't tell us about this fork. It could be either one."

Lewis called to Sergeants Ordway and Gass. "Each of you take a canoe and crew up a different one of these forks and decide which direction it comes from. Be sure to get back by nightfall."

As the expedition awaited their return, the men dressed skins to make clothing while Lewis and Clark took celestial calculations to fix the location for Clark's map, still puzzling over the identity of the two wide-flowing forks.

"The north fork is larger than the south fork, and its muddy water is more turbulent," Lewis noted. "The south fork, on the other hand, is clear and calm."

"The north fork looks and acts like the Missouri River we have known all these weeks, so the men will think it's the continuation of the Missouri," Clark reasoned.

Both leaders studied the water and the terrain. Lewis commented, " The north fork is so muddy that it must have run a great distance through prairie, which would indicate that it can't be the true source of the Missouri." Gesturing, he added, "The south fork is so clear that it must have come directly out of the mountains, don't you think? It could prove that the true source of the Missouri lies north, in the mountains."

Positive identification was crucial for the expedition to continue to the west coast. When Ordway and Gass returned with inconclusive information, the captains decided they would each lead a party far enough up the different forks to determine which one was the continuation of the Missouri. Lewis took Pryor, Drouillard, Shields, Windsor, Cruzatte, and Labiche to explore the north fork. Clark selected the Fields brothers, Gass, Shannon, and York to go with him up the south fork. Each team was to travel a day and a half up the fork, and then return to camp.

Clark's party explored fifty miles up the southern fork and then returned—but when Lewis and his party came to no conclusion, they continued up the northern fork another twenty miles, convinced that it could not be the Missouri because it bore too far north. They built rafts to ride the current back to camp, but it rained all night making the river hazardous, so they walked back to camp.

"The northern fork goes too far north," Lewis said when his group returned, "so I'm convinced that the southern fork is the Missouri." Still, the problem hung in the air.

Private Cruzatte ("St. Peter" to the men) was an experienced Missouri River navigator whose knowledge and skill had earned the respect of everyone in the Corps.

"I think the north fork is the Missouri," he announced to the men, which convinced them.

But Lewis stuck with his opinion that the south fork was the one they needed. He was so certain of it that he named the north fork "Maria's River" in honor of his teenaged cousin, Miss Maria Wood.

The captains decided that Lewis would lead a team up the south fork until they found the Falls of the Missouri, which would leave no doubt in anyone's mind—provided they found it. Clark was to follow with the pirogues and canoes the next day. Before Lewis and his party left in search of the falls, the captains decided to hide the large red pirogue in thick brush and undergrowth and prepare a cache for all the heavy baggage they could do without, thereby lightening the loads in the remaining vessels and adding men to their crews. Seven men under Cruzatte, who had experience building caches, dug a huge hole in which to bury the baggage. The men filled the cache with ammunition, axes, beaver traps, blacksmith tools, tents, and superfluous baggage of every kind, totaling about a thousand pounds. Then the captains gave out a dram of whiskey, Cruzatte broke out his fiddle, and the men had a frolic. To commemorate their presence in this place, they branded several trees with Captain Lewis's branding iron. That evening, Sacagawea was ill, becoming nauseous and unable to hold food down. She thought she had eaten something that disagreed with her and hoped she would feel better the next morning.

At sunrise, Lewis and his party started up the south fork in search of the falls. Before following, the main party with Clark put out all of the merchandise to dry, and John Shields repaired the main spring of the air gun. Although Shields had never served an apprenticeship at any trade, he was so gifted that he even made his own tools, working extremely well in either wood or metal. He was very important to the functioning of the Corps of Discovery because he seemed able to repair anything. With great satisfaction, Lewis felt that he and Clark had done well in selecting the men, except for Reed and Newman.

Meanwhile, Lewis and his detachment proceeded up the south fork in search of the Falls of the Missouri. They passed through an open and level plain that continued as far as they could see, populated with great numbers of buffalo, as well as some wolves and antelopes. The prickly pears were so numerous that it required half of their attention to avoid them. Near the river, the level plain was cut by deep ravines.

With Clark's following party, the rapid current made handling the boats difficult, and the men were in the water from morning until night struggling to get the boats upstream. Sacagawea was now very sick, and Captain Clark put her in the covered part of the white pirogue where it was cool. He tried to coax her to take some medicine, but she refused.

Farther on up the southern fork, where high cliffs and crags ended the prairie and fronted the river, Captain Lewis had gone ahead to survey the land. There had been a sudden afternoon downpour, creating slippery grass and oozing mud. Suddenly Lewis slipped and nearly fell from a craggy precipice that dropped ninety feet to the river and rocks below. At the last moment, he stopped his fall with his espontoon, and at that same moment heard someone cry out, "Help!!" Windsor had lost his footing and slid to the very edge of the precipice, his right arm and leg dangling over it.

"Your knife!" Lewis shouted. "Take your knife and dig a foothold for your foot!"

Windsor was terrified and slipped a few inches more before he could pull his knife from its sheath and twist his body so he could carve a quick foothold in the cliff. Lewis watched intently, trying to come up with an alternate plan if he failed. Windsor painstakingly gouged out a hole and stuck his left foot in it, scrambling up and over the top—safe and grateful in the wet grass. He lay there for a few moments as Lewis walked over to him.

"It's a long way down there, lad. I'm mighty glad you didn't take the short cut."

"Me, too!" he said with relief.

That night Lewis's group camped in an old Indian lodge made of sticks and mud, and the next morning they continued up the southern fork of the river. Suddenly, Collins yelled, "Listen! Do you hear a roar? I think I hear the falls!"

Everyone stopped and listened. Sure enough, they heard a faint roar in the distance. The sound increased as they continued, and soon they began to see a spray of mist rising like a column of smoke above the trees.. By noon they reached the deafening roar of the Great Falls of the Missouri River.

"My God! Look at that!" someone yelled over the din.

Shouting over the roar of falling water, George Gibson slapped Captain Lewis's back, "You were right, Captain! All the rest of us were wrong!"

"Lucky guess!" Lewis yelled back at Gibson with false modesty. He had been certain that the south fork was the correct one all the time.

He immediately sent Joseph Fields back down the river to find Clark's party and give them the good news.

The falls presented a truly breathtaking scene. The river above the falls was eight-hundred yards wide, of which one-hundred yards formed a smooth sheet of water that fell about eighty feet to the river below. The remaining seven hundred yards of the river fell onto rocks, creating a jumble of rising, swirling spray measuring fifteen or twenty feet before it was caught by the falling water and slammed back upon the rocks.

The falls created a spectacular sight of sheer spray that was two-hundred yards wide and eighty feet high, which caught the arching reflections of the sun and created a huge rainbow. The men stared at the scene, enraptured by the beauty and majesty of nature. Lewis climbed a nearby hill to get an even better look. From the hill, he also looked out over an expansive plain that reached from the river to the snow-clad mountains in the south and southwest. He could also see the meandering Missouri cutting its way through the land. What beauty! The falls of the Missouri were actually a series of five large falls spread over a distance of eighteen miles. A second river, which the Indians called the Medicine River, emptied into the Missouri just above the falls.

Fields returned with further news. "Captain Clark and the others have arrived at the foot of a rapid about five miles below and are waiting there for you to come and examine Sacagawea, who is very sick," he reported.

As Lewis hiked to Clark's group, he came upon a herd of buffalo and decided to kill one and leave it there so he could camp there and dine on the buffalo on his return trip. The buffalo, shot through the lungs, stood dumbly, stunned and gushing blood from its mouth and nostrils. Watching and waiting for the buffalo to fall, Lewis neglected to reload his rifle. A grizzly, not twenty yards away, suddenly startled him, and without thinking, he raised his empty gun to shoot again. The bear charged! With no tree within three-hundred yards, Lewis turned and ran toward the river. He leaped into the water and went twenty yards, then turned back, intending to use his espontoon against his attacker, which would be in water over its head and at a disadvantage. The grizzly, however, instead of attacking, suddenly wheeled at the river's edge, and ran back the way it had come, looking behind as if frightened. *I'll be damned!* Lewis thought. *He couldn't have been afraid of me, so what was he running from?* He would never know.

"Where is Sacagawea?" Lewis asked upon arrival at Clark's location.

Clark was truly distressed. "If we lose Janey, Meriwether, the baby will die! We'll have no way to feed Pomp—and no one to translate with the Shoshones for us either."

Sacagawea lay in pain, drenched in sweat. Lewis gave her thirty drops of laudanum to help her sleep and offered to take Pomp so she could rest. As ill as she was, she wanted to keep Pomp with her. When hunters found a sulfur spring, Lewis decided to try the sulfur water on Sacagawea. He also gave her barks and opium, which quickly produced a stronger pulse. He decided to stay at the lower camp, both to restore Sacagawea to health and to record celestial observations.

Next morning, Captain Clark called the men at the lower camp together. "Sergeant Gass, take six men and cut enough timber to make two wagons," he instructed. "It's eighteen miles around the falls, and we can't portage these canoes that distance on our backs. Look for some big trees to make wheels. We can use the masts from the pirogues as axles and tongues.

While Gass and the carpenters felled trees and built the wagons, Clark and five others went out to mark a portage route around the falls. Meanwhile, Lewis had other men hide the white pirogue among the willows on an island. Then he had them take the canoes out of the river and up a three-mile gradual ascent to a plain, where they could be loaded onto the wagons.

Sacagawea, who was finally improving, walked the area for the first time with Pomp who cooed and smiled at his mother and the men, who enjoyed pausing in their labors to greet them both. Lewis continued the same regimen of medicine for Sacagawea and cautioned both her and Charbonneau about foods she must avoid and foods she should eat for the next few days.

When a party of men went out to retrieve the meat from a kill, a grizzly suddenly crashed out of the brush and charged Alexander Willard, who instinctively turned and ran, zigzagging around trees to try to confuse the bear. Colter, Collins, and Howard chased and wounded the bear, only to have it wheel about and turn on them, charging straight for Howard, who dashed headlong into the river. When Colter and Collins ran after it to try rescue Howard, the bear became confused and ran away. Colter and Collins chased it, firing shots into it repeatedly, finally killing it a half mile away.

"Wow! That was close!" a winded Willard said, his heart racing.

"Those big guys don't take kindly to being shot," a dripping wet Howard agreed.

When they butchered the beast, they found nine musket balls in its carcass, including one lodged in its heart.

"No wonder the Mandans told us grizzlies were hard to kill!" Collins marveled. "Imagine trying to fight that monster with bows and arrows."

Back at camp, Sacagawea's fever returned after she ate some apples and dried fish.

"Why did you allow her to eat such food?" an angry Lewis demanded of Charbonneau. "I told you what she should eat."

Lewis gave her thirty drops of laudanum, which gave her a tolerable night's sleep.

The carpenters took great pride in building the two wagons and were especially proud of their wooden wheels made from crosscuts of large tree trunks. Clark sketched a map of the area around the falls for the men, having marked the route the wagons would take.

"Sergeant Ordway, I'm leaving you in charge of the camp while the rest of us make the first trip around the falls," Lewis said. The personable Ordway had become popular among the men. "I'll leave Goodrich to catch fish for you and York to cut firewood. Of course, Sacagawea and the baby will stay with you also."

Up on the plain, the men lifted canoes onto the wagons. "All right, men," Clark called out, "let's get into harness and make like mules!"

With Shannon braying playfully like a donkey, the men fitted the makeshift harness to their bodies and started the eighteen-mile obstacle course around the falls. Prickly pear plants quickly became a problem on the portage, their thorns painfully piercing the men's moccasins. They also discovered that great herds of buffalo had trampled the ground so badly after the last rain that their sharp hooves had left it uneven, and by now it had dried that way as though it had been frozen solid, making footing precarious and painful. They hoisted the sail of the largest canoe, which helped the men in harness as long as the wind blew in their favor. During the exhausting journey, one wagon tongue and two wagon wheels broke, forcing the men to stop and make repairs.

They arrived at the end of the portage after dark on the second day, extremely fatigued, and established the upper camp under some shady willows on White Bear Island, named for an albino bear they had seen. Lewis planned to stay there with several men to assemble and cover the iron-framed boat, which was thirty-six feet long, four and a half feet wide, and twenty-six inches deep. It was so light that five men could carry it.

The next morning the still weary men started the return trek to the lower Portage Creek Camp with the empty wagons, arriving very late in the day. They reloaded the wagons before turning in and started out the next morning with their second load. After several miles, one of the wagon tongues broke again, delaying them for a short time. At every halt, the poor fellows in harness dropped to the ground, so utterly exhausted that they fell asleep instantly and had to be wakened to continue the brutal trip. Some were limping from sore feet, and others became faint with the heat—yet no one complained. All were determined to complete this journey to the Pacific Ocean or die in the attempt. When they got within three miles of the upper camp, a violent rainstorm struck and within a few minutes the ground was covered with water. The men trudged on through the rain and arrived at the upper camp soaked and exhausted.

"You men look like the dregs off a slave ship," Lewis greeted them. "You have sure as hell earned a double ration of whiskey."

The whiskey revived them before they took to their bedding and slept the sleep of the dead throughout the night. The next day they returned again to the lower camp, where they got new loads ready to start out again the following morning.

At the upper White Bear Island Camp, Seaman was in a constant state of agitation with the frequent sightings of bears. Whitehouse and Frazier sewed elk skins onto the iron frame of the collapsible boat, which the men called "The Experiment," while Gass and Shields fit horizontal bars of wood to it.

The hunters discovered an enormous spring that they estimated to be three to four hundred feet wide, forming a falls into the river.

"Good God, did you ever see a spring that goldarn big?" Shannon marveled.

"Not even close," Willard agreed. "We don't have springs that size back in the States. This country is unbelievable."

The cold water was clear, and the men thought it was the best water they had ever tasted.

The next day, Drouillard and his hunting party were struck by a fierce storm of rain, causing them to take refuge under a ledge in a creek bank. The sky darkened, lightning lit up the sky, thunder pierced the air, and the creek rose precipitously.

"We can't stay here," Drouillard shouted as the water rose.

When they scrambled from under their ledge, they were accosted by fierce sleet driven so hard by the wind that the men could barely stay on their feet as they continued toward the upper camp, where they arrived shortly before dark. The party with the wagons was already there, and Captain Lewis gave them all a gill of whiskey.

"Damn, the whiskey almost makes it worthwhile," Drouillard grinned.

"It helps," Colter agreed, "but I'd trade it for a dry, warm bed."

At the lower Portage Camp, some of the men set out to carry the remaining canoe and the last of the baggage three miles to the top of the staging hill, to be left there until morning. Others made last-minute repairs to the wagons. They broke camp the next morning and all hands set out for the upper camp, deciding to leave some boxes and kegs of pork and flour for another load. They struggled with the heavy load all day. When they camped at the end of the day, another storm struck and it rained all night. The men had to search individually for shelter because they had cached their tents. The rain stopped the next morning, and the weather cleared up. When they reached the upper camp, Clark sent everyone back for the goods they had left on the hill.

York, Sacagawea, Pomp, and Charbonneau, who hadn't yet seen the falls, wanted to go and see them. Sacagawea begged Charbonneau to ask Captain to go see the great falls. Clark agreed and set out to guide them and show them the natural phenomenon.

As the wagon party was returning to the upper camp with the final load, a fierce black cloud in the west promised trouble. The party hurried but had not got halfway before a violent storm of hail hit them. Hugh McNeal was knocked down by a single huge ball of hail, and all the men were bruised. Abandoning the wagon, the men ran for the camp in great confusion. Some of the men arrived with bleeding heads. Soon after they arrived, the storm stopped, leaving more than an inch of hail on the ground.

"My God, this is strange country!" Labiche pronounced. "God only knows what's going to happen from one minute to the next."

Clark and his party returned at about the same time. Clark had also seen the storm coming and sought shelter under a ledge in a deep ravine. The violent rain at first wasn't terribly alarming, but then the extremely violent hailstorm struck, sending a wall of water hurtling down the ravine, driving rocks and anything it encountered before it.

"Get out of here, quick!" Clark shouted at Charbonneau and Sacagawea.

Clark pushed Sacagawea, with Pomp strapped to her back, up the side of the ravine while Charbonneau pulled her from above. When they got to the top, they found York searching frantically for them. He had left them shortly before to pursue some buffalo,

"I thought you had all been washed away," he said with great relief.

One moment longer and the water rushing down the ravine would have swept them into the river just above the eighty-seven-foot falls, where they would certainly have plunged to their deaths. As it was, they lost their compass, a tomahawk, Charbonneau's gun and shot pouch, a horn with powder and ball, moccasins, Pomp's clothes, and their bedding. They set out for the upper camp as quickly as possible because the baby was naked and cold and Sacagawea was just recovering from her severe illness.

The men at the upper camp were safely ensconced under a copse of trees.

"Let's make some punch with the hail," Captain Lewis said to try to lighten the mood and ease the tension.

"Let's measure the biggest hailstone," Shannon said enthusiastically. "I bet this is a record."

Lewis measured the largest hailstone at seven inches in circumference and weighed it at three ounces. Then he used some of the hail to make the punch.

The next morning, some of the men went for the abandoned wagon. Two men went to search for the lost compass while four more made new axles and repaired the wagons. The men returned with the wagon and baggage from the hill, and the others brought back the compass—but they found nothing else that had been lost.

At the upper camp, Frazier and Whitehouse sewed skins to the iron-framed boat, Gass and Shields shaved bark for wadding, and Joseph Fields made cross braces. They finished the skin covering and put it into the water to toughen before being sewed onto the frame the next day. Twenty-eight elk skins and four buffalo skins were required to cover the boat.

Both mosquitoes and grizzly bears continued to be a constant problem at the upper camp. Lewis made it a policy never to send only one man on any errand, lest he run afoul of a grizzly. The bears didn't attack the men in the camp, but they prowled close around the camp every night. Seaman patrolled the perimeter of the camp with the sentry at night and gave the men timely notice when the bears were around. Lewis also ordered the men to sleep with their guns within easy reach.

CHAPTER 19

Into the Rocky Mountains

July, 1805

As the last load arrived at White Bear Camp, Shields and Bratton worked at a tar kiln they had built to make pitch for sealing the seams of the skins covering the iron-frame boat. Their attempts were proving futile because they lacked pitch-pine, a crucial ingredient. Pitch pine trees had been so plentiful in the East that Lewis hadn't anticipated that pitch pines would not be growing near the Falls of the Missouri River. He was beginning to worry that the iron-frame boat could prove to be a mistake.

Men of the Corps not otherwise engaged busied themselves making moccasins from the hides of the animals they had killed. Unfortunately, the first day of wear wore holes in the new moccasins, which the men patched for the second day, then discarded as worthless. The river above the falls looked smooth and gentle, and the men were eager to be on their way. Meanwhile, the hunters camped on the Medicine River killed sixteen buffalo and cured the meat for the uncertain future.

July 4 was a beautiful day—deep blue skies, warm sun, and a refreshing breeze. Mosquitoes, black gnats, and prickly pears continued to assault the men, but to celebrate Independence Day, the Corps of Discovery were treated to the last of their whiskey supply, except for a few ounces Lewis saved for illnesses. That evening, Cruzatte broke out his fiddle and the men danced until ten o'clock to such tunes as "Miss McLeod's Reel" and "Durang's Hornpipe." Privately, each man suspected they would soon enter upon the most difficult and perilous part of their journey—the great mountain range looming ahead of them—and they relished their fun this evening all the more.

The hunters had killed and prepared enough buffalo to feed the Corps of Discovery for days ahead, but they could have killed hundreds more because the herds were penned in by steep cliffs and could not have escaped. Joseph Whitehouse, the former tailor, was kept busy making new clothes with the skins the hunters brought in. Meanwhile, those working on the collapsible iron boat applied buffalo tallow, charcoal, and beeswax as a substitute for pitch to the seams of the boat covering without success. The seams continued to leak.

"Clark, I hate like hell to give up on the iron-framed boat, but we can't wait any longer," Lewis admitted with frustration. "It has taken nearly a month just to portage our supplies around the falls, and during that time, we have moved only twenty miles upriver. It seems clear now that the iron-frame boat was a mistake."

Clark grimaced and shook his head. "In that case, we need to make more canoes to carry what the collapsible boat could have held. We can't carry our necessities in the few canoes we have."

Clark set out to find trees that were big enough to make suitable canoes, and they finally found a grove of cottonwoods that filled the bill. Selecting two of the trees—one twenty-five feet tall and another thirty-three feet tall—he returned to camp for a ten-man detachment to do the work. They had no tents now and only boat sails for shelter. The men worked in the hot sun, cursing swarms of pesky mosquitoes and black gnats that were attracted to the men's eyes.

A week later, the Corps of Discovery pushed off in eight canoes—two large ones and six small ones—packed with their supplies. At first, the current was gentle and smooth, but soon the river narrowed, the current quickened, and they entered a majestic canyon bounded by cliffs as high as fourteen-hundred feet.

"We'll call this The Gates to the Mountains," Lewis announced to his awestruck men.

Without a shore to walk on to tow the boats, the men rowed hard against the swift-flowing current in water that was too deep for the help of poles. When they finally emerged from the canyon, they were delighted to see rolling plains populated with herds of buffalo. Beaver were also plentiful in the river.

"At least we'll eat well," Gass said with a big smile.

"Yeah, and that's half the battle," Colter agreed.

Coming to wild whitewater rapids, the men towed the canoes until huge rocks blocked their way with a current so powerful that they could neither row nor pole. For hours, the men had to tow with all their strength against the fierce current while navigating between gigantic rocks. The sun baked their shoulders and backs as the cold water numbed their legs, and the ever-present mosquitoes and gnats buzzed their faces and bare skin. Sometimes the insects even got into the men's mouths and throats.

"God damn these bugs!" Cruzette cursed as he batted them away.

"They are bloody hell!" Shannon agreed.

"Have heart, men," Clark said cheerfully as he swatted his neck. "They can't last forever."

Now, in the middle of summer, the days seemed interminably long and the strain of work exhausting. Only the realization that the Corps of Discovery was making history and that this would be the most important mission of their lives gave the men the necessary courage, pride, and endurance to meet and overcome the challenges and discomforts. The life of every member of the expedition, including Sacagawea, Pomp, and York, was dependent on the others. By now, they all knew each other's backgrounds, habits, skills, weaknesses, and dreams. They could identify one another in the dark by voice, and they were determined to triumph or die together.

Still, they looked with dread at the snowy peaks of the Rocky Mountains that pierced the sky ahead of them. The craggy peaks appeared to be forming several ranges, with each succeeding range rising higher than the last. The captains had made a plan for crossing them that they desperately trusted would work. Sacagawea's tribe, the Shoshones, lived on the eastern side of the mountains, and the Mandans had told the captains that the Shoshones had plenty of horses that could carry them and their supplies across the mountains. With Sacagawea as their translator, the captains hoped to trade for enough horses to get their expedition over the mountains. They also hoped the Shoshones would provide them with an experienced guide.

In this region east of the Rockies, the expedition noticed that pine trees had been stripped of bark, and Sacagawea explained that the Shoshones did this to get the sap and then use the soft part of the bark as food. Lewis, walking on shore, encountered the remains of an extraordinary abandoned Indian lodge that had been built with sixteen large cottonwood tree trunks, each about fifty feet long. The larger end of each trunk—as thick as a man's body—rested on the ground in a circle. Then were slanted upward and tied together with willow branches at the top. The area inside the lodge was 216 feet in circumference. Lewis decided that it had been a council house for matters of the greatest importance.

All evidence pointed to this being Shoshone territory, and the captains decided to search for them. Captain Clark with York, Potts, and Reuben Field would form an advance party, locate a Shoshone village, and establish friendly relations, assuring the Indians that the gunfire they may have heard was simply their hunters, and no threat to them.

Captain Lewis and the main party found themselves in a confined valley that featured suffocating heat as well as an abundance of wild onions and currants, which the men eagerly gathered. Suddenly a large column of smoke several miles away became visible—so large that Lewis knew it had been intentionally set.

"That fire was surely set by Indians," Lewis said, "almost certainly by Shoshones, probably as a warning to the rest of their tribe to retreat into the mountains for safety to avoid us," he muttered with disappointment to Ordway.

The main party entered a plain that was ten to twelve miles long, bordered by parallel mountains with snow-covered peaks. Willow trees were thick along the banks of the river. The men marveled at a large herd of big-horned animals that bounded calmly from rock to rock on nearly perpendicular cliffs, apparently oblivious to the fact that one false step would send them plummeting five-hundred feet to their deaths. Lewis recalled that Joseph Fields had found a horn on the Yellowstone River that looked identical to those of these animals.

"There's a whole herd of *Josephus Fielduses*," Lewis teased Joseph Fields, recalling their earlier experience.

"Aw, you're joshing me, Captain," Field replied, cracking his knuckles self-conscientiously.

Nearby buttes rose to over two-hundred feet, the tops of which appeared to be perfectly level. There were also numerous islands in the river. The water was so clear that when an otter sank to the bottom after being shot, Lewis dove in to retrieve it, delighting the men.

Clark and his party returned the next evening. "We found no Shoshones," he said, downcast.

"I think they are afraid of us because they heard the guns of our hunters," Lewis replied, disappointment showing in his face.

"Well, we can't blame them. They don't have guns, and they know we do," Clark agreed. "Somehow, we have to make personal contact with them and prove our good intentions."

Clark set out again with the same three men while Lewis and the flotilla of canoes continued up the river. Clark was determined to find the Shoshones this time and convince them that the Corps of Discovery was on a peaceful mission.

"It would help if we had Janie along to translate for us when we find them," he said to the others. "It's too bad she has the baby to take care of."

Great swarms of mosquitoes and black gnats increased near the river in the summer heat while prickly pears covering the ground pierced the feet of every person in the main party. Although not life-threatening, these constant harassments caused pain and discomfort. To add to their torment, the men began to encounter another new discovery— needle grass, a plant with sharp seeds that penetrated buckskin clothing, caused sharp pain until removed, and had to be tediously plucked out one by one. Seaman seemed to suffer most from this plague. He constantly scratched himself, to no avail. George Shannon took pity on the group's mascot and each evening plucked the needle-like seeds from his paws. Seaman, understandably grateful, wagged his tail and licked Shannon's hand.

Each day was exhausting because of these pests of nature, but even so, the men averaged eighteen miles per day. The broad landscape lacked trees, but currant and berry bushes abounded. Finally, Clark and his party returned to report that they had found many signs of Indians, but no flesh-and-blood Shoshones.

Sacagawea began to recognize the country they were passing through. She passed the news along to Charbonneau, who sent it on up the translation chain to Lewis. Meanwhile, Clark calculated they had come one-hundred-sixty miles from the Falls of the Missouri. As the expedition continued upriver, Clark and his advance party went out again on their continuing search for the Shoshone Indians.

With Lewis and the main party, conditions on the river were increasingly miserable. Plagued by heat, mosquitoes, gnats, needle grass, and prickly pears, they sometimes measured their progress in yards. The labor was so fatiguing that Lewis worked alongside the men to encourage them. His pride in them was so great that he couldn't find words that didn't sound maudlin.

When they arrived at a fork of three rivers in an open valley, they found a note from Clark. He wrote that his group would rejoin them at this fork unless they encountered fresh signs of Shoshones in the area.

Lewis viewed the three forks and decided to follow the one that went west, naming it the Jefferson River. He named the other two the Madison River and the Gallatin River. The three rivers were named in honor of President Jefferson, Secretary of State James Madison, and Secretary of the Treasury Albert Gallatin.

Clark returned to camp sick with a high fever, frequent chills, and constant pain in his muscles. Lewis recommended that he take a dozen of Dr. Rush's laxative pills, but Clark would take only five.

"If I took a dozen of those thunderclaps, I'd dig a new cache for us, and we don't need one," Clark joked.

He also soaked his feet in warm water, but at the end of the day he was still ill and his fever lingered. Despite Clark's illness, the Corps continued up the river, passing a red cliff that caught Sacagawea's attention.

"My people made paint from that cliff!" she told Charbonneau, who passed the information along to the captains.

Lewis was feeling deep anxiety about the expedition's inability to make contact with the Shoshones. He had imagined it would be the highlight of this leg of the journey—especially now, with Sacagawea to translate for them.

"We'll soon be in the mountains and game will become very scarce, maybe even nonexistent," he said to Clark. "Without Shoshone horses and a guide's knowledge of the mountains, I doubt the we really have a chance."

Clark sipped his bark tea. "Well, it's at least possible that the Jefferson River could lead us to tributaries of the Columbia," he speculated hopefully, even though recognizing that it was a very slim possibility.

Sacagawea, sitting nearby, stiffened suddenly as she looked around. She searched out Charbonneau. "This is where my people were camped when the Hidatsas attacked us," she told him excitedly. "We ran three miles up the river and hid in the brush, but the Hidatsas found us, killed four men, four women, and some of our boys. They captured the rest of the women and girls, including me." She shuddered visibly at the memory, and Charbonneau comforted her—the first time any of the men had ever seen tenderness between them.

Captain Clark admired Sacagawea's ability to adapt to whatever life handed her, and he was completely taken with little Pomp. He made over Pomp and played with him so much that the men nicknamed him "nursemaid."

The captains named creeks after Gass, Howard, Frazier, and Reuben Fields. The river eventually became crooked, filled with grassy islands and beaver dams. Cottonwood trees grew in the river bottoms, but no trees grew away from the river. The hills now met the river on both sides, and the mountains showed more snow on their summits. Game was becoming more and more scarce.

Lewis, filled with premonition about venturing into the Rockies without horses and a guide, took three men and set out to search for the Shoshones. He planned to be gone four or five days while Clark continued to recuperate as the main party progressed westward on the river.

CHAPTER 20

Meeting the Shoshones

August, 1805

Captain Clark and the main party noted that the hills were getting higher and more pine trees were growing on the hillsides and riverbanks. Even though they could see snow on the mountaintops, the windless heat in the valley was suffocating. The river was crooked and rapid, and they began to pass many beaver lodges where beavers had dammed up the water at the mouths of tributaries with a series of dams, one above the other. The men were now spending half their time in the water, towing their vessels over shoals and rapids that grew ever stronger.

Increasingly, the hunters returned from the day's hunting with no game to show for their labor. "There's very little life out there," Drouillard reported. "But about three miles ahead, the river forks again."

When they came to the fork, Clark and Hugh McNeal looked over the scene. The right fork was the larger of the two.

"My guess is that Captain Lewis would probably have taken the bigger fork," McNeal suggested, batting away a swarm of gnats from his face.

Clark considered his comment. "I think you're right, but to be safe I'll leave a note telling him which fork we took in case he returns here."

The right fork presented the men with rapids that occasionally dropped three to four feet within the length of a canoe. With great effort, they passed over them, but the current was so swift that they found it difficult to stay on their feet. They camped after covering only eight miles. The next day, George Drouillard arrived from Lewis's party.

"You took the wrong fork," he told Clark.

Clark turned to McNeal. "Since Shannon is out hunting and won't know we're turning back, you wait for him here."

Then Clark and Drouillard reversed course and headed back down the rapids. At the forks, Captain Lewis was waiting for them.

"I've been thirty miles up the other fork, and it is much easier to navigate," he announced.

McNeal returned that evening without Shannon. "I gave him plenty of time before I left," he told Clark, whose expression showed disapproval.

"Blow the horn to let him know where we are," Clark said to Ordway. "Then fire the cannon, wait a few minutes, and fire a volley of rifle shots."

But the signals didn't work. Shannon didn't show up.

Deciding that they had one more canoe than they needed to carry supplies, the captains ordered it hidden in a nearby grove of cottonwood trees where they could retrieve it on their return trip. The men put damp goods out in the sun to dry as Captain Lewis recorded the latitude and longitude of the location. Sunflowers and thistles, as well as a variety of rye grass that grew three feet tall, grew everywhere.

Shannon still had not returned, and Captain Clark sent Reuben Fields out in search of him. When Fields returned alone, they decided to pack up their goods and continue, assuming that Shannon would find them. A summer storm arose, but the party continued, passing smooth prairie on each side of the very crooked river. After seven miles, they camped, and the hunters finally brought in two deer, to everyone's great relief.

At sunrise, the group set out again, having seen nothing of Shannon. Clark had developed a boil on one ankle, which was swollen and inflamed, causing him to limp in pain. Gass, Charbonneau, and several of the other men complained of various ailments. Everyone was exhausted, weakening their ability to stay healthy. As their energy level sank, morale began to suffer as well. Sacagawea lifted the spirits of the group when she recognized a plain as being near her tribe's summer camping ground.

"My people will be either on this river or on the river west of here," she told Lewis through the convoluted translation chain.

Lewis turned to Clark. "In that case, I think we should send out another greeting party, this time to stay out until they contact the Shoshones,"

"I'll be ready to leave in the morning," Clark responded.

"Not with your swollen ankle, my friend. You stay here in charge of the main party while I take your place in the search."

Clark started to protest, but he knew Lewis was right.

Lewis lowered his voice. "This is a do-or-die situation. If we don't get Shoshone horses and a Shoshone guide, our mission could end in these mountains." He glanced toward Sacagawea. "I hope they'll welcome us. They should because they need contact with white men so they can arm themselves to protect their people from the Blackfoot and Hidatsas."

"Of course we aren't bringing guns now," Clark said softly, "only the promise to bring them later. Actually, we need the Shoshones more than they need us right now. In the long run, that situation will reverse, but convincing them may be one of our greatest challenges—if we can find them."

"Then let's pray that we make contact this time," Lewis said.

The main party with Clark came to a valley where the three forks of the river converged. The valley appeared to be ten to twelve miles wide, all open prairie covered with tall grass and prickly pears, except for a few scattered groves of cottonwood and willow trees. The river was only twenty-five yards wide now and so shallow that in some places the men again had to get into the water and drag the canoes.

When they halted for breakfast, George Shannon finally walked into camp. He had been lost for three days after they had reversed course without telling him. He was greeted with shouts of welcome and slaps on the back Shannon was weak and hungry, but he was greatly relieved that he had found the expedition.

"I think you goldarn guys are trying to get rid of me," he teased good-naturedly.

"Yeah, but you just keep coming back no matter how hard we try," John Colter joked.

Lewis's party, searching for the Shoshones, spread out across a valley in search of an Indian trail. Drouillard went to the right, Shields to the left, and McNeal stayed with Lewis in the center.

"If you find a trail, put your hat on the muzzle of your rifle and lift it up so we can see your signal," Lewis told Drouillard and Shields.

They marched in a widely-spaced line for five miles with no luck. Then Lewis squinted and took out his telescope. He saw an Indian on horseback, armed with a bow and a quiver of arrows, about two miles distant and coming toward them. From his unfamiliar dress, Lewis knew the man was from an unknown Indian tribe.

Lewis continued walking at his normal pace as the Indian approached. When he was a half-mile away, the Indian suddenly stopped. As an invitation to talk, Lewis pulled a blanket from his pack, shook it out, and spread it on the ground. But the Indian glanced suspiciously at Drouillard and Shields. He saw four armed men coming toward him rather than a friendly invitation to talk. The Indian was becoming alarmed, and his horse pranced as if ready to race away. Lewis laid his rifle on the blanket and walked on toward the Indian with hands and arms outstretched in a gesture of friendship.

The Indian watched as Lewis approached. Lewis called out, "*Tab ba bone*," which Sacagawea had told him was Shoshone for "*white man*." The Indian kept glancing at Drouillard and Shields as they also advanced toward him. Lewis was furious with the two men, but he knew if he shouted at them to stop, the Indian might think it was a command to attack. Lewis signaled the other two men to stop, but

Shields failed to see his command and continued walking. Now only one-hundred-fifty yards from the Indian, Lewis repeated "*Tab ba bone*" and pulled up his sleeves to show his white skin. After a few more moments, the Indian turned his horse and galloped away. Lewis was uncharacteristically angry that Shields had not stopped walking and had frightened away their first opportunity to connect with Indians who could be the Shoshones.

"When you saw that I was trying to make contact with the Indian, you should have stopped," he admonished Shields.

"Sorry, Captain," a chastened Shields responded. "I guess I wasn't paying enough attention."

The four men continued walking, following the trail of the Indian's horse.

"The Shoshones could be camped in the hills over there," Lewis said after a long silence, "and we don't want them to think that white men are advancing on them. Let's stop and build a fire of willow brush and eat before going on."

However, as they started out again, a heavy downpour raised the grass, wiping out the horse tracks. Continuing in that direction, the men noticed several places where Indians had been digging for roots, an indication that they were on the right track. After a few more miles, the men made camp for the night.

The next morning, they found a wide Indian trail, where they halted at a stream to breakfast on the venison in their backpacks. Several miles farther, they saw what they took to be the headwaters of the mighty Missouri River.

"This must be it, Captain," McNeal said, thoughtfully assessing the possible source of one of America's greatest rivers.

"I think so," Lewis agreed, marveling that this calm spot might have spawned the beauty and treachery of the immense river they had traveled.

Lewis drank of the water, and Shields stood triumphantly astride the rivulet, as if posing for a painting. They proceeded to the top of the dividing ridge, from where they could see the immense ranges of towering mountains to the west, their peaks covered with snow—shattering any remaining hope of an easy passage to a branch of the Columbia River. They took their first steps on the western side of the dividing ridge, went through Lemhi Pass, and continued another ten miles before making camp. The next morning they followed a trail that led to a long valley, where they suddenly spotted two Indian women and a man. Coming within a half-mile of them, Lewis stopped.

"You men wait here and do nothing to make them suspicious of us," he said. Lewis unslung his pack, put it and his rifle on the ground, and advanced alone at a slow but steady pace.

Lewis called out, "*Tub ba bone*" repeatedly, but the Indians fled. Lewis hurried to the hill where they had stood, but they were not in sight. Their dogs were less shy and came near Lewis. *Maybe I can tie some beads and other trinkets in a kerchief around the dog's neck to let them know I come in peace*, Lewis thought. But the dogs would not let him touch them despite their curiosity about him.

Topping a rise less than a mile later, Lewis and his men surprised three Indian females sitting on the ground no more than thirty yards away—an elderly woman, a teenager, and a half-grown child. Lewis put down his rifle and advanced slowly. The teenager ran away, but the old woman and the child remained. Seeing no chance of escaping with a stranger so close, they sat with their heads bowed as if expecting to die.

Lewis walked up slowly and took the hand of the old woman, raising her to her feet, saying, "*Tab ba bone.*" He pulled up his sleeve to show the color of his skin. His clothes were made entirely of buckskin, and his face and hands were so tanned that he could have easily been an Indian. He gave the woman some beads, a few moccasin awls, a mirror, and some paint. The color of his skin, the gifts, and his friendly manner seemed to calm her.

Drouillard had followed Lewis, and now Lewis turned to him saying, "Ask her to call back the teenager." He didn't want the girl to raise an alarm in the village.

When she returned, Lewis gave her some trinkets and painted the cheeks of all three with vermillion. All three females smiled at Lewis with delight.

"Take us to your village to meet your chiefs," Drouillard signed to the old squaw at Lewis's request.

She agreed, and the group set off with the Indians leading. Suddenly, sixty mounted Shoshone warriors startled Lewis and his party when they thundered down upon them at full speed, halting just in front of the small party. They rode fine horses and were armed with bows and arrows. Lewis and his men put down their rifles to signal no hostile intent.

"Keep still, men," Lewis ordered. "Don't do anything to alarm them."

The old squaw told the Indian who was apparently the chief that these were white men and showed him the presents they had given her. The Shoshone warriors could have overpowered Lewis's small party easily and taken their rifles, knives, and more trade goods than they had ever seen, but the chief dismounted and approached Lewis, saying *"Ah-hi-e,"* which Lewis later learned meant, *"I am much pleased."* The chief put his left arm over Lewis's right shoulder and touched his cheek to Lewis's repeating, *"Ah-hi-e."* The warriors dismounted and approached, and all of them made the same greeting to the white men. Lewis smiled. This was going far better than he could have hoped!

Lewis learned that his party was very lucky because the war party had ridden out in response to the alarm raised by the Indian who had fled from Lewis earlier. The Shoshones had expected their enemies, the Blackfoot, and might have attacked immediately except for the old squaw. Lewis brought out his pipe and sat down, signaling to the Indians that they should do the same. They did so, removing their moccasins, a custom among the Shoshones to indicate sincerity or friendship. Lewis lit the pipe and passed it around. Then he distributed small presents. The Shoshones were particularly pleased with the blue beads and vermillion paint.

Lewis was greatly pleased that he and his men had at last met these calm and welcoming members of the Shoshone tribe. The chief's name was Cameahwait, and Lewis gave him an American flag, telling him it represented a bond between the Indians and the white men.

Cameahwait sent a few young men ahead to tell their village to prepare for their arrival. Then he spoke to the warriors, and soon the entire party set out for the Shoshone village.

When they arrived, Lewis and his men were ushered into an old buffalo-hide tepee and ceremoniously seated on green boughs covered with antelope skins. The chief lit a pipe from a fire in the center of the tepee and then gave a speech in his own language that lasted several minutes. After pointing the stem of the pipe to the four points of the compass, he presented it to Lewis, but when Lewis reached for it he pulled it back and repeated the ceremony, this time pointing the pipe stem to the heavens. He smoked three puffs and held the pipe while Lewis took three puffs, then extended it to each white man who also took three puffs. Then he gave the pipe to his warriors.

Lewis gave his standard speech through Drouillard's sign language, although he couldn't tell if the Shoshones understood—he needed Sacagawea to interpret, but she was still with the Clark group. Lewis distributed his remaining presents to the Indians, who were delighted to receive them.

Lewis and his men had not eaten for twenty-four hours, and when he mentioned this to Cameahwait, the chief immediately ordered that cakes of serviceberries and chokeberries be brought to them.

All the women and children of the camp gathered to inspect the white men, the first they had ever seen. The Shoshones were small people, with thick ankles, bowed legs, and flat feet. Men and women alike wore their hair loose over their shoulders, although a few of the men wore it in two braids that fell in front. All adults wore robes that hung to the middle of their legs. The robes either hung loose or were held together with their hands. Made of the skin of buffalo, antelope, or bighorn sheep, the robe served as clothing during the day and as a blanket at night. The men also wore collarless long shirts made of animal skins that retained the animal's tail and fell to mid-thigh. The edges of the shirts were fringed and ornamented with porcupine quills. Beads were also sewn on some shirts by using sinews from the animal's body as thread. The men also wore leggings made from antelope skin from which the hair had been scraped. Each legging required almost an entire animal skin, complete with tail and with fringed and ornamented edges.

From Cameahwait, Lewis confirmed finally that there was definitely no all-water route across the continent. Cameahwait also told Lewis, through Drouillard's sign language, that it was time for the Shoshones to cross the dividing ridge to meet other tribes of Shoshones and Flatheads and hunt buffalo on the Missouri River. Horses were the most needed commodity for the Corps of Discovery in the months ahead in the mountains, but if the Shoshones needed all their horses for the buffalo hunt, it spelled disaster to the Corps.

That night, the Shoshones entertained Lewis and his men with a dance, during which their women sang, that lasted almost until dawn.

CHAPTER 21

With the Shoshones

Mid-August, 1805

In the Shoshone village, Captain Lewis spent the morning writing in his journal and the afternoon getting additional information about the country to the west. He talked with Cameahwait through Drouillard.

"Have you crossed the high mountains?" he had Drouillard signal to the Shoshone chief.

"No," he responded, "but we have an old man with us who has, a Nez Perce. He and other Nez Perce have told me that a river west of the mountains runs a long way toward the setting sun and ends in a great lake of bad-tasting water." Lewis had never heard of the Nez Perce, who proved to be the major tribe living west of the mountains. "The Nez Perce come east across the mountains to hunt buffalo on the Missouri each year," the chief added.

"Ask him what trail they take across the mountains," Lewis said.

Drouillard shared the disappointing answer: "A very bad trail that they call the Lolo Trail. There is no game, and they must live for many days on berries only. They say the trail is broken, rocky, and covered with many fallen trees."

For a few silent moments Lewis pondered the chief's description. *If the Indians can bring their women and children over the mountains,* he told himself, *surely our seasoned and tough soldiers can cross them. It will be difficult and dangerous, but the men have already proven they can do more than they ever thought they were capable of doing—ascending the Missouri River against its mighty current with the keelboat, surviving the brutally cold winter at Fort Mandan, and performing the incredible labor at the Great Falls portage. Every time they have left such an experience behind them, they have believed it surely had to be the worst, only to have it get even worse the next time. We can do this!*

"There are no buffalo west of the mountains," Cameahwait continued. "People there live on salmon and roots." He also had a complaint. "The Spanish west of the mountains refuse to sell us guns, but the English to the east of the mountains sell guns to the Blackfoot, Hidatsa, and other tribes that are enemies of the Shoshone. With guns, the tribes east of the mountains constantly bully and attack us, and we are forced to flee to the mountains."

Lewis saw the opportunity to induce Cameahwait to help his expedition take their supplies over the Continental Divide and provide horses to get them over the Rocky Mountain range.

"When we return to our country from our journey to the great lake that tastes bad, we will send men with many guns for the Shoshone," he assured Cameahwait through Drouillard. "Bring your young men and come with me tomorrow to meet the rest of my men and help us bring our supplies over the mountain pass. Then we will remain among you and trade with you for horses."

The next morning, Lewis faced a problem in the Shoshone village. The Shoshone warriors refused to move when Cameahwait tried to lead them out to meet Clark and the main expedition. A mischievous Shoshone had spread a rumor that the white men were in league with the Blackfoot and had come to lead them into an ambush.

Cameahwait tried to reason with them. "If we don't help them, the white men will bring no guns." When that didn't work, he challenged their manhood. "I hope there are still some of you who are not afraid to die!" he announced loudly. Then he mounted his horse. "I will go with the white men and convince myself of the truth of what they say, and I hope that at least some of you will have the courage to join me."

Six Shoshone warriors mounted their horses, and the small party set out with Lewis and his men. Soon, six more warriors and three women joined them, making a party of sixteen Indians and four white men. Shoshones continued to ride up and join them until it appeared to Lewis that all the men of the village were with them.

Lewis sent Drouillard and Shields out to hunt for game because neither the Indians nor the white men had anything to eat. He asked Cameahwait to keep his young men in camp so they wouldn't spook the game. This renewed the suspicion of the Shoshone warriors, who feared that the white men were trying to make contact with the Blackfoot. Two parties of Shoshone braves set out on each side of the valley to spy on Drouillard and Shields.

When Drouillard at last killed a deer, the excited Indians took off at a run to share in the prize. They were starved, and yet they took only the parts of the deer that Drouillard threw away. They ate ravenously of the still-warm kidneys, spleen, and liver, blood dripping from their chins. One of the last warriors to arrive picked up nine feet of the small intestine, chewing on one end while squeezing the contents out the other end. Lewis viewed the scene with a combination of horror, pity, and compassion for these starving people. He saved a hindquarter for himself and his men and gave the rest of the meat to Cameahwait to divide among his people. The Indians devoured it without bothering to cook it. As they moved on, Drouillard killed another deer, and the same scene was repeated. Then Drouillard killed a third deer, and the Indians were in good humor. When Shields killed an antelope, the problem of food was solved temporarily. All of this made clear to the white men the severe limitations faced by Indian hunters using only bows and arrows.

As they approached the forks where Lewis had told the Shoshones they would meet Captain Clark, Cameahwait halted. He spoke to his people, and with much ceremony he had the warriors remove the tippets they wore around their necks and place them on the white men. Tippets were a kind of scarf or short robe made from skins of ermine. Lewis realized that the chief's suspicions of treachery were still

strong because wearing the tippets would make the white men look like
Shoshones in case the Blackfoot were waiting at the fork rather than
Clark. Lewis took off his hat and put it on Cameahwait, instructing
his men to follow his example. Now the white men looked like Indians,
and the Indians looked like white men. The fears of the Shoshone were
somewhat relieved.

As they neared the fork, Lewis saw with a sinking feeling that
Clark had not yet arrived, greatly increasing the distrust of the
Shoshone. Desperate to demonstrate his good will, Lewis gave his rifle
to Cameahwait.

"If Blackfoot attack, you can use it to defend yourself," he said. "And
if you think I have deceived you, you can kill me with my own gun."

Lewis ordered his men to give up their rifles to Shoshone warriors
as well, which gave the Indians considerably more confidence in the
white men. Recalling that he had left a note for Clark at the forks, Lewis
decided to use a little deception.

"I will send one of my men down the river to see if our other chief
has sent a man ahead to leave us a message," he told Cameahwait. "You
send one of your men with him to verify anything they find."

He sent Drouillard and an Indian to get his own note. They
returned with the note and the warrior's confirmation that they had
picked it up at the forks.

Looking at the note, he announced, "Our other chief has sent us
a message that they are just below and coming on and that we should
wait for them at the forks."

He knew he wasn't out of danger yet. He really had no idea where
Clark was. Clark could have found navigation impossible and returned
to camp many miles below where his team would wait for Lewis.

Lewis had Drouillard signal to Cameahwait. "In the morning, I
will send a man ahead to meet the rest of our expedition. You send
one of your men with him to see the truth of my words." This was
an enormous gamble because the Indians had the rifles, and if Clark
wasn't coming up the Jefferson River, they could easily kill the white
men—and probably would.

"A Shoshone woman is with our other party," Lewis told Cameahwait, hoping to pique his interest with the news. "We also have a black man with short, curly hair."

The disbelieving Indians were eager to see this oddity. The idea of a black man aroused their curiosity, and they chattered about it among themselves. Lewis slept very little that night. He knew that if the Shoshone left him, they would hide in the mountains where it would be impossible to find them, and they would spread the alarm to all other Shoshone villages in the area. Without horses, the Corps of Discovery would have to cross the Rocky Mountains on foot, carrying their provisions and equipment on their backs, vastly increasing the labor of their journey. Lewis feared that such a demanding prospect could so discourage the men as to defeat the expedition. Lewis equated the Corps of Discovery with his own life, and he saw its fate now subject to the caprice of a few primitive natives who were capable of being as fickle as the wind.

With the Clark party, the river was very cold, causing the men's feet and legs to ache when they had to wade in it—and they were in it almost constantly, hauling their canoes over rapids and shoals. The river bottom and shores were rocky, the current continued swift all day, and the wind was hard from the southwest. They covered fourteen miles and camped in a little copse of trees in the upper part of the valley.

As they set up camp, Charbonneau struck Sacagawea, drawing a severe reprimand from Captain Clark.

"I will not tolerate that kind of behavior," he sternly admonished Charbonneau. "There will be no violence between members of the Corps of Discovery. She may be your slave in the Hidatsa village, but here she is as much a member of the Corps of Discovery as you are. Do not hit her again as long as you are under my command."

Lewis had just observed his thirty-first birthday, and he was convinced that even though he had lived half of his expected life span, he had accomplished nothing that would advance the condition of mankind. If he completed this expedition successfully, he would have achieved something vastly worthwhile, but if he failed… He pushed such gloomy thoughts from his mind and tried once again to find sleep. Several of the young warriors were bedded below in the willow brush, hiding from an enemy they feared would attack during the night. Cameahwait and several of his Shoshones slept nearby, and Lewis could hear their measured breathing in the stillness of the night. To the west, the mountains loomed like great sleeping giant shadows, their secrets shrouded by the dark night. *Lord, give me wisdom and strength,* he prayed. Overhead, the sky looked like a huge blanket of black velvet in which millions of shining diamonds hung over the Earth.

Captain Clark and his main party were finding conditions worse. The temperature at this altitude was forty-seven degrees, the river current was swift, the cold river was shallow, and the men had to tow the canoes most of the time. They covered fourteen miles during the day and then camped in a narrow bottom. There was no timber, so they had to collect willow sticks to build a fire to cook their venison. For several nights they had been sleeping under two blankets or robes, and they awakened now to a light frost. They ate breakfast at dawn and prepared to set out again.

Suddenly, they saw two Indians on the opposite side of the river. "It's Drouillard!" one of the men shouted. Drouillard, wearing the tippet of a Shoshone, and his Indian companion came up on horseback.

"Captain Lewis and the others are waiting at the forks with the Shoshone," Drouillard said.

"Thank God, he's found the Shoshones!" Clark exclaimed. "Let's go, everyone!"

At the forks, Clark was shocked to see Lewis with a whole company of Indians, some of whom were armed with U.S. Army rifles. However, the Shoshones seemed friendly.

"I am happier to see you than you know," Lewis said softly, smiling and slapping his friend's back. "Our lives were literally in your hands!"

They heard two women shout excitedly and saw that one of the Shoshone women had recognized Sacagawea. The two women cried and hugged, talking at the same time. Sacagawea showed off little

Pomp, and the other Shoshone women gathered around to greet her and admire her baby boy.

Lewis had a canopy raised and called a conference. Sacagawea translated, but it was a translation chain that ran from Sacagawea speaking Shoshone to the Indians and translating their responses into Hidatsa to Charbonneau, who translated the Hidatsa to French for Drouillard, who translated the French into English for the captains.

Then, to the amazement of the Corps, Sacagawea recognized Cameahwait as her brother! She jumped up, ran to him, and began crying profusely. Perplexity changed to elation when Lewis learned what was happening. What a stroke of luck for the expedition! Eventually, Sacagawea recovered her composure and the council began.

Lewis tailored his standard speech to make it appear that the primary objective of the expedition was to help the Shoshones by finding a more direct route to bring arms to them. He made it clear that to do so, the expedition had to have Shoshone horses and a guide to lead them over the mountains.

"We will help you," Cameahwait said, "but I am sad that it will be more time before you bring us guns. We don't have enough horses to carry all the supplies over the pass now, but we will take what we can back to the village in the morning and encourage all our people to come and help."

Lewis then distributed presents. Everything seemed to astonish the Shoshones, especially the air gun and York. It was clear that horses were the only Shoshone economic asset, although they were dressed well in antelope and mountain goat skins. A few colorful beads hung from their ears, and muscle shells adorned their hair.

"The Spanish must have brought the horses originally, don't you think?" Lewis speculated.

"Probably," Clark agreed, "but they seem to have no knives, metal tomahawks, or other metal weapons—only bows and arrows—so we have to assume that they've had no contact with white men in a very long time."

The soldiers spread their provisions out to dry as the expedition waited for Cameahwait to return from the Shoshone village. Lewis recorded the Shoshones' dress and customs in his journal. He found them to be frank, communicative, fair, generous, and honest.

This was the time of year that the entire Shoshone nation gathered at the forks in the river for its annual buffalo hunt on the plains. Cameahwait and his village joined with different Shoshone bands that were arriving daily from throughout the area.

The Corps was out of fresh meat, so the soldiers joined with the Shoshones to make a fish drag of willows tied together and stretched across the river. They caught more than five hundred pan fish. The Shoshones also killed three deer during the day, chasing them on horseback until the deer were too fatigued to continue, then killing them with bows and arrows. In the afternoon, the Shoshones helped the expedition prepare to cross the mountain pass by sinking the canoes in the river and anchoring them with large rocks to preserve them for their return trip the following spring.

"The Shoshones could bring them up and steal them, Captain," Shields warned.

"Yes, they could, but we'll have to take that chance," Lewis said.

During the evening, Sacagawea overheard her brother instruct some of his young braves to tell many others to meet him the next day so they could go to the prairie to hunt buffalo, which she reported to the captains through the translation chain.

"If that happens, we'll be stuck without horses and have no guide to lead us over the mountains," Lewis said to Clark, his heart and hopes sinking.

"We have to convince them to keep their promise to help us, my friend," Clark added. "We're very fortunate that Janie's loyalty is to us rather than her brother."

"We are indeed!" Lewis said. "I guess the hardships and dangers of our journey have bonded her pretty solidly to us."

Deciding to confront Cameahwait directly, Lewis invited him for a smoke. He knew that bravery and honesty were primary virtues among the Indians, and if an Indian gave his word he was expected to keep it. He took Drouillard as interpreter instead of Sacagawea out of respect for her and her relationship with her brother

"You promised to help us get our supplies over the pass," Lewis reminded the chief through Drouillard's sign language.

Cameahwait nodded his head.

"Now you are planning to abandon us and go to the Missouri River to hunt buffalo."

Cameahwait's eyes darted. Then he looked at the ground and nodded again.

"Why are you breaking your promise?"

Cameahwait was silent for a moment. "What we were about to do is wrong," he admitted finally. "I did it because my people are hungry and I must provide for them. But now I will do as I promised you."

The next day they loaded all the pack horses for the trip over the mountain pass and set out at noon. Private Weiser was very ill, and Captain Lewis gave him peppermint and laudanum, which helped. Weiser rode Captain Lewis' horse while Lewis walked. The mountains on both sides of the trail were very high and occasionally covered with pine trees. The expanded party covered fifteen miles before camping. Hunters came in with a deer, which the captains gave to the Shoshones because they were starving. During that day's travel, Clark had seen squaws digging roots to feed their children, and he found it distressing to witness such hunger.

When they resumed the journey the next day, one of the Indian women paused to give birth to a baby, then hurried to catch up. They finally came to the Shoshone village. Cameahwait asked Lewis to have the soldiers fire their guns. Lewis had the men form a single rank and fire two rounds. The Shoshone were much pleased with this exhibition. The village consisted of thirty-two lodges made of willow bushes and earth that surrounded a large ceremonial lodge for guests. Lewis paid the Indians who had helped them carry supplies across the mountain pass with beads, needles, and other such items.

Then he began trading with the Shoshones for horses. He had decided that the expedition needed twenty-five horses to carry their supplies over the mountains, but he first wanted horses that would enable the hunters to bring in the meat they killed. He got three horses for a uniform coat, a pair of leggings, a few handkerchiefs, three knives, and some trinkets. Private John Boley bought a horse for an old checked shirt, a pair of leggings, and a knife. Some of the other men also bought their own horses.

"I need twenty more horses," Lewis told Cameahwait through Sacagawea.

The price of Shoshone horses had increased considerably because the Indians knew they had a precious commodity and a desperate buyer. Lewis paid a higher price for nine more horses, but the Shoshones would not sell more without a still higher price. Altogether, the expedition now had twenty-five horses, which Lewis thought would be sufficient.

"Will we be able to hire your old Nez Perce who has been over the mountains to guide us over them?" he asked Cameahwait.

"I have spoken to him and he is willing to guide you," Cameahwait responded through Sacagawea.

"Excellent!" a delighted Lewis responded. "This calls for a celebration. Cruzatte, break out your fiddle!"

The soldiers danced to the lively tunes, much to the amusement of the Shoshones, but the state of Lewis's mind did not fit the mirth of his men. He worried that the caprice of the Shoshones might lead them to change their minds about the horses, possibly destroying any hope of completing the Corp's journey.

He confided to Clark under the noise and gaiety of the moment, "Our experience has been that the Indians are unpredictable and not entirely trustworthy. I fear our horses may not materialize."

"Well, let's assume the best until the worst happens."

The next day the two captains talked with the old Nez Perce guide who had crossed the Rocky Mountains and now would lead the Corps of Discovery. Because they couldn't pronounce his name, they called him Old Toby, even though he was probably not over fifty. They found him to be a friendly and intelligent man.

"The mountains are very high," he told them through the translation chain. "There is no game there. When we crossed the mountains, we lived for days on berries. Hunger and weakness were severe problems."

The Shoshones refused to sell more horses for anything less than guns, which the Corps could not afford to part with. They now had twenty-seven horses, and they planned to depart the next morning with Old Toby as their guide.

"Sacagawea doesn't show any special reluctance to leave her people again," John Potts commented to Shields as they prepared to leave. "I think if she has little Pomp, enough to eat, and a few trinkets to wear, she's contented anywhere—even with Charbonneau."

Shields, chewing on his ever-present twig, paused to remove it from his mouth before answering his friend. "Could be, but remember that she was only nine years old when she was captured, and she probably just accepts her fate as inevitable. She seems awfully nice. I think life has just dealt her a bad hand."

CHAPTER 22

Through the Rockies

September, 1805

The Corps of Discovery followed Old Toby into the high, rugged foothills of the Rocky Mountains where there were no trails to follow. The men struggled through dense, thorny underbrush that snagged their buckskin clothing and scratched their faces and hands as they climbed hillsides as steep as the roof of a house. The passage, narrow and filled with stones, bruised the hooves of their horses because they had no horseshoes.

York's feet became so sore that Captain Clark unloaded the packsaddle of one horse and distributed the load to the other horses so York could ride.

At last they reached the peak of the first mountain of the foothills and began to descend into a wide valley. Once there, their passage was relatively easy for the next three days—but the men kept looking with trepidation at the massive mountains still ahead of them, their peaks hidden high in the clouds. This forbidding range was a barrier that must be endured—crossing it was essential to the success of their mission. Each man considered the challenges ahead, imagining what might be demanded of him.

Ordway, usually optimistic, was worried. "I can't imagine such a large group of men successfully crossing those mountains with tons of supplies."

"I can't either," Colter replied, sharing his friend's concern. "But the captains haven't done anything stupid or led us wrong yet. I wouldn't bet against them."

At the evening campfire, Old Toby approached the captains, who had finished eating their dried venison stew. "Tomorrow we will begin the hardest part of our journey over the high mountains," he told them through Sacagawea and the translation chain. He traced an enormous mountain in the air with his finger.

Not long after setting out the next morning, one of horses fell backwards because of the steep angle of the climb. Men hurried to recover the supplies that had broken loose from the pack saddle and quickly rearranged the animal's load as it struggled to find firm footing again. Fallen tree trunks created serious obstacles, and the men often had to stop to lift them out of the way. At other times the brush was so thick they had to cut paths for the horses—a time-consuming job. At times the ascent was so steep and rocky that the weaker pack horses and colts sometimes lost their footing, stumbling and even falling. Simply moving ahead was fatiguing, and the expedition covered only five miles that entire day.

Hunters soon found that game animals were practically nonexistent in the mountains. They killed only a few pheasants—meager fare that sent the expedition to bed hungry. To make matters worse, constant rain made the night uncomfortable. The next day they battled the rugged terrain again, marveling that some fir trees were one-hundred-fifty feet tall. They ate the last of their salt pork and once again went to bed hungry.

"Why don't we kill one of the colts?" Collins suggested to Ordway. "We're working too damned hard to go hungry. We're going to be too weak to do anything if this continues."

"The captains want to wait one more day to see if our hunters find game before we do that," Ordway said. "We have to conserve our supply of food as much as possible if we want to make it over these mountains."

When they camped that night, they were wet, hungry, and tired to the bone. The expedition had traveled only eleven miles that day. Their horses, too, were weak and listless.

"It's time to kill one of the colts," Lewis decided. "We can't go on like this."

The colt provided a skimpy meal for more than thirty adults and Seaman, but it was enough to keep them going. The next day's travel took them down to a river where they found a band of four hundred Flathead Indians with about five hundred horses who were coming east across the mountains. Eighty of the men were warriors, who greeted the Corps with friendship, putting white robes over the captains' shoulders and smoking the pipe of peace with them. The Flatheads had stout physiques, and their complexions were lighter than other Indian tribes the Corps had met. They were well-dressed in the skins of mountain goats and buffalo robes.

"Drouillard, take Old Toby and see if you can communicate with them," Lewis instructed.

The Flathead Indians were allies of the Shoshones, and the presence of Old Toby and Sacagawea was fortunate. Translations still took a convoluted path, but the captains were able to communicate with them. Their language had a sort of gurgling sound because they spoke much through their throats. Captain Lewis recorded a vocabulary of their language to the extent he could. Because of the very different language, some of the soldiers wondered if this tribe could be related to the rumored Indians of Welsh descent they had heard so much about back home.

This tribe had never seen white men before, and York was the center of attention as the first black man they had ever seen. This large group was on its way to join Cameahwait's band at Three Forks, where they would go together for a great buffalo hunt on the plains.

Lewis gave the Indians presents and bought eleven horses from them for only a few articles of merchandise. The Flatheads even traded fresh horses for the Corps' worn-out Shoshone horses. The Corps of Discovery now had thirty-nine horses and three colts for packing, riding, or food if necessary.

The Flathead chief told Lewis that the Corps of Discovery must cross four more mountains before reaching a place where other men with hair on their faces live. These Indians helped the expedition in every way they could, selling them pack saddles and ropes for cheap prices. Finally, the Flatheads departed for the Missouri River and their annual buffalo hunt.

When the Corps continued, now with a total of forty horses, falling snow covered the men's moccasins. Some of them wrapped their feet with rags, and their fingers on their rifles ached from the cold. There was nothing to eat except berries and a little corn, which they parched. The area they were passing through was filled with tall, green pines and balsam trees that contrasted sharply with the whiteness of the snow-clad land. They noticed that the bark of some pine trees had been peeled away, and Toby explained that Indians eat the inside of the bark in the spring. The men rejoiced when the hunters returned with a dozen pheasants and, almost miraculously it seemed to the men, a deer and an elk.

"God will provide!" one of the deeply religious men proclaimed, and he bowed in prayer to give thanks.

That day as they climbed to higher elevations, the falling snow turned into a pelting, cold rain that left them drenched and shivering. Prickly pear cactus was again penetrating their moccasins and piercing their feet.

The captains decided to send out four hunters on horses to search constantly for game. John Colter, one of the hunters, met three Indians on horseback, who were afraid of him until he put his gun on the ground to show that he meant them no harm. Then they approached him in a friendly manner, and Colter led them back to camp to meet the captains. They were Flatheads who said that they had heard the white men's guns all day, but were afraid to approach them because they had no guns. They were tracking two Shoshone Indians who had stolen horses from them. One of them told Lewis, through sign language

Drouillard had trouble understanding, that the Corps could cross the mountains in six days. This was good news to Lewis, who fretted constantly because their lives depended on getting over the mountains before the deep, impassable snows of winter began.

"Look at that tree!" Shannon exclaimed to the men nearby. All eyes turned to see a tree on which a number of images had been painted. From a large branch hung a white bearskin. "What do you think this is?" he asked.

"Looks almost like a place of worship," someone suggested.

"Yeah, I agree," Whitehouse joined in. "I'd say they must believe in a power greater than themselves, just like we do."

A little farther on, the men were astonished to see a spring of steaming water pouring from rocks. A handsome small green meadow bordered the spring as steam rose in the air, and the men dismounted to examine such strange phenomena.

"The f-f-folks back home will n-never b-b-believe this!" Reuben Fields was certain.

"Hell, I'm not even sure I believe it, and I'm right here to see it," his brother said, cracking his knuckles. "What could possibly heat that water?"

No one had answers or even a speculation, but the delighted men found that hot water springs were all over this area, and they eagerly left their clothes in piles and relaxed in a soothing hot bath, their first in weeks. When the expedition reassembled, the men felt refreshed and relaxed. The Corps continued its journey and had to keep going until they found water at ten o'clock that night. They had covered eighteen exhausting, but interesting miles that day.

The next day brought rain, hail, and snow. Even worse, Old Toby got lost. The steep, rocky ground was covered with fallen trees, and the horses kept slipping on the wet ground. By the time they made camp, men and horses could scarcely move, and all were ravenously hungry.

"Kill another colt," Lewis ordered Drouillard. "We have to have nourishing food. We can't keep expending the energy these mountains demand unless we have food in our stomachs."

They also had the dried soup that Lewis had wisely decided to bring along. It wasn't favored by the men, but they were very glad to get it now.

The next day, Old Toby recognized his mistake and corrected it, but the footing in the trail was still extremely difficult. The steep ascent was made worse by the immense number of fallen trees. One of the horses slipped and rolled forty yards down the mountain before it lodged against a tree. It was shaken, but unhurt. The expedition had made only twelve miles by the end of the day in spite of tremendous exertion. Worse, they could see even higher mountains ahead of them. York melted snow to cook the remainder of yesterday's colt and some of the portable soup.

"I never thought I'd be glad to eat the captain's portable soup," Shannon said grimly.

The next morning they awoke covered with snow. During the night, the hungry horses had strayed in search of grass, and it took all morning to find them and bring them in. The trail was very difficult and they made only ten miles that day over slippery terrain that was littered with fallen trees. Their hunters managed to kill only a few grouse, which York cooked, but it was a scant supper and everyone went to sleep still hungry.

Snow continued to fall, depositing several inches. It collected on the branches of trees, and as the men brushed against the branches, the snow fell in their faces and down their collars. Lewis felt that he had never been so cold and wet in his life. Again, their camp was wet, hungry, and miserable. Although the members of the expedition were extremely uncomfortable, they performed their duties without complaint. Lewis was proud of the spirit the men continued to show under such adverse conditions.

"We've got to kill the last colt," Lewis ordered Drouillard.

Then in an aside to Clark, he added in a low voice, "But only God knows where our next meal is coming from."

As days passed, only a few canisters of dried soup and a bit of bear oil remained in the depleted stock of foodstuffs. Lewis, aware that both men and horses were approaching the limits of their endurance, was beginning to despair. Naturally inclined to melancholy anyway, his spirits were plummeting. *God, please let my people survive,* he prayed. *The fault is mine if anyone's, not theirs.*

Clark conferred with Lewis. "There is no real hope of finding game in these mountains, and we can't sacrifice any of the packhorses without abandoning essential supplies."

"Yes, and retreat would only compound our problems," Lewis said, sitting on a rock in utter despair. The two were sitting apart from the men, who were scattered across the stony slope, silent or dozing. "Backtracking is impossible because a journey back to the Mandan villages is beyond our strength and endurance."

"But we have to do something!" Clark insisted. "Suppose I take six hunters ahead and try to reach level country where there's sure to be game and send meat back to the main party?"

"That may be our only hope," Lewis conceded.

Clark selected six men and struck out at first light, climbing over rugged terrain filled with fallen tree trunks and, at times, nearly impenetrable thickets of brambly undergrowth. Eight hours later they halted to melt snow for their scant supply of portable soup and to let their horses graze. When darkness fell, they found places to sleep on the mountainside.

Meanwhile, Lewis and the main party struggled ahead across eighteen difficult miles and broke out the last of the portable soup when they camped. Every member of the group realized how critical their situation had become. For the most part, the men were quiet, conserving the energy required to talk and laugh. Only little Pomp, now nearly eight months old and almost ready to walk, was his happy, active self, and Sacagawea maintained her pleasant, easy ways as she cared for her young son. Pomp delighted in playing with Seaman.

The next day the entire company was excited when Robert Frazier began cheering and pumping his fist westward into the air. Within seconds, more cheers arose from the ranks as eager eyes searched miles ahead and below, where a large tract of prairie land had come into view.

"Prairie!" exclaimed Ordway. "That means game! Food is ahead!"

"We'll be there tomorrow," Old Toby signed happily.

The way ahead was a stony passage that ran along the edge of a steep precipice, and the men tried to avoid looking over the edge to the abyss below. All day long, they followed the ridge without mishap, but at dusk their luck changed. One of the pack horses lost its footing and began to slide. The party watched in horror as the horse slid three hundred feet down the precipice, landing in a creek at the bottom. Three men immediately began the steep descent to save what they could of the supplies. Certainly, the horse would be hopelessly injured, and perhaps would need to be put out of its misery.

As the others watched the precarious descent, fearing for their comrades' safety, the three men quickly untied the horse's load and then watched in amazement as the animal climbed shakily to its feet. The men shouldered the packs of supplies and then led the trembling animal back up the steep slope to the stunned crowd at the top.

The next day, to their unspeakable joy, they found a bundle of fresh meat that Clark and his hunters had left tied to a tree limb for them, along with a note. Clark had found and slaughtered a horse.

"God bless him!" Charbonneau said, almost in tears, then adding self-consciously, "My baby won't die."

Colter leaned over and whispered to Shields, "I suspect he's far more concerned about himself than Pomp."

"Yeah, I've never seen the baby eat meat. He's doing just fine on his mother's milk. It's Charbonneau that's hungry, not the baby."

"It seems to me that he should be more concerned about Sacagawea getting enough to eat so she can feed Pomp." The two men shook their heads.

The men immediately built a fire and prepared the food, which lifted their morale as much as it filled their growling stomachs. Dark circles had begun to form menacingly under their eyes. The meat of the horse didn't last long, however, and the party continued to grow weaker as the days passed. The constant cramp of hunger, the extreme physical exertion, and the dark specter of death from starvation in these mountains were testing the limits of even the most indomitable men. Still, they never lashed out or demanded an explanation for their plight. Even though they were literally starving, they remained a disciplined military unit, each man performing his designated duties without complaint.

Captain Clark reached a plain where he and his men came upon three young Indian boys, ranging in age from ten to twelve years, who ran from the strangers and hid in tall grass. Clark dismounted and gave his gun and horse to one of his men. Talking in a friendly tone, knowing they wouldn't understand his words, he gave the boys some ribbon and trinkets, and they quickly scampered off.

.In a short time, an adult male Indian approached them with great caution. Clark greeted him with a smile and friendly gestures. Returning Clark's smile, the Indian motioned for the white men to follow him, and they went together to a large lodge. Through improvised sign language, Clark learned that the lodge belonged to a great chief who was away on a raid with tribal warriors. The squaws at the lodge gave the white men berries, dried salmon, and roots, and Clark gave them presents in return. Then the Indian signaled that Clark and his men should follow him again and led them to a Nez Perce village of about thirty lodges. The squaws, children, and old men of the village gathered to inspect Clark and his men. They treated the white men kindly, feeding them and making them comfortable.

The Nez Perce were darker than the Flatheads and spoke a different language. Although their dress was similar, they wore more beads and also sported brass and copper jewelry as well as shells. The men were large and portly, and the women were small and attractive. Near the Indian village ran a clear river that was about two hundred yards wide and two to five feet deep, with a rocky bottom. Clark and his men saw salmon swimming in the river, which Clark decided to call *Clearwater River.*

Eating too much food too quickly made Clark and his men sick. Nevertheless, Clark purchased as much dried salmon, roots, and berries as possible with the few articles his party had in their packs, and then sent Reuben Field, with an Indian, back to the main party with the food. Clark sent the other men out to hunt while he began getting information from the Nez Perce about the route west. He was taken to the camp of Twisted Hair, a Nez Perce chief who was about sixty years of age.

"Let's smoke," Clark signaled, taking his pipe from his pack.

Twisted Hair seated himself and motioned for Clark to sit.

"Where does this river go?" Clark signaled by pointing in the river's downstream direction.

"To a bigger river," Twisted Hair motioned. Then he made an undulating motion like a snake.

Clark turned to York and asked, "Do you suppose he means the river curves and twists?"

:"Maybe, but he could also mean that they call it the Snake River," York answered intuitively.

Lewis and the main party had not yet arrived at the wide prairie ahead of them. They were on a heavily wooded slope where fallen trees from a forest fire littered the ground. It was an exceptionally difficult passage. They camped near dusk at a large creek surrounded by grass for the horses. The hunters returned with a wolf and three pheasants they had killed, not enough to provide a hearty meal for the group. Everyone was weak and starving, and some were even staggering in their effort to walk.

Lewis cautioned the men to hobble the horses to prevent delay in the morning. He was determined to make a forced march the next day to reach the open prairie, if at all possible. The beautiful wide prairie had turned out to be more distant than Old Toby had thought.

Lewis discovered the next morning to his chagrin that one of the men had not hobbled his horse properly, and by the time the animal was found and returned to camp it was mid-day. The party had gone only two miles before they encountered Reuben Fields with provisions of dried fish and roots.

"What a godsend you are!" exclaimed Lewis. "We are completely out of food."

Smiling with the knowledge that he was serving the needs of the Corps, Fields shared his news: "There is a N-N-Nez Perce village only s-seven m-miles from here."

"Thank God!" Lewis said with heart-felt relief. He added to himself, *I really was afraid we were going to die here, and I'm sure the men were too.*

Lewis and his men straggled into the Nez Perce village, ragged and weak from hunger, but with radiant faces—they had defied death by crossing the monumental mountains! Lewis felt triumphant that the Corps had endured all the trials and deprivations and were now descending at last to level and fertile country where game surely was roaming. Eight-month-old Pomp was no worse for the journey. Sacagawea's milk had held up in spite of her scant diet, and the baby was actually the only member of the Corps of Discovery who appeared robust. The Corps was nearly giddy with relief that they were safe again. Hundreds of Indians gathered to inspect these tattered, gaunt strangers with their weak, bony horses.

"These good people will want to feed you, but don't eat too much," Captain Clark cautioned Lewis's men. "If you do, after enduring such near starvation, you'll get sick."

The Nez Perce Indians were a much larger nation than the Shoshones. They lived well and were dressed well in the skins of mountain goats, deer, and elk. Their homes were leather lodges where they lived in relative comfort. Their curiosity at seeing white men—and especially a black man—was evident. For the first time in his life, York found his black skin a point of pride because it made him unique among the entire gathering of Indians and the Corps of Discovery.

The Nez Perce were friendly and fed the men dried salmon and bread made from the root of a plant called *camas*, which grew in abundance on the prairie. Despite Clark's warning, the starving men ate too much, and that night they were all sick. Most of them, including

Captain Lewis, were ill for a week. They suffered from dysentery, with acute diarrhea and vomiting.

Had the Nez Perce been hostile, they could have killed the entire Corps in a few minutes and stolen all their goods and guns, gaining an arsenal that was vast by their standards. As with most Indian tribes, they had only a couple of old and inferior guns, and like the Shoshones, they were constantly harassed by the Blackfoot tribe when they made their annual trip to hunt buffalo.

While Lewis was ill, Clark moved their camp to the nearby Clearwater River, where they found Ponderosa pines of sufficient size to make canoes. The Nez Perce could not understand any of the languages spoken by members of the expedition, nor could they understand the sign language that had been universal among the Plains Indians. The two groups tried to develop their own hand signals. Chief Twisted Hair advised the captains about the route to the Pacific Ocean by drawing pictures in the dirt and a map on an elk skin. According to his map, the Clearwater River flowed west and joined the Columbia River.

Twisted Hair signed to the captains that it was a five-sleep journey to the Columbia River by means of the Clearwater River and Snake Rivers, and then another five sleeps to the falls of the Columbia. If Twisted Hair was right, and if their interpretation of his signs was correct, the Corps of Discovery was only two weeks from the ocean. However, the captains had learned from experience that Indian estimates of distance were either too optimistic or the Indians traveled much faster than white men. The latter was probably true because of the tons of supplies the Corps was carrying. In any case, they weren't going anywhere until they could rest, regain their strength, and build canoes.

Lewis named their camp near the Nez Perce village *Traveler's Rest*. Over the next couple of days, the captains awarded medals to Twisted Hair and three lesser chiefs, along with shirts, knives, handkerchiefs, and tobacco. These trifles did not satisfy the Indians, however, and at the end of the second day the Nez Perce signaled that the food for the Corps would no longer be free. The captains were forced to trade from their diminishing supply of goods for more roots, berries, and dried fish.

"We are on our way to the great bad-tasting lake where the sun goes down," Clark signaled to Twisted Hair. "We will go by canoe, and we need to leave our horses here until we come back. I will give you two army rifles when we return if you will care for our horses until then."

Twisted Hair promised to look after the expedition's herd of thirty-eight horses until the expedition returned in the spring on their journey back home. He probably figured that if the white men didn't return, the Nez Perce would be that much richer in horses, and if they did return he would have acquired two excellent guns.

"I have a branding iron of my initials," Lewis told Clark. "We can brand our horses to distinguish them from those of the Nez Perce."

"That's a bit of good luck," Clark agreed. "That will probably avoid problems on our return trip."

Clark took a work party to the stand of ponderosa pines and divided the party into five teams, each to make one canoe. However, the heat was stifling and many of the men were still ill. Because he had so few healthy men, Clark decided to use the Indian method for making canoes. Instead of hewing out the inside of the canoe with chisels and axes, a very strenuous job, they put the tree trunk over a slow-burning fire trench, a process that Twisted Hair showed them how to do. Using this method, it took ten days to complete four large canoes and one small one.

As work on the canoes progressed, the members of the expedition continued to live on dried fish bought from the Nez Perce. In this level and fertile countryside, the Corps expected to find game animals, but their hunters returned empty-handed every day, and the men were not regaining their strength. Lewis decided to slaughter a horse, and at last the men ate heartily.

It was soon time to leave Traveler's Rest.

CHAPTER 23

Adventures on the Columbia River

October, 1805

Before the Corps of Discovery departed Traveler's Rest, Captain Clark directed the men to dig a cache in which to hide their pack saddles, which they wouldn't need until their return trip. Toward evening, they put their five new canoes into the Clearwater River (which soon became the Snake River), and packed their gear and supplies into them. After dark, they buried the pack saddles in the hidden cache. Then Captain Lewis went to search for Chief Twisted Hair.

"Can we hire you to guide us to the Columbia River?" he signaled.

Twisted Hair signaled his consent, but when the expedition was ready to leave, he couldn't be found.

"We can't wait for him," Lewis decided. "Let's go on and leave word for him to catch up with us."

It was a joy for the men to be going downstream with the current in the river, the first time that had happened since they had left the Ohio River two years earlier. Encountering wild rapids, the men were forced to get into the cold water and guide the canoes, but for the most part, the river was deep and the current gentle. When a canoe steered by Sergeant Gass struck a rock in a rapid, swinging around and striking another rock, the canoe broke and sank. Fortunately, the water was only waist deep, but it was roaring forcefully over the rocks, and the men who couldn't swim were frightened. "Just stand still until we can get another canoe to you," Sergeant Pryor yelled to the stranded non-swimmers, who were too frightened to respond.

Men who could face down a grizzly bear with their long rifles, were terrified of being stranded in the raging, turbulent river. Other men unloaded one of the other canoes and retrieved the stranded non-swimmers, finally calming their fears. When they had retrieved the men and transferred the supplies to shore, the expedition camped and spread the baggage out to dry. They delayed resuming their journey to allow Gass, Pryor, Joseph Fields, and Shields to repair the badly damaged canoe. Local Indians brought food for sale, and the captains bought a considerable amount of fresh salmon, two dogs (which the men had begun to eat and enjoy), and some camas roots from them. Here, to the captains' relief, Twisted Hair caught up with them.

When the men finished repairing the canoe, Cruzatte tuned up his fiddle and the men danced to "Columbus Cotillion," "MacDonald's Reel," and "The Country Courtship." One of the Indian squaws began singing and distributing her camas roots and bracelets. When one of the soldiers declined her offer, she angrily threw her remaining roots and bracelets into the fire, grabbed a sharp flint from her husband, and cut both of her arms in many places. The men were stunned into silence as they watched. She then scraped blood from the cuts and licked it from her hand. She tore beads and pieces of copper from a necklace she was wearing and gave them to those near her. Suddenly she collapsed, unconscious. Her friends revived her with water and then took care of her. Captain Clark gave her some small presents, and she smiled at him gratefully.

"What kind of strange behavior was that?" Ordway whispered to Clark.

"I don't know," Clark whispered back, "but her behavior was strange, and the way her friends reacted was also strange. I'd say she must be important to them."

Within a week, they were on the Columbia River, which the men estimated to be about four hundred yards wide. The area contrasted with the wooded mountains the expedition had recently passed, for the area here was a barren landscape. Local Indians lined both banks of the river to inspect the Corps' small fleet of canoes.

Indian villages were numerous on the banks of the Columbia, and the natives must have been part of the extended Nez Perce nation because Twisted Hair conversed fluently with them. These Nez Perce owned a large number of dogs and horses, which seemed to be their medium of exchange. Members of the expedition by this time were accustomed to supplementing their usual fare of fish and roots with the meat of dogs and horses.

"I wonder if we wouldn't be better off just buying food from the Indians instead of losing time by sending out hunters," Lewis suggested. "We finally have the river current working in our favor, and I hate to let anything interfere with our progress now."

"I agree," Clark said. "The Nez Perce might ridicule us for eating dogs, calling us 'dog eaters', but our men are working very hard and need something more nourishing than the salmon and roots the Indians live on."

When the expedition came to a swirling rapids followed by a particularly dangerous one littered with boulders, they halted and took one canoe at a time past the obstruction. The river was still four hundred yards wide, with barren shores except for a few straggly willows. When they stopped at a large Indian fishing camp to buy salmon and dogs, they saw copper kettles and trinkets that could have come only from white traders.

"Ask them where they got these things," Lewis had Drouillard signal Twisted Hair to find out from a local man.

"From a white man with hair on his face," was the reply.

"That's a good sign," Clark said. "We must be getting close to the Pacific Ocean where white settlers live."

The land along the Columbia continued to be devoid of trees, and the men could scarcely find enough wood to cook their food. Lewis hired two local Flathead Indians to pilot the canoes through a two-mile long swirling rapid that was filled with dangerous rocks. Many more frightening stretches like this one were ahead, and the men shouted with jubilation when the Columbia once again became calm. But the falls of the Columbia River finally lay before them.

"I hate to stop to portage," Lewis told Clark. "We're on the last leg of our journey and the current is working for us.'

Clark had an idea. "Why don't we send the men who can't swim to portage around the falls with the instruments and rifles while the rest of us run the rapids with the canoes?"

"Good idea!" Lewis shot back. "We'll hire local Indians who know these rapids to pilot our canoes through them."

The plan worked perfectly, and once they were past the falls, the Columbia River was so clear that the men could see pebbles and even grains of sand on the river bottom. As they continued, their cumbersome dugout canoes sometimes scraped on rocks, sprang leaks, swamped, and even overturned. Supplies were often damaged or lost, but the expedition successfully ran nearly fifteen additional rapids in their determination to increase their pace. Their goal was almost in view!

One evening when they camped, they found wood that Indians had hidden under stones. Although they had never taken anything that belonged to any Indians, they gave in to necessity this time because wood was so scarce, and one of the hunters had killed eight ducks that needed to cook.

Salmon, which had just spawned, were thick in the river. Most were dead or dying, but Seaman enjoyed leaping into the river and returning with a wriggling live one in his mouth.

The expedition came to a treacherous rapid that the Indians had told them would be the last dangerous one. Approaching it cautiously, they halted above it, and the captains sent the non-swimmers around it with their most precious supplies. Then, with lightened canoes, the crews successfully ran the rapid.

The country was totally barren, without a single tree, but they passed a fork in the river where about two hundred Indians were camped. The Corps also camped here, and that evening a band of Indians wearing copper and brass trinkets came singing and dancing into the camp. The captains greeted them cordially and smoked pipes with them.

"Where did you get these shiny decorations?" Lewis had Twisted Hair ask them.

"From white traders on a river north of here," was the answer.

A number of them wore red and blue cloth, but there were no buffalo robes among them—verifying that there were no buffalo west of the mountains, as the Mandans had told them. The captains bought seven dogs, a quantity of salmon, and dried horsemeat from these Indians who were members of another tribe of the Flathead nation.

The captains presented them with needles, flags, and other small articles, and Lewis recorded some of their words. The Corps of Discovery remained in this camp a day so the captains could record celestial observations and update the map they were creating. Meanwhile, the soldiers dressed animal skins, mended clothes and shoes, and put their weapons in working order. Clark measured the width of the smooth and gentle Columbia River at this point and entered eight hundred and sixty yards in his journal.

When the Corps departed the next morning, the land along the river was flat for the first ten miles, and then it became broken hills. They passed Indian fishing camps occupying several islands and saw Indian scaffolds holding an enormous number of salmon drying in the sun. Dead salmon floated in the river, and live salmon leaped from the water.

After traveling thirty-six miles, the men made camp across the river from an Indian camp. When several of the Indians crossed the river to visit, Cruzatte played some lively tunes on his fiddle, pleasing the guests. The next day, the Corps came to another village where, strangely, the Indians hid from them. Captain Clark entered one of their lodges and found more than thirty people, who cringed at the sight of him.

"Don't be afraid," he said, hoping the tone of his voice would convey a friendly message.

He gave them a few small presents, but they remained terrified. Drouillard and the Fields brothers arrived and also tried unsuccessfully to persuade them of their friendly intentions. Only when Sacagawea appeared did this local tribe relax, knowing that no squaw ever accompanied a war party.

As the expedition continued downstream, it met many natives, some of whom had firewood to sell—a welcome commodity because it had become so scarce. Cruzatte and Gibson played their violins whenever they camped, and the Indians always left happy and smiling. Another time the men came upon an island where Indians had left giant canoes filled to the tops with human skeletons covered with mats, fish nets, and small trinkets.

The treeless land here was brown tundra-like plains, and the river remained calm and smooth. Birds of many types filled the air with chirping as they swarmed along the river to feed on the dead salmon. When the Corps stopped at an Indian village, the men were surprised to see the natives wearing white men's clothing.

"We're getting close now!" Clark commented happily. Everyone strained to look ahead to be the first to see the ocean.

The river now contained deep channels that created dangerous whirlpools, and the men steered carefully to avoid them. After traveling thirty-two miles, they camped near some Indian lodges where scattered pine trees dotted the area. These Indians, wearing elk and deer skins, had pierced noses and were not as cordial as the earlier tribes had been.

Huge boulders divided the river into channels, creating roaring rapids that filled with fear some of the men who couldn't swim. Chinook Indians gathered on the bank to see if the white men would venture into the rapids, but the men unloaded the canoes and guided the empty vessels with elk-skin ropes through the dangerous waters.

A great chief named Yellept with a few sub-chiefs visited the captains to smoke with them and learn about the purpose of their mission. Yellept was a handsome man of about thirty-five years, about 5'8" tall, with a well-proportioned physique.

"Stay with us a day so my people can meet you," Yellept signaled.

"We are in a great hurry," Lewis responded through Drouillard. "When we return from the great lake that tastes bad, we will visit your people."

This satisfied Yellept and his party of Chinook Indians.

The Chinooks didn't look, dress, or speak like the Nez Perce, Twisted Hair's people. They were shorter, had large feet, and wore short robes of fur around their necks, arms, and legs. A few wore raccoon skins, leading the captains to deduce that timber must be nearby. They were eager to trade, but they would not sell fish, so the captains bought dogs from them. The Chinooks made lightweight canoes that were sturdier and easier to handle than the dugouts used by the Corps, so Lewis bought one from them.

The expedition had become aware that everything Indian along the Columbia River was infested with fleas, and by now all the members of the Lewis and Clark team were infested and scratching also. They had learned that the Chinooks were at war with the Nez Perce, which explained Twisted Hair's sudden unannounced departure.

Arriving at a place called the Short Narrows, where the river shrank to only forty-five yards in width, creating a two-mile stretch of water that surged and swirled in every direction, the captains had to decide how to advance.

"We'll send the men who can't swim on shore again," Lewis decided. "The rest of us will have to run the rapids."

The Indians, experts with canoes, didn't believe the soldiers could stay afloat in their big, heavy dugout canoes and gathered to watch the soldiers drown, so their tribe could claim the lost equipment. But the Indians were surprised and disappointed. The run was successful except for one canoe that crashed into an enormous rock.

The Corps of Discovery camped that night at an Indian village of twenty-one strange-looking structures. The lower half of each house was underground, and the upper part was covered with white cedar bark. Each house was about thirty feet long and twenty feet wide and was occupied by three families. Half of each house was used for storing dried and pounded fish. Beds were on the side walls with a fireplace in the center of the house.

Whenever they camped, Cruzatte and Gibson played their fiddles while Shannon sang, and the men of the expedition danced for the local Indians, which always seemed to establish friendly relations.

Back on the river, the expedition passed some falls and moved into a calm three-mile stretch. The captains stopped here to record celestial observations and update their maps. Meanwhile, several men who went out to find and collect pitch pine to repair their canoes, returned with five deer, one goose, a gray squirrel, and one salmon.

"It's good to have game available again," Drouillard said as the other men clustered around to help clean the animals.

"Yeah, dried fish and roots get old in a hurry, and then we're still hungry," Shields agreed, spitting out the pine twig he had been chewing.

Progressing on the Columbia, which continued to widen and then narrow with rapids, the expedition passed safely, camping at night under the stars, singing and dancing with high spirits. Eight-month-old Pomp crawled from person to person, bouncing with the music, and sometimes, swinging and laughing in the arms of a dancer. Each man enjoyed picking him up, talking to him, tickling him, and then passing him to the next person. The men loved little Pomp and considered him their mascot.

The Corps of Discovery now began to have problems with local Indians stealing from them. Anything that was laid aside for a moment vanished. It was not only a vexing problem but a serious one.

"I'm going to kill the next damned Indian that steals from me!" an exasperated John Colter exploded.

"No!" Captain Lewis said sternly. "We have to keep good relations with them so we will have a friendly reception when we return. For the sake of our mission, be patient with them."

Two Chinook chiefs and fifteen warriors crossed the river in a canoe, bringing presents of deer meat and bread made from roots. The captains gave medals to the chiefs and trinkets to his men. Cruzatte brought out his fiddle, and York danced a jig for the Indians, delighting them. Hunters from the Corps brought in five deer, so there was plenty of meat for the party. One of the men had gigged a steelhead trout and fried it in bear oil provided by one of the Indians. The Indians spent the night, which was beneficial to Corps-Chinook relations. The captains recorded celestial observations, updated maps, and recorded some of the vocabulary of this nation of Indians.

Next day, the Corps continued past a number of Indian villages on both sides of the river, and the terrain again become mountainous with springs falling nearly a hundred feet from the cliffs. The country back from the river was covered with pine and cottonwood trees, while willow trees grew in the bottoms. Rain fell all day, and the expedition made camp that night at the head of the last great drop in the river, which the Indians called the Great Chute. It was a half-mile long, with the river compressed into narrows where the water rushed, violent and foaming, over many boulders before pitching over a twenty-foot waterfall.

Lewis took a party of five men to visit a nearby Indian village where the natives gave them berries, nuts, and fish to eat. Because of the language barrier, Lewis could get no information from them about the land ahead. Nearby, they came upon an oddity: a towering rock standing on land—about eight-hundred feet high and four hundred paces around. They saw something else they had never seen before when an Indian war party passed by with the chief wearing a vest of shingled wood, apparently designed to stop an arrow.

"By God, they can be inventive, too!" Colter marveled.

A four-mile stretch ahead of them was filled with beautiful but dangerous rapids and waterfalls. Huge rocks projected from the river, looking as if they had fallen from the high cliffs. The Corps portaged around the largest falls, but whenever possible, they ran the rapids— hurtling through the gushing water and steering around boulders. They spent two days passing this treacherous area.

Cottonwood, oak, ash, and hazelnut trees—all wearing the yellow and brown leaves of autumn—along with heavy underbrush were thick on both sides of the river. The expedition passed the mouth of a tributary that was close to forty yards wide, and then they camped on an island at the head of a great rapid. A number of Indians came to their camp and indicated that they were surprised to see them.

"Were you rained from the sky?" they asked with sign language. This amused everyone in the expedition, but they kept their laughter to themselves.

Captain Clark pointed to the river and then pointed upstream, indicating that they had come down the river with all its rapids and dangers, which seemed to relieve their Indian visitors.

CHAPTER 24

The Pacific Ocean

November, 1805

When the Corps of Discovery encountered a number of Indians traveling east who were portaging around the rapids, they stopped to exchange greetings with them. The Indians were taking pounded salmon to trade with other tribes upriver. After catching the salmon, they cleaned them, dried them, and then pounded them between two stones. Placing the pounded salmon into a basket lined with dried and stretched salmon skin, they pressed it down as hard as possible and continued to add layers until the basket was full. Then they covered the contents of the basket with more dried and stretched salmon skin, which they tied securely through the handles of the basket. They then stacked the baskets, each weighing about a hundred pounds. The Indians informed the captains that the pounded salmon would keep for several years.

Clark was intrigued by the industry of these people. He commented to those around him, "This is clearly a thriving trade route of a commercially sophisticated people." Those nearby nodded in agreement as they surveyed the many stacks of baskets, all expertly packed and neatly stacked.

Soon, the expedition reached the beginning of the tidewater of the Columbia River, and from here on the rising and falling of ocean tides introduced the Corps to a very different world.

"It can't be far now!" Ordway announced. "We must be near the ocean. I can hardly wait to see it!"

The riverbanks were thick with fir, spruce, ash, and alder trees. Migrating water fowl were everywhere, and the honking of geese resounded through the countryside as they called to one another in mid-flight. A damp, gray blanket of fog now chilled the river each morning, and Indian villages dotted the landscape. The river again became extremely wide, with a smooth current. Sand islands were scattered at the mouth of a wide, shallow tributary to the Columbia River. Local Indians signed to the captains that they would see white men's vessels farther down the river.

"Good news!" Lewis said. "At last we'll be able to use President Jefferson's letter of credit to buy the goods we need for the return trip."

"And they will probably be able to give us information about local Indians," Clark added. "It will be interesting to see how many white settlers there are."

The expedition camped on a large island where ponds full of migrating geese, brants, and ducks provided a bountiful supper. Several Indians camped with them, and a Snake tribal woman tried unsuccessfully to talk with Sacagawea. Lewis had Drouillard sign them as best he could to ask how much farther it was to the Pacific Ocean.

"Two more sleeps to the bad-tasting water," was the reply.

As they progressed, the soldiers noted that the local Indians were much better canoeists than the men of the Corps, and their canoes were better designed to ride the waves than the Corps' dugout canoes. However, the soldiers were not impressed with the local Indians, finding them physically unattractive and very inclined to steal. The natives looked healthy, although eye infection was a common malady. Great numbers of them had lost vision in one eye, and many had lost their sight entirely. They also had bad teeth, which was rare among other Indians the Corps had met. One of the Indians could speak a few words of English, but the soldiers were amused that the words he so proudly pronounced were curse words—not useful for communication. These western Indians also drove hard bargains, charging inflated prices for their food and goods.

The expedition continued past many islands and timbered bottoms. They met some Indians in handsome canoes that were unlike any the men had seen before. The canoes were very light weight, high in the middle and tapered at each end, with curious figures carved into the prow of each. Wind and high waves did not seem to hinder these canoes, which rode the highest waves with apparent ease. Captain Lewis traded the expedition's smallest canoe plus a hatchet and a few trinkets for one of these excellent canoes.

After passing several mostly barren large islands, the Corps came to a river that was 120 yards wide at its narrowest point, where the men were astonished to find a bed of quicksand. Captain Clark named it Quicksand River. The expedition continued on the Columbia River until after dark in an effort to escape the constant intrusion of Indians, but they were unsuccessful at doing so. Four canoes of Indians followed them until they camped and then stayed near them all night.

After eight miles the next day, the expedition came upon a large Indian village where some of the natives wore manufactured clothes. When the expedition camped nearby, several local Indians came from the village to visit. They were colorfully dressed, some wearing sailor jackets, shirts, and hats while others wore scarlet and blue blankets. They gave the captains some roots that were about the size of hen's eggs, called *wappato*, which the Indians roasted. Although they seemed friendly, they brought along a show of weaponry that included war axes, spears, bows and arrows, and pistols, as well as some trinkets.

This was a meeting fraught with danger! Two groups of armed young men from two very different cultures, unable to communicate with spoken language, faced each other, . Even though the captains thought the native men pompous and disagreeable, they smoked with them in an attentive and friendly manner to try to make friends. The atmosphere changed quickly, however, when Clark discovered that one of them had made off with his pipe tomahawk, which they had all been smoking.

"This is too much!" he said angrily. "Men, search every Indian and all their canoes." Clark was determined to find his pipe.

The soldiers couldn't find the tomahawk pipe, and while the search went on, one of the Indians stole Drouillard's capote—a long, hooded blanket-coat made of heavy wool.

"Goddammit! Stop stealing from us!" a furious Clark shouted. "We came here to be friends with you, but we will fight if you keep stealing from us!" His face was red with anger. The captains found Drouillard's capote, but not the pipe. Seeing the captains' anger, the Indians left without further incident.

The Corps of Discovery proceeded ten miles to another large Indian village on an island. Natives who came out in canoes to meet them wanted to trade for guns, but the captains refused. The expedition continued another thirty-one miles before making camp. The next day they passed a small village where Indians came out in canoes to offer them roots, trout, and furs at bargain prices.

"They really have a thriving river trade going on here," Lewis commented.

"They are fairly advanced in many ways," Clark agreed. "They just haven't figured out yet how to create metal and things like that yet."

"To be honest, we didn't either," Lewis mused. "We're just lucky that our ancestors invented written language so they could pass their knowledge down to us." As a brisk wind rose from the west, whipping up waves and whistling through the trees, the expedition continued past large bottom lands with cottonwood trees. The wind brought heavy rain, and after traveling twenty-nine miles the Corps camped under an overhanging cliff. It rained heavily all night long, making conditions wet and disagreeable. They no longer had shelter from the rain, having left their tents in the caches on the Missouri River. Sacagawea wrapped herself and Pomp in her buffalo robe so Pomp could draw warmth from her body and be protected from the rain. The next day, the men built large fires to try to dry out their bedding and kill the fleas in them, which had multiplied by every contact with Indian tribes.

The expedition passed low, marshy islands that were partly covered with willows. Fowl of every variety were plentiful: geese, brants, ducks, cranes, loons, and seagulls. The expedition made thirty-four miles in the rain. When they camped, Pryor cocked his ear toward the western horizon.

"Listen!" he shouted. "Everybody be quiet a minute."

Even the rain couldn't drown out the sound of waves breaking on rocks in the distance.

"We've done it!" shouted Hugh Hall.

"It's the Pacific Ocean!" Ordway shouted, throwing his cap in the air and then straining to catch it before it landed in the river.

But there was no real celebration for the Corps of Discovery because it was raining too hard for Cruzatte and Gibson to bring out their fiddles. Still, each person was filled with pride, and there was great joy in camp that night despite the wet conditions. They had conquered over half a continent, against all odds for a small group of men living off the land and constantly encountering strange bands of Indians whom folks back home described as "savages," although the Corps of Discovery had been greeted amiably and assisted by all the tribes they had encountered except the Teton Sioux.

The next day, they rounded a point into what they assumed was a bay because the river was suddenly five to six miles wide. When the expedition halted to eat, several Indians showed up with fresh fish for sale, which the captains bought. The river became so brackish now that the men couldn't drink from it. In addition, some of the men began to feel nauseated from the constant movement of the tide.

"Hang the supplies on trees to keep them above the tide," Captain Clark advised the men when they camped.

It didn't make much difference, however, because rain fell all evening and all night.

"Does the rain ever stop in this part of the world?" wondered Private Alexander Carson. "I'm mighty tired of it."

During the night the wind became so strong that it added to their discomfort. Although the tide didn't reach their campsite, the canoes in the river had to be tended all night long. These were disagreeable circumstances, but the expedition had to spend a second night in this camp because the waves were too high for travel. Nevertheless, the men were so elated at reaching their goal that their cheerfulness was inextinguishable.

"When do we get to see the ocean?" Sacagawea asked Clark through the translation chain.

"Just as soon as we find it, Janie. It has to be very close."

All the members of the expedition were excited in anticipation of seeing the ocean.

"After all the rivers we've had to fight our way up, I thought I'd seen enough goldarn water to last me the rest of my life, but the ocean is different!" Shannon grinned.

November 10 brought another day and night of rain, and it was still raining the next morning. The waves were not as high as the day before, so the men loaded the canoes and set out, passing rocky cliffs and flowing springs. They watched playful porpoises and sea otters in the river, as well as noisy seagulls and ducks.

The rainstorm was unrelenting, and at noon the next day the expedition finally pulled into a cove for shelter until the storm abated. Then they searched again for a better harbor, camping in a place they called Point Ellice. They thought this place with its high cliffs would shelter them from the wind, but when a violent storm arose, high water battered the shore and they were trapped. Point Ellice became a virtual prison for them for the next eleven days as the storm continued. Spirits that had remained high for so long began to plummet.

"This is God-forsaken weather and a God-forsaken place," Shields groused.

"It sure ain't the Garden of Eden," Colter agreed.

At high tide, immense waves uprooted trees, tearing them out of the ground and strewing them across the already confined campsite. Fires were extremely difficult to start and nearly impossible to maintain. Hunters reported back to the captains that the surrounding hills were covered with fallen timber, and the underbrush was so thick it was impassable.

Eventually, they all began to look like survivors from a shipwreck. They were constantly chilled and forced to sleep in wet clothing and soaked bedding, which were rotting as a result of being wet all the time.

The odor of wetness pervaded everything. Their canoes were always at the mercy of wind and waves. The men began to despair, fearing that they might be permanently trapped.

"Surely to God, this weather has to break soon," Lewis agonized.

"It doesn't show any sign of it," Clark responded, his voice betraying his loss of optimism.

Then the men spied a dark shape bobbing in the water in the distance, occasionally vanishing and then reappearing on the crest of a high wave.

"It's a boat!" someone yelled.

"Thank God!" Lewis exclaimed. "If we're lucky, they'll have food."

They were Clatsop Indians, relatives of the Chinooks, who unloaded baskets of roots and fish into the eager hands of the men.

"We are glad to see you! Welcome!" Lewis had Drouillard signal them as best he could. "Does this rain ever stop?"

One Clatsop Indian smiled and with a sweeping gesture indicated that the goods they brought were for sale. If he understood the question about the rain, he ignored it. The captains gratefully bought all the food while the men of the expedition inspected with great interest the remarkable canoe that had brought the Indians through such turbulent water.

The Clatsops departed, apparently pleased with the success of their mission. The men hoped they would return with more food in a few days because the Corps' dugouts could not travel through such violent water and they would not be able to leave their waterlogged prison until the weather let up.

Rain continued every day and night, making the unsheltered men more and more miserable. Finally, four Indians came to their camp with salmon trout, which the captains bought. Trying to communicate with them, the captains learned that they had visited a ship anchored in the mouth of the river where a white man named Mr. Haley had traded with them, but both the ship and Mr. Haley had now gone.

Out of desperation, the captains finally sent Privates Colter, Willard, and Shannon in the Indian canoe they had recently bought to explore the shoreline beyond Point Ellice and see if they could find a better campsite. The three men explored the coastline until they finally found a sandy beach.

"Let's go see if there is any game in the area," Colter suggested.

After quickly spotting a pair of elks, they were satisfied.

"Tell you what," Colter said to Willard and Shannon, "you men start clearing an area for a camp while I report back to the captain."

When Colter returned to report that they had found a sandy beach in a bay beyond Point Ellice where there was also game, Captain Lewis decided to explore the site himself. Taking Drouillard and three privates with them, he and Colter returned to the site.

However, Willard and Shannon were missing. Searching and calling for them, they finally found them—in a very precarious position. After Colter left, they had gone hunting and spent the night with five Chinook Indians they had met enroute. While they slept, the Indians stole their rifles. Upon discovering this in the morning, Willard informed the Indians with crude but emphatic signs that a larger party of soldiers was coming and would shoot the thieves. At that propitious moment, Lewis and his party appeared, and the Indians sheepishly handed back the rifles and hastily departed.

For Clark and the main party at Point Ellice, the never-ending storm continued. They survived under miserable conditions with only pounded salmon to eat—but it was food, and they were grateful for it. As the weeks-long storm finally eased, Lewis and his detachment returned and reported that they had explored thirty miles downriver from the new site to the ocean.

"It is something to behold!" Lewis reported enthusiastically to Clark and the main group. "Have the men break camp, and we'll all go together to see our grand destination—the Pacific Ocean."

When the expedition reached the mouth of the Columbia River on the Pacific Coast, the men stood silently, staring at the vast Pacific Ocean with joy, reverence, and an enormous sense of achievement. Foam-tipped breakers swept the rocky shore constantly, pulsating like the heart beat of a living thing.

"This moment may be the high point of our lives," Ordway said.

"It's a historic event, for sure," Colter added.

"Yes, we have made history today," Clark added wistfully.

"Children will learn about us as part of their schooling," an awed Shannon predicted almost reverently.

"We have indeed become a part of our country's history," Lewis added. "President Jefferson will be proud of us."

After a meal and an evening of celebration, the expedition turned south, continued along the coast, and camped at a place called Haley's Bay, where local Indians lived in great numbers. These Indians were very friendly, and their women flirted openly with men of the expedition, as their husbands watched approvingly. In their culture, husbands of the squaws showed respect to visitors by offering their wives for a night of sexual pleasure.

The weather remained rainy, with a high wind coming out of the southwest. The tide was so high that one of the expedition's canoes smashed against logs driven in by the tide and was nearly destroyed before they could get it out of the water.

The next day was clear and sunny for a most welcome change. Many of the men tried to dry their soggy belongings, and several went out to hunt, while the captains recorded longitude and latitude. The expedition was visited by a group of Chinook Indians that included two chiefs. The captains sat for a smoke with them and gave them medals and an American flag. One of the chiefs wore a beautiful robe made expertly from sea otter skins.

"That is a nice robe," Clark signed. "I will give you fishhooks for it."

At first, the chief declined. Then he looked at the belt made of blue beads that Sacagawea was wearing and pointed to it. Clark looked at Janie questioningly, but she did not want to part with such a prized possession.

"You must give me something for it," she finally insisted through Charbonneau.

"I'll give you a blue cloth coat," Clark promised, and she reluctantly handed over her prized belt of blue beads.

A Clatsop chief named Cusealah offered a woman to each captain, and when they declined, the women were highly insulted. Later, the captains teased each other about their missed opportunity.

"Before I joined the Corps, I resolved to always set a perfect example for the men," Clark said, smiling impishly at Lewis. "But my determination could break down if the Indians keep offering us women—and we must remember, turning them down is insulting to them." He heard Lewis chuckle.

"Well, we do want the Indians to be America's friends." Still smiling, Lewis looked at the red-haired Clark. "I guess some people would think it our patriotic duty."

The next morning, an old Chinook woman appeared with six daughters and nieces in tow, offering to sell their sexual services. The soldiers were eager to accommodate them. The young Indian women wore their hair loose, flowing over their shoulders and down their back. They had decorated themselves with beads hanging from their ears and around their necks, brass bracelets around their wrists, and a string with some curious kind of trinkets tied above one ankle. They had tattoos of various designs on their arms and were very proud of their appearance. The captains did not want to part with their most valuable articles, so they divided pieces of ribbon among the men to pay for the favors of the Indian lasses.

Word got out among the Clatsops that the captains would pay a high price in blue beads for sea-otter furs. That night a group came over the estuary with two robes to sell. The captains wanted the robes, but the price was too high. Clark offered his watch, a handkerchief, red beads, and a dollar in American coin, but his offer was rejected. The Indians wanted blue beads, but the captains knew that their remaining blue beads had to be preserved for more serious use.

"I guess we should have brought only blue beads with us," Lewis said ruefully.

"Yes, if we had only known," Clark responded, pausing for a moment before adding, "These Clatsops are more likeable than the Chinooks, don't you agree?"

"At least they aren't thieves," Lewis said with a sigh. "That alone makes them more likeable."

The honesty and affability of the Clatsops became a factor in the decision about where the expedition would spend the winter. The captains knew their supply of beads and trinkets would not last, and Chinook prices were so high that the Corps would not be able to get through the winter if they had to buy food from them. The expedition needed a sure source of meat, and the Clatsops told them that elk were plentiful in Clatsop territory. The captains wanted to remain close to the ocean so they could extract salt from seawater for seasoning as well as for preserving meat for the trip home. They also hoped that if they stayed near the ocean, a trading ship might sail into the area.

In searching for a site for camp, the expedition encountered another village of friendly Clatsops, and the captains bought roots from them. The day was rainy and cold, and the expedition passed several low, marshy islands covered with coarse grass and stunted willows. They camped in some thick woods.

"This is a gloomy goldarn country," Shannon complained. "It's always dismal and wet, and the sun almost never shines."

"I think we'd better get used to it," Thomas Howard replied. "We're going to spend the winter here whether we like it or not. There's no place else to go."

Storms struck the next morning with strong wind from the northwest. Waves broke with ferocity on shore, throwing seawater into the camp of the Corps of Discovery. The men were wet and miserable as they huddled in their makeshift shelters. To add to their misery, their attempts to burn wet wood caused great clouds of smoke that irritated everyone's eyes and breathing.

Vultures, eagles, hawks, and crows filled the sky in large numbers, while bugs, flies, spiders, and small lizards swarmed in the camp. The Corps had only a little pounded fish to eat, and their clothes were rotting on their bodies. Even so, Captain Lewis took Drouillard, Reuben Field, Shannon, Colter, and Labiche and set out in search of a suitable location for winter quarters.

They found a promising location on a small bluff rising thirty feet above the high-tide mark. It was about two hundred feet from the river and about three miles from the mouth of the Columbia River. A spring with fresh water was nearby, and there were plenty of big trees to use in building a fort. Best of all, this location promised good hunting. The scouting group liked the location.

"You know," Lewis said to his team, "there are more than thirty of us, counting York and Sacagawea, and this will be our third winter together. Maybe I'm getting sentimental, but we have survived incredible hardships together, and it would be nice to give everyone a say about where we spend this winter."

Back with the rest of the expedition, Clark responded to Lewis' idea. "Well, we are a military unit. Still, I've never heard of a military unit that has bonded as closely as this one has. Let's put it to a vote—including York and Sacagawea."

The captains called the entire group together.

"We must decide where we're going to build our fort for the winter," Lewis began. "We could build it on the coast so we can watch for a ship and make our salt, but it's wet and stormy by the ocean. We could build it inland under the shelter of trees. Or we could return to the Nez Perce Indians and winter where we have our horses. We want to get everyone's opinion before making a decision."

The issue was debated, with every person invited to offer an opinion and the reasons for it. When a vote was finally taken, the group had decided to build the fort on the site the group had found. It was inland, on the southern side of the Columbia River estuary. They were eager to get started.

CHAPTER 25

Fort Clatsop

December, 1805

December began with illness among the men, which Lewis attributed to eating too much pounded salmon.

"Have the men stop boiling it in salt water and boil it only in fresh water," he instructed Ordway, hoping that would solve the problem.

Storms continued all day, causing the river to rise two feet higher than normal while the men scrambled to get their belongings out of its reach. When the storm had blown itself out, the expedition proceeded to the site they had selected for their winter fort. They unloaded their canoes and camped amid tall, straight pine and balsam fir trees. The hunters went out in search of game while the other men mended their clothing and dressed skins for new clothes.

The captains designed the new fort, which included seven huts, and named it Fort Clatsop. The men went to work under Sergeant Gass's supervision while Captain Clark and a few others searched for a place to establish a salt camp. Rain continued to fall every day, and many of the men building the fort became ill—some with dysentery and some with boils. Every person was fighting fleas, which had infested the group many weeks before and were inescapable, tormenting them at night and preventing sound sleep.

The hunters went out every day to hunt elk, while the rest of the party cut down trees to construct their fort. The area around the site was covered with a heavy growth of several species of fir trees, as well as black alder trees that often reached a height of sixty to seventy feet, with trunks two to four feet thick. Fires were used to burn branches from the trees, but the wet branches caused irritated eyes and difficult breathing.

Clark and the men with him, searching for a location to build a salt camp, encountered bogs in which the men sank to their hips in mud and water. They camped on a small knoll, using an elk skin as shelter from the rain. Dry wood was very scarce, but they collected what they could find and built a tolerable fire to cook their supper.

"Lord! I wish we was back in the dry country," Collins said, moving closer to the fire. "I don't think I've been completely dry or warm since we first saw the Pacific Ocean."

"It's all part of soldiering," Clark assured him. "Never in the history of mankind has a soldier's life been easy."

They finally established a salt camp at a place where the salt-makers would have ready access to saltwater and wood for their fires, as well as enough game to sustain the salt-making crew. The process was to boil sea water in large kettles until it boiled away, leaving its salt stuck to the sides of the kettles. Then they would scrape the salt from the kettles and store it in barrels for transport to the fort. In time, they found that they could produce nearly a gallon of salt per day.

At the main camp, workers began to raise one line of huts under the supervision of Sergeant Gass, while Sergeant Pryor and eight men crossed the bay in canoes and gathered boards from an abandoned Indian lodge. The chief of a neighboring Clatsop village visited them, and Lewis bought some lynx and otter pelts from him.

"We are pleased that you will build your fort near us," he signed. "We will sell food and other goods to you."

Clatsop prices were reasonable one day and outrageous the next. The captains were learning that dealing and trading with the Indians took much of their time. The men had now cut enough timber for their fort and were ready to start splitting logs. The men were elated that even the thickest logs split beautifully. The first hut they built was a smokehouse for the preservation of meat in this wet climate. Two men began splitting planks for the ceilings of the fort while others began installing them over the smokehouse to make it available for use as quickly as possible.

When Drouillard and his crew of hunters returned from a successful trip, Shannon shouted proudly, "We killed seventeen elk!"

"Well, I guess we finished the smokehouse just in time," Lewis said, smiling at Shannon's enthusiasm.

Most of the men set out several miles with canoes to retrieve and dress the meat. After cleaning and butchering the elk, each man carried a load of meat back to his canoe, then returned for another load. When they returned for a third load, night had overtaken them. When a sudden and ferocious storm blew in, Ordway's canoe crew of Whitehouse, Colter, Collins, and McNeal got lost in the dark and couldn't find their way back.

"We'll never find our canoe in such a black and moonless night," Ordway decided. "We're going to have to camp here and return in the morning."

They soon discovered that the wind and rain made building a fire impossible.

"Damn, this is going to be a long, miserable night without a fire, supper, or shelter," Colter groaned.

The storm worsened, lightning split the night sky, and thunder seemed to threaten the very existence of the world. Hail, driven by ferocious hurricane-force winds that uprooted old trees, brutalized the men. They searched earnestly for any kind of cover, but the best they could find in the dark was a large fallen tree. They huddled on the leeward side of the trunk as the howling wind screamed over them with frightening fury.

"God! What would you give for a warm, dry bed right now?" McNeal asked..

"A year's pay," came a laconic reply.

To survive the long, miserable, sleepless night, the men lay in spooning positions to try to draw warmth from each other. When dawn finally began to lighten the eastern sky, the forlorn group roused their wet bodies, straggled back to their canoe, and returned to the fort—only to be teased by the men who had spent the night in warm and dry bedding.

"You're so slow that you got trapped out at nightfall in the storm?" someone teased,'

Potts added to the prodding. "My grandma was slow, but she was old."

"Yeah, Old Mose, back home, was the same way, but his hair was snow white," chimed in another. More laughter.

The four men took their ribbing gracefully, but it was an experience they would never forget.

The walls of the fort were up, and some of the men began filling the chinks between the logs with clay and mud. Others worked at splitting planks and curing elk meat. Finally, the captains carried their bedrolls into their unfinished quarters as the roof was being laid on the other buildings. The men joyously carried their own gear into their new, dry sleeping quarters and built cozy fires.

"At last! A warm place to sleep and dry bedding to sleep in!" Potts exulted.

"Almost feels like we're back in civilization!" McNeal said happily as he dropped his belongings in a corner.

Seaman had made a great favorite of Shannon and followed him about more than he followed anyone, even Lewis. Seaman was also fascinated with the baby, Pomp. Sacagawea had watched Seaman carefully at first when he came to the baby. She worried that a 140-pound dog might unintentionally hurt her 20-pound baby, but Seaman was as careful in his attentions to the baby as the men in the expedition. Sacagawea finally accepted Seaman's attentions to Pomp as part of their daily routine.

Christmas, 1805, was rainy, wet, and miserable. Still, the men woke the camp with a rifle volley and a rendition of "The First Noel" to celebrate the day. Christmas dinner was elk meat that was beginning to spoil, fish that was none too fresh, and a few soggy roots. The captains distributed tobacco to the men who smoked or chewed, and handkerchiefs to the others. The men exchanged little gifts, and Sacagawea gave Captain Clark two dozen white weasel tails. The liquor was all gone, but in their dry and warm quarters, the men didn't mind.

"Hell, if I'm dry and warm and have a full belly, I'm happy<" Bratton purred.

"Well, if you throw a woman into the bargain, I'll agree with you," Shields added.

"Yeah, that's the one thing I envy Charbonneau—he's got a woman," Cruzatte said, casually spitting tobacco juice into the fire.

Fort Clatsop was two long structures facing each other and joined by palisade walls. It featured a main gate at the front and a smaller one at the rear that provided easy access to a spring some thirty yards distant. One of the structures was divided into three huts that served as the enlisted men's quarters. The other structure contained four huts: one for the captains, one for Charbonneau and his family, one for the smokehouse, and one as an orderly room. Between the buildings was a fifty-by-twenty-foot parade ground.

December 26 was another day of high winds and fierce rain. Some Indians came in the evening and informed the men that a very large fish, later identified as a whale, had washed ashore, and their squaws were bringing back oil and meat from it. Captain Lewis and three men prepared to go in a canoe to see it, but the storm became suddenly violent and they were prevented from leaving. For the next few days the men were kept busy as they cut and brought in huge logs for the palisade at the fort. The captains also bought wapato roots and dried salmon from the Indians.

December 30 was a fair morning with a little sunshine, which amazed the happy men. They finished building the palisade and the gate to the fort. A sentinel was posted and the captains told the Clatsops that when darkness fell, all visitors must leave the fort. The men built a shelter to protect the sentinel from the weather. Lewis wrote an order for the governance of the garrison that was based on principles used at United States Army frontier fortifications during the previous thirty years. First, there would at all times be a sergeant-of-the-guard and three privates on duty in the orderly room. The sergeant-of-the-guard would be responsible for the smokehouse and seeing that fires were kept burning at all times to smoke the meat. He would also check the canoes each day to make sure they were safely secured. A sentinel would be posted at the palisade both day and night.

During this last week of the year, the Corps of Discovery was visited by a young man—half-Indian, half-white—about twenty-five years old with red hair and freckles. His father was an English sailor, and he had "Jack Ramsay" tattooed on his arm. He spoke no English and had all the habits and mannerisms of the Indians, having lived with them all his life. The men in the expedition who had lain with Indian women couldn't help wondering if some day one of their own offspring might be a curiosity such as this young man.

Chapter 26

Life at Fort Clatsop

January, 1806

The men barely took time to celebrate New Year's Day, but they were grateful that the fort was finished and they had warm quarters with a roof to protect them from the constant rain. Several Indians visited the fort, offering some of the whale meat they had salvaged for sale. That afternoon two soldiers arrived at the fort from the salt camp with two barrels of salt.

Each hut at Fort Clatsop had its own cooking accessories, kettle, and fireplace, as well as an axe to provide firewood. All other tools, except those issued to John Shields on a permanent basis for his metal work, were kept in the captains' quarters. Only with their permission could the tools be borrowed, and the borrower had to return them immediately after use to prevent a trade with Indians for furs or sexual favors.

Despite the benefits of warm, dry quarters, complaints were still common. "*Mon Dieu*, this damned weather is always wet and miserable! Doesn't it ever change?" Labiche complained.

Gass added to the litany: "Yeah, it's never a biting cold, but the chill goes right through you, the sun hardly ever shines, and the insects drive you crazy!"

The daily coming and going of the Clatsops made an Indian presence in the fort routine. The Clatsops went barelegged and barefoot all year round and wore a little cape over their shoulders. The women wore short skirts made of grass that was twisted like twine. Both sexes wore hats, conic in shape and made of woven bark and grass, They were cleverly designed to cast off rain. Held in place by a chin strap, the hats seemed so practical and attractive that the captains ordered two and were so pleased with them that they ordered hats for all members of the expedition.

The captains often gave permission to a chief with a small mixed party to spend the night, and the soldiers had frequent sexual contact with the Indian women.

Clark observed, "They seem to place small value on the virtue of their women."

"Apparently, it's a cultural thing," Lewis agreed. "We've seen it before with other tribes. Our people seem to idolize our women, placing them on pedestals, but the Indians treat them as practical commodities."

Smiling, Clark responded. "I'm sure that all women would prefer our way, and all men would prefer the Indians' way. Just a difference in cultures."

Communication with the Clatsops was difficult from the beginning. The sign language of the Plains Indians didn't work with them, so the expedition learned some Clatsop words, and the Clatsops learned some English words and phrases, such as *mosquito, powder, knife, damned rascal,* and *son of a bitch.*

The Clatsops were unlike any other Indians the expedition had encountered. They were mild and cooperative, but they were tough hagglers during a trade—a consequence of long and regular contact with trading ships. If a buyer walked away, however, the seller would return the next day with a better price. The expedition engaged in a thriving trade among the various Indian villages, using colored beads as their most common unit of exchange. The Clatsops were loquacious and inquisitive, small in stature, and not built as well as the Plains Indians. The entire people smelled of smoke and fish because they slept close to the fire in their dwellings, where fish and meat were constantly drying. Their houses were dim and smoky and always smelled like fish because that was the staple of their diet. They used wooden bowls and spoons and wove large, decorated baskets, filled them with roots and seeds, and lined the walls of their houses with them.

The Clatsops were likable, easygoing, and always cheerful. Gambling appealed to them, and they loved to play games. They were extremely fond of smoking tobacco, inhaling it deeply and then slowly exhaling it through their mouths and noses. Apparently, they were unacquainted with liquor because they never asked for it.

They used bows and arrows, but their arrows were only two-and-a-half feet long, good for small game and fish, but ineffective for elk. Their method for killing elk was to trap them in deadfalls and pits. The Corps of Discovery could not have survived without the Clatsops, who provided not only critical fish and roots, but also priceless information about the location of elk herds and the availability of meat and oil from the beached whale.

Clatsop women did every kind of labor for their families. Although the women were treated poorly, the Clatsop men showed more respect for their wives' judgment and opinions than any of the other Indian tribes the Corps had encountered. Clatsop women were permitted to speak freely before their men and sometimes even appeared to command with a tone of authority. On the other hand, the men would prostitute their wives and daughters for a fish hook or a string of beads. Nevertheless, the Clatsops treated their old people with greater deference and respect than the Plains Indians.

Both the Chinooks and the Clatsops buried their dead in canoes, which they placed on a scaffold along with a paddle, furs, eating implements, and other articles. Then they fitted a larger canoe over the canoe/casket, securing it with ropes.

The soldiers had never seen better canoes that those of the Clatsops. Some of the larger ones were up to fifty feet long and could carry five tons or thirty people. Their paddles, too, were of superior design.

"People back east will never believe how intelligent and inventive these so-called "savage" are," Clark said. "They know how to adapt to their land and its weather."

"As far as I'm concerned, all the Indians we've met can cope with their environment with the most educated of mankind," Lewis agreed. "It's too bad they don't have a written language to pass on their wisdom to succeeding generations."

Life at Fort Clatsop was generally dull, and the constant rain did not help the disposition of the men. To some of them, the fort seemed more like a prison than a fort. Their main diversion was sex with the Clatsop women, which usually led to venereal disease. Men who were not out hunting spent their days scraping elk hides, making clothing, cutting firewood, keeping the fire going in the smokehouse, and carrying out other tasks that they hated and regarded as "women's work." Captain Lewis was busy writing in his journals each day as he recorded natural history and the culture of the Indians. Captain Clark worked on his maps and their journal.

There was no soap for the expedition because the pine wood the expedition burned did not produce the essential lye in the small amount of ashes it left. In making axe handles, they used wood from crabapple trees because it was so hard. And as a substitute for chewing tobacco, the men used the bark of that same tree, laughing with good nature that Cruzatte's spitting was no longer up to par.

Their menu also contributed to the monotony. Getting enough of it was no longer a worry, but getting variety into it was impossible. They lived on elk. At breakfast and supper, day after day, they ate boiled elk, dried elk, and sometimes even slightly spoiled elk. When there was fresh elk meat that could be roasted, the men gorged themselves. The meat was seldom fresh, however, because as time passed, the hunters had to extend their hunting range farther and farther away from fort. By mid-January their kills were taking place so far from the fort that the trip to go out to bring in the meat sometimes took days. The captains had to trade with the Clatsop Indians for more fish, roots, and dogs.

During the winter, Lewis discovered and documented ten new plants and trees. He collected, labeled, and preserved dozens of plants, leaves, and cones to take home. He also described many new animals—thirty-five mammals, fifty birds, ten reptiles and fish, and five invertebrates. Clark painstakingly worked on his largest map, which covered the country from the mouth of the Missouri River to Fort Clatsop. On February 11, he finally finished it.

"Here is my contribution to the world's knowledge!" he told Lewis proudly. "It's not perfect, but I'm convinced that we have found the only navigable passage across the continent of North America."

"It may not be the easy passage many want," Lewis agreed, "but the reality of geography can't be wished away—this is the only water route from the Atlantic to the Pacific—and most of the time, the land was beautiful!"

"You're right, my friend. I estimate that we have covered four thousand miles from the mouth of the Missouri to the Pacific Ocean, including all the twists and turns the various rivers gave us." Looking at the detail of his map, Clark remembered and glimpsed again the breathtaking splendor of mountains, prairies, and waterfalls.

Some of the men wanted to see the remains of the great whale that had been beached a few weeks ago, south of the expedition's salt camp. Clark volunteered to lead the group, which included Sacagawea. She had been denied at first, but she argued her case skillfully. With stumbling words and signs, she said, "I have traveled a long way with you to see the great waters and now that the monstrous fish is also to be seen, I think it is very hard that I am not permitted to see it."

Always compassionate where Janie and Pomp were concerned, Clark relented and included the two of them in the group. An Indian guide led them. At one point they climbed a high, steep hill from which they could see the ocean and shore, and Clark felt it was one of the grandest scenes he had ever beheld: the rolling blue ocean extending farther than the eye could see and rhythmic waves tipped with white foam, gently caressing the beach.

By the time the group reached the whale, the Indians tribes had already stripped off the meat, leaving only the bones. The soldiers measured the skeleton and announced that it was one hundred and five feet long. They traded with the local Indians for three hundred pounds of whale meat and oil, and the men were delighted to have a new food to vary their daily diet of elk. They found the whale blubber to be tender, with a slightly sweet taste that they liked.

Hugh McNeal had become comfortable and complacent with the constant presence of Clatsop Indians in the fort every day, and he decided to go to a nearby Clatsop village alone and unarmed. A friendly person, he wanted to make some new friends among the easy-going Clatsops. He met a young brave who seemed to fit the bill, a strapping young man about twenty years old.

"Hello," the Indian signaled to McNeal.

"Hello," McNeal responded with a nod of his head, smiling broadly and offering to shake hands with the young man.

An Indian woman was watching the encounter.

"Come with me," the young brave gestured.

McNeal raised his eyebrows and gestured palms up. "Where to?"

The young brave smiled mischievously and formed an hourglass figure with his hands. McNeal smiled, pulling at his nose from habit. The brave took him by the arm and motioned to a stand of trees outside the village as he looked at the blanket McNeal had slung over his shoulder. McNeal had brought the blanket as an object to trade if he found something in the village he wanted. The Clatsop woman, who had continued to watch the unfolding scene, now turned and ran toward Fort Clatsop.

McNeal went with the young brave, thinking he might have found a pleasant purchase for his blanket. When they reached the stand of trees, the Indian motioned toward something deeper in the woods. McNeal peered in the direction indicated and then turned back to the brave to ask where he meant. McNeal was stunned! The brave had raised his tomahawk and was preparing to crash it into McNeal's head. McNeal's heart leaped as he instinctively grabbed the Indian's arm holding the tomahawk, deflecting the blow. McNeal tried to twist the brave's arm as he wrestled him to the ground. The Indian fought fiercely to free his arm and strike McNeal with the tomahawk. All the physical exertion of the past two years began to pay off for McNeal as he proved the stronger of the two. Still, the Indian fought savagely to kill him.

Suddenly, they were being pulled apart by Captain Clark and three other soldiers from the fort. The young brave glared at the Indian woman who had observed the meeting of the two men and had left immediately for the soldiers' fort. The woman, guessing that the young brave was luring McNeal into the woods to kill him and take his blanket, had run swiftly to bring soldiers to save his life.

McNeal thanked his rescuers and the woman profusely, and he gave the blanket to her as a reward. The woman, surprised and pleased, rushed into the village to show the reward to her friends.

CHAPTER 27

Homeward Bound

March. 1806

Excitement in Fort Clatsop was mounting each day as the Corps of Discovery began making plans to start the homeward trek. The captains checked the ammunition. Four pounds of powder was encased in each eight-pound lead canister. The canisters would be used to make lead minnie balls—a system Lewis had devised back in Pittsburgh.

"That was an ingenious method you invented," Clark told him as they finished the inventory of the expedition's supplies.

"Thanks. It has worked out well. And it looks like we have plenty of ammunition to get us back home safely," Lewis responded as Clark made notations in their journal.

Rain continued daily, and winter on the Pacific Coast brought strong winds, heavy clouds, and crashing tides. At night, the Corps' prized Indian canoe broke loose and floated away. Sergeant Gass discovered its loss when he checked the moorings at daybreak. Losing that canoe would be a considerable loss because it was so well made and so lightweight that four men could carry it on their shoulders a mile or more without resting. It could carry up to fifteen hundred pounds of supplies along with three men. Captain Clark sent seven men to search for it and also to retrieve elk meat the hunters had killed and dressed the day before. Toward evening, the men returned with the meat but without the canoe. Next day three men were sent out to find the missing canoe, but failed. Evidently it had floated far out of the area. On the third day, Sergeant Gass and a party of five determined men set out to find the canoe and finally spotted it trapped in a marsh.

"Good work, men," Lewis said with relief. "We damned sure can't afford to lose that canoe."

Two men from the salt camp arrived at the fort to report illness there. "Gibson and Bratton are very sick, Captain Lewis," Henry Cooper said with obvious concern.

"What's wrong with them?"

"We have no idea."

"Sergeant Pryor, take five men and a canoe and bring those two men back to the fort," Lewis ordered. "Leave two men there to replace them."

By nightfall, Pryor's group carried in the two ailing soldiers wrapped in blankets. Lewis and Clark spent the night trying to diagnose the men's ailments. Administering laudanum and Glauber salts, they managed to make the men comfortable enough to sleep through the night, and by morning both men were a little better.

Candlefish—another species new to science—began to run in immense numbers in the numerous waterways. The Clatsops netted them and brought them to the fort to sell to the captains.

"What are these, and what would we do with them?" Lewis asked. "They're too small to provide anybody with a meal."

The fish were only seven inches long, but the Clatsops insisted they were good food.

"How do you cook them?" Lewis inquired.

One Clatsop took a dozen candlefish and gutted them, then built a fire and strung the fish on a spit over the fire. When they were roasted, he handed one to Lewis.

The captain accepted the fish with low expectations and finished it off in three bites. "Say! These are really good!"

The Indians smiled and nodded as Lewis passed the remaining candlefish to curious men around him. Their approval came with smiles and nods. The sale was completed and roast candlefish became a welcome relief from the monotony of elk meat for all meals.

To the captains, the health of the men was becoming a major concern. Someone was always down with a cold, the flu, a venereal disease, or strained muscles. Lewis could treat their health conditions, but he could do nothing about their diet, the climate with its endless rain, or boredom from monotony of camp life.

There was a bright spot in February, however. On Pomp's first birthday, Captain Clark made a "birthday cake" from Indian bread, and all the men gathered around the baby, wishing him a happy birthday. Clark had carved a little toy horse as a gift, and some of the other men had made similar toys for the occasion. Seaman, sensing that something out of the ordinary was happening, inspected every toy at great length while the men laughed and patted him affectionately. Sacagawea showed Pomp his gifts, explaining each as though he could understand her words. He gleefully waved his fat little arms and jabbered as if he knew what the occasion was, his dark eyes sparkling with excitement.

"It's too bad he won't remember this, Janie," Clark said.

"But we will," Sacagawea smiled.

Bratton became much worse, suffering great pain in his back. Lewis prepared a liniment from alcohol, camphor, and castile soap and rubbed Bratton's back thoroughly and carefully. Then he bathed and massaged Bratton's feet to help with circulation. Nothing seemed to help.

With spring finally approaching, the men hauled their canoes out of the water and corked and pitched them. Drouillard went to the nearest Clatsop village to try to buy another Indian canoe for their journey home, set to begin March 23. Drouillard returned not only with a canoe but with the Indians who sold it to him.

"They want to stay in the fort tonight," he told Captain Clark.

Lewis, walking up at that moment, said, "Well, if that will get us the canoe, they're welcome."

Unfortunately, by morning the Clatsops had changed their minds about selling the canoe.'

"Damn!" Lewis exclaimed. "We desperately need another one of their excellent canoes. Our dugouts just don't measure up. Drouillard, take some men to another village and see if you can buy one of theirs."

But Drouillard's quests in other villages were also unsuccessful.

When the old hag showed up again with her six young girls to barter their sexual services, the captains called all the men together.

Lewis spoke. "These are the same women who gave many of you venereal diseases last fall." Surveying the faces of the many men he had treated, he added, "I'm asking you now to have nothing more to do with them because we can't afford to have you getting sick again. Besides, you want to be healthy when we get home." Faces lit up at the very thought of being home again. The men agreed, and the disappointed old bawd left the fort with her girls.

The men continued to repair their canoes and goods for departure, even as the weather continued to bring rain, hail, thunder, and lightning. Upon inspecting the vessels available for their return journey, Lewis frowned.

"Clark, somehow or other we've got to get another of those Clatsop canoes," Lewis said with real concern. "Our dugout canoes are just too heavy and awkward to fight the current on the Columbia River."

"Well, I have an idea, but you may not like it." He glanced at his friend and raised his eyebrows. "We've tried every way possible to buy one, and the Indians—even our friends—refuse to sell us one."

"You're right, I'm sorry to say."

"I'd hate to do it, but we might have to steal one, Meriwether."

Shocked, Lewis looked at his co-commander with surprise. A moment of consideration followed. "Our return trip will be one of scarcity and uncertainty," Lewis said. "We don't have enough canoes that can deal with the Columbia River current and to carry all our supplies. Getting another of their canoes is crucial to our survival—it may mean the difference between arriving home with all our team and our records or bemoaning their loss to the river."

Clark was contemplating the possibilities. "Well," he said, "we won't be back this way. We'll never see the Clatsops again."

"If it's a matter of the success or failure of our mission, I think we can justify stealing one canoe. We have to have one. I just hate to ruin the good relations we have built with the Clatsops."

Clark brightened. "We can give them Fort Clatsop as compensation," he suggested.

"Excellent idea! What could we do with it anyway?" Lewis was smiling.

Four men were dispatched that day to travel to a distant Clatsop village down the coast, far from the fort, where they stole a Clatsop canoe. They brought it back and hid it until departure of the Corps of Discovery. The fort would be given to the nearby Clatsops.

"Sergeant Ordway, take six men and go close down the salt camp," Lewis instructed as the departure date drew near. "Bring back the men working there and everything else of value."

When Ordway set out, he decided to save time by going directly overland instead of by canoe. Shortly after leaving the fort, however, his detachment was struck by a sudden, fierce storm. The wind blew stinging, freezing rain into the men's faces, and thunder, lightning, and high wind tormented them further. They came across an abandoned Indian lodge and decided to spend the night in it.

"Gather some wood and let's build a fire and try to dry out our wet clothes," Ordway shouted above the roaring wind.

They built a fire, cooked some elk meat, and settled down to spend a comfortable night indoors while the storm raged outside.

"I'm really glad to be going home," Shannon said to no one in particular. "Sitting inside with a warm fire and a full belly while the goldarn wind and thunder threaten outside makes me think of home. I miss it. I guess I'm homesick for my folks and my own bed."

McNeal was sitting on the floor close to the fire. "For sure, it will be good to get out of this damned climate with constant rain where everything mildews and smells musty," he said. He pulled absent-mindedly at his nose and added, "I just can't wait to get started!"

At morning light, wind from the northwest continued to blow fiercely into their faces as they struggled toward the salt camp. When they reached the coast, the storm had churned the ocean into huge waves that crashed violently against the shore. The men, a desolate group, walked along the coast with the storm driving into them head-on until they finally reached the salt camp.

"God! Are we ever glad to get here!" Ordway exclaimed as he greeted the salt crew. The men entered the hut, slapping their dripping hats against their legs and hands to dislodge the rain. "I made a big mistake by deciding to come overland."

"Come on in and get warm and dry," Gass greeted his comrades from the fort. "No one should be out in this weather—it isn't fit for man or beast."

"Or plants either," Ordway added.

The group enjoyed the camaraderie as well as a comfortable night while the storm blew outside. In the morning Ordway's party and the men from the salt camp returned to the fort by canoes, loaded with supplies.

The captains checked and double-checked supplies for the return trip, especially rifles and ammunition, their only means of hunting and defending themselves on their two-thousand-miles trip through Indian country. In the past three months the men had made 368 pairs of moccasins for the return journey. They wanted to be sure to avoid the discomfort and danger of being barefoot when rocks and nettles were underfoot.

The Corps of Discovery was desperately poor now, starting for home with only a handful of trading items to barter for food when necessary. They had one red robe and six blue ones, Clark's one uniform coat and hat, five robes made from a large flag, and a few other lightweight clothes. They had supplies and trading goods buried in their caches along the Missouri River, if those items had not been discovered and stolen.

Drouillard came down with a pain in his side, much like pleurisy, and Captain Clark bled him. Several other men were also ill. Bratton remained very weak and had lost so much weight that Lewis worried about his recovery. The captains hoped the men would be in better health on the homeward trip than they had been in the unhealthy climate at Fort Clatsop.

Lewis gave several Clatsop chiefs a list of the names of all the people in the Corps of Discovery to provide proof they had crossed the continent and had arrived at the Pacific Ocean. Proof of this accomplishment could be needed in the future to certify that the United States owned the right of discovery to establish ownership and settlement.

Before starting their return journey at noon on March 23, the captains held a formal ceremony to present Fort Clatsop to the nearby Clatsop people. They called together all the members of the Corps of Discovery and invited the local Clatsop village.

"To honor the friendship of the Clatsop people and our people, I bestow Fort Clatsop upon your village," Captain Lewis announced. "We have lived among you and have grown fond of you. We will always consider you our friends. We wish you well in the future."

The chief of the local village stepped forward and shook Lewis's hand.

"We are sorry to see you go," he signed. "We have been good friends. We wish you good fortune on your journey."

It was a touching moment for the Indians and the members of the expedition as both parties recalled their mutual support and friendship. The soldiers, however, were excited and eager to begin their long trip. After a short prayer by Captain Clark calling upon God's blessing and protection, the Corps of Discovery began its return voyage in three large canoes and two small ones.

The Columbia River was very high from the long season of constant rain, and progress was difficult. They hadn't gone far when they saw the old bawd and her six girls, who had come in a canoe carrying the skin of a sea otter, dried fish, and hats for sale in addition to an offer of the girls' services. The captains bought the skin only, and with a strong breeze from the southwest, the men set out in high spirits.

Paddling up the Columbia River against the current and high waves was a real challenge—worse than the entry on the Missouri had been so long ago. Just as with the Missouri, they had to tow the canoes at the rapids and portage around the falls. They passed several Indian villages and were frequently joined by a fleet of canoes filled with Indians who stayed with them for several miles, evidently looking them over. The expedition camped on Quicksand River and remained a day or so to make celestial observations and to hunt—but game was scarce.

White cedars were plentiful here, and vast stands were stripped of their bark, indicating that Indians had been there during the past few months. As days passed, finding adequate food became a real problem, as were multitudes of Indians along the entire length of the Columbia River who observed them with unsettling curiosity.

Drouillard communicated with passing Indians in sign language and reported to Clark, "Captain, the Indians all say that the people up river are starving, and the salmon won't begin to run for another month."

"That's bad news," Clark told Lewis. "We know there will be no game in the mountains."

"I think we'd better stop for a few days and try to lay in enough meat to last at least until we get to the mountains," Lewis responded.

Men who were not hunting collected wood to make a scaffold on which to smoke the meat. Some of the meat was cut into thin strips to be smoked and dried. Natives descending the river stopped to visit the expedition camp, scavenging bones and little pieces of gristle the soldiers had thrown away. One Indian was brash and foolish enough to try to forcibly wrest a tomahawk from John Colter, who looked like the smallest of all the soldiers. The brave had unknowingly chosen one of the toughest of the soldiers, however, and Colter soundly thrashed him. The Indians constantly loitered near the expedition until Lewis decided it was time to get rid of them.

"Sergeant Ordway, set up a target. Let's have a little target practice and see if we can motivate these people to leave us alone," he ordered.

Ordway selected the five best shots in the Corps and demonstrated their expertise with firearms. The Indians left immediately. As the expedition worked its way up the river, however, more Indians were always present and ready to steal anything left unguarded even for an instant, forcing the captains to detail guards to protect the supplies. The expedition had not yet left stormy weather behind, and twice the crashing tide forced them to move their camp to higher ground.

"Damn this weather and the thieving Indians!" Lewis muttered one evening with uncharacteristic disgust.

"Be patient, Meriwether," Clark counseled. "We'll be rid of both soon."

The Corps stopped at an Indian village long enough to buy wapato roots and fish, then proceeded to the mouth of a river, where they camped. Clark sent six hunters ahead to Deer Island while the rest of the men brought the small canoes into camp to repair them.

Next morning, the expedition encountered a large Indian village of joined huts and stayed three hours while Clark bought dogs and wapato roots from them. Then the expedition proceeded to an abandoned Indian village, where they camped. Local Indians visited them. Their women, instead of wearing the straw-and-bark skirts of the Clatsops and Chinooks, wore a soft leather breach cloth and nothing more.

The next day the river rose so high that the roaring tide could not affect it. The expedition passed two Indian villages on a large island that was twenty-five miles long, partly timbered, and partly open prairie with surrounding countryside that was low and level. They passed an Indian village that had been large and heavily populated when they passed it last fall, but now the Indians were scattered up and down the river, and only two lodges remained in the village.

"I wonder what happened to them," Clark mused.

"I would guess that some disease struck the village," Lewis said as he recalled the large community and the activity they had seen here previously.

CHAPTER 28

Gratitude to Indian Friends

May, 1806

Through high plains, near river bottoms where cottonwood trees grew in dense stands, the expedition continued toward the mountains. Heavily timbered country was visible in the southeast, and after traveling twenty-six miles, the expedition camped where water was abundant. The next morning, one of the horses was missing, and men went out in different directions to search for it. Colter returned to where they had stopped to eat yesterday, and there he met a Walla Walla Indian preparing to return the horse to them.

"I'm bringing your horse," the Indian signed.

Colter nodded and smiled, not knowing enough sign language to respond. The Indian had an open, pleasant countenance that inspired Colter's friendly response. He motioned for the Indian to follow him back to camp where the captains rewarded his kindness with a tomahawk and a knife.

The Corps continued through this high country, with mountains that were filled with timber and partly covered with snow on their right. Pushing forward to the forks of the Missouri River, they came upon an Indian chief they had met last fall, in the company of several other Indians.

"We are happy to see you!" Lewis had Drouillard signal the chief as the two parties met.

"We thought we would never see you again," the chief signed. "We thought you had perished."

"We are very much alive," Lewis assured him with a smile. The captains decided to stop and smoke with the chief to renew good relations with his tribe.

As the expedition continued to ascend the high plains, they came to a small Indian village where they bought root bread, fresh fish, and two dogs before pressing onward. That afternoon they came to another Indian village where they bought one dog and camped for the night. Next morning they moved on to the mouth of the Kooskooskee River and saw many horses on the high plains. Indian villages dotted the area and the Corps of Discovery camped near a group they had met last fall. This village had little to eat, and no food was for sale. Their women were pounding roots to make cakes in preparation for their own crossing of the mountains. Several inhabitants came to the captains for medical treatment, promising to give them a horse in payment. As with the other Indian villages they had encountered on the way west, Clark had gained a reputation as an effective doctor.

"Please stay with us two or three days and help our people," their chief signaled. A native brought the horse they had promised, which the men immediately slaughtered for supper.

Two days later, the expedition finally set out again, proceeding up a rocky road along the Kooskooskee River and camping near a distant village. Here an Indian came to them with two canisters of powder his dog had dug up from the cache the Corps had buried last October. Impressed with the honesty of the brave, the captains rewarded him with a few trinkets. The mountains loomed before them, and this Indian shared unwelcome news.

"Snow has been very heavy," he told the captains through Drouillard. "The mountains won't be passable until at least June."

"Lord! I hope he's wrong," Lewis groaned to Clark.

The captains dreaded crossing the mountains again, unable to forget the cold and hunger of their first crossing. They particularly hated to stop their progress now because they knew that beyond the mountains were buffalo hump and tongue, Charbonneau's *boudin blanc* sausage, and their caches containing tobacco, tools, and kettles. The men had been dreaming for weeks about feasting on buffalo, and with this news, morale began to sink.

Then the expedition encountered Chief Cut Nose, with a hunting party of braves from a branch of the Nez Perce. They had not met this chief last fall, but they had heard about him. He was a stocky man in his forties with a pleasant smile and disposition.

"We are happy to meet you!" Lewis had Drouillard signal to him. "We have been told many good things about you."

Chief Cut Nose, smiling broadly, signed, "My people have told me many good things about you."

He was a more important chief than their old friend, Twisted Hair, whom they met next with another half dozen braves. It was Twisted Hair with whom they had left their horses last fall, but he now greeted the expedition coolly, which greatly puzzled the captains.

"I wonder what's wrong." Lewis muttered to Clark.

"I don't know, but I hope it doesn't bode ill for us," Clark answered. "It doesn't look good."

For twenty minutes, Cut Nose and Twisted Hair shouted at each other and gestured angrily. Lewis and Clark did not know what was going on, but they knew they needed the friendship of both chiefs. They also needed to recover the horses they had left with Twisted Hair and the caches hidden in the area. As the expedition moved forward, the two Indian factions fell in behind them, staying a distance apart from each other.

When it came time to stop for the day, the two small bands of Indians made separate camps. The captains decided to call a council to try to calm the situation. A Shoshone teenager was with Cut Nose, and they asked him to be interpreter for the meeting because he could converse with Sacagawea as well as both chiefs. However, the young man refused because he did not want to be caught between the two antagonistic chiefs. Without an interpreter, the captains gave up the idea of a meeting, and everyone returned to separate camps.

Lewis was worried. "Damn! This dispute must be resolved. It could cripple our mission."

"You're right," Clark agreed. "Not only might the Indians blame us for their discord, turning both chiefs against us, but we also need our horses and supplies before we enter the mountains."

Lewis said, "Let's wait until Drouillard returns from hunting so he can sign for us."

When Drouillard returned, the captains invited Twisted Hair for a smoke. He accepted and explained to Drouillard that when he returned from guiding the Corps last fall, he collected the expedition's horses and took charge of them, as they had agreed. Cut Nose then returned from his war excursion and asserted his primary leadership among the Nez Perce. He said that Twisted Hair should not have accepted responsibility for the expedition's horses. He claimed that as leader, he, Cut Nose, should be in charge of the white men's horses. Consequently, the horses scattered, but many of them were with Chief Broken Arm, a chief of great eminence whose village was up river.

Then the captains invited Cut Nose to join their campfire. He told the captains, in the presence of Twisted Hair, that Twisted Hair was two-faced and had never taken care of the horses. Instead, he had allowed his young men to ride and misuse them. This is the reason, he insisted, that he had forbidden Twisted Hair to be responsible for the horses.

"We will go to Broken Arm's camp in the morning and see how many horses and saddles we can collect," Lewis had Drouillard sign.

This plan was satisfactory to the two chiefs, who calmed down considerably after being able to tell their respective sides of the story. The next day, everyone moved to Broken Arm's lodge, which was one-hundred-and-fifty feet long and built of sticks, mud, and grass. It contained twenty-four campfires and twice that many families.

"I have twenty-one of your horses and about half the saddles," Broken Arm signed. "Twisted Hair must find and bring in the rest of the horses and saddles."

Lewis paid Twisted Hair one rifle, a hundred musket balls, and two pounds of powder for his services to this point and told him that the other promised rifle would be paid when he brought in the rest of the horses and saddles.

Broken Arm had erected a large conic lodge of leather and laid a supply of wood at the door. He signaled that the captains should make the lodge their home while they were visiting him. Various other chiefs arrived at Broken Arm's village to visit him. Next morning, the captains' lodge was crowded with sleeping Indians, including Broken Arm. Many were strangers, so Captain Lewis explained the United States to them and drew a map for them. All this had to go through the translation chain and took half a day.

One of Lewis's goals was to convince the Indians to send guides and peacemakers with the Corps of Discovery to Blackfoot country. He had promised the Nez Perce that he would make peace between their two peoples so that the Nez Perce could move to the buffalo-hunting side of the great dividing ridge. Lewis no longer referred to the Indians as President Jefferson's children or to Jefferson as their father in his speeches—he had learned a great deal of respect for these people. He asked that as many as three chiefs accompany the soldiers back to Washington to meet the President. Lewis showed them his spyglass, compass, watch, and the air gun, which were all amazements to them.

The chiefs seemed pleased by his invitation to meet the President, but said they would have to consult among themselves. The next day, the chiefs told the captains they had decided to accept the invitation, but they also needed the approval of their people. Broken Arm held a plebiscite of sorts. He cooked a huge pot of pounded roots and soup, and then he gave a speech. He announced the chiefs' decision to do as the white men wished, and then he asked all those who agreed to come forward and eat. Those who were opposed should not eat. There was no dissenting vote.

What the Nez Perce agreed to, however, was not exactly what Lewis had asked for. The Indians said they were willing to move east of the mountains—but only after the United States Army had built a fort on the Missouri River where they could trade for arms and ammunition in order to defend themselves against the Blackfoot tribes. As for sending a delegate to the Blackfoot, they thought not. As for sending a delegation to the President, they said maybe after the army fort had been built east of the mountains.

The captains told the Indians of their wish to camp where they could fish, hunt, and graze their horses until the snow in the mountains melted enough to allow them to continue. The chiefs also warned that it was too soon to think of crossing the mountains. Snow in the passes would be much too deep, and there would be no grass for the horses for at least another three weeks.

"This is very disappointing!" Lewis said to Clark. "This is a delay that I would never have expected in May."

Chief Broken Arm approached the captains with a gift. "I give you two fat colts," he signed, obviously apologizing that the other two chiefs were still at odds with each other, creating a bad impression of the Nez Perce. The captains accepted his gift with sincere appreciation and then led the expedition to Twisted Hair's village to get most of the remaining horses.

The high plains leading into the mountains contained rich soil filled with camas, wild onions, and other roots that provided most of the food that sustained the Indians at this time of year. The weather turned cold, rainy, and windy. Then the wind slackened, and the rain turned to snow.

By morning, six inches had accumulated, and the Corps of Discovery gathered their horses and set out, traveling over open, treeless plains. They descended a steep hill into a valley, crossed a creek, and camped that evening near a village of Cut Nose's tribe, a village of about fifteen lodges. The natives hoisted their American flag and appeared happy to see the expedition. Although they had little food, they served the men camas roots and dried fish. They had many horses and gave two to the men to butcher for food, one of which the men slaughtered immediately because they had not eaten all day. Some of the squaws pitched a buffalo-hide lodge, brought wood, and made a fire. The chiefs invited the captains to stay in the lodge. A number of Indians came from neighboring villages to see the members of the Corps of Discovery, and during the evening Cruzatte played his fiddle and the men danced.

When the expedition departed next morning, the snow had melted in the valley but remained on the hills and high plains. Cottonwood and chokecherry trees abounded along the creek, and a scattering of pine trees grew on the edges of the hills. The day was cold, but the sun was shining and spring was in the air. The expedition, now with sixty horses, followed a stream that was about fifteen yards wide and led to a heavily timbered plain four miles away. The expedition was now as close to the mountains as it dared go until the snow melted in the passes.

"This is the place Cut Nose recommended," Lewis announced. "Sergeant Pryor, get some men and take our supplies over to the other side of the river. Sergeant Gass, take as many men as you need and swim the horses across the river."

The Clearwater River at this point was rapid and one-hundred-and-fifty yards wide. When all the horses, supplies, and men were safely on the opposite shore, they moved downstream to a location that had been an old habitation of the Indians. It was an excellent location for defense. Here the surface was sunken about four feet into the earth, fronted by a wall of earth rising almost four feet above ground level. The spot was about thirty feet in diameter. The men placed supplies into the sunken area and began to construct their own shelter, using willow poles and prairie grass around the shelter.

The soldiers built a bower for the captains because their old leather lodge had rotted and become unfit for use. They erected an old sail over the bower for protection against rain. Their new camp was within forty paces of the river, located in an extensive bottom covered with pine trees. The men put their goods out to dry in the sun, and Captain Lewis recorded the latitude and longitude of the location. There was good hunting and plenty of grazing for the horses. They called the place Clearwater River Camp. The soldiers also established a hunting camp several miles away, and the captains sent five men to build a canoe for fishing and for crossing the river when necessary.

Snow was still many feet deep near the base of the mountains. Clark commented that they had spring, summer, and winter all within twenty miles of the camp. As the Corps of Discovery waited for the passes to clear, Lewis and Clark practiced medicine. Every morning, their Indian patients came to Clearwater River Camp, lining up for treatment. The captains used eyewash for sore eyes and hot rubdowns for rheumatism and similar ailments. One case was particularly difficult. An old chief had been suffering from paralysis and was unable to move his arms or legs. Yet he ate well, digested his food normally, had a clear mind and a good pulse. He also retained a strong-looking body. Nothing the captains did or tried eased his paralysis.

"Captain, I have seen paralysis cured by sweating," John Shields suggested as he chewed on the ever-present twig.

Deciding to give sweating a try, Lewis directed a small sweat-lodge to be built and heated stones placed inside. The chief went into the lodge naked, with a bucket of water to sprinkle on the hot stones to create steam. After twenty minutes of sweating, he was taken out and plunged into the frigid river. It worked! The chief regained the use of his hands and arms immediately and soon even his legs and feet began to function. Lewis's reputation now was legendary among the Nez Perce Indians, and the captains' medical practice became responsible for creating a continuing food supply for the Corps.

The food acquired through barter for medical treatment was roots and fish, but the captains knew that their men could not subsist on such a diet. Captain Lewis offered to trade a horse that was worn down but would recover for a young horse they could slaughter for meat.

"Our men are not accustomed to living on roots alone and must have meat to keep up their strength," he explained.

"No trade," the chief signaled. "Take whatever you want from our herd for your food."

The captains were stunned by the generous offer. This was greater goodwill than what they would expect even from their own countrymen back East.

The Indians asked the captains to repeat the sweat treatment for the lame chief in hopes of curing him further. The captains could not make him sweat as much as they wished, but they gave him laudanum, which calmed him, enabling him to rest comfortably. The next day, he was much better, and the captains asked that he remain at Clearwater River Camp so they could continue the sweat baths.

Sacagawea worked at laying in a supply of fennel roots to help see them over the Rocky Mountains. The expedition was out of trading goods to use as currency, but the captains discovered that brass buttons were items the Indians prized. Lewis and Clark both cut the brass buttons from their dress uniforms and traded for three bushels of roots. Because so many Indians had sore eyes, the captains put eye wash into vials and used them as currency also.

Three hunters crossed the river and returned with three bears and several prairie hens. They gave the Indians some of the bear meat because the Nez Perce had been so generous to them. From the bears, the men stored five gallons of oil in a keg for their journey over the mountains.

"Captain," Ordway said to Clark one day, "what would you say to butchering a couple of those stallions that are always giving us so much trouble? It seems to me that we could solve two problems at the same time. We really don't need sixty horses."

"Ordway, I can see why you're a sergeant," Clark responded genially. "I think that's a damned smart idea!"

Before the day was over, the stallions were butchered and being smoked over a large, slow fire.

The captains decided now that each man should make his own deal for roots to see him over the mountains. Each man was given one awl, one knitting pin, a half-ounce of vermilion, two needles, a few spools of thread, and about a yard of ribbon as trading goods. The captains comforted themselves now with the knowledge that they had enough horses for travel and food to sustain them when they crossed the mountains.

Pomp was cutting teeth and running a fever. His neck was also swollen. As Sacagawea watched, Captain Lewis gave him a dose of cream of tartar and applied a warm poultice of boiled onions to his neck. The child was understandably fussy and crying. Sacagawea cooed and soothed him as much as she could. Even Seaman seemed concerned and inspected the baby several times throughout the day.

Private William Bratton had been virtually disabled with a mysterious ailment that had all but paralyzed him for some time, and Lewis decided to try Shields' sweat treatment on him. Bratton was subjected to twenty minutes of sweating, then taken out and plunged into the cold river, and immediately returned to the sweat hole for forty-five minutes, during which time he drank large amounts of horsemint tea. He was soon walking again.

Chapter 29

DANGEROUS TRAILS

June, 1806

Captain Clark had an idea and smiled as he approached Captain Lewis. "Meriwether, we have seen that the young Indian braves are fond of games and gambling, just as our young soldiers are. Why don't we sponsor some athletic competitions for them? I think it would be entertaining as well as challenging."

"That's an excellent idea!" Lewis said immediately. "It will stave off boredom as we wait for the mountain snows to melt, and it will also keep them fit and out of trouble." Both leaders were enthusiastic and began to lay plans for the games. There would be foot races, target shooting, horseback riding, and feats of strength.

The young men of the Corps and the local villages were eager and excited as they gathered to participate in the contests. Each man had a favorite event that he thought he could win, but they all participated in all events, and victories were pretty evenly distributed among both sides. One of the most hotly contested games was a shooting match that Captain Lewis finally won with two hits at two-hundred-and-twenty yards, greatly impressing the Indians. But when it came to horseback riding, the Nez Perce put the soldiers to shame. They did feats that the soldiers could only gasp at and admire. Clearly, the braves had spent their lives on horseback, learning movements of daring that only very reckless young men would even attempt. While galloping at full speed, they hid themselves on the far side of their horses and shot arrows accurately from under their horses' necks. Members of the Corps cheered and shouted approval from the sidelines.

The soldiers pitted the speed of their horses against each other and against the Indians. The two competitive groups raced from point to point over a pleasant green valley with beautiful snow-capped mountains looming behind them, while crowds of onlookers cheered them on. Horses—their care, training, trading, and racing—bonded the white and red men. These exciting events provided an experience that both groups of men would remember fondly.

The soldiers were interested to learn that Indian saddles were made of wood that was jointed and covered with freshly killed animal skin. When the skin dried, it bound every part of the saddle tightly, keeping the joints in place. A buffalo robe thrown over the wooden saddle softened the ride.

Every day now, members of the Corps of Discovery watched the snow on the mountains to see if it had receded. It was June, a time for snow in the lower passes to be gone, but the snow seemed immovable in the heights.

"Snowfall last winter was more than normal," Cut Nose signed. "It might be July before you can leave."

"God! I hope he's wrong," Clark told Lewis.

When the river began to rise in the valley, the soldiers were optimistic because it meant that the snow in the mountains was melting at last. All the men except the hunters and wood cutters made pack saddles and prepared loads of provisions for their anticipated departure. Captain Lewis spent his time compiling a list of the native tribes they had met in the lands west of the Rocky Mountains. He estimated that they had encountered a total of 80,000 people of the tribes.

Private Frazier was fascinated with trying to learn the Nez Perce language. "I think if I stayed six months, I could learn to speak it," he told Sergeant Ordway.

"You do show a talent for it," Ordway responded. "I think you could do it."

Stallions in the expedition's herd became so troublesome that the captains offered to trade two of them for one of the Indian geldings. When the Indians refused, the captains decided they must undertake the risky procedure of castrating the stallions. When Drouillard and some assistants began the operation, a young Indian watched the procedure.

"We do it a different way," he signed to Drouillard.

"How do you do it?" Drouillard asked.

"We let the wound bleed openly instead of tying off the sac."

As an experiment, the captains had him castrate two of their stallions the Indian way while Drouillard did two the white man's way. The Indian way proved superior.

The greatest asset of each Nez Perce village in this area was its vast herd of horses. An individual Nez Perce might own fifty to a hundred head of horses.

"You know, their horses could be a source of economic profit to them in ways they can't imagine," Lewis speculated to Clark. "They could actually make up for the lack of a commercially navigable water route across the continent by creating large trains of packhorses to carry spices and other desirable goods from the Far East and California to the United States, and the reverse: mercantile goods from the United States and Europe back to California."

"I guess I'd classify that as an ambitious plan for white men," Clark responded doubtfully. "I'd be very surprised if it would interest the Indians. Besides, that would require a permanent peace between the Nez Perce and the Blackfoot, which seems very unlikely to me."

"I'd like to think it could be possible, with such large profits to be made," Lewis added.

"I don't know, Meriweather. The Indians place much more importance on bravery in battle than on wealth. They'd have to give up that aspect of their culture, which I doubt they'd be willing to do."

Lewis considered his friend's comments and slowly nodded his head.

In his journal, Lewis described new plants and wildlife of the area. He wrote lengthy descriptions of a black woodpecker and the western tanager. He collected and described nearly fifty new plants, such as the mariposa lily, yellow bells, purple trillium, and ragged robin. In spring these wildflowers grew in abundant patches of color, dotting the landscape under the warming blue skies.

When Lewis learned that the Indians had sent a teenaged boy alone over the mountains to Traveler's Rest to ask the Flatheads what winter had done to the eastern side of the mountains, he was ecstatic.

"If a boy can cross the mountains, so can we!" he insisted, and went with Drouillard to tell Chief Cut Nose.

"No. It is too soon," Cut Nose told him. "One boy who knows the trail can do it, but thirty men who do not know the trail and have sixty horses to feed cannot do it. The creeks are not yet high, the trails are covered with fifteen feet of snow, and there is not enough grass for your horses. Be patient and wait."

But Lewis was not patient, and he had made up his mind.

"Will you send some guides with us?" Lewis asked Cut Nose and Twisted Hair.

The chiefs stalled, very reluctant to agree. They conferred with each other.

Finally, they signaled, "We do not want to be responsible for your deaths."

Later, Lewis talked with Clark. "Clark, if a fifteen-year-old boy can get through the mountains, I know we can, too!"

"But what the chiefs said makes sense, Meriwether," Clark insisted. "We must remember our starving time when we crossed the mountains during the trip west, which I doubt any of us will ever forget. It's a very dangerous crossing."

"But we can do it!" Lewis insisted. Nothing more was said.

Lewis inspected the men's packs and decided that the expedition had enough dried meat, bread, and roots to make the trip. In addition, they had enough horses that they could afford to butcher some if necessary.

"I know we can do it," Lewis kept insisting confidently.

Clark wondered briefly if it might be time to assume sole command, as he and Lewis had discussed earlier, but he quickly put the thought out of his mind.

The men prepared their supplies and pack saddles for departure. First, the captains planned to move their camp eastward from the banks of the Clearwater River to higher ground where they had first met the Nez Perce the preceding September. There, they would make final preparations for their challenge to the mountains. The captains sent out hunters every day and directed the men to cut the venison into thin strips to dry in the sun. This jerky would be tasty and nourishing.

Before they departed for the new camp, the captains held a farewell party with the Nez Perce at the Clearwater River Camp they had occupied for nearly a month. The festive afternoon featured horse and foot races and games. In the evening, Cruzatte's fiddle came out and the dancing began to the tunes of "Rye Whiskey," "My Love Is But a Lassie," "Jefferson and Liberty," and others. As the festivities continued, the worried chiefs tried to convince Lewis that the snow was still too deep, and they would not be able to cross the mountains until the beginning of July.

"Your horses will be too long without food," they cautioned.

Even when the Indian boy who had tried to cross the mountains alone returned and reported that he had been forced back by heavy snow, Lewis still insisted on leaving. He was absolutely convinced that the Corps could do it. Finally, everything was ready, and the men's mood was exuberant.

"If a lone boy who knows the trail cannot make it, you cannot make it," Cut Nose signaled, still trying to convince Lewis to wait.

"What he's saying is logical, Meriwether," Clark agreed, now even more skeptical after the boy's return. "Maybe we'd better listen to them."

Stubbornly dismissing all warnings, Lewis insisted, "We can make it."

"Well, since you're determined, let's hope you're right," Clark said with uncertainty. "All of our lives are at stake."

On June 15 the Corps of Discovery gathered its sixty horses and set out in a light rain. They marched through the wet morning and afternoon, every member of the expedition riding one horse and leading a pack horse. The going was difficult because fallen trees were lying in the trail, and the ground was slippery from the rain that was turning to sleet. Still, they made twenty-two miles that first day and camped in a small glade where there was good grazing for the horses. The glade was bursting with new plant life.

Well, so far, so good," Clark announced.

"We'll be fine," Lewis assured him confidently. "We'll save at least a couple of weeks by going now."

On the second day, the expedition continued to climb and finally halted at a creek to eat and allow the horses to graze. The new grass was shorter this time, and the foliage on the bushes was just starting to bud. The captains allowed the horses to graze for two hours before setting out again. As they climbed, deeper snow covered the ground at this elevation.

"Actually, the snow makes traveling easier because it covers the fallen trees," Lewis commented, still supporting his decision to venture onward.

However, snow also covered the trail, making progress slow. Toward evening, they came to a creek and followed it to the place where Captain Clark had found and killed a horse the previous fall. They camped here, having made fifteen miles that day.

"This place has real memories from last year," Shields said to Willard, chewing his twig contemplatively. "Remember how starved we were when we found the horsemeat Captain Clark had left for us?"

"Who could forget?" Willard responded. "We all thought we were going to die."

The young grass was not sufficient for the horses now, and it was becoming clear that as they continued to gain altitude there would be even less grass.

"The lack of grass could become a real problem," Clark began to worry.

"Well, nothing ventured, nothing gained," Lewis asserted. "If we had been timid about taking risks, we wouldn't have made it to the Pacific Ocean."

By the time they had ascended half way up the mountain, they were walking on snow three to four feet deep. As they continued, the snow got deeper, until at the top of the mountain it was twelve to fifteen feet deep, although it was so packed that it easily held the weight of the horses. But here was winter with all its rigors—the wind was wild and frigid, the hands and feet of the men became numb, and the Corps of Discovery was still six or seven days from Traveler's Rest, provided they didn't lose their way. Drouillard, their chief woodsman and the closest thing they had to a guide, approached Lewis.

"Captain, we could lose our way very easily," he warned, obviously worried. "We don't know these mountains, and we can't be sure where the trail is under all this snow. If we wander away from the trail without knowing it, we could end up roaming aimlessly around these mountains with no idea where we are," he said.

Lewis conferred with Clark.

"If we get lost in these mountains, we'll have to use our horses for food, and without them we would have to abandon all our equipment and supplies," Lewis said, finally realizing their predicament. "Then we'd all die of starvation."

Clark squelched his impulse to refer to all the warnings the Indians had given them. "Our main concern must be for the safety of the men," he offered. "If we get lost here, the Corps of Discovery is doomed."

Lewis loathed the very thought of admitting defeat and returning back, but his common sense finally won. "You're right," he said dejectedly. "It would be madness to continue without a guide. Let's return to that former campsite where there was enough grass to feed the horses and wait there while we send someone back to the Nez Perce villages to hire a guide. We can continue when the chiefs say it is safe."

"We may even be able to add to our supply of food while we wait," Clark suggested, already beginning to feel better about their delay.

The captains selected Drouillard and Shannon to return to the Nez Perce and hire guides who would lead them whenever the chiefs thought it was safe for them to go.

"Take an army rifle to pay for a guide to lead us to Traveler's Rest," Lewis instructed them. This was an unprecedented price, but he went even further. "Offer two additional army rifles and ten horses to any guide willing to lead us to the Great Falls of the Missouri."

The men made a cache for all the supplies they wouldn't need immediately, including their instruments and journals, concealing it on scaffolds before starting back down the mountain. The men were unaccustomed to retreating in defeat and were not happy about it, but they trusted the decision of the captains whose wisdom had seen them through all their dangers so far. When four men led the disappointed column, clearing tree limbs and bushes from their path as they descended, one man fell and cut his leg severely. The party halted while Lewis sewed up and bound the wound. Then they continued and arrived at their former camp toward evening. While the horses eagerly grazed, the men made camp and settled in to hunt and to wait.

As the group waited, the captains mulled over the rest of the return trip.

"We could add a couple of dimensions to our mission as we return to St. Louis," Lewis said speculatively. "We could separate into two groups at Traveler's Rest and accomplish two different objectives." Clark listened attentively as Lewis continued with enthusiasm. "I could follow the Nez Perce buffalo route to the Great Falls of the Missouri and then from there conduct an exploration of Maria's River to its source. If the Maria's source proves to be north of forty-nine degrees, that would extend the size of the Louisiana Territory, which would be very important to the United States."

"But, Meriwether, you'd be going deep into Blackfoot territory, and you know how greatly the other Indian tribes fear them," Clark warned.

"Yes, but if I could meet with the Blackfoot chiefs and convince them to become part of a new American trading empire, it would be worth the risk."

"It could also get you and your men killed." Clark was always the realist.

"Well, we're professional soldiers. It's our job to risk our lives for the benefit of our country." Lewis stood and stretched his back. "At any rate, let's think it over. We don't have to decide until we get to Traveler's Rest."

Clark was becoming more and more concerned about Lewis's judgment. Could it really be approaching the time to speak up about his concern? But all he said was, "And what would I be doing meanwhile?"

Lewis showed that he had that figured out also. "You would follow the Jefferson River to Three Forks, cross into the Yellowstone Valley, and proceed down the Yellowstone River to the Missouri, exploring and mapping the new country as you go, extending our knowledge of the area. We could then meet at the Missouri River. What a great contribution you would make to our knowledge of this vast territory!"

After a few days, two young Nez Perce Indians who were on their way to visit friends on the other side of the mountain arrived at the Corps of Discovery camp. Without Drouillard, Lewis found it difficult to follow their sign language. They seemed to be saying that Drouillard and Shannon would not be returning for two more days, but Lewis couldn't understand why.

"Stay with us until our two men return," he signed them. "Then you can guide us over the mountain."

"We will wait two days," they signed.

But two days later, Drouillard and Shannon still had not shown up, and Lewis feared the young braves would set off that morning. He called for Sergeant Gass.

"Gass, take a few men and accompany these braves to Traveler's Rest," he instructed. "Blaze the trail as you go by marking trees so we can follow you."

But a few minutes later, Drouillard and Shannon came riding up, appearing out of the morning mist.

"We're really glad to see you!" Lewis greeted them. "What held you up?"

"Some hard bargaining," Drouillard said.

The delay proved to be worth the wait, however, because they had brought three guides with them. One was the brother of Cut Nose, a young man called Brave Eagle.

"We are happy you will guide us," Lewis had Drouillard signal.

Brave Eagle responded, "We are glad to help you."

The expedition set out the next morning, and by noon they reached the cache they had left nine days earlier. Everything was in good order, and the snow by now had thinned from eleven feet to seven. Some of the men loaded the supplies from the cache into the horses' pack saddles while others prepared a meal of boiled venison.

"We must hurry," Brave Eagle signed urgently to Drouillard. "It is far to the place we must reach today before dark. It is the only place where there is enough grass for the horses."

The guides led them up the steep sides of a mountain covered with snow, and they arrived at the desired grassy area in late evening, camping near a spring. As Brave Eagle had predicted, there was an abundance of lush grass that was no more than ten days old.

"These Indians know what they're doing," Lewis admitted ruefully. "If we'd waited two more weeks, we'd have been all right."

Next day, the expedition came across a cone-shaped mound of stones that had been stacked eight feet high, before which the Indians stopped for a ceremonial smoke. Evidently, the monument had religious significance for them. Ahead of the expedition were towering mountains that filled the men with both awe and dread—increasing their respect for the guides.

"Without our guides, we'd have been trapped in these mountains forever," Lewis finally admitted to Clark.

The young Indian guides had an uncanny ability to follow the snow-covered trails. Miraculously, wherever the snow had melted away, the expedition found itself on the trail. That day, they made twenty-eight miles. When they camped, there was no grass in sight for the horses, and the Corps found itself without meat. Not yet willing to butcher a horse, they ate roots boiled in bear oil. After darkness had descended, the Indians set fire to a fir tree. The tree had a great number of dry limbs near the ground, and when the Indians set the lower branches ablaze, the fire flashed all the way to the top of the tree.

"Is there a purpose for this?" Clark asked Brave Eagle out of curiosity..

"It is to bring good weather for our journey," was his response.

The burning fir tree, flaming from bottom to top, created a spectacular sight, lighting up the night like a Fourth of July celebration.

"I hope they don't set the whole goldarn mountain on fire," Shannon muttered to Seaman, who wagged his tail at the sound of Shannon's voice and stared at the burning tree.

Next morning, one of the guides said he was sick.

"I hope this doesn't bode ill for us," Lewis confided to Clark. "That usually means that Indians are getting ready to abandon whatever they're doing."

"I'm afraid we have to risk leaving them here to care for him," Clark said. "All we can do is hope they join us later."

Two hours after stopping that evening, their Indian guides walked into camp with the sick man, who had recovered enough to walk. When he lay down with only a hairless elk skin to cover him, a relieved Captain Lewis gently placed a buffalo robe over him.

"You keep the buffalo robe," he signed to the man. "We appreciate your help."

The next day, their guides took them along a ridge on a different route than the one they had followed west the previous fall. They were surrounded by sky-high mountains covered with snow. At noon they halted on the south side of a mountain and remained there during the afternoon to let the horses rest.

"Drouillard, ask how far it is to the next grazing place," Lewis requested.

"Farther than we can march today," the Indians replied.

"In that case, let's camp here," he decided. "The horses are tired and we'll be better off in the long run to give them a good rest."

Thick fog rose from the hollows the next day as the party continued along a ridge that descended to a creek. They were delighted to find a supply of meat which their advance hunters had left hanging from high tree limbs to protect it from grizzly bears and wolves. They ascended another high mountain and endured a hail storm accompanied by thunder and lightning. Finally, they arrived at the headwaters of Lolo Creek, and toward evening came to the hot springs where they had bathed last fall.

"I c-c-can't wait to get in there and enjoy a hot b-b-bath!" Reuben Fields exclaimed.

"Yeah, I bet I could wash five pounds of dirt off me," his brother said, anticipating the pleasure of hot water.

After setting up camp, the men and guides stripped off their clothes and jumped into the springs. The Indians stayed in the hot water as long as they could bear it and then leaped out, ran to the creek, and jumped into the frigid water, whooping and splashing with glee. When the cold water became unbearable, they ran back to the hot springs. Lewis took a hot bath only, staying in the steaming water for nineteen minutes. Remaining in the hot water that long brought on profuse sweats, but there were no complaints. Sacagawea gave Pomp an unaccustomed hot bath, talking to him animatedly to assure him that the hot water was a rare treat.

The Corps traveled twenty-eight miles the next day without relieving the horses of their packs. Their meat was gone, so Ordway issued a pint of bear oil to each mess for the cooks to boil roots for supper.

"I would welcome even portable soup right now," McNeal said, pulling absently at his nose.

Nearby, Shields agreed. "Yeah, you don't appreciate something until you don't have it anymore," he said, spitting out a chewed-up twig.

They were out of the deep snow now, but the trail was still difficult and dangerous. On one steep slope, Lewis's horse slipped and Lewis fell off backward, sliding forty feet before he could grab a bush to stop his fall. Finally, the Corps of Discovery reached its old camp at Traveler's Rest just before sunset.

Clark smiled with relief as he said, "This almost feels like coming home."

Lewis, with only a few bruises and scratches, agreed. "In a way, it is. At least it's coming back to something familiar."

They had covered one-hundred-and-sixty-five miles in six days because the Indians had led them through a shortcut. Last fall, this trip going west had taken eleven days to cover the same distance, but some days had been wasted then because Old Toby lost his way. The horses had survived this journey in good condition and needed only a few days' rest to restore them completely, thanks to the skill of their Indian guides.

"Our guides' sense of distance and timing, their inborn sense of direction, and their ability to follow a trail buried under many feet of snow are truly remarkable," Lewis marveled. "Most of the trail was in dense forest, and these guides are very young men, not yet twenty years old."

"These are not primitive people by any means," Clark added. "They are supremely capable, and they have skills that we can only envy."

The expedition stayed at Traveler's Rest for three days.

"Clark, we have to decide whether we'll split up here as we discussed," Lewis said the first evening. "I think we should do it. I will take nine men and seventeen horses and follow the Nez Perce trail to the Falls of the Missouri, where I'll leave Thompson, McNeal, and Goodrich to dig up the cache we left there last fall. Then we'll prepare the wagons for the portage around the falls. I'll take Drouillard, the Fields brothers, Werner, Frazier, and Gass and go up Maria's River to discover if it goes as far north as Latitude 50°. If I meet the Blackfoot, I'll try to convince them to join President Jefferson's proposed trading system. Then I'll return to the mouth of Maria's River to meet the ten men coming down the Missouri River under Sergeant Ordway."

"That's a new twist to your plan," Clark interjected. Lewis's plan was becoming far too complex, Clark worried, especially with a large part of it being led by an enlisted man. Clark was becoming less and less certain of Lewis's judgment.

Lewis continued. "Ordway's detachment will proceed with you and your men to the head of the Jefferson River, where we left canoes and a cache before we crossed the Lemhi Pass with the Shoshones. Ordway's party will leave you there to explore the Jefferson River where it meets the Missouri, and there join the men I will send to help make the portage around the falls. These fourteen men will then go to the mouth of Maria's River to meet me and my detachment. Then together we'll go to the mouth of the Yellowstone River to meet you and your men."

Clark was silent, considering his partner's complicated plan. After a few moments, he said, "That's a very complex and ambitious plan, Meriwether, and it requires charging a non-commissioned officer with great responsibilities."

"Yes, but we know Sergeant Ordway is an intelligent and dependable man."

"Clearly, you have given your plan a lot of thought."

"To be honest, I really began formulating this plan back in Fort Clatsop."

Clark was considering the benefits and drawbacks in the plan. "That would give me ten men, in addition to Sacagawea and Pomp, to lead across the dividing ridge and down between the Missouri and Yellowstone Rivers."

"Yes, that's right," Lewis agreed. "When you reach the Yellowstone, you can build canoes and descend to the junction with the Missouri— where the entire expedition will come together again."

"You haven't accounted for Sergeant Pryor and couple of other men," Clark pointed out.

"I want to send them on an independent mission to take a letter to Mr. Heney of the Northwest Company to seek help in getting Sioux chiefs to go to Washington. Pryor will go with you until you make canoes, and when you set off in the canoes, he and his men will take the horses to the Mandan villages as gifts to the Mandan before continuing on to meet Mr. Heney and deliver my letter."

Clark answered quickly. "That's a very complex plan that demands some very exact timing. We both know that exact timing can be dangerous in military planning."

"Yes, but we're soldiers, and the things we have already accomplished almost defy belief. I want this expedition to be as successful as possible and to bring back all the valuable information we can possibly gather. I also want to make every effort to establish peace between the warring tribes, and I want to do everything possible to create the American trading empire. I am absolutely convinced we can do this, Clark."

"The goal is worthwhile, but I am concerned that we will be dividing our forces into four different detachments in the heart of a country that is filled with roaming bands of Crow, Blackfoot, Hidatsa, and others." Clark continued, "We'll all be scattered so widely that we won't be able to support each other. You and your men will be at risk from the Blackfoot and have the most dangerous mission." Clark believed he would be shirking his duty if he failed to share his doubts about Lewis's plans.

"I know we can do it, Clark."

Captain Clark remembered the last time his co-leader had spoken those words. He looked down, his hand on his chin. "Well, if you're convinced we should…"

Lewis immediately sat down to write the letter to Mr. Heney. His secondary goal was to coax Heney to leave the British Northwest Company and join the American commercial effort. He had met Heney and felt he was the right man to help establish the American trading empire. He had become convinced that Heney was the only white man who could convince the Sioux to abandon their warlike ways and join President Jefferson's hoped-for trading system.

CHAPTER 30

Contending with Treachery

July, 1806

On horseback, Lewis led nine soldiers and five Indians northwest along the Bitterroot River. After going five miles, they headed up the Blackfoot River through heavily timbered country, where high, precipitous mountains brought feelings of awe. The Corps of Discovery was now divided into four groups, each with a mission of its own as they made their way back home. In three weeks they would all reassemble at the mouth of the Yellowstone River—if everything went as planned.

On the second day out, Drouillard returned from hunting to report, "I found tracks of a very large Indian party, Captain."

Lewis was not surprised. "I imagine it's a Hidatsa hunting party. Let's be ready to meet them soon."

They encountered no Indians, however, and continued to travel up the Blackfoot River through beautiful country. After eleven miles, the river dwindled to little more than a creek.

"I sure hope we find some b-b-buffalo soon," Reuben Fields commented. "I've b-b-been dreaming of delicious b-b-buffalo hump all winter, and I w-want to eat some."

But they saw no buffalo even though tantalizing signs of their passage through this valley were all around them. They covered a total of thirty-one miles before camping the third day. That night, Lewis fought off nagging doubts about whether he and Clark had made the right decision to split up. Too many things could go wrong. Still, his duty was to extract the maximum advantage from this mission, and he was determined to fulfill that pledge to President Jefferson.

Brave Eagle approached Drouillard the next day. "You don't need us any longer because the trail is so easy that even a white man couldn't get lost," he signed, stating an obvious fact and meaning no disrespect. "We will return to our village tomorrow."

"Our hunters will provide you with meat for your journey," Lewis had Drouillard sign.

Lewis ordered the hunters to turn out early the next morning to find meat for the returning guides. He was unwilling to let them leave without a good supply of provisions after they had so expertly guided the expedition over such dangerous mountain snows.

This was a sad day for the men because it was their last contact with the Nez Perce, their friends and companions for the past two months. The Nez Perce had seen the soldiers of the Corps starving and fed them, confused and given them good advice, lost and guided them. They had ridden together, eaten together, played together, danced together, lived together, and crossed the Lolo Trail together. Although the two groups could communicate only through sign language, they had shared experiences that firmly bonded them. They had managed to master their communication and cultural barriers to become true friends.

Now traveling without guides, Lewis and his men crossed one river and camped at another after covering thirty-one miles.

"Hey, Reuben!" Joseph Fields called to his brother as he came in from hunting. "We've got your buffalo hump!"

The hunters had finally found and killed a fat buffalo. When the next day turned out to be blustery and rainy, they stayed at their campsite all day and feasted on buffalo.

"Man, this is good eating!" Shields said gleefully.

"T-t-too b-b-bad we don't have Charbonneau with us to make his *b-b-boudin b-b-blanc*," Reuben Fields added.

They rejoiced at being on the plains of the Missouri River again, which abounded with game. They saw herds of buffalo farther down the river. It was mating season, and the continuous roar of bellowing bulls kept the party awake at night. The sound echoed and amplified across the plains, frightening the tethered horses so much that the men had to roust themselves from their bedrolls to calm them down.

The party continued traveling through high plains that were heavily populated with buffalo, providing meat as well as hides to make boats. Lewis and his men used the boats to cross the wide Missouri to get to their cache on the eastern bank. Lewis ordered eleven buffalo killed so that the men of his party who would be left at the Great Falls of the Missouri would not run out of food.

Next morning brought a serious problem. "Captain, seven of our horses are missing," Hugh McNeal reported, pulling nervously at his nose.

Lewis grimaced. "Indians have stolen them," he guessed. "Drouillard, track them and see what you can find out."

Drouillard rode off, and the remaining men swam the few horses they had across the river and then paddled the bull-boats over. They were now just above the Great Falls of the Missouri, and they camped at the upper White Bear campsite where they had unsuccessfully tried last fall to build the iron-frame boat. Eagerly, the men dug up the cache they had left at the site, but they were bitterly disappointed when they discovered that high water during the spring runoff had soaked everything. The bearskins, most of the medicine, and Lewis's plant specimens had been ruined.

"Damn!" Lewis agonized. He was devastated at the loss of the dozens and dozens of flora that he had so painstakingly labeled, dried, and preserved. However, the papers, illustrations, and maps were still legible.

"Well, let's hope the wagon wheels we buried fared better," he said hopefully. "Let's dig them up."

The wagon wheels were in good shape, so the men began to reassemble the wagons. The missing horses, however, could not be found. The men responsible for hobbling them had not done their job adequately, and the horses had freed themselves and wandered off. The men searched all day, but the horses were not to be found.

"Well, let's load two canoes onto the wagons anyway and hope we find the horses tomorrow," Lewis said.

Next morning, the men spread out to search in different directions. Near noon, they found the horses at the falls and brought them back to last night's campsite. They harnessed them to the wagons and set out to haul the large canoes over the portage to their old camp below the falls. One of the wagon axles broke after going only five miles, so they made another axle and resumed travel. The wheels on the wagon carrying the larger canoe had a series of breakdowns. With much difficulty, they finally moved the canoes and some of their supplies close to a creek where they camped. As night approached, rain and wind pounded them, and the men lacked shelter because their tents were in a cache farther east.

"Turn the canoes upside down and try to sleep under them," Lewis suggested. Some of the men lay under the canoes, and others sat by the fire, enduring the rain under whatever covering they could find.

They continued the next day, halting frequently to rest the horses, which struggled to continue when wagon wheels sank into the mud nearly to the hubs. After much fatiguing labor for both horses and men, they managed to arrive at Portage Creek, the old lower campsite. Next morning, they opened the cache they had left there nine months earlier. A few beaver skins and robes had rotted, but everything else was in good shape. The men hauled the white pirogue out of the bushes to repair it. When they went to do the same with the red pirogue, however, they found that it had rotted and was now useless.

"Well, we can't expect everything to go right," Lewis said with resignation.

McNeal, out hunting alone, suddenly found himself face-to-face with a grizzly that roared up not more than ten feet from him. His heart leaped, and his startled horse reared, throwing McNeal to the ground as it galloped away. McNeal leaped to his feet and with all his strength clubbed the grizzly's head with the stock of his gun. McNeal was shaking with fear, the adrenalin pumping. Frantically, not waiting to see the effect of the clubbing, he dashed for the nearest tree and scrambled for high branches. The dazed grizzly momentarily fell to its knees and began pawing at the pain in its head. Then it recovered and angrily charged the tree where McNeal had taken refuge. Knowing that grizzlies do not climb trees, McNeal felt that he was temporarily safe. Growling ferociously, the grizzly waited at the base of the tree until dusk, reminding McNeal of a hound dog with a treed raccoon Finally, the bear gave up its futile vigil and abandoned his prey. McNeal slipped cautiously down the tree, tracked his horse by hard-to-see hoof prints, and returned to camp in the dark. He had a story to tell around the campfire that evening.

Drouillard hadn't returned after several days, and Lewis began to fear that a grizzly had attacked him also. "He's been gone too long. He's never gone this long, and I'm afraid something may have happened to him."

But later that day Drouillard rode into camp. "I followed the trail for two days and found where the thieves had crossed the river with our horses," he reported. "I kept following their tracks, but they had too big a head start, so I finally gave up."

"How many were there?" someone asked.

"It was a large group—maybe fifteen lodges. I wouldn't have been able to get our horses back even if I had found them.

As hunters brought in a good supply of fresh meat, the men cut it into strips and put it out to dry in the bright sunlight. This food would sustain the group that planned a trip up Maria's River. Lewis reduced the size of his party from nine to four, leaving more men at the falls than originally planned. Before departing for Maria's River, he sketched the Great Falls of the Missouri for his records.

He and his small party set out across treeless plains toward the upper reaches of Maria's River. They proceeded along the river for several miles until they reached a place where they decided to cross the hundred-and-fifty yard span. They collected wood and built three small rafts to take their supplies across the swiftly moving river. With supplies safely across, they drove their horses into the river and swam them across. But in this entire area, mosquitoes filled the air in great swarms, so thick and troublesome that they flew into men's mouths as they talked. The men built two huge fires—one for the horses and one for themselves—so that the flames and smoke would deter the mosquitoes. Both men and horses were so tortured by the devilish insects that they willingly placed themselves in the densest smoke.

"Any other time, the fire would make the horses frantic," Lewis said to Drouillard at they fanned the smoke toward their faces.

"I guess it's a matter of the lesser evil," Drouillard remarked. When the air cooled an hour after dark, the mosquitoes disappeared.

The countryside now was broken and filled with steep ravines, and the river was confined between narrow cliffs. The land was so rocky that the horses developed sore hooves. After many miles, the land became more level and less rocky, but no timber or underbrush was to be seen. High cliffs had given way to normal river banks three or four feet high. Lewis's small group had to make their fires using buffalo dung, which served the purpose quite well.

The main reason Lewis had taken this small detachment so far north was to see if the source of Maria's River lay within the boundaries of the Louisiana Purchase. A secondary purpose was to meet the Blackfoot Indians and add them to the tribes of those interested in establishing a system of trade across the vast territory. But now, Lewis's desire to meet with the Blackfoot was starting to give way to a nagging fear. When he had planned this excursion, he had hoped to have some leading Nez Perce with him to help make peace, but that safeguard was now gone. He had also planned for a party of nine men, and now he had only four. Finally, what the Nez Perce chiefs said about the Blackfoot—that they were a vicious and lawless set of wretches—was beginning to affect Lewis's thinking. He decided to avoid the Blackfoot if at all possible. He felt sure now that the Blackfoot, finding a small and vulnerable party of white men, would attack and rob them. These dangers were close to his mind as he stepped up to take his turn on sentinel duty.

For the next three days, the small party followed Maria's River upstream. When the river forked into two branches, they took the northern fork. The horses' feet were still sore, and clouds of mosquitoes still harassed every man and beast, slowing the pace and bringing great discomfort to all.

"It's beginning to look like Maria's River doesn't go as far north as I had hoped," Lewis told his companions, "but we need to know for sure."

They went twenty-four miles before stopping to eat and let the horses graze and rest. Then they continued twelve more miles and camped in a grove of cottonwood tress that was only ten miles from the base of the northern Rocky Mountains. After making and recording celestial observations, Captain Lewis decided that there was no point in going any farther up Maria's River.

"We'll call this place Camp Disappointment," he told the men glumly.

He decided to stay there two days to rest both the men and the horses from the trying journey. Drouillard returned from a scouting mission to report many signs of Indians in the area. The men went out to hunt, but without success—a sure sign that a great number of Indians had been hunting in the area.

"We're probably lucky we haven't met the Blackfoot," Lewis told Drouillard.

"I think you're right. From what we've heard about them, and the fact we are such a small group, that is a good thing," Drouillard agreed.

They left Camp Disappointment and rode south. There was no game in the area, but the hunters killed some pigeons and cooked them with roots for a tasty meal. After grazing the horses, they continued, with Drouillard out in front hunting. Lewis and the Fields brothers ascended to a high plain while Drouillard remained in the valley.

When Lewis reached the high plain and looked around at the beauty of the place, he was alarmed to see a herd of about thirty horses a mile away. He got out his telescope and discovered several Indians astride their horses, staring intently into the valley. Lewis could tell they were watching Drouillard. If there were as many men as there were horses, Lewis's little party would be vastly outnumbered. He resolved to make the best of the situation.

"Show the flag," he ordered Joseph Fields.

Fields unfurled the flag. Lewis and both Fields brothers advanced slowly toward the Indians, who were now milling about as if much alarmed. Suddenly one of the Indians broke out of the milling group and whipped his horse full-speed toward Lewis's party. Lewis dismounted and stood waiting for the onrushing horse and rider. His behavior seemed to confuse the Indian, who probably expected the three men to flee from him. When the Indian halted a hundred yards away, Lewis held out his hand in calm greeting, but the Indian wheeled his horse and galloped back to his companions. Lewis could count them now: there were eight young men. Lewis suspected that others were hidden behind the bluffs because there were many other saddled horses. Lewis and the Fields brothers advanced cautiously.

"If they are hostile, we have to fight to the death," Lewis said soberly as they walked. The Fields brothers both nodded in grim-faced assent. The Indian party could possibly outnumbered Lewis's group by as many as eight to one.

"If they are friendly, or at least not violent, we might be able to establish contact with the Blackfoot chiefs and have a chance to talk to them about a trading system," Lewis said hopefully.

"Well, let's hope they're friendly," Joseph Fields said, cracking his knuckles nervously. Down on the plain, Drouillard was unaware of the drama taking place behind him.

When they advanced to within a hundred yards of the Indians, they stopped. Lewis continued alone to meet the Indian who had ridden out in front of his group. He was a young brave of nineteen or twenty years, very thin and dressed in buckskin, his hair pulled back into a single braid. He eyed Lewis cautiously. These two men from vastly different cultures met and shook hands, nodding at each other tentatively. Then both moved on to shake hands with the others of their respective parties. The Indians signaled they would like to smoke. Using his limited sign-language skills, Lewis told them that his pipe was with his hunter in the valley. He proposed that Reuben Fields and one of the Indians ride down to find Drouillard and bring him back, which was done.

Lewis had Drouillard sign, "What nation are you from?"

"Blackfoot nation," was the reply.

"Who is your chief?"

Three of them stepped forward. Lewis knew they were too young and too many to be chiefs, but he decided to humor them. He handed out a medal, a flag, and a handkerchief to the three who had stepped forward. By now, Lewis was confident that there were only eight of them in the immediate vicinity. He was relieved because he was convinced that he and his men could handle eight of them if they became hostile. The sun was sinking, and when Lewis proposed that they camp together, they agreed.

They came to a favorable spot in a bend of the river, a bowl-like bottom with three large cottonwood trees in the center and excellent grazing for the horses. With Drouillard flashing signs, Lewis asked question after question. The Indians said they were part of a large band that was one day's march away, near the foot of the mountains. They said a white man was living among them. They also said another large band of their nation was hunting buffalo while on the way to the mouth of Maria's River. Lewis had no way of knowing how much of this was true and how much of it was meant to intimidate. If it was all true, it meant that he and his men were in the middle of the Blackfoot nation and that a Canadian trader was living with them—which meant they had firearms, although this group of eight had only two muskets. Lewis asked about trading patterns of the Blackfoot.

"We ride six days to a British post on the North Saskatchewan River to buy guns, ammunition, whiskey, and blankets in exchange for wolf and beaver skins," was the reply.

Lewis explained that they would get a much better deal from the Americans once the Americans arrived on the high plains. He gave his peace speech. He said he had come from the rising sun and had gone to where the sun set and had made peace among warring nations on both sides of the mountains. He said he had come to their country to invite the Blackfoot nation to join the American trading empire. To his delight, they readily gave their assent.

The young Indians were willing to talk the sign language as long as the smoking continued. They were extremely fond of tobacco, and Lewis plied them with it until late that night. He told them that he had other men in the area, a party of soldiers he would be meeting at the mouth of Maria's River. He asked them to send messengers to nearby bands of their nation to meet in three days at the mouth of Maria's River for a council about peace and trade. He concluded by asking them to accompany him to the mouth of Maria's River and promised them ten horses and some tobacco if they would do so. They made no reply to his invitation.

Lewis took the first watch that night. At 11:30 he roused Reuben Fields to take his place as sentinel.

"Watch the Indians carefully, lest they try to steal our horses," he whispered.

During the night, as the Blackfoot braves slept in an area apart from Lewis and his men, they began talking in low voices among themselves. Lewis and Drouillard, awakened by the murmur, could hear occasional phrases and words as they spoke their native language, but neither could understand the words. However, from the tones of their voices and the intensity of various phrases, the white men perceived that they were brewing a plot against them.

Lewis fell back to sleep, but awoke before daybreak when Drouillard shouted, "Damn you! Let go of my gun!" Lewis saw Drouillard scuffling with an Indian for his rifle. Lewis leaped to his feet and frantically reached for his rifle, but it was gone. He drew his pistol, and when he saw a second Indian running away with his rifle, he ran after him, shouting in English and aiming his pistol.

"Lay down my rifle or I will shoot you!"

Understanding Lewis's tone of voice, the brave lowered the rifle as Drouillard rushed in.

"Let me kill the bastard, Captain!"

Lewis extended his arm to halt Drouillard's action while keeping his eyes on the would-be thief. "No! We have our rifles, and the Indians are falling back."

Simultaneously, the Fields brothers woke to see two Indians running off with their rifles which had been lying beside them as they slept. Dashing at full speed after the thieves, they tackled them at fifty yards and wrestled their rifles from their grasp. During the scuffle, Reuben pulled his knife and plunged it into one young man's chest, killing him instantly. The Fields brothers leaped to their feet and took off after the horses.

Lewis was running after two Blackfoot who were trying to drive off the white men's horses. He sprinted some three hundred yards, at which point the Indians had reached a vertical bluff. Lewis, out of breath, could pursue no farther. He shouted that he would shoot if they didn't return the horses. When one Indian aimed a British musket at him, Lewis shot him in the stomach. The wounded Indian raised himself to one knee and fired at Lewis, who felt the wind of the bullet as it passed his head. Unable to reload because his shot pouch was back at camp, Lewis turned and made his way back.

"Call the Fields boys back! We have enough horses!" Lewis shouted to Drouillard. But the Fields brothers were too far away.

Lewis and Drouillard began to saddle the horses as the Fields brothers returned leading four of the Blackfoot horses. Lewis appraised his herd and selected the four Indian horses because they were fresh and rested, as well as four of his original herd. As the men arranged saddles and the placement of supplies on the packhorses, Lewis began burning the articles the Indians had left behind, including two bows and two quivers of arrows. Only the musket the Indians had left behind and the flag Lewis had given the Indians the previous evening escaped the fire. Angry at Indian treachery, Lewis found the medal he had awarded at last night's campfire ceremony and left it hanging around the neck of the dead Indian to let his friends know who his killers were.

But Drouillard, familiar with Indian ways, asked, "Do you think it's wise to taunt them that way?"

"Let them know who they are dealing with!" Lewis answered grimly.

Minutes later, Lewis told the others, "The surviving young Blackfoot braves will ride at top speed to the nearest village and report what happened. Then a big party of warriors will set out to kill any white men they can find. I just hope we don't find a band of Blackfoot Indians between us and Maria's River."

With one Blackfoot brave dead and another fatally wounded, Lewis and his group knew they were in deadly danger. They were four white men in the middle of a land of hundreds of Blackfoot warriors who would surely seek revenge the instant they heard the news. They must leave the area immediately.

They struck out toward the mouth of Maria's River, the horses proceeding at a trot that covered eight miles per hour. They rode through the morning and midday, not stopping until three o'clock, when they finally halted to eat and let the horses graze. They had covered sixty-three miles. After an hour-and-a-half break, they covered another seventeen miles before dark. Seeing a buffalo, they killed and ate it for supper, setting off again at a walk across flat plains by moonlight. At two o'clock in the morning, Lewis finally ordered a halt. They had started the day with an Indian fight and followed that with a hundred-mile ride. Now they turned their horses out to graze and finally lay down to sleep. Everyone was extremely tired and since there were only four of them, Lewis didn't post a sentinel, deciding they would risk danger so all could get some uninterrupted sleep Lewis woke at first light, so stiff he could hardly move.

"Wake up, men," he called. "We've got to keep moving. Let's get saddled up."

Joseph Fields was dragging his aching body from his bedroll. "Can't we rest just a little longer, Captain?" he pleaded.

"Our lives depend on the distance we can put between us and the Blackfoot warriors," Lewis said, shaking his head.

With that, the men became alert, and their retreat was resumed. After twelve miles, they reached the Missouri River and continued alongside it for eight more miles. Suddenly they heard rifle shots. Staring anxiously upriver—fearing that a Blackfoot war party would ride into view—they suddenly saw Corps of Discovery canoes coming down the river. It was Sergeant Ordway's party!

"You will never know how happy we are to see you!" Lewis shouted to them as they put in to shore. "We killed two Blackfoot braves who tried to rob us. A war party is probably searching for us. Help us quickly transfer our supplies from our horses to your canoes, and then we'll turn the horses loose."

Down the Missouri River the enlarged party went, sharing their separate experiences and still on the lookout for angry Blackfoot warriors. Finally, they arrived at the mouth of Maria's River, the very place Lewis had told the Blackfoot braves his group would be.

Lewis gave orders. "Quickly! Dig up the caches we buried here last summer. We have to keep moving!"

Skins and furs had been damaged in the cache, but the gunpowder, corn, flour, pork, and salt were all in fairly good condition. They returned to the canoes in record time and continued downstream. After fifteen miles, Lewis decided they had left the Blackfoot warriors safely behind, so they made camp across the river facing the direction from which the Blackfoot could appear.

Lewis's exploration of Maria's River was finished.

"Separating into small groups was a mistake," he admitted privately to Sergeant Ordway. "All I accomplished was to make enemies of the Blackfoot nation."

The only objective now was to reunite with Clark and his party and arrive at the safety of the Mandan villages. Next morning, they shoved off and sailed along with the current at seven miles per hour. Progress continued uneventfully over the next five days. Game was so plentiful that at one stop the men killed twenty-nine deer. They stayed over to cut the meat into strips and dry it in the sun. The canoes passed large timbered bottoms, eventually arriving at last year's camp at the three forks of the Missouri River.

Through heavy rain, thunder, and hail, they continued the next day before camping that night. The next morning, they entered the high country with the white clay cliffs that resembled ancient towns and buildings. When they spotted bighorn sheep on the cliffs, the Fields brothers went out and killed two large rams. Lewis saved the skeletons, horns, and skin to take to Washington.

Every day they felt closer to home.

CHAPTER 31

Problems For the Corps of Discovery

End of Summer, 1806

"The sheepskins are beginning to spoil, and we need to save them to take back to Washington," Captain Lewis told the men, holding up a skin from a longhorn sheep to display the black mold along the edges. "Let's set up camp at these abandoned Indian lodges and catch up on our work."

Their boats pulled into shore, and the men unloaded all the goods and the recently killed venison that required drying in the sun. As they worked, Shannon suddenly shouted. "Hey! Look out!" A grizzly had wandered into their midst, sniffing at the objects strewn on the ground. As the men scrambled out of its way, the bear reared up, ready to attack. Shields was ready with his gun and fired point blank at the grizzly's head. The huge beast crashed heavily to the ground.

"Good shot!" Ordway complimented Shields. "We can use his skin and lard. But with so many deer in this area, we really don't need his meat."

After skinning the grizzly, rendering his fat, jerking the venison, and drying the sheepskins, they continued two days later downriver past Two Thousand Mile Creek before high wind forced them to put in and make camp. The following day, the hunters killed twenty-five deer, and the group stayed longer to make jerky to last them for several days. These members of the Corps were eager to reach the mouth of the Yellowstone River and meet Captain Clark's party, but the wind became so violent that travel was out of the question. They camped near a site they had used on their way west.

A week later, they reached the mouth of the Yellowstone River. Clark was not there, but signs of an encampment indicated that he had been there a week earlier. Lewis found a note from Clark saying that this site had too little game and too many mosquitoes, so he and his detachment were moving farther downstream to await the main party. Seeing elk on shore, Lewis called out, "Put in, men, and let's get some more meat."

Lewis and Cruzatte went ashore to hunt for elk. Lewis killed one elk, and Cruzatte wounded one. The two men headed into the willows to search for the wounded elk and decided to separate. Several minutes later, a tremendously violent force struck Lewis's body, spinning him around. He hit the ground clutching at his buttocks, and when he looked at his hand, it was covered with blood. A bullet had struck him just below his hip joint on his left side and passed through his buttocks, lodging in his leather breeches without striking bone. Lewis's first thought was that Cruzatte—who was blind in one eye and nearsighted in the other one—had mistaken Lewis's buckskin clothing for the wounded elk and had shot him.

"Cruzatte! You shot me!" he called. "Come help me!"

When Cruzatte didn't answer, Lewis assumed that he must have been shot by an Indian. In these thick willows, it was impossible to know whether it was just one warrior or an entire party.

"Cruzatte! Indian attack! Retreat to the canoes," Lewis shouted.

Dragging himself as he tried to run, Lewis set out for the canoes, but after the first hundred paces, his wound forced him to stop. He could see the Corps' canoes, so he shouted to the men waiting there.

"To arms, men! We're under attack!"

The waiting men grabbed their rifles and rushed to help Lewis, who was obviously hurt.

"I'm wounded, and Cruzatte is missing!" he shouted at the men rushing toward him. "Keep going, men! Find Cruzatte!"

He struggled to the pirogue, where he placed his pistol on his left side and his rifle on his right. He also made sure the air gun was close at hand, determined to sell his life as dearly as possible, should the Indians attack him. He was alone for about twenty minutes, in a state of great anxiety, suspense, and pain. Finally the men returned with Cruzatte.

"There are no Indians around," Drouillard reported. "It had to be Cruzatte who shot you."

"Mais non, mon Capitan," Cruzatte protested, reverting to his native French in his frightened agitation. "I did not shoot you." Cruzatte fidgeted in distress.

"Didn't you hear me call to you? You were only forty yards away."

"No, Captain."

But the bullet that had ended up in his breeches was a .54 caliber musket ball from a U.S. Army rifle, not a weapon any Indian west of the Mississippi River was at all likely to have. Lewis knew that Cruzatte had accidentally shot him and was afraid to admit it. Sergeant Gass helped Lewis out of his clothes, and Lewis dressed his own wounds as best he could. The detachment continued downriver, with Lewis lying on his stomach in the pirogue. His wound had become so painful by the time the party made camp that he couldn't bear to be moved from the pirogue. After having a poultice of Peruvian bark applied to his wounds, he spent a sleepless and painful night with a high fever. By morning the fever was gone, but he was extremely stiff and sore. During the morning, Lewis's detachment rounded a bend and found the camp of Captain Clark and his party.

"Hello, the camp!" shouted Sergeant Gass from the bow of the pirogue.

"Hello, the boat!" Clark shouted in return, a huge smile on his face.

The pirogue fired its cannon to celebrate the reunion of all the members of the Corps of Discovery on the banks of the Missouri River.

"Am I ever glad to see you!" Lewis exclaimed to Clark. "Please take charge of the expedition." Then he explained what had happened to him.

"My God! That's a nasty-looking wound!" Clark said, frowning. He assigned Sacagawea as Lewis's caregiver until he recovered.

Clark spent the next half hour telling Lewis the story of his group's journey down the Yellowstone Valley. Clark and his party of twenty men, plus Sacagawea and Pomp and forty-nine horses, had turned south when they left the main group. They were going through Sacagawea's home territory at the time, and she was able to guide them over the best routes. They covered one-hundred-sixty-four miles in five days and reached the cache at the mouth of the Yellowstone River where the expedition had left supplies more than a year before. To their delight, the cache was still intact and the canoes still in good condition. Finally, they reached the Forks of the Missouri, having covered in one day the same distance that had taken them six days on the way west.

Then Sergeant Ordway had taken six canoes and ten men to explore the Jefferson River to its mouth near the Great Falls of the Missouri, about six days away, where they expected to meet Captain Lewis and his detachment.

After Ordway's departure with his group, Captain Clark and his small remaining party left on horseback to go cross-country to the Yellowstone River. They reached the Yellowstone River two days later and began to search for trees large enough to make dug-out canoes. Finally, they found two cottonwood trees that would make two twenty-eight-foot canoes, which they planned to lash together for sturdiness.

The next morning Colter discovered that half of their horses were missing. They couldn't understand how the Indians could sneak in and make off with so many of their horses without being heard by the sentinel. Colter suggested that the Indians had a lot of practice at stealing horses and reminded the captain that, to the Indians, stealing horses was an act of bravery.

There was nothing to be done about the missing horses. Because the Corps had been divided into small groups, each group was now too weak to be a fighting force. Clark ordered Sergeant Pryor to take the remaining horses to the Mandan villages as a gift and to deliver Captain Lewis's letter to Mr. Heney who was living there

When the canoes were finished, Clark and his party took to the river. At one point, they came to a rock butte beside the river. Clark christened it "Pompey's Tower" after little Pomp. Charbonneau carried his son to the top of the butte, showed him the vast countryside below, and told him, "You will be famous in history because this place is named for you." Pomp laughed and pointed, enjoying the attention he was getting. Clark impulsively wrote his name and the date on Pompey's Tower.

Clark related that his men had become so short of clothing that they were now killing deer for their skins to make clothes, although no meat was allowed to go to waste. With the river current in their favor, they were averaging seventy miles per day. Once, they were forced to stop for an hour while a huge herd of buffalo swam across the river in front of them. They had plenty of venison to eat, so they killed none of the buffalo. On another day, a bear doggedly pursued them down the river, attracted by the smell of the venison in their canoes.

Shortly before rejoining Lewis's party, Sergeant Pryor and his men had suddenly and unexpectedly shown up, floating down the river in two canoes made of buffalo skins. Pryor said that all their horses were stolen by Indians. Not only were they unable to give the horses to the Mandan, but Mr. Heney had left and wasn't expected to return, so Lewis's letter was undelivered also. Without horses, they killed two buffalo and made two buffalo-boats, as the Arikara had taught them.

"Well, that's the end of that dream," Lewis said when Clark finished relating his group's adventures. "Mr. Heney was our only hope for pacifying the Sioux and bringing them into the American trading system. Even worse, it looks like our Indian policy is coming apart. We have hostile Blackfoot behind us and hostile Sioux in front of us—and these two nations can block the whole middle section of the Missouri River to American traders. Our mission clearly isn't as successful as I had hoped." Lewis sighed deeply as he readjusted his position on his bedroll.

"But we have had a very successful journey of discovery," Clark argued. "We have accomplished more than anyone could have expected."

Lewis shook his head. "We'll never establish a trading empire with the Indians fighting each other constantly."

"I agree with you there," Clark agreed. "War is such an ingrained part of their culture that it's unlikely they will abandon it willingly. Nevertheless, the Corps has been extremely successful. Think of all the information we have gathered."

Lewis attempted to smile at his co-captain and said softly, "I guess you're right—I hope you are."

The Corps of Discovery continued down the Missouri River, hunting as they went, mostly for skins. They wanted skins not only to make clothing, but also to use as trade goods to buy food from the Indians with when they reached the Mandan villages. Two days later, the Mandan villages came into view. The members of the Corps of Discovery saluted their old friends with their cannon. The Mandans, led by Big White, Black Cat, and Raven Man, greeted the captains with hugs and a smoking ceremony.

"We are happy to see you again," Big White signed. "We weren't sure you would return."

"Well, I can't blame you for that," Clark smiled. "In truth, I doubt that we were at all sure we'd ever return."

The news from the Mandan chiefs was all bad. The Arikaras and the Mandans were at war, the Hidatsas had sent a war party into the Rockies and killed some Shoshones, the Sioux had raided the Mandans, and the Mandans were divided by internal quarrels.

"It looks like the whole upper Missouri is at war," Clark reported to Lewis aboard the pirogue. "It's just like we'd never been here and never received promises of peaceful relations among the Indians."

Lewis shook his head. "We'll never establish a trading empire with the Indians fighting each other constantly."

"I'm afraid not," Clark agreed. "And war is such an ingrained part of their culture that it's unlikely they will abandon it willingly."

"I would like to visit your country and meet your Great Father," Big White signed, "but I don't want to fight the Sioux of the river."

"We will protect you from the Sioux," Clark promised. Then, to provide an incentive, he added, "If you go to Washington with us, an American trading post will be built among you soon."

But the chief still refused. Finally, after much pleading from Jessaume, Big White agreed to go if the captains also agreed to take his wife and son, as well as Jessaume and his wife and two sons. Such a plan would dangerously overload the canoes, but the captains were desperate to take the chiefs to Washington, so Clark reluctantly agreed.

Two fur trappers, white men, Joseph Dickson of Illinois and Forrest Hancock of Boone's Settlement, arrived at the Mandan villages. They had set out in 1804, spent the winter in Iowa country, and been robbed by Indians; nevertheless, they were heading to the Yellowstone River to trap beaver. It seemed clear to Clark that American trappers and frontiersmen would soon be arriving in great numbers to work in the Louisiana Territory.

John Colter approached Captain Clark that evening. "Captain, Dickson and Hancock have asked me to join them on their trapping expedition, and I'd like to go with them," he said.

Clark was surprised that Colter would want to return into the deep wilderness instead of going home to his family. But Clark knew that Colter was quick-minded, courageous, and a good hunter—all excellent qualities for Dickson and Hancock's endeavor. Colter's request presented a problem. If the captains allowed Colter to cut his enlistment short, would other men follow with the same request? Clark went to Lewis's bedside to consult with him, and he, too, was taken aback.

Lewis pulled himself up on one elbow to voice his reaction. "Colter has been a good soldier all the way to the Pacific and back," he said. "I would be in favor of accommodating him, but we must make sure no other soldier is going to ask for the same privilege."

After obtaining the pledge from every other man that he would not ask to leave the Corps early, Clark had Ordway draw up discharge papers for Colter.

"You have served the Corps of Discovery faithfully and well," Clark said, clapping him on the shoulder. "Go with our blessings, and good luck to you."

He paid Colter his final wages, and Sergeant Ordway fitted him out with powder, lead, and other supplies. Lewis, still eager to help establish an American presence in the upper Louisiana Territory, gave Dickson and Hancock information about impediments ahead of them and told them where they could find beaver in abundance. He also gave them an extra rifle, lead, and powder.

As the expedition prepared to resume its journey, many of the men traded deerskins with the Mandan Indians for corn, beans, robes, and moccasins. The captains gave the swivel gun to One Eye, the great chief of the Hidatsa in an elaborate celebration designed to impress the Indians.

Before departing, Clark settled with Charbonneau, paying him five hundred dollars for his services, his horse, and his tepee. Sacagawea received nothing, which made Clark feel terrible. Janie had not only been very useful in their dealings with the Shoshones, but she had guided Clark's small group through the Yellowstone territory. She had borne the dangers and hunger of the long expedition without complaint while being encumbered with the constant care of her baby, who was even now only nineteen months old.

With open hands gesturing his futility, Clark apologized. "I'm sorry, Janie. You have earned pay of your own, but I have no authority to pay you. You deserve more thanks than we can convey to you with mere words."

She didn't understand Clark's words, but she could read his meaning and his sentiment in his face. She grasped his hand and smiled. Clark called to Drouillard to come and translate for him.

"Janie, I would like to take Pomp home to St. Louis with me and raise him as my own son." He watched her hopefully as Drouillard signed. "He will have a much better life with me than he could ever have here."

Sacagawea frowned, surprised by Clark's request. She hesitated only a moment before responding.

"She says maybe next summer, after Pompey is weaned."

"Then I will return next summer," Clark said, smiling and nodding as a solemn promise to Sacagawea.

When the Corps of Discovery resumed its journey, the captains directed the men to lash their two largest canoes together to make them steadier in the water for Big White, Jessaume, and their families. As they progressed, Big White pointed out several places where he and his nation had formerly lived. He also told Captain Clark the story of the Mandan's origin.

"We came out of the ground, where we had lived in a great underground village," Big White began as Drouillard signed. "A grapevine grew down from the earth to the village and the people saw the light at the top of the grapevine. Some of the people climbed the grapevine and emerged onto the plains, where they saw buffalo and every kind of animal and plant. They took some grapes back to their underground village, where the people found them good and decided to go up and live on the plains. Before they could all climb the grapevine, the weight of a fat woman broke it, and all the people that were left below ground had to remain there. Mandans who die now return to that underground village."

Still nursing his painful wounds, Lewis was confined to the pirogue. He was healing, but his wounds were so painful that he couldn't walk. The men, however, were all in good spirits. When they arrived at the first Arikara village, Clark ordered a halt and fired the blunderbusses in greeting. Arikara Indians gathered on the banks in great numbers.

"What has happened since we have been gone?" Drouillard signed for Clark.

The Arikara responded that the Sioux had gone to war with the Mandans.

Clark was furious and spat out the words, "Damn the Sioux!"

The captains asked the Arikara chiefs to go with them to Washington, but they were afraid to pass through Sioux territory. In the evening, the expedition moved downriver to the lower village of the Arikara where they camped and traded for robes and moccasins. The chiefs of this village were also afraid to go east with the expedition.

"All the tribes are afraid of the Sioux," Clark lamented.

"The Sioux are going to have to be controlled if President Jefferson's trading empire is to succeed," Lewis predicted from his bed.

"It seems unlikely to me that such a trading empire will ever be established," Clark commented. "The only way to stop the Indians from fighting each other is to subjugate them, and that would take a bigger army than the United States has."

The Corps of Discovery continued the next morning and stopped at mid-day for a meal at the mouth of the Cheyenne River. Then they passed the mouth of the Teton River and camped on a bluff. Lewis was now able to walk a little, but he overdid it and suffered a relapse, spending another miserable night in pain.

The expedition arrived at a site where they had camped on the journey west and camped there again. Their hunters killed three deer and two buffalo, and the men worked on jerking the meat and dressing the skins to make clothing. They pushed off into the river at ten o'clock the next morning. In the afternoon, they were surprised to find two-hundred unknown Indians waiting for them on the bank as they traveled down the river.

Lewis was immediately cautious. "We are in Sioux territory," he warned Clark. "Let's put in to shore on the opposite side of the river."

The Indians whooped and fired their guns, and the expedition answered by firing their noisy blunderbusses.

"This could mean trouble," Lewis cautioned Clark.

Some of the Indians began to swim across the river, but Clark took three men in a small canoe and met them on a sandbar. Drouillard said softly, "This is the same band of Teton Sioux that caused us trouble last year."

"Tell them to stay away from us," Clark instructed Drouillard. "We want nothing to do with them."

Most of the Indians left then, but some remained on the sandbar, signing that they were friends and the white men should come over to their side of the river. Drouillard signaled them again to stay away from the expedition. The Indians returned to their comrades and continued to call over to the white men. Jessaume could understand some of their words.

"They are threatening to kill us if we go over to their side of the river," he said.

After a tense period of facing each other, most of the Sioux left except for a few, and the expedition set out again. At dark, they camped on a large sandbar and doubled their sentinels. They stayed on the sandbar through a stormy and disagreeable night and then set out in the morning, rowing hard all day without stopping to eat. This was still Sioux country, and they remained on full alert.

Nine Sioux warriors suddenly appeared on the riverbank and signed for the expedition to come ashore. At first, Clark ignored them, but reconsidered because one of the Corps' canoes was still out of sight behind them. Clark continued around a bend and then put into shore and waited for the canoe to catch up. In about fifteen minutes, Clark and his party heard shots ring out.

Assuming that the Sioux were attacking their last canoe, Clark took fifteen men and ran along the shore toward the sound of the guns. Lewis hobbled out of his pirogue and quickly moved the rest of the men into a defensive position. Then Clark saw the expedition's last canoe coming serenely down the river, undisturbed. The Indians turned out to be Yankton Sioux, who were merely shooting at targets. The band was the group that had been friendly on the Corps' westward route two years earlier.

Clark invited them to come into their boats for a smoke. The Yankton Sioux saluted Big White, the Mandan chief with the expedition, and all smoked several pipes of tobacco in friendship.

CHAPTER 32

Return to Civilization

September, 1806

The Corps of Discovery had been gone two years and five months, and now, on their way home, the men began to watch for trappers and traders coming upriver who could give them news of what had been happening in the world. Who had been elected President of the United States during their absence? What was happening in St. Louis? In Washington? Who had been appointed governor of the Louisiana Territory? Finally, they encountered a trading party in two canoes coming upriver. The leader was James Aird, a Scotsman from Wisconsin, who had a license to trade with the Sioux. He was a large, fair-haired, friendly man who greeted the captains warmly.

"We are just putting in to make camp," he said with big smile. "Join me in my tent and let's talk."

The captains had no sooner entered Aird's tent than a thunderstorm struck. Sheltered from the torrent and gusty wind, Aird relayed all the current news he knew: Jefferson had been re-elected to a second term, and General Wilkinson had been named governor of the Louisiana Territory with headquarters in St. Louis. Aaron Burr and Alexander Hamilton had fought a duel, and Hamilton was dead.

Captain Lewis commented, "From what I know of those two gentlemen, the country would be better off if the duel had gone the other way."

Before departing upriver next morning, Aird gave to each of the soldiers who wanted it enough tobacco to last until the expedition reached St. Louis. The men relaxed as they interacted comfortably with a group who spoke their own language.

The Corps stopped at Floyd's Bluff and climbed the hill to pay their respects at the gravesite of Sergeant Floyd, the only man who had died during their entire trip west. Finding the grave in disrepair, they worked to restore it to its original condition. Captain Lewis insisted on accompanying the party to Floyd's grave, but the climb proved to be too strenuous for him and he suffered another painful relapse. When they camped that night, the expedition had covered seventy-five miles during the day. They camped on a sandbar in an effort to evade the mosquitoes which were still swarming around them.

At noon the next day, they met a keelboat carrying twelve Frenchmen who were going upriver to winter with the Yankton Sioux.

"It's s-so g-g-good to see civilized p-p-people again!" Reuben Fields said, speaking the words that each soldier felt

The Frenchmen gave the men of the expedition a little whiskey, the first they had tasted in more than a year. The men toasted each other and the Corps's achievements. Ordway traded a beaver skin for a gentleman's hat and a store-bought shirt.

"Now I know I'm back in the real world!" he exclaimed exultantly, showing off his new clothes.

The following day, the expedition covered fifty-eight miles and camped twelve miles above the mouth of the Platte River at Camp White Catfish, where they had stayed several days on their way west. The river bottoms here had rich, black soil with massive timber of oak, elm, ash, walnut, and hickory.

Traveling down the Missouri to the Mississippi River, they passed the Platte River the next day and made good time by stopping for nothing in their intense desire to get back home. The met four more Frenchmen who were going upriver with a load of trading goods. They waved and called to the Frenchmen, but didn't take time to stop. Then a large keelboat loaded with merchandise appeared. The leader of the keelboat, a man named McClellan who knew both Lewis and Clark, told them that people in the States had given the expedition up for dead months before. Pierre Dorion and Joseph Gravelines, who had been members of the Corps party, were with McClellan, returning from Washington after accompanying the Arikara chief to meet President Jefferson.

"It's good to see you again," Captain Clark told Dorion and Gravelines. "Captain Lewis and I are glad to know you were able to deliver the Arikara chief safely to Washington."

"President Jefferson was greatly concerned for your safety and well-being," Gravelines reported. "He is very anxious for your return."

The two parties camped together that night, and some of the soldiers traded buffalo robes for civilian clothing. In the morning, McClellan gave each man of the expedition a gill of whiskey, and the parties set off in opposite directions. Next day, the Corps of Discovery encountered three keelboats of French traders from St. Louis. Another party of traders appeared and gave the men whiskey, biscuits, pork, and onions—all most welcome treats. When the expedition camped at dark, the captains distributed a gill of whiskey to each man, and they happily sang and danced until nearly midnight. The Corps was almost home!

Continuing down the Missouri, the expedition was meeting trading parties every day. They met eight Frenchmen in a pirogue loaded with merchandise who were headed for the Pawnee nation on the Platte River. At noon, they met a keelboat and two canoes that were loaded with trading goods headed upriver to trade with the Indians.

"The American people have been deeply concerned about your fate," their leader said. "Rumors spread that you had all been killed or that the Spaniards had captured you and were working you as slave laborers in their mines."

The men laughed, happy that their success had avoided those sad ends.

"We didn't see a Spaniard the whole time we were gone," Captain Lewis said, joining in the laughter. He was now recovering quickly.

The expedition passed the Kansas River and was on extra alert because the Kansas Indians were known to rob passing boats. When they stopped to eat, Silas Goodrich caught an enormous catfish they judged to weigh a hundred pounds. It was obvious that they were nearing the Mississippi River. As they continued, they saw thirty-seven deer along the banks and stopped to shoot and clean five of them. Then they passed through a part of the river so filled with tree trunks and debris that merely passing them was a challenge.

That afternoon, they encountered a large boat carrying fifteen American soldiers commanded by Captain McCann, whose mission was to cross the mountains, continue southwest into Spanish territory, and convince the Spaniards to trade their silver and gold for the Americans' goods and supplies. The Corps aired their dwindling number of supplies under the late summer sun while several hunters were sent ahead in two canoes to hunt. Joyous at the prospect of arriving soon at St. Louis, the happy party again danced and sang until almost midnight.

Sore, itchy eyes—which Captain Lewis assumed was caused by the dazzling reflection of the sun on the river day after day—became a serious problem. Potts, Shannon, and Shields were so incapacitated by eye problems that their inflamed eyes were swollen shut. The affliction was extremely painful, especially in sunlight. Lewis treated their eyes with the same solution he had used on various Indian tribes who had suffered from eye ailments. With three oarsmen unable to work, the captains abandoned one canoe and distributed its crew among the other canoes.

By September 18, the expedition was within one-hundred-and-fifty miles of American settlements, but the Corps had run completely out of provisions and trade goods. They had plenty of rifles, powder, and lead for hunting, but the busy passage of traders' boats had caused the deer and bear to move away from the river. Gathering meat for daily meals required hunters to go farther from the river to find it, considerably slowing the expedition's progress. However, nearby were so many ripe plums, which the men called pawpaws, that gathering a bushel of them took only a few minutes. The squaws of Chief Big White and Jessaume were the principle gatherers. When the men assured the captains that they would accept pawpaws as their only food, the hunters stopped searching for game.

"Save what meat we have for Seaman," Lewis announced. "We'll go the rest of the way on pawpaws."

Late the next evening, after covering eighty-four miles, they arrived at the mouth of the Osage River. Not long after, the expedition began seeing milk cows in the fields, evoking shouts of joy from the men.

"Look at them goldarn cows!" shouted Shannon joyfully, happy to see again the sure signs of American life. "Now I know we're back in civilization!"

Everyone knew now that they had survived their long, historical journey. They reached the tiny village of La Charette, near St. Louis—the first white settlement they had seen in more than two years. Because it was Sunday, they even saw a number of ladies and gentlemen walking along the riverbank—a veritable picture of domesticity to these men who had almost forgotten what civilization looked like. When they pulled their boats into the banks of the village, the soldiers asked permission to fire a salute.

"Fire away!" Lewis commanded with enthusiasm.

The men fired three volleys, which were answered by three rounds from five trading boats at the riverbank. Curious citizens rushed to check the commotion, then told the men they thought they had been lost long ago. This was the Corps of Discovery's first celebration of their incredible trip. The captains were invited to dine with prominent families, and another generous man supplied the expedition with needed provisions. The captains bought two gallons of whiskey for eight dollars, which they considered an exorbitant price.

The Corps began to pass scattered houses along the riverbank and clapped each other on the back, pointing excitedly. When they arrived at St. Charles toward evening, the townspeople gathered on the riverbank to welcome the famous expedition. Local citizens feted the heroes with refreshments and provided sleeping quarters in the town. The men laughed and enjoyed their celebrity, thankful to be back among fellow citizens.

The next morning, a hard rain continued until eleven o'clock when the party was reunited to continue downriver. Toward evening, they arrived at Fort Bellefontaine on the south shore of the Missouri River, a community that had been built while they were gone. The Corps camped a short distance below the fort. Artillery at the fort fired seventeen rounds to honor the successful return of the Corps of Discovery. Most of Lewis and Clark's men quartered in the fort that night and discovered that a number of soldiers stationed there were acquaintances.

Continuing downriver, they entered the Mississippi and stopped briefly at Fort Dubois where they had wintered in 1804. At noon on September 23, St. Louis finally came into view. It was very exciting for the members of the Corps to be back where they had started.

"There it is, men!" Lewis shouted to all their canoes. "St. Louis!"

With great excitement, the men raised three lusty cheers.

"Prepare the blunderbusses to fire three rounds!" Clark yelled.

The inhabitants of St. Louis had somehow learned that the Corps of Discovery—that valiant group that had been feared lost—was returning to St. Louis, their starting point for exploring the Louisiana Territory. Hundreds of excited people jammed the harbor, waiting to see the heroes.

Lewis docked the pirogue and the canoes followed suit as civilians cheered and applauded the Corps of Discovery. The men leaped from their vessels, some laughing and some teary-eyed, to shake hands with everyone in sight. To be sure, they were proud of themselves, even though they still wore the filthy, ragged buckskins that had endured months of treacherous pathways.

Lewis choked back tears of relief and joy. The great dream that President Jefferson and he had shared had been realized. To give himself time to regain his composure, he busied himself with mundane tasks while the tumultuous crowd greeted his men. He looked around to find his co-captain.

"Well, Clark, we did it!" Lewis managed finally. "We took twenty-eight unruly soldiers, added a few trappers and an Indian girl, and molded them all into an elite team of tough, hardy, resourceful, and disciplined people and accomplished our mission with them." It was a moment of dreams-come-true for both men.

"These men accomplished incredible feats," Clark agreed. "We also had a few failures with the Sioux and the Blackfoot who remain enemies of the United States. But we discovered that there is no all-water route to the Pacific Ocean, and that tributaries of the Missouri River do not extend north of forty-nine degrees latitude. These are important things President Jefferson needs to know, and we discovered them."

"One of our most amazing accomplishments was that we established peaceful relations with most of the Indian tribes we met," Lewis added proudly. "We also discovered more than a hundred animals new to science, including the prairie dog, blacktail deer, jackrabbit, and trumpeter swan. We discovered almost two hundred new species of plants, including grasses, shrubs, fruits, and flowers. What valuable discoveries!"

Next morning, Lewis called all the men of the Corps of Discovery together for the last time. He had purchased whiskey, and now he dispensed a gill to each man.

"Gentlemen of the Corps of Discovery, I salute you and your remarkable accomplishments!" He raised his glass to salute his constant comrades of the past twenty-eight months. "You have carved out a niche in the history of your country that will remain in its annals for all time. You have all shown remarkable endurance, fortitude, determination, and bravery every day of our journey. Your country will forever be proud of you. Captain Clark and I salute you with heart-felt appreciation and admiration."

He raised his glass higher as a gesture to the noble men under his command, and then smiled humbly at the triumphant shouts of those brave men.

EPILOGUE

The men of the Corps of Discovery had shared every day for nearly two and a half years of their lives together. Surely no other military unit in history has formed such a close bond. They faced nearly impossible odds and achieved monumental accomplishments in spite of those odds. They had learned to know and care deeply for one another and the land. They had conquered half a continent of unmapped wilderness that was inhabited by countless numbers of heretofore unknown Indian tribes whom their country had labeled as "savages," although with the single exception of the Teton Sioux, the Indian tribes they encountered proved to be accommodating and extremely helpful. The Corps of Discovery could not have achieved its unbelievable march to the Pacific Ocean and back without them. The soldiers of the expedition were unassuming men of great courage and tenacity who conquered not only the wilderness but also the great Rocky Mountains—and they did it all on modest river boats, on foot, and on horseback. They suffered near starvation, the dreadful stormy weather of the Fort Clatsop period, and the incredible physical exertion demanded of them daily.

For the most part during the ensuing years, the men of the Corps of Discovery lost track of each other due to the undeveloped means of communication at the time. What is known of the principle members of the expedition after they returned follows:

MERIWETHER LEWIS was born at Locust Hill Plantation near Charlottesville, Virginia. He was well educated for his time. He was particular, precise, serious, and reserved. According to President Jefferson, the Lewis family was "subject to hypochondriac affectations. It was a constitutional disposition in the family." Jefferson also called it melancholy, and it would later become known as depression.

In his boyhood, Lewis developed a love of hunting and exploring. He enhanced his skills as a hunter and outdoorsman and developed an interest in plants, animals, and geology which served him well during the twenty-eight months duration of the Corps of Discovery.

As a young man in the army, he fought against Indians in the Northwest Territory, where he learned much about Indians, their character, and their languages. He served in the First Infantry of General Anthony Wayne's northwestern campaign. In 1801, he was appointed President Jefferson's private secretary, a position in which he learned much about diplomacy, statesmanship, and national policy.

He became governor of the Louisiana Territory upon the return of the expedition. He died October 11, 1809 on a trip to Washington as he worked to settle financial problems arising from the expedition. An inevitable "conspiracy theory" arose that he had been murdered, but in view of his known genealogical history of depression, both William Clark and President Thomas Jefferson believed it was suicide. A monument was erected in his honor at the place of his death near Nashville, Tennessee.

WILLIAM CLARK was born near Charlottesville, Virginia, of Scottish ancestry. His family was of the lesser gentry, owners of modest estates and a few slaves. His family migrated to Kentucky in 1785 before it was a state, and he came to adulthood near Louisville. His famous oldest brother, General George Rogers Clark, taught him wilderness survival skills.

Blending fairness, honesty, and physical strength with patience, respect, and understanding, Clark recognized the personal dignity of the Indians, honoring their cultures and religious beliefs. He learned military command, engineering, construction and typography during four years as a young army officer with the western branch of the United States Army.

After the Corps of Discovery expedition, he served as head of the Indian Bureau and became governor of Missouri upon the death the Meriwether Lewis. He died in St. Louis in 1838.

SACAGAWEA After returning to the Mandan Villages, details of her life become elusive. It is known that she and her husband, Charbonneau, traveled to St. Louis in 1809 to deliver Pomp to William Clark as they had agreed. Three years later, she gave birth to a daughter but died three months later. Captain Clark raised both Pomp and his sister as his own, providing them with benefits they could never have known with the Shoshone tribe.

POMPEY Baby Pomp, formally Jean Baptiste Charbonneau, was given to Clark by his parents and was raised by Clark as his own. As an adult, Pomp trapped in the Rocky Mountains, scouted for the army, and joined the California gold rush. Nothing more is known of him.

SEAMAN Nothing definite is known about Seaman after the expedition, but he is reported to have been with Lewis on his last fateful journey. When Lewis was buried, Seaman reportedly refused to leave the grave, refusing food and eventually starving to death.

BEN YORK, a slave of the Clark family since birth, was given his freedom by Captain Clark after returning from the expedition. Clark also gave him a dray and six horses, and York engaged in the draying business between Nashville, Tennessee and Richmond, Kentucky. He died of cholera at an unknown date.

JOHN ORDWAY was born in New Hampshire. He was highly regarded by his commanding officers. He kept the orderly books and performed other important duties. After returning from the expedition, Ordway settled in Missouri and became the owner of an extensive estate that included two plantations. He died in 1887, at a ripe old age.

GEORGE DROUILLARD was the son of a French-Canadian father and a Shawnee mother. He was very adept at Indian sign language. He seemed to always be with one of the captains when emergencies occurred that required skill, nerve, endurance, and cool judgment. After returning from the expedition, Drouillard returned to the Rocky Mountains, where he gathered information that contributed to Captain Clark's final map of the area. He was killed by the Blackfoot tribe in 1810, near the site of Lewis's scrape with them.

GEORGE SHANNON was born in Pennsylvania. When part of a military party returning an Indian chief to the Mandan villages in 1807, Shannon was shot in the leg by the Arikara Indians. The leg was amputated, and he received a pension from the government for the loss of his leg. He studied law and opened a law practice in Lexington, Kentucky. He was elected to the House of Representatives from Kentucky and later to the United States Senate from Missouri. He died in 1836.

JOHN SHIELDS, born in Virginia, had been a blacksmith, and as such became one of the most valuable men on the expedition as head blacksmith, gunsmith, boat builder, and general repairman for anything. After his discharge from the army, Shields trapped for a year in Missouri with Daniel Boone. He died in 1809 in Indiana.

NATHANIEL PRYOR was born in Virginia, but his family moved to Kentucky when he was eleven. He was one of the few married men on the expedition. Lewis and Clark knew him to be a man of character and ability. Pryor remained in the army and became an officer, serving in the Battle of New Orleans. After his discharge from the army, he married an Osage girl and lived with the Osage tribe until he died in 1831.

PIERRE CRUZATTE was half French and half Omaha Indian. He had been a river man and trader on the Missouri, and he could speak the Omaha language and was skilled in the sign language. He was valuable assistance at the Indian councils and encounters with the various Indian tribes on the lower Missouri. He played the fiddle to entertain the men of the expedition as well as the Indian tribes they encountered, which in no small part helped to achieve and maintain the good will of the native tribes the expedition encountered. Nothing is known of him after the expedition.

JOSEPH FIELDS was born in Virginia, but moved to Kentucky with his family as a child. The Fields brothers were considered two of the expedition's most valuable men. Both were excellent woodsmen and hunters. He was discharged from the army on October 10, 1806. He is thought to have died in the late 1820's.

REUBEN FIELDS was discharged from the army with his brother on October 10, 1806. He settled in Indiana, where he died in late 1822.

PATRICK GASS was born near Chambersburg, Pennsylvania, of Irish descent. He was a fine carpenter, boat builder, and woodsman. He led the construction of the expedition's forts at St. Louis, the Mandan Villages, and Fort Clatsop, as well as the making of the wagons at the falls of the Missouri. Gass is known to have served in the military during the War of 1812. He lost an eye in battle and was discharged with a pension in 1831. He died in 1870, at the age of ninety-eight.

SILAS GOODRICH was born in Massachusetts. After the expedition, he re-enlisted in the army and was known to have died by the late 1820's.

JOHN COLTER was born in Virginia, but his family moved to Kentucky in his childhood. He was quick-minded, courageous, and a fine hunter and was trusted with many special missions. After the expedition, he fell out with Hancock and Dixon within six weeks of being discharged from the Corps of Discovery. He continued in the mountains as a trapper until 1811, when he returned to St. Louis and settled on a farm. He died of jaundice on November 11, 1813.

WILLIAM BRATTON was born in 1778 in Virginia, of Irish parentage. The family migrated to Kentucky. He was a blacksmith and gunsmith as well as a hunter. After the expedition, Bratton returned to Kentucky and re-enlisted in the army during the War of 1812. He later married and settled on a farm in Indiana. He died on November 11, 1841.

TOUSSAINT CHARBONNEAU was born March 20, 1767 in Boucherville, Quebec. He was French-Canadian. He was a trapper, laborer, and interpreter of the Hidatsas language. He could not speak English, and he really didn't speak Hidatsas very well. Nothing is known of him after his return from the expedition except that he worked for a fur company from 1811-1838 as a translator for the Upper Missouri Agency's Indian Bureau. He is thought to have died at the Mandan Villages.

FRANCOIS LABICHE was half French and half Omaha Indian. He served as an interpreter and as headman of one of the pirogues during the time with Lewis and Clark.. He was adept in French, English, and several Indian languages, which made him valuable. He was an excellent tracker, hunter, and waterman. Nothing is known of him after the expedition.

JOHN POTTS was born in Germany. After the expedition, he became a trapper in the upper Missouri area, where he was killed by the Blackfoot Indians in 1810.

JOSEPH WHITEHOUSE was born in Virginia, but his family migrated to Kentucky. He kept a journal of the expedition and worked on publishing it after its completion. Nothing more is known of him.

ALEXANDER WILLARD was born in New Hampshire. He was a proficient blacksmith, gunsmith, and hunter. Willard was employed as a blacksmith in Missouri in 1808, served with the army in the War of 1812, and lived in Wisconsin from 1824 to 1852. In 1852, he and his family migrated by covered wagon to California, where he died in 1865 at the age of eighty-seven.

CPSIA information can be obtained
at www.ICGtesting.com
Printed in the USA
FSHW020638010319
56012FS